The Way We Were

ELIZABETH NOBLE

MICHAEL JOSEPH
an imprint of
PENGUIN BOOKS

MICHAEL JOSEPH

Published by the Penguin Group
Penguin Books Ltd, 80 Strand, London WC2R 0RL, England
Penguin Group (USA) Inc., 375 Hudson Street, New York, New York 10014, USA
Penguin Group (Canada), 90 Eglinton Avenue East, Suite 700, Toronto, Ontario, Canada M4P 2Y3
(a division of Pearson Penguin Canada Inc.)
Penguin Ireland, 25 St Stephen's Green, Dublin 2, Ireland (a division of Penguin Books Ltd)
Penguin Group (Australia), 250 Camberwell Road, Camberwell, Victoria 3124, Australia
(a division of Pearson Australia Group Pty Ltd)
Penguin Books India Pvt Ltd, 11 Community Centre, Panchsheel Park, New Delhi – 110 017, India
Penguin Group (NZ), 67 Apollo Drive, Rosedale, North Shore 0632, New Zealand
(a division of Pearson New Zealand Ltd)
Penguin Books (South Africa) (Pty) Ltd, 24 Sturdee Avenue, Rosebank,
Johannesburg 2196, South Africa

Penguin Books Ltd, Registered Offices: 80 Strand, London WC2R 0RL, England

www.penguin.com

First published 2010
1

Set in Garamond MT Std 13.75/16.25 pt
Typeset by Palimpsest Book Production Limited, Grangemouth, Stirlingshire
Printed in Great Britain by Clays Ltd, St Ives plc

A CIP catalogue record for this book is available from the British Library

HARDBACK ISBN: 978–0–718–15535–3
TRADE PAPERBACK ISBN: 978–0–718–15536–0

www.greenpenguin.co.uk

The Way We Were

Also by Elizabeth Noble

The Reading Group
The Friendship Test
Alphabet Weekends
Things I Want My Daughters To Know
The Girl Next Door

For A and L, with my love and my thanks

Prologue

June

The kiss, like everything else about the day, was picture-perfect. Not too chaste, not too intimate. The groom, an ideal several inches taller than the slender woman beside him, took his bride's face in his hands, tender and possessive. He laid his forehead against hers for a second or two before their lips met. Her eyes shone with tears of joy. There was an appropriate collective sigh among the congregation. It was like watching a Hallmark card come to life.

First married kiss over, the beaming newly-weds turned to face the congregation, their cheeks touching, her retroussé nose wrinkling in shy self-deprecation, and the veil that had been lifted from her face a few minutes earlier framed them both in a cloud of fairytale tulle.

The vicar raised his hands in an expansive gesture. 'Ladies and gentlemen, Mr and Mrs Hammond,' and the whole church erupted into spontaneous applause.

In the second pew on the groom's side questions raced through Susannah's brain so fast she could barely put them in order.

1. Since when did we applaud in church?
2. How is it that my little brother is old enough to get married?
3. Was I really ever as naive as they appear?
4. Just when did I get so cynical, and so bitter?

The answers didn't come quite so quickly. Except about the clapping. It was modern. Not for the first time, Susannah found herself strangely at odds with the practices of her own generation. This wasn't a performance. This was a solemn, dignified ceremony.

Her 'baby' brother Alexander was thirty-three. Not young to marry, by most people's standards. It was the fact that his being thirty-three meant that she was thirty-nine that choked her a little bit. She remembered him being born so vividly – a living Tiny Tears, a six-year-old girl's dream come true.

Yes, yes – of course she'd been that naive – all that, and more. Naive and delirious with the same joy she'd seen on their faces, and certain, so very certain, that she'd be married for ever. She'd stood at that very altar, exactly where Alex and Chloe stood now, and she imagined she'd felt exactly as they did (though she also remembered a disconcerting sensation that the strangely uncomfortable garter she was wearing was slipping down her thigh towards her knee). The certainty was the part that had deserted her. She couldn't have lived without him. Back then, she'd have viewed it almost as a physical impossibility – that her heart, the one she'd just finished giving him, would literally stop beating in her chest if he wasn't beside her. She wasn't certain about anything any more.

And the getting cynical and bitter part? That . . . that question she couldn't answer. If she'd known it was happening – if she'd stood apart from herself and watched – she wouldn't have let it. Would she?

Chloe was radiant. Really. Everyone said it about every bride – it was one of the required words for days like today – but it wasn't true about every bride. At least, not as true as it was about Chloe today. (Had everyone said it about her? Was it true, about her?) Chloe was Canadian and, actually, she always 'glowed' with North American wholesome health. All straight white teeth and smooth blonde waves. She looked, Susannah acknowledged, particularly lovely today. Her dress was a long sheath of heavy ivory duchesse satin. Elegant and timeless, it suited Chloe perfectly. As she passed, she shook her bouquet slightly at Susannah in triumphant greeting, and Susannah felt herself shaking her clenched fists in response, her shoulders hunched.

Alex's chest was puffed out with pride. Chloe's arm was through his, and he had clasped her fingers with his other hand. He kept looking from her to their guests, and quickly back to her, as though he still couldn't believe she was his wife, at last.

It was hard not to believe in these two, watching them now. Even for Susannah.

Maybe Alex and Chloe would be okay. Some people were, weren't they?

Susannah's mother, Rosemary, turned now to her only daughter. Her face was wet with what Susannah had called 'happy tears' when she was little, and she dabbed carefully at her eyes with a white lacy handkerchief saved for just such an occasion. 'Wasn't that wonderful?'

Susannah smiled indulgently, which was easier said than done, given that she found her teeth were clenched. Another required word. 'It was. Wonderful!'

'And didn't she look beautiful?'

'Absolutely!'

This Q&A could take a while. Although most of her mother's Q's seemed to be rhetorical, and she probably needn't bother with the A's. This and the photos. Susannah wondered how far she was from her first glass of champagne. Too long, almost certainly. Perhaps she should have slipped a hip flask into her handbag.

'I'm so thrilled they did it here.'

This was not news. St Gabriel's Parish Church was at the geographical centre of the village and the spiritual centre of Rosemary Hammond's life, inextricably linked to her and her family. She felt a glow of pleasure and satisfaction, remembering her own marriage here on the July day England had won the World Cup in 1966. All three of her children had been christened and confirmed here, and her parents were buried beside each other, though twelve years apart, in the churchyard outside. Before she and her husband had joined the French invasion and bought a converted barn there, she never missed a Sunday service – except when she was away on holiday, and twice, after the hysterectomy she'd had in 2005 – and on almost every Friday afternoon for the last fifteen years, she'd dusted and polished the pews with three or four of her friends. Clive, her husband, called it 'dusting for Jesus' and was always rewarded with a harmless flick of the yellow duster as she left.

Alastair, the eldest and the first of her children to marry, had married from Kathryn's home near Cambridge. Of course. It was the right thing to do, although Rosemary knew, and was slightly resentful of the fact, that no one in Kathryn's family seemed particularly religious, and Kathryn herself had never even met the vicar who performed the service before they started planning the wedding. Rosemary hadn't liked the flowers much (gerberas – so casual), and she was pretty sure that the pulpit hadn't seen Pledge for a few weeks.

Alastair and Kathryn's daughters were Alex and Chloe's bridesmaids today. Millie and Sadie were tripping excitedly down the aisle behind Chloe, delighted by the swoosh of their tulle petticoats and the elaborately styled hair they'd had done at the hairdresser's.

Susannah had married Sean here, sixteen years ago. She had joked about eloping in the early days of her engagement, but Rosemary knew she would never do

that to her. Susannah was her only daughter, after all
– her only chance to really organize a wedding. Rosemary had been daydreaming about her little girl's
wedding since the day Susannah had been born.
Saving for it, too – squirrelling away money from her
housekeeping. There hadn't been any money when
she and Clive had married, not for extras – 'bells and
whistles' Clive called them. She'd been determined
that Susannah should have them all. Floral arrangements at the end of each pew – not just at the altar –
real champagne, and not just one glass for the toast . . .

But Alex's wedding had been a bonus. Alex had been
a bonus all his life, in fact, conceived five years after
Susannah – and long after she'd stopped hoping it
might happen, and had determined to be content with
the two children God had already given her and Clive.
Chloe, bless her, had wanted a traditional English
wedding, and she'd loved St Gabriel's since she'd spent
her first holiday with the Hammonds, three years earlier,
and they'd all traipsed up there for midnight mass on
Christmas Eve. Alex had proposed three months ago,
on a walking holiday in Scotland. They'd telephoned
from a pub, and Chloe had said then, straight away,
drunk on happiness and sentiment (and a couple of
whisky macs), that she wanted to marry at St Gabriel's,
that she couldn't imagine doing it anywhere else. It had
all been a bit of a rush, if Rosemary was honest. They'd
been lucky this Saturday was free. It was the first one
since Easter the Reverend Trevor had had free, and

would be the last one until after October half-term. She suspected – though she hadn't asked, since it seemed like bad luck – there might have been a cancellation . . . St Gabriel's was a very picturesque *Four Weddings and a Funeral* type of church, and always in demand, and no amount of polishing or praying could get you a Saturday at short notice in the summer.

It had all been worth it, though – all the hard work to get it organized. The pews shone, the flowers were truly gorgeous. Back at the house the marquee had looked heavenly, and somehow made the house look more heavenly too, the champagne was on ice, and the jazz ensemble was warming up. Chloe's parents had insisted on writing a generous cheque, and the 'bells and whistles' had been truly rung and blown. Chloe's mother had said, when she'd arrived at the house to see the marquee before the service, that she half expected Hugh Grant to pop up from behind an urn in morning dress, and Rosemary took this to be high praise. Rosemary watched the tall, straight back of her younger son, and her beloved granddaughters, and felt suffused with joy. She squeezed her husband's hand, and he stroked back, a bit choked himself. The two of them had been married for more than forty years. These were the wonderful days that they had dreamed of in the years when 'O' levels and mortgage payments and squabbling siblings had sometimes seemed overwhelming. The moments of joy that Clive always joked had to be paid for.

'What is wrong with this picture?' Susannah asked

herself, looking around at her siblings and her parents and her nieces and nephew. Only one thing. One blot on this picture-perfect landscape. Next to her euphoric mum and dad, her sister-in-law Kathryn was making her baby, Oscar, giggle by blowing raspberries against his neck while he reached for the feathers on her hat, the ones that tickled his nose when she bent her face to him.

It was Susannah. She was the only one who didn't fit. Her eyes filled with sudden tears. Christ. Looking down immediately, she opened her handbag and fumbled among the detritus within for a tissue. She felt a tear run down the side of her nose, where she feared it might imminently mingle with snot. These were not the pretty, appropriate tears one should cry at a wedding. These were just a minute or so away from being full-blown, shoulder-shaking sobs, and she was determined that wasn't going to happen. She dug the fingernails of her left hand into her palm, and clenched her teeth again. Susannah was an ugly crier, and she knew it. A minute of proper crying would leave an hour of red, swollen eyes and an even redder nose. And would mean looks, and questions – and questions she could do without today.

Her brother Alastair took her arm at the elbow, squeezing quite hard, and pushed a plaid cotton hand-kerchief into her hand. 'Oh no, you don't.'

The others had filtered into the aisle, and joined the melee of guests heading towards the steps of the church. Susannah's brother pulled her by the arm in the opposite direction from all of them, back towards the altar, and she let herself be led.

'Wait just a minute.' His voice was firm, but not unkind. He could have been talking to Sadie.

The choir was changing out of their surplices in the small vestibule at the back of the church.

'Don't mind us . . . taking the short cut,' he announced, as he led Susannah through them to a door which opened into the quiet graveyard. He didn't let go of her elbow until he'd guided her on to a bench, and then he sat down beside her.

Susannah pulled her pillbox hat off and ran her fingers through her hair. 'Thanks.'

He sat back, not answering her, but running his finger between his collar and his neck, and pushing his hair back from his forehead. For a few moments they sat in a silence punctuated only by Susannah's occasional sniffing, and by the hum of noise from the front of the church.

Alastair crossed his long legs. 'I had my first cigarette on this bench. Thirteen years old. Threw up ten minutes later . . . just over there.' He gestured to a tree ten yards away.

Susannah smiled. He'd never been much of a smoker. She had been — ten a day, for almost exactly the three years she was away at university, as though it were a course requirement, until graduation, when she'd stopped as suddenly as she'd started. He'd always tortured her about it, given half the chance. Mum and Dad had never known, despite his threats: he'd never betray her.

'And I might have lost my virginity on this bench, too, if Sally Harris hadn't had extremely tight jeans and a 10 p.m. curfew.'

She laughed out loud. 'Sally Harris. God!'

'Apparently her dad had to pull the zipper up with a coathanger before she came out, and I think she was honestly afraid if she took them off she might never get them back on and she'd have to go home in her knickers . . .'

'At least, that's what she told you . . .'

'They were bloody tight, too. I could hardly get my hand in . . .'

'Eew. That's so disgusting.'

He smirked at her. 'Stopped you blubbing, though, hasn't it?'

'Stopped me eating at the reception, too, I should think . . .'

'Well, that won't hurt you either, Chunky.'

He'd called her Chunky, and only Chunky, for some two years, when she was about ten until twelve, and had been, it would be fair to say . . . chunky. She'd slimmed down that summer, and been unvaryingly slim ever since, but he still called her Chunky some-times when they were on their own.

She slapped his chest. 'Oy!'

That was Alastair. The archetypal big brother. When

they were younger, when they'd lived together as children, he'd often been dismissive, or unkind, and sometimes given the outward impression that all he did all day was think of ways to torture her, but let anyone else – anyone – mess with her, and he morphed instantly into her rescuer. Her champion. He still was, she supposed.

'So?' He was looking right at her now, one eyebrow raised.

'So, what?' She didn't quite meet his gaze.

'So . . . why the tears?'

'Everyone cries at weddings, don't they? Mum was getting through the Kleenex like it was going out of style. Kathryn, too . . .'

'Right. So, you're not saying?'

'Saying what?' Just because he'd rescued her, didn't mean she had to tell him.

'Okay – just because I rescued you, doesn't mean you have to tell me.' It was spooky how he did that. 'But if you want to . . . I'm all ears. And this is your window of opportunity, because I've got Kath's permission to drink all afternoon, and I fully intend to be insensible by the time they cut the cake . . . Oscar has been on a bloody bender the last four or five nights, and I'm exhausted, so I'm going to go quick. So . . . if you want to talk, the doctor is in . . .'

'I suppose I must have been thinking about Sean.'

'Bullshit.'

'Do doctors usually talk to their patients like that?'

'They should do, if they don't.'

'So, why don't you believe me?'

'Because I haven't seen you cry over Sean in years. I'm not buying it. Those weren't nostalgia, regret tears. Those were very much present-tense tears, if you ask me.'

'Really? How do you know so much . . . ?'

'Look, Sis – you might not want to say, but you don't have to be a genius to clock that something isn't right. You haven't been around much for months now. You've avoided all the family stuff – not just the reunions . . . you didn't come to Oscar's christening.'

She started to speak, to reiterate the excuse she had used and had been so sure had been believed, but Alastair raised his hand to stop her. 'And that doesn't matter. That's not what I'm saying. And today you've shown up, but Doug's not with you . . . yet again . . .'

'He had the kids . . . last minute.' She sounded pathetic, even to herself.

Again, the hand. The hand was quite annoying, actually, even if it was entirely justified . . . 'Maybe he did. Maybe he didn't. Maybe it's none of my damn business. But I'm worried about you, Suze. That's all. We're all a bit worried about you.'

'Have you "all" been talking about me, then?' She hated the thought of that. All of them sitting around in their various states of contentment, talking about her. The only one who didn't seem happy.

'It's not like that. I don't mean Mum and Dad. God

knows, Mum hasn't heard a word that isn't about Alex and Chloe's wedding for weeks now. And you know Dad. He never gives much away. I mean me and Kathryn. And actually, she's been busy with the baby. Okay. I mean me.'

'Great.' She almost giggled. 'So, no one else cares a damn about me, then?'

They both smiled at her contrariness.

Alastair put an arm around Susannah, and she leant her head on his shoulder.

'I'm just saying . . .'

'I know.'

They sat there for a few minutes, without speaking, in the warm sunshine. Susannah felt her heart rate slow, and the urge to cry slowly recede, until she was quite calm.

Then Alastair sat up. 'We should get back. After you've done something about that mascara gloop . . . They'll be furious if they can't find us for the photos.'

'You're right.' She fished in her bag for a compact, and licked the corner of his handkerchief before dabbing away the black smudges beneath her eyes.

'Usually.'

'I don't know how Kathryn puts up with you.' She reapplied her lipgloss, closed the handbag and handed the handkerchief back to Alastair, who looked revolted, then balled it up and shoved it in his pocket.

'What do you mean put up with me? She worships the very ground I walk on.'

The two of them stood up and began to wander towards the sound of the crowd, hand in hand.

'Poor, deluded girl.'

This was the familiar banter of her childhood.

'And I'm amazing in bed. Sally Harris had no idea what she was missing.'

She snorted. It was comforting, distracting, and helpful.

Just before they rounded the corner, he squeezed her hand and then dropped it gently. 'Think you can keep the wailing and gnashing of teeth at bay now?' He rolled his eyes at her in mock exasperation. So unfair.

'Think I can. Just about.'

'Good. Do. For God's sake. Put that prissy hat back on. And stay off the booze, will you? Nothing worse at a wedding than a middle-aged woman on her own, drunk and trying to get off with one of the ushers.' He nudged her with his shoulder.

'I'll try to remember that.'

Their mother descended on them as they appeared, looking mildly irritated and a little flushed. She tutted at them, and smoothed a strand of Susannah's hair that was escaping the elastic holding the hat on her head, as though she was a recalcitrant child. She didn't appear to notice that there had been tears. 'Where have you two been?' She didn't wait for an answer. She never really did. 'We've finished Chloe's lot. Hardly any of them, of course. You're up. Groom's family. Come on . . . he's got the ladder out for us.'

Douglas was supposed to be here. It was her fault he wasn't, she supposed. She'd told him not to come. She hadn't meant it – 'Don't bother coming,' she'd said. He knew she hadn't meant it, too. But he still hadn't come.

He'd crossed a line. Not coming today, when he knew perfectly well that people would wonder why. There would be a place laid for him in the marquee, on her table. His name, in perfect calligraphic script. An empty chair. He knew she'd have to explain his absence, to nosy aunts and concerned friends and well-meaning strangers. That her explanation, however plausible, however light and funny her delivery, would probably not be believed. That crossed a line – made something private public. He knew how she hated that. But then they were crossing lines more and more, the two of them, lately. And now she didn't even know where they were drawing the lines. She used to know where they were – the lines. She used to know how he'd react, how he'd behave in any given situation. They'd learnt the rhythm of each other. She wasn't so sure any more. Of him, or of herself. She wasn't ever certain. Once upon a time, they hadn't quarrelled. Later, when they did, she'd never have gone to bed without making it up. Then they'd begun to fall asleep angry, or resentful, edging ever further from the centre of their king-size bed, back to tense back. Now, twice in the last few months, she'd slept in the spare bedroom. And, although on the first occasion, when they'd both had too much wine, he'd come in the middle of the night to try and coax her back to their bed, the second time, when they'd both been sober, he hadn't. Crossing lines.

The nervous young photographer was running through his small repertoire of corny lines, trying to make everyone laugh for his family shot. Apparently, though, he wasn't as good at it as four-year-old Sadie, who was currently lifting her bridesmaid dress over her head, displaying her round tummy, and her days-of-the-week knickers. 'I wouldn't mind so much if she wasn't wearing Wednesday,' Kathryn laughed, as she tried to hold on to a wriggling and increasingly irate Oscar, and smooth down Sadie's dress at the same time.

'That's it. Got it. Thanks, everyone.' The relief in the photographer's voice was obvious. This was only his fourth wedding, and none of the others had had quite so many people, or a flashing bridesmaid. Looking at him, red-cheeked and sweating, Susannah wondered how the poor devil was going to make it through the reception. This lot was hard enough to corral sober. A couple of glasses of champagne, and it would be like herding cats.

Susannah's parents' home was a five-minute stroll from the church, across the common and down a small lane. People had begun wandering in that general direction, led by a neighbour, thirsty, and hoping for at least a vol-au-vent before the next round of picture-taking.

A small crowd of villagers, uninvited but still keen to see the bride, and the guests in their wedding finery, had gathered around the entrance to the churchyard during the service. Susannah remembered doing the same thing when she'd been a young girl. When curly perms and bell sleeves were all the rage for brides, and the grooms all had sideburns and Kevin Keegan haircuts. There'd been a wedding most Saturdays in the summer. She'd watch the guests arrive, the bride climb out of the smart car, smooth her dress nervously before she took her father's arm. Then she'd cycle to the village shop and spend her pocket money on fruit salad sweets and sherbet fountains and *Smash Hits* magazine, returning in time to watch as the newly-weds stepped out into the sound of the bells. She loved the dresses and the bridesmaids and the flowers, the beribboned cars (and once a carriage pulled by two dappled horses) and all the guests resplendent in hats and high heels. She loved the bells; she thought it was the happiest sound in the world. Mostly she loved the bit when the couple kissed in a shower of confetti or rose petals.

As Chloe and Alexander made their way through the guests – they were walking over to the house, too (endlessly romantic, Chloe loved that – she said she'd feel like a heroine in a Thomas Hardy or a Jane Austen novel) – the elderly ladies of the WI cooed and aahed at them. 'You look smashing, love.' 'God Bless.' It was old-fashioned, but it was lovely. Their well wishes seemed, to Susannah, more poignant and more affecting than those of the people who'd had the copperplate invitations on their mantels for six weeks, who'd spent their £50 on the John Lewis wedding list and bought a new dress for last year's too-expensive hat. These were the real romantics, just as she'd been, once. They'd no other reason to be here at all. They weren't Alexander's college room-mate, or Chloe's senior partner, or somebody's elderly aunt.

Then she saw someone she knew among them, and her breath caught in her throat. She hadn't thought to see her. As soon as she did, she wondered why it hadn't occurred to her that she might. They'd been here together, the two of them, after all, more than once, standing outside the church, waiting to see brides, a million years ago.

Most of the people at the gates were unfamiliar to her now – she hadn't lived here for years, and she came back fairly irregularly, only stopping at Mum and Dad's house when she did visit. But this was someone she'd once known well, though it had been two decades since they'd last met. Lois Rossi. Older, and definitely a little plumper. Her hair, which she'd once worn in a shiny brunette bob that swung across her shoulders, was now shining silver, and shorter. Lois was smiling broadly, and right at her. Susannah wondered if she recognized her, almost looked over her shoulder to check who else the smile might be intended for. Maybe it was generic.

Behind Lois, much, much taller, and this time she was absolutely certain it was on her the same deep brown eyes were focused, was her son.

Roberto Rossi. Rob.

The tall, dark, handsome boy she'd fallen in love with – for the first, exquisite time – when she was 16 years old. And now the man she hadn't seen for twenty years.

For a moment, Susannah didn't know what to do. She wanted to run, but she was rooted to the spot, as though their collective gazes had trapped her, made her incapable of movement. And she was standing on grass in four-inch heels, so it wouldn't so much be running, as aerating . . . She looked around for her brother but she couldn't see him, or anyone she knew. She was standing still, frozen in a moment, while hordes of hat-wearing strangers were spilling past her – friends of Chloe and Alex's, she supposed – all laughing and chatting noisily. A thronging sea of pastel and feathers in a heady fog of perfume and hairspray. It almost made her dizzy.

There had been a time, many years ago, when bumping into Lois, or Rob, had been her greatest preoccupation and fear when any trip to her parents' home had been mooted. She'd once pulled into the Texaco filling station on the outskirts of the village with the petrol gauge reading 'you should have filled up thirty miles ago, you moron', only to see Rob's father, Frank, at the opposite pump. She'd hared out again without actually stopping, desperate not to make eye contact with him, and sputtered to a humiliating dead stop about five miles later. She and Sean hadn't been to hear their banns read at St Gabriel's for the same reason. Lois and Frank had been away on holiday for the wedding itself – not that they'd have come to wish her well, she didn't think. Not after what had happened.

The fear had subsided, as fears usually do. Her visits home had tapered off, too. She'd been too happily self-absorbed to come, at first. Too humiliated, once things started to go wrong, and too wretched to do much of anything once it really all fell apart with Sean.

And she and Douglas hadn't been frequent visitors in recent years either. The kids, Doug's beloved boat in Chichester Harbour, her job . . . life pulled them in so many directions. And it just sped up. Weeks, months, seasons, years . . . passed. Mum and Dad were retired, and spent a few months each year at the place they'd bought in France. (A major triumph, from Dad's point of view – he had doubted even his persuasive persistence would convince Mum to leave the village, and St Gabriel's.) When they were home, they were happy to 'gallivant', as Dad called it. Mum always said she'd cooked enough Sunday dinners for a lifetime, and she was pleased to have someone else slave over a stove on her behalf. And then Alastair and Kathryn had hogged them, too – luring them for Christmas and Easter and mini-breaks in Cornwall with their succession of ever more adorable grandbabies.

And so by now she'd forgotten to look over her shoulder, or wear her big Jackie O sunglasses. And so now she'd seen them. That figured. Could this day get any more difficult?

Lois Rossi was walking towards her, her arms outstretched. God. Yes, it could. It could get worse. Now she remembered. Frank, Lois's husband, was ill. Really ill.

He'd been diagnosed with motor neurone disease about three years ago. Mum had told her – part of the litany of village gossip she ran through whenever she saw her, most of which was about members of the congregation Susannah wouldn't know if they fell on her. She'd thought about writing to Lois, when she'd heard. But what would she say? If someone had died, the platitudes flowed easily enough. But it wasn't so easy to know what to write about Frank – she didn't know much about the disease, except that it was devastating and that Stephen Hawking was pretty much the only person, so far as she knew, who had survived it for any real length of time. For most people, she was sure, it was a death sentence. Mum's story had come with no details. And so she hadn't written. And now, as they moved towards each other across the grass, she really wished she had. Writing something about it would have been infinitely easier than trying to think of the right thing to say, now, here, in the middle of all of this wedding gaiety.

Lois spoke first, as she tramped forwards. 'Susannah!'

That was all she said. And then, up close to her, she opened her arms even wider and pulled Susannah into a still-familiar embrace. Susannah felt almost weak with relief. Of course, she reasoned, of course Lois wouldn't still be angry with her. Maybe she never had been. Not all these years later. Lifetimes later.

1987

September

Alastair and Susannah stood at the unmarked bus stop at 8.15 a.m., waiting for their coach. They, along with probably eighty per cent of the thousand or so kids at their school, were bussed by a procession of coaches each morning the five miles to the enormous grey concrete building in the nearest town. Their coach made five stops along its route, and theirs was the second, and the busiest. There were maybe twenty-five other kids who got picked up here, most of whom lived in the detached houses on the quiet roads around this side of the common. A different coach collected kids from the opposite side, as well as the new estate the other side of the high street, and another from the outlying farms and remote properties. They were all blinking in the early morning sunshine, faintly outraged at being up so early after six weeks of lie-ins and lazy days.

Alex was still at the primary school in the village, which the two of them had also attended. Mum would take him, about thirty minutes later than she and Al had to leave to catch the bus. Alex still got the full-on

Mum treatment – a sitting-down breakfast, a 'have you brushed properly?' teeth inspection and the escorted walk. The two of them would walk across the common, and then Mum would stand at the bottom of the lane and watch him walk the last 100 yards or so, until he went through the gate and became, for the next few hours, the responsibility of the school.

This was the last year they'd catch the bus together. Alastair was in the upper sixth now. He would do his 'A' levels next summer and go off to university this time next year. Exeter, to read Engineering, if he got the grades he needed, which everyone assumed he would.

Susannah was just a year behind him, although Al was eighteen months older. She'd finished her 'O' levels this past summer, and was just going into the sixth form. The college was next door to the school – fifty yards, a B road and a world apart from the kids still in the lower forms. It was, really, an affront to still have to ride on the bus with them.

She knew from last year how it worked. Sixth-formers didn't wear uniform, and with mufti, came power. They stood a way apart from everyone else at the bus stop. They commandeered the last six or seven rows of the coach. It was an unwritten rule, and they boarded the bus last, many of them ostentatiously stubbing out cigarettes on their way. Sixth-formers did not talk to anyone else. When she'd been in the fifth form, Alastair had never once spoken to her at the bus stop. On the walk to and from it, of course he had – they'd always been close. But once they got there, and for the duration of the ride each day, she was a stranger to him, and she accepted it. Alex would be a first-former next year, in her last year. And it would be exactly the same. She'd look past him while there were other people around, and then stroll the last part of the walk home companionably with him.

God knows what state Mum would be in next year. The church would be clean, at least. Alastair would be gone altogether, and Alex would be on the coach. And the year after . . . God help Alex. He'd be the only one left . . .

Today Susannah was most excited to be out of the unflattering bottle-green uniform the school required. They still had to wear a tie, for God's sake, and no amount of skilful tying, or artfully untucked shirt, could make that look good. Especially if you had boobs, which she – much to her consternation – had. Mum and Dad had given her an unprecedented £250 when she'd got her results in August – as a reward, and to buy a new wardrobe for sixth form – and she'd spent every penny in a breathless one-day trip to Oxford Street. Today, she was carefully dressed in drainpipe jeans and a black sweater, with a long black and royal-blue stripy scarf wrapped several times around her neck. Slouchy suede boots from Chelsea Girl. And today Al, and the others, could talk to her at last, although, so far, they weren't, really.

This new cool made the first day back even cooler.

She'd always been a start-of-term girl. New stationery, a new bag, a new start. She'd probably never admit it to anyone, but she'd been looking forward to today. You were supposed to lament the end of summer, and act like going back to school was the end of the world. But actually, Susannah didn't love the aimless freedom of summer as much as everyone else seemed to. This year had seemed even longer, sweating on her 'O' level results, which didn't come out until the middle of August. By contrast, Alastair didn't ever seem to sweat about anything, and was definitely an end-of-term kind of a boy. This morning, Mum had practically had to pour cold water on his head to get him out of bed, but she'd been up and dressed and eating breakfast before even Dad came down – far too early.

She'd got eight A's and a B (in Geography). A new family record. Alastair had done well last year, but not quite that well. Susannah knew, really, that Alastair was every bit as clever as she was. He could have done just as well. If he cared enough. But he didn't. Alastair was, she acknowledged, much more of an all-rounder than she was. He worked just hard enough to get a handful of A's and B's in his exams. And the rest of the time, he did different things. Did them all pretty well. He played most sports well, he had a huge gang of friends, he had an encyclopedic knowledge of music and a vast collection of records. He went fishing with Dad, and tinkered with his BMX bike, on which he could perform tricks dramatic enough to scare the hell out of their mum. He went out with girls – had already had a stream of girlfriends. Alastair was balanced. Susannah had always suspected that she wasn't, not particularly.

She was clever, she knew that. Really quite clever. The kind of clever that could come top of the class without really trying, and which, when effort was applied, made teachers excited. The kind that made the other kids treat her with a mix of awe and disdain that she'd never got used to. Of everything else about herself, she wasn't quite so certain. That's why this – the start of school – felt like solid ground to her.

'Hey, Suze!'

It was Amelia Lloyd. Calling from fifty yards away, and waving at her manically, oblivious to the stares it earned her. They'd been best friends since the Lloyds had come to the village in the third year of junior school. Amelia lived alone with her parents in the big old rectory behind the church. Her mum had spent two years doing it up after they moved there, with a big conservatory on the side and a swimming pool in the garden. They had the most amazing dining table that sat twelve but converted into a snooker table if you turned it over and pulled the pockets out. Her dad was a solicitor – a partner in a London law firm. They seemed rich to Susannah. They went skiing every Easter, to a gingerbread house sort of chalet Amelia's grandparents owned in Switzerland, and took long summer holidays to cool-sounding places. Amelia was an only child, with an en suite bathroom and a pony, and she was only at state school because of her parents' left-wing political convictions, she said. They'd suggested, left of centre or not, that she went away for sixth form, to Roedean or Marlborough, or St Mary's Ascot, but a horrified Amelia had mounted a major campaign of resistance the previous year, with Susannah as her campaign manager, and they'd relented, agreeing that she could stay for sixth form on the condition that her 'O' level results were good enough.

She should probably have been awful – spoilt and indulged. But she wasn't. Okay, she was spoilt, but Amelia was also sunny and funny and generous, fearless and fierce. If she'd been able to articulate it, Susannah might have said that her childhood sprang into Technicolor when Amelia arrived in the village – the way Dorothy's did in *The Wizard of Oz* after she woke up from the hurricane. They'd met at Brownies, of which Susannah's mother was Brown Owl that whole decade, long after Susannah had given it up. When Amelia was sworn into the Pixies, along with Susannah, they'd become inseparable almost straight away, to Susannah's great surprise and Amelia's great relief. Susannah had been so afraid, when they first all went to senior school, that she'd lose her, that Amelia would be seduced away from her by the cool girls. But that hadn't happened, thank God. Amelia had made Susannah a little cooler, and Susannah, Amelia claimed, had made her a smidge cleverer, and the exchange was something much valued by both of them.

Now, though, they hadn't seen each other since Amelia got back from her summer holiday yesterday. That had been part of the reason summer had dragged – she'd been gone for ages . . . and Susannah had missed her badly. Amelia had telephoned last night to squeal delightedly about her results: five A's, three B's and a C (in Maths). But it was good enough to force her parents to let her stay, and that was all either of them really cared about. They were both going to do three 'A' levels – Amelia had chosen English, History and French, and Susannah Maths, English and Economics – and their plan was to end up at the same university. They didn't know which one yet, although they were currently keen on Bristol, if they could get offers once they'd started the dreadful process of UCCA. Amelia had a cousin who'd been to Bristol and said it was brilliant and cool. Amelia had alluded to something important she had to tell her, but gave no clues. It would have to wait, she said, until the coach the next day . . . Susannah had known there was no point trying to wrangle it out of her – Amelia loved drama. Something more important than 'O' level results . . .

And now here she was, tanned a deep dirty brown, with white-blonde highlights in her golden hair. ('Sun-In!') The two girls hugged, and Amelia swung her friend boisterously. The younger kids stared at them.

'Suze! I can't believe how much I missed you!'

'You look so great. I can't believe how brown you are. I hate you.'

Amelia preened. She was wearing a white shirt, of course, with short sleeves despite the definite autumn chill in the air this morning, and with more buttons undone than Susannah's mother would have allowed when she left the house. Probably Amelia's mum, too – she doubtless undid them on her walk to the bus stop. Her long, skinny legs looked even longer and skinnier. 'I know. I don't think I've ever been this brown. This tan took me three weeks of concerted effort, you know.'

'Lucky devil. How was Italy?'

'Fantastic. Can't wait to tell you *all* about it!'

The coach had pulled up now, and the kids in uniform had climbed on, the first-formers looking nervous, the others affectedly bored. Susannah mounted the steps, nodded a greeting to the driver, who she did not recognize from last year, and walked with studied indifference down the aisle to the hallowed ground of the back rows, where she slid into an empty seat three rows in front of Alastair. He smiled briefly at her and waved a casual greeting to Amelia, who blew him a kiss in return before sitting down next to Susannah, her whole body leaning in conspiratorially. The driver turned on Radio 1, presumably to drown out the din, and Paul Young blared out.

When Amelia spoke again, it was in a rapid-fire

whisper. 'So, Italy . . . Italy was beautiful. We went to Venice and Rome and did all the museums and galleries Mum wanted to, plus a bit of shopping, and everything was great. Venice was *amazing*. Definitely going there on my honeymoon. Rome was pretty cool, too. But the last week – the last week was *the best*.'

'Where were you the last week, again?'

Susannah and her brothers had spent a week at their granny's in Suffolk, and then the entire family had shivered through a week in a self-catering bungalow in a rainy and chilly Pembrokeshire. She wasn't exactly jealous of Amelia, but she'd kill to see all those places in real life. She was determined to go InterRailing after 'A' levels, and Amelia had said she'd go with her, although Susannah wasn't sure why Amelia would want to retrace her steps in hostels and cheap bed and breakfasts after the four-star hotels and resorts she was used to.

'The Amalfi Coast.' Amelia said it in a hammy Italian accent. 'Most romantic place in the world. Sorrento.'

'And . . .'

'And I met a boy . . .' Amelia was beaming.

'An Italian boy?!'

'An English boy. Tristan. He was staying at the hotel with his parents. We met the first night. He's an only child, too, so we were sort of twiddling our thumbs round the pool, and then I got in and swam a bit, and he did, too, and then he sort of accidentally on purpose bumped into me, near the shallow end, and we got chatting in the water and we stayed in until we were practically prunes, we were so waterlogged.

'And from then on, we were like Siamese twins, practically joined at the hip. We spent every minute together. It was *so* romantic.'

'What about your mum and dad?'

'They were hardly ever there. I don't know what got into them – they've never given me so much freedom. Perhaps they've finally decided I've grown up a bit. They kept going on these day trips – they went to Capri, this island off the Amalfi Coast, and to the ruins at Pompeii, you know, all those people under the volcano. And for these boring, long lunches – because they wanted to be out of the sun in the hottest part of the day – have you ever heard anything so ridiculous? . . . So, most of the time, it was just the two of us. His parents weren't around that much either. They didn't hang around the pool . . .'

'But you two did?'

'When we weren't hanging around in my room . . .' Amelia left a very pregnant pause and winked lasciviously.

Susannah clamped her hand over her mouth, in no doubt, suddenly, what it was her friend was making such a pantomime of telling her. 'You didn't?'

She didn't answer straight away. Then she laughed triumphantly. 'Oh yes, I did.'

Susannah felt herself blush, though Amelia did not. 'You have to tell me everything.'

'I'm not telling you everything, you perv.' Amelia punched her in the arm, but she was still smiling. 'But I'll tell you how it happened. You'll see why I did it. It couldn't have been more perfect. I didn't want my first time to be in a car, or behind the science block or upstairs at some seedy party, under a pile of coats. I wanted it to be . . . perfect. And it was.'

'I can't believe you went all the way with him.'

'You would have, too, believe me.'

Susannah didn't think so. She was so very far away from even imagining that.

Amelia settled into her story. 'So . . . we had this incredibly romantic dinner together. On the terrace. Tristan was allowed to put it on his parents' bill. Mum and Dad had gone down the coast to some town called Ravello – they'd been gone all day. I don't know where his parents were – somewhere else having dinner, I suppose. They were kind of not interested in him at all. It was all candlelit and gorgeous, and I was all brown, and I wore that silver strappy dress, you know the one?'

Susannah nodded.

'And afterwards . . . it just happened. We were kissing, and stuff, by the pool, on the loungers, and then he just asked me, if I wanted to go back to his room. And I said yes.'

'What about your parents?'

Amelia brushed the question off with a wave of her hand. 'I left them a note, saying I was exhausted – that I'd had too much sun – and I'd gone to bed early . . .'

Susannah knew her own mother would have come knocking to check on her, armed with after-sun and paracetamol. She'd never have had the nerve to lie like that in the first place. Never have been brave enough to go to a boy's room . . . let alone do anything once she'd gone.

'You're so funny, Suze – my parents were the last thing on my mind, but *that's* your burning question . . . !'

She was making a goofy face, and Susannah felt a bit foolish. 'I have other questions. How was it . . . you know . . . ?!'

'That's more like it.' Amelia lowered her voice to a whisper, and put her mouth close to Susannah's ear. 'It was lovely.'

'That's it, lovely?'

'Lovely. Very lovely. Much, much nicer than I'd even expected. That's all you're getting.'

Susannah doubted that. Amelia would just eke the story out.

'So, are you going to see this Tristan again?'

'I don't know. We swapped numbers, and addresses and stuff. He's a year older than we are. He lives some-where near Lincoln, goes to boarding school around there. We might get together, I suppose.'

Susannah was a little shocked, though she'd never dare say so. It seemed so . . . so casual. That you would meet a guy and sleep with him – as a virgin – and not even be sure of whether you were going to see him again. She wondered whether Amelia was

34

pretending, for her benefit, not to care as much as she did.

'Listen.' Amelia smiled benevolently at her, reading her face. 'This isn't the guy I'm going to marry, Suze. He was gorgeous, and we had so much fun, and I'm so, so glad I chose him, you know, to be the first one, because, like I said, it was perfect. He doesn't have to be the love of my life, you know. And that doesn't mean I'm suddenly going to become this slut who sleeps with everyone. I just feel like I got the first time out of the way, and I did it right, you know?'

Susannah had never thought of losing her virginity as something to be got out of the way. 'I thought getting it right meant waiting for someone you really loved.'

'No offence, Suze, but you really are the most old-fashioned, soppy thing. You're going to be waiting and waiting.'

Susannah snorted derisively. 'It's not exactly like I'm fighting them off, is it?'

'That's just because you're not giving out the right vibes. You're pretty, you're fun and clever. You just have this "don't even think about it" sign on your forehead. It's . . . off-putting.' Amelia wrinkled her nose, and gave a small shake of her head.

Susannah wiped her forehead with the back of her hand. 'I do not.'

Amelia folded her arms. 'Kiss anyone this summer? Anyone at all?'

'No, but . . .'

'But nothing. I rest my case. You're sixteen years old – not far off seventeen – and you haven't even ever been kissed. Not properly. What kind of a state to be in is that?'

They were both laughing now. Susannah hoped no one was listening, but when she put her head up above the top of the seat and looked around, everyone seemed to be engrossed in their own conversations. No one was even looking at her.

'That's my mission, in fact.'

'What's your mission?'

'I'm going to get you a boyfriend this year.'

Susannah blew a raspberry at her friend.

'If it kills me.'

'And it might.'

'What were you and Amelia in cahoots about, then?' Alastair had caught her up. The coach had pulled up and the kids all spilt out and began the unwilling trudge towards their various new forms. Amelia had stopped to talk to a group of girls she knew from the stables where her pony was boarded.

Susannah had thought, for the last couple of years at least, that Alastair had something of a crush on her best friend, although he always denied it. It was just that he was always just a little bit more interested in Susannah when Amelia was round at their house. And sometimes, she swore, he brushed his hair before he came down from his bedroom, when he knew she was around. Even Alex had noticed, although their mum told them off when they teased him.

'None of your business.' She smirked at him.

'Was it me? Did she miss me?'

Susannah knew he was only half joking. 'Not sure she actually remembers your name.'

Alastair clutched his heart theatrically. 'You wound me, Sis.'

'Have a good day, Romeo.'

'You too, Chunky.'

'Does anyone know what the origin of the term "kitchen-sink drama" is?'

No one answered. Of course. What did he expect, this early in the class? In the year? In the 'A' level course? Points for trying, Mr Blythe, Susannah thought. He'd taught her 'O' level last year, too – some teachers taught in both buildings. They'd done *The Great Gatsby* and *Othello* together, and she really liked him. But he was one of those teachers most kids found it easier to mock than to be inspired by. He had a huge Adam's apple, a permanent shaving rash, and terrible taste in clothes. Amelia had christened him Ichabod years ago and the nickname had stuck (although most of the class hadn't a clue where it came from). Poor Mr Blythe. He so loved all things English Literature, she could tell, but he was facing a room full of blank-faced, lazy-eyed teenagers who'd rather be out on the grass in the sunshine talking about something – anything – else.

'Has anyone actually read this play?'

Susannah had, of course, but even she wasn't going to raise her hand straight away. She knew he'd know she'd read it. He'd know she knew exactly what a kitchen-sink drama was. And even something about the historical context of this kind of theatre. She didn't need the social handicap of everyone else knowing it, too. Not yet – too early in the year for that. He was getting exasperated now, although they were only five minutes into the class. They were all supposed to have read it over the summer – they'd all been given a copy. This didn't bode well for the rest of the double period.

People looked down and shuffled their papers, fiddling with the contents of their pencil cases and, in some of the more blatant cases, make-up bags.

Mr Blythe clasped his hands behind his back, legs apart, swallowed so that his Adam's apple bobbed violently in his throat, and launched into a monologue about the British New Wave of the late 1950s and early 1960s, and the playwrights determined to bring realism to theatre in that era. Susannah was interested, though she expended some energy trying to look as though she wasn't. He didn't really look right at them while he talked. It was as if he was lecturing to the back of the room, at some mythical motivated students in his own imagination. Satisfied that he had warmed to his theme, and would talk for at least ten to fifteen minutes without requiring any feedback from them, most of the kids in the room started doodling and daydreaming, and mouthing things to each other across the floor.

Susannah looked around. The classroom was one of the rooms in the new block, on the second floor. Arranged in a horseshoe of desks, she had a clear view of everyone, or as clear a view as you could have when most of the kids were slouched down behind their bags. Next to her, Amelia was happily drawing elaborate and exotic flowers on the front of her new pink binder with Tipp-Ex. There were about twenty more of them, mostly kids she knew from her 'O' level class last year, although it was astonishing how different everyone looked out of the familiar uniform. Today sort of proved the point that uniform was a great leveller. Now, what you wore was going to create a pecking order that hadn't existed before.

And there was one new boy.

She'd noticed him straight away. He'd come in a couple of minutes late – presumably he wasn't sure where he should be – and he'd mumbled an apology. Then he'd sat down at a desk by the window. He didn't slouch – he sat forward, his feet crossed at the ankles.

He was incredibly tall. She'd noticed that first, as soon as he came into the room. Much taller than most of the guys in the room, and at least five inches taller than Ichabod.

Now, with Ichabod's voice droning in the background, she was free to study him more carefully.

His hair was unfashionably short, but she liked it. She thought the late 1980s were an unfortunate era for the male hairstyle, and a cursory glance around the room revealed a number of scrawny ponytails and a few cases of Limahl-inspired, salt-and-pepper-highlighted mullets. His was dark brown, and just long enough to fall in a slight wave on the top of his head, short above his ears and around his neck. His eyes were very, very brown. And he shaved – there was a clear shadow on his top lip and chin. He was olive-skinned – he looked a little like he might be Mediterranean – Spanish or something . . . Mum would probably say he was swarthy (she suspected, but did not know for sure, that her mum was ever so slightly racist), but she quite liked it. He was big. A lot of the guys in this room were skinny – still lanky. Boys. Not him. He was more . . . manly. Just saying the word in her own head made her blush. Silly. Manly was such a romance novel word.

Susannah raised her gaze to his face again, and found he was looking right at her. She felt herself colour up even more, and then he smiled. His smile was broad and slightly wonky. He raised one eyebrow in a silent challenge, and Susannah stared down at her text, feeling her breath come fast, and not knowing why.

At the end of the interminable class, she stayed in her seat until most of the kids had left, rushing to lunch. Looking down intently at the contents of her bag, she watched his feet come across the room, pause slightly in front of her desk, and then carry on out of the room.

Present Day

Behind Lois, Rob smiled at her, almost shyly – a smile that revealed no teeth behind his lips. That same wonky smile.

'Hi, Susie.'

Strangely, no one else had ever called her Susie (and, while they'd been together, he had never called her anything else), and the use of the familiar nickname jolted her like a volt of electricity. She was struggling, for the moment, to separate past and present. Memories, long buried and almost forgotten, had flooded back unexpectedly and vividly when she saw him, swamping her brain. She had to consciously drag herself back to this moment.

'How are you, sweetheart? You look gorgeous . . . !' Lois was holding both her hands, but leaning back, looking her up and down.

'Thanks.' She felt as self-conscious as a teenager. 'I'm well. Very well, thank you. And how are you?' Then, without really meaning to, she blurted out, 'All of you – how's Frank?' She wished she'd written. 'I was so sorry . . . Lois . . . so sorry to hear that he was ill.'

Lois waved away the apology, not unkindly. 'Bless

43

you, love. He's not too bad . . . considering . . .' But she looked tired.

Now Rob spoke. 'He's been in hospital. They've been changing some of his drugs. That's why I'm home. I've been here, helping Mum, for a few days.'

Lois didn't drive. At least, she didn't used to.

'He's coming home tomorrow.' Lois put her arm up around Rob's waist now, and leant her head in towards his chest. He was such a lot taller than she was. 'He's been a great help, my boy. Lovely to have him here . . .'

'I'm sure he is.' The memory of his calm, quiet strength brushed past her like a ghost. Susannah was still watching Rob's face. He looked good. Hardly the boy his mother pronounced him to be, but still boyish, somehow. There were a few fine lines around his eyes, and on either side of his mouth. His hair had receded a little, but it was still thick and dark, with just a smattering of salt and pepper at each temple. His eyes were as brown as ever. Usually olive, he was quite tanned today – his blue check shirt was open at the neck . . . She realized she was staring at him. And no one was saying anything. Where was all this coming from? She didn't remember the last time she had felt this vulnerable, this emotional . . .

For a long moment the three of them smiled at each other. It felt to Susannah as though there was so much to say that none of them could start to speak.

Then, suddenly, Sadie was pulling on Susannah's skirt. 'Auntie Susannah!'

Relieved, Susannah lifted Sadie on to her hip. Over her shoulder she saw Alastair standing, waiting for her. He must have sent Sadie over.

'So, this is one of Alastair's, is it?'

She nodded. 'This is Sadie.'

Lois clucked a little at Sadie, who preened and glowed with pleasure. Then, 'Daddy says you have to come now, Auntie Susannah . . .'

'Of course.' Lois smiled, and stepped back. 'Of course, you must go . . . it's been just lovely to see you.'

'You, too, Lois.' And she meant it. 'And you, Rob. Good to see you.'

The same shy smile. 'And you, too, Susie.'

The name again. All of them so polite. She put Sadie down, and the little girl grabbed her wrist, pulling her away. She mock-grimaced, and let herself be dragged, giving them a small wave.

When she reached Alastair, Sadie considered her duty discharged – she dropped Susannah's hand and headed off at a trot towards the house in search of her mother.

'Just call me Sir Galahad.'

'Did I look like I needed rescuing, then?'

'I just figured you could do without a blast from the past today.'

'Probably.' She looked back at Lois and Rob, but they had turned and were walking back across the common, arm in arm. She was disappointed – she wanted to see his face again. How ridiculous.

'Hey! Earth to Chunky.'

She shook her head and smiled at her brother.

Alastair put one arm around her shoulder. 'Come on, snap out of it, or I'm going to have to slap you. Let's get you a glass of champagne . . . Actually, forget you, let's get me one . . .'

In just a minute or two more they were reabsorbed by the party – it was impossible not to be. The bride and groom beamed, the marquee was as lovely as Mum had boasted. A small jazz ensemble was playing, and 120 guests distracted Susannah from her reverie. Almost.

Susannah didn't go into the house straight away when she got back to Islington later that night. She was tired, and strangely drained by the day. That wasn't how you were supposed to feel at the end of a wedding – especially when it was the marriage of people you loved. You were supposed to feel suffused with joy, and bathed in the reflected glow of the newly-weds' love for each other, weren't you? Or at least, if you couldn't manage that, full of catty observations about the guests, and criticisms of how this particular couple had chosen to do it. She had the beginnings of a blister on one toe, as it happened, but that wasn't it. Maybe she should have stayed at Mum's. (Maybe not – if the wedding itself had been tiring, the clean-up tomorrow was going to be a hundred times more so . . . the party had still been close to full swing when she'd left, entering a pretty dangerous 'requests of the DJ' phase. Madness had just started playing when she made her escape, and Alex and Chloe's young lawyer friends looked pretty set in for the night.) She found a parking space a few houses down from home – how she longed for a drive-way – and sat in the car with her head laid back against the headrest. She'd only had a couple of drinks across the whole day – two glasses of champagne – but the beginnings of a nasty headache were stirring in her temples anyway. It was almost dark outside now, and all the lights in her house were blaring already. Alastair was right about one thing – things weren't right here. Bright, maybe, but not right. It wasn't right that she'd been alone at her brother's wedding today, and it wasn't alright to be sitting in the car now, slightly dreading going into her own home.

The kids were all there, she knew. It wasn't Doug's weekend to have them, but the arrangement was, as Douglas always said with a touch of pride (as though it proved how civilized he was), a 'fluid' one. If 'fluid' meant that the two of them were always at the mercy of his ex-wife, Sylvie, and her whims, then he'd be right. He'd have picked them up from their mother's this morning, after she'd left.

That's what the fight had been about. Nominally, at least. These days the fights were about lots of things but, like icebergs, only ten per cent ever surfaced. He'd waited until last night to tell her, although it turned out Sylvie had called on Wednesday to ask him to have them. He wasn't brave. She'd been furious. He'd presented the problem with no solution — glad to unload it on to her. What was he supposed to do? He was supposed to say no, she said. Unless he was actually glad to have the excuse to get out of coming. He said that wasn't true, said he'd wanted to come. Shrugged, as though he expected her to call her mum, who she knew had been laying tables in the marquee all after-noon, and suddenly find space for three kids she barely knew. No, she'd screamed, hearing herself sound ugly and mean. No. Enough was enough. He should have said no. And now it was his problem. Don't bother coming, she'd said. And he hadn't. Had she expected him to do anything different? Call Sylvie and say he'd changed his mind? Not for a minute.

She could already visualize what she'd find when she went in — it was always the same. Sylvie lived in a tip, and the kids had picked up their housekeeping skills from her and could not be persuaded that things were different in this house. The kitchen would be a mess — dishes in the sink, the detritus of meal prepa-ration left across the counters, cheese going hard, and a knife left in the butter. She had this peculiar sensa-tion, whenever the children were there, even after all these years, that it wasn't her house any more.

It wasn't her house, actually. Technical point. She did have her own home, though she never thought of it in those terms — just a little flat she'd bought after Sean and before Douglas, and had never really lived in. But this house belonged to Douglas. He'd lived here when they first met. Not with Sylvie – this was the house he'd bought after the divorce had split their assets and reduced both their circumstances. Much smaller than the one he'd lived in with her, apparently. That had been a detached house in a better road, with off-street parking. This was a terraced house with three bedrooms and a pocket handkerchief lawn. But it felt like hers, when they weren't here. When they were, she definitely felt invaded. And then felt guilty about feeling that way. And then irritated by feeling guilty. This was a very, very familiar pattern. Daisy would be shut in her room, doubtless with the phone from the landing pulled to the limit of its cord, playing music too loud. Susannah had never understood how teenagers could listen to their stereo at full blast and talk to their friends on the phone at the same time, but couldn't hear you ask them to make their beds if you were standing right beside them and all around was silence. No doubt she'd be talking to Seth – 'the boyfriend'. Rosie would be watching some rubbish on the TV. (Sylvie limited 'screen time'; she and Doug didn't. So there was a real feast and famine thing going on that Susannah didn't think was at all healthy – the kids were all plugged into something or other 24/7 when they were with them. Rosie had tried to wear the earbuds of her iPod shuffle through dinner last week.) And Fin, who should probably be in bed by now, would be plugged into his DS Lite, far too wired by the game to realize he was sleepy.

*

It hadn't always been like this. She'd never meant it to turn out this way. She sounded like a mother, and she had the workload of a mother, but she'd never had a Mother's Day card.

It wasn't the kids. She'd wanted to love the kids. She'd always thought that would come in time. Maybe not the instant punch of unconditional love that assaults a biological parent in the delivery suite, but a gradual sweet affection, and that then they'd be a family – the five of them. A blended, chaotic family, dysfunctional, maybe, but no more than anyone else was. They worked – you saw them all around you. The children weren't a surprise, after all. She'd worked with Doug before the two of them got together, so she'd known – known perfectly well –that there was an ex-wife, and three young children. They hadn't seemed like a barrier then. They'd even seemed a little like a bonus. It was time. She was in her thirties. She thought she was ready. And here they were. She wasn't hung up like some women might be about them not being her own. At least, that's what she told herself.

But that wasn't quite how it had been. That wasn't, it seemed, what Douglas had wanted.

The Douglas of back then seemed like a whole different person. (Did everyone feel that way, after a few years, when they woke up and looked at the guy in the bed next to them?) She'd been thirty-one, divorced from Sean by then, damaged. Certainly not 'actively looking'. And certainly not looking in his direction. She was doing the classic 'focusing on her career' thing, and office romances were not in her plan. He was a colleague – a senior colleague at that – not her boss, but the boss of several of her peers, and a partner in the firm – and he was twelve years older than her. They were friends, she supposed, in the beginning. He was kind, and seemed sweet. Sad, even. And maybe just a little bit grateful that she would spend time with him. It was such a gradual thing, falling in love with him. Which didn't sound romantic, or sexy, or all that convincing. But at the time, she thought it was just what she needed. Sean had more than bruised her. Maybe Sylvie had done the same thing to Doug. They needed a slow burn. Time to trust again. They were both more careful with their hearts this time around.

She'd honestly thought he was being the same way when it came to the children. Protecting them. She loved him for it, at first. Like she loved him, at first, for a hundred things that drove her crazy now, like the way he always fell asleep in front of the news and couldn't make a decent cup of tea. It was ages before he introduced her to them. They'd been sleeping together for nine months when she was first invited to go for pizza with them. She remembered vividly standing in her underwear, the phone tucked on her shoulder with Amelia on the end of the line, talking her through what to wear. Amelia, her touchstone for so many years, had taken on, since Susannah had met Douglas, the stature of a goddess – mother to three small children, including her god-daughter Elizabeth and godson Sam, and thus the expert on all things 'small people'.

'I've got to get it right. It's really important, first impressions.'

'Don't make such a big deal of it. To them, it isn't. They probably couldn't care less. Well, except the oldest one, maybe. Daisy?'

'Yes. Daisy's eight. Rose is three.'

'What's with all the flower names?' Amelia was a traditionalist.

'I don't know. He says it was Sylvie.' Sylvie was not.

'And the boy child?' Amelia always called Sam 'the boy child'. Or 'Bub', which was short for Beelzebub, and directly attributable, at that time, to his penchant for emptying drawers out on to the floor.

'Fin. He's just two.' She thought he looked like an angel in his photographs. A blond, curly-haired angel.

'So, that's easy. Fin and Rose are like Sam and Victoria. They just want you to get down to their level, talk to them, be a bit silly, you know? Show an interest, but not like a teacher, you know. Like a cool babysitter.'

'You say that as if I know how to be one of those.'

'You're kidding, right? You're *the* cool babysitter. They love it when you come round here. You're a bloody baby whisperer. Victoria still hasn't forgiven me for not asking you to be her godmother, too.'

'Yes, well. Me, too, now that you mention it . . .'

'Oh, bugger off. You know we had to ask J's sister . . .'

She laughed. 'But Daisy?'

'Daisy'll be the tricky one. She's your Elizabeth, and Lord knows I have to watch myself around mine . . . Eight is the new thirteen. She's old enough to know what's going on. Sylvie sounds like enough of a head-case to have told her stuff she's not old enough to understand, too. And most of it is probably rubbish. I bet you she's told Daisy it's *your* fault their dad left them.'

'That's not even physically possible. I hadn't met him.'

'That won't stop a wacky ex, I'm telling you. Hell hath no fury like a forty-something woman whose husband has moved on. They'll say anything . . .'

'How do you know so much about this stuff?'

'I watch *EastEnders* while I do the ironing,' Amelia deadpanned. 'So, this Daisy, she could be tricky. They close?'

'Who – Sylvie and Daisy?'

'No, Douglas and Daisy.'

'I don't know. In either case, as it goes. I've never seen them together, have I?'

'That's right – you haven't.' Amelia said this thought-fully, in the style of Inspector Poirot, and then let the line fall silent for a moment, making her point. 'Have I mentioned that's weird . . . ?'

She *had* mentioned it, of course, more than once. If by 'mentioned' you meant endlessly harangued and gone on about. And, apparently, she was going to again, if Susannah didn't stop her . . . 'I mean, you've been practically living there with him for the last six months, and you haven't met his kids yet?'

'Give it a rest, Meels. I'm meeting them now, aren't I? Could we focus? Wardrobe?'

'Right. Ask a woman who hasn't worn anything without an elasticated waistband for . . . I don't know . . . about a thousand years – yeah, ask her for fashion advice . . .'

'I have to leave in about six minutes . . .'

'Okay, okay.' Amelia finally got down to business. 'Jeans. Dark wash, low rise. No mum jeans.'

'I don't have any mum jeans.'

'Right. Forgot. Sorry. The biker boots, that suede jacket. Dangly earrings. Cool but not too cool. Casual.'

Susannah was pulling clothes out of the wardrobe. 'Thanks a million. Love you.'

'Love you, too. Call me after . . .'

Amelia had been so right about Daisy. She was eight almost nine, she said, but she seemed more like eight going on eighteen to Susannah. There was something knowing and slightly hard about her that was unnerving in a child so young. Maybe Amelia was right, and Sylvie *had* been trying to poison her against Susannah. Rose was just a pretty, pouty princess with a big baby belly, who came to dinner in a tutu and a tiara. And Fin was little more than a baby, with a dummy firmly plugged into his little rosebud mouth, and a large grubby square of satin that smelt like socks gripped tightly in his hand, every bit as delectable as he had appeared in his pictures – just considerably noisier.

Of course, at first, it touched her to see Douglas,

the man she had fallen in love with, with his children. At the beginning. It was touching, and it was sexy, all at the same time. For about five minutes. Until Rosie threw a fit because they didn't serve chips, and Fin started crying loudly, no one knew why . . . And until she realized that he didn't apparently know them a great deal better than she did. Couldn't calm the tantrum or quell the tears. Or at least, didn't have a clue how to relate to them. His questions to Daisy were prescriptive and mechanical, her answers bland and delivered parrot-fashion. The next stage was to feel sorry for him – the displaced dad. Just after that was the irritation. The kind only a childless woman can feel while sitting in a booth with ill-mannered children for whom she is not responsible, with a father who blustered ineffectually and kept making threats he didn't follow through on.

That first time had been a real eye-opener. Beyond a frank up-and-down perusal at the beginning of the evening by Daisy – and the dubious honour, at the end, of wiping Rosie's bum on a trip to the loo – the kids had shown almost no interest in her, or her assumed cool babysitter demeanour, or her coolish outfit. And the suede jacket had a mozzarella grease stain on the right lapel to this day. It remained one of the most exhausting and least pleasurable evenings she had ever spent, right up there with most New Year's Eves for the disappointment of anticipation.

But it wasn't on the occasion of that initial meeting

that Susannah had first tried to intervene (however much she might have wanted to). Douglas had smiled winsomely and apologetically at her in the cab on the way home (having left her, carefully invisible, around the corner from Sylvie's while he dropped them off with their mother) and held her hand and told her how happy he was that she'd met them at last. And then they'd had distinctly childless-couple-type sex on the sofa at home, which had been wonderfully distracting.

That wasn't until months later − after she and Douglas had become an established item and she'd left the firm they both worked at (Amelia had been really cross about that, gone all feminist on her over it, but Susannah knew one of them had to leave, and Doug was the partner) and she had moved in with him officially. They'd all been in the park, Susannah giving it her best shot, and Rosie had been earnestly torturing Fin in the sandpit − taking toys from him, deliberately filling in the holes he'd painstakingly dug, and stamping on his castles. Douglas had been on the other side of the park, helping Daisy stay upright on the roller-blades Susannah had persuaded him to buy her for her birthday. Susannah had first remonstrated with Rosie, then shouted, and finally, in exasperation, slapped her hand, hard. Douglas had watched the whole thing from a distance, and he was tight-lipped and white-faced for the rest of the afternoon. It hadn't helped that Daisy had fallen off the skates moments later, twisting her ankle so hard she howled for a full ten minutes.

Later that night, when the kids had gone to bed, and he'd gone up to tuck them in, she'd poured two big glasses of Pinot Noir, ready to talk about what they were going to do about Rosie's increasingly unkind behaviour towards her little brother. But when Douglas had come down, he hadn't sat beside her at the kitchen table as she had thought he would. He'd stood, formally, in front of her, with the table between them, and delivered a speech he'd clearly been rehearsing in his own head all afternoon.

It was a tone of voice she hadn't heard him use before outside of a boardroom, and it shocked her to hear it in their home. 'We need to get something straight if we have any kind of a future, Susannah.' (If? They were living together . . .) 'These are *my* kids. They have a mother. I'm not about to confuse them by having you come on to the scene and trying to be another mother to them. You can be their friend. But don't try and be a parent. That's not what I want. And I never, ever, ever want you to raise a hand against any one of them.'

She felt like he'd slapped her. That was the first night they'd fallen asleep without making friends. She was bewildered, angry and hurt, and she'd lain stiffly in the bed beside him, trying to figure out what to do.

She never told anyone what he'd said that night. Not her mother, and definitely not Amelia. No one. She knew what Amelia would have said. She'd have said she should get the hell out before it was too late. And maybe she was right. Maybe she should have done. But she loved him. (Hear the refrain of women throughout the history of the world and time.) She didn't want to start again. She didn't want to be on her own. So she made excuses for him in her head, made them until she'd convinced herself she'd been out of line. That he was right – she shouldn't interfere.

And truthfully, she didn't believe, back then, that it would always be that way. She told herself she wouldn't have stayed if she had, although she wasn't sure that she believed herself, even as she said it. Time, she felt, would be bound to change things. Maybe she'd pushed too hard, too soon. But things would change. They would all, surely, find a level, grow together into some-thing that worked. And, in a way, it did. They'd been together for eight years. She'd done the school run, and sat through the school plays and concerts. She'd admin-istered the Calpol, done the algebra problems and trawled through Toys R Us looking for the Christmas gift 'du jour'. It just wasn't the way she had ever thought it would be. She didn't feel like they belonged to her, not in any way. If they loved each other, it was never articulated, or even assumed, by her, them, or their father. These days, she wondered if she'd been right to stay. Or at least, right to stay on Douglas's terms. Once the patterns of a relationship were set, it was hard – or was it more like impossible? – to change them.

Outside the house now, she took a deep breath, and put her key in the lock. Inside, the kids barely registered her presence – Fin didn't look up from his game and Rosie threw only a vague greeting and a wave in her direction, her eyes never leaving the flickering screen. Simon Cowell was bashing someone. It was always Simon Cowell these days. And he was always bashing someone. All the sofa cushions were on the rug, and Fin was lying prostrate on them like a little emperor, while Rosie sprawled across all three of the sofa's seats. Douglas and Daisy were nowhere to be seen.

Her 'hi, guys' didn't get much sensible response. She decided against the kitchen – she knew she'd feel compelled to start clearing up, and she really wasn't in the mood, plus she was in a pale-coloured and not inexpensive dress that wasn't intended for domestic tasks – and headed instead straight for the stairs. As she'd thought she would be, Daisy was squirrelled away in the room she shared – much to her consternation – with Rosie, with the phone cord shut in the door, and Death Cab for Cutie playing on the iPod dock. It amazed her that she even knew who was making the noise, but she did. Elizabeth had loaded some stuff on to her iPod a few weeks ago, when she'd been round at Amelia's house. She didn't hate all of it . . . She assumed that Douglas was closeted away in his top-floor study. That was his primary refuge from all things domestic, these days. He kept an old-fashioned stereo up there, and a collection of jazz CDs, as well as a bottle of Maker's Mark whisky and an ancient, peeling leather recliner. Daisy called it, in the disparaging tone she had adopted in recent years, his 'man cave'. But he was, instead, in their room. The bed – which she'd left unmade – was made now, with all the extraneous pillows he complained about neatly in place, just as she would have done it herself. Through the open door to their en suite bathroom she could see that the bath was running. He was pouring bath salts under the tap. He turned when he heard her, and smiled almost sheepishly. The same pizzeria smile. He looked about twenty-five years old when he smiled that way. 'I heard you come in. Thought you'd like a hot bath.'

Then he came to her, and folded her into an embrace. 'I'm so sorry, Susannah.' He spoke into her neck, his hand stroking her hair. 'I was a shit last night, and I'm sorry.' He peeled the jacket off her shoulders, and kissed the side of her neck.

He was good at this. She didn't know if it was deliberate, or just dumb luck, but his apologies were always issued when she was tired enough to accept them rather than prolong whatever aggravation he was apologizing for. So she stood and let him hold her for a moment. Everything about him was so very familiar to her. His touch, his scent, the sound of his voice. She let him unzip the dress, so that it fell to the floor, then let him lead her into the bathroom.

The bath was half full, and he leant over to turn off the taps, pulling a hand through the water to check the temperature. 'It's ready. Why don't you climb in, and I'll go down and get you a drink. What do you want? A cup of tea, or something stronger? Then you'll tell me all about it.'

'Tea. I've got a headache.' She knew she sounded sulky.

His face was full of concern. 'I'm sorry. I'll bring you a pill, shall I?'

She shrugged and smiled, really trying. 'Can't blame you for the headache, at least.'

She shucked off her bra and knickers, and stepped, naked, into the hot bath. Douglas stroked her shoulder as she sat down. There was nothing sexual about the gesture, or about the feeling in the room, despite her nakedness. There never was, when the kids were in the house. She'd learnt that a long time ago.

Amelia had once told her that she and her ex-husband, Jonathan, when they were still married, liked to 'do it' in the mornings on weekends when the kids were small. If the kids were in front of the TV, watching cartoons, she said, they'd be happy and quiet for just long enough. Their dad would come down and settle them, with a bowl of Cheerios and the remote control, make a cup of tea, bring it back up and lock the door behind him. Best fifteen minutes of the weekend, she said. They could be done, she laughed, in time to drink the tea before it got cold.

That didn't work with Douglas. Certainly not in the mornings, and not even at night. Not even if the kids were sound asleep in their beds. At first it had frustrated her, not only sexually, but because it seemed wrong – wrong to keep these two key parts of his life so separate and compartmentalized. He'd been insatiable, in the early days. He couldn't get enough of her. Any time, any place. Making up for lost years in a largely sexless marriage, he said. They'd had sex almost every day, in those first few months. She didn't know how he could turn it all off just like that. She'd tried everything to weaken his resolve, used every weapon in her sexual arsenal to persuade him that it was okay, that having quiet, quick sex behind the locked door of their bedroom wasn't going to hurt the kids, but nothing had worked and eventually she'd given up. Sex went absolutely off the agenda when the kids were at home. Another thing she'd never confessed to Amelia.

She lay back in the deep bath and closed her eyes. And the moment she did she saw Rob.

Not as he'd been today. As he'd been then . . .

1987

Rob Rossi had moved with his parents into the village during the summer, apparently. They didn't go to St Gabriel's – they were Catholic, not that they went to any church at all – which explained why they hadn't registered on Mum's radar. They lived in a house on the other side of the common. Different coach.

For weeks, they didn't speak. But Susannah got very used to looking for him during the day. He was easy to spot, being so tall. And every time she spotted him, her breath caught in her throat. She found herself thinking about him at odd times of the day, and lying in bed at night. She started looking hard at herself in the mirror in the morning. Trying to see what he saw. Wondering if he saw her at all.

Susannah was a typically self-conscious teenager, a little taller than she wanted to be, acutely aware of the relatively new curves in her shape. Amelia had had boobs for ever, but Susannah's were a much more recent development. She recognized, in moments of objective appraisal, that her skin was clearer than most people's her own age, that her eyes – a disappointing hazel most of the time – were green around the edges, and sparkled when she was happy. Amelia said she had a ski-jump nose and bee-stung lips, damn her, but Susannah knew Amelia was prettier – and anyway, she sometimes thought she'd swap all the good bits for her best friend's confident swagger.

She and Rob only had one class together – English. He was very quiet there, but if Ichabod called on him, his answers were full, his voice deep. He would smile at her sometimes, shyly, but his eyes always dropped away from her gaze before the smile left his mouth. She wondered if he was making fun of her, if she was staring. He was something of a loner – he seemed to be friendly with lots of guys, but no one in particular, and she never saw him talking to girls. He sometimes played football at lunchtime, and sometimes read a magazine – she didn't know what – sitting against a tree next to the science block. Amelia said he had a sexy-broody thing going on. She said he reminded her of Heathcliff, but Susannah didn't see it – she didn't have her best friend's flair for drama – to her, he seemed coolly self-contained. Like he didn't need any of them.

One Friday night, sometime in late October, Amelia's mother was driving the two of them home from the cinema – and a graphic retelling of the plot of *Fatal Attraction* was under way – when they both saw him, walking along the main road from the bus stop towards his house. He was wearing military-style clothes – unfashionably flared blue trousers and a ribbed sweater, with a black beret. There was a girl with him – dressed the same way. At first Susannah thought she was a guy.

The following Monday, Amelia – who wasn't in the least shy around him, or anyone else – sat on the edge of his desk and asked him about it, while they were waiting for English class to start.

'Are you a soldier, then?' Her tone sounded vaguely mocking to Susannah.

Rob looked uncomfortable, as though she'd caught him off guard, though he didn't ask her why she was asking. He shook his head. 'Air cadet.'

'What does that mean?'

'I'm going to be an airman. In the RAF. After "A" levels.'

'We saw you, the other night. Susannah and me.'

He looked at Susannah, then nodded.

'With a girl. Is that your girlfriend?'

He was still looking straight at her, and his cheeks pinked up.

Amelia could be mean when she wanted to be, Susannah thought, even as she felt herself sit forward to hear his answer.

'No. I don't have a girlfriend.'

Amelia nudged Susannah significantly – just, thank God, at the moment Mr Blythe walked in and asked them to open the play at page 110, and just before Susannah pinched Amelia's thigh, hard, across the desk.

But despite Amelia's teasing and goading, it was November before Susannah worked up the courage to talk to him herself. They smiled at each other, and there were moments when she convinced herself he was looking for her, too, among a crowd. Sometimes he held her gaze for just a bit longer than he needed to. She always felt, after that happened, that the Ready Brek glow from the television was fuzzing and glowing around her. There was always a huge bonfire in the village, on the common, for Guy Fawkes. They started building it in October – everyone in the village contributing – and by November the Fifth it was usually vast enough to roast a multitude of guys. The Rotary set up a fireworks display in a field to the north, and a travelling fairground with a small Ferris wheel and bumper cars usually erected its rides on the other side of the common. The whole village came out, so long as it wasn't raining, for the lighting of the bonfire, and the fireworks. Ever since Susannah was a little girl she'd found it exciting – something about the darkness, and the unusual presence of everyone on the common at night, along with the relaxation of school-night bedtime. She loved the fireworks best of all. She couldn't watch a fireworks display without getting a lump in her throat. They always made her want to cry.

The bonfire had really taken hold now, having been lit from six or seven different points around its perimeter, and flames licked at the branches near the top. The guys were all ablaze. The fire crackled fantastically, and smelt delicious. It was weird how your front could be so hot your cheeks hurt, while you were still cold in the back. Amelia had gone with Alastair to buy hot cider and toffee apples before the fireworks

66

started. Separated from her parents and Alex, who'd found friends of their own on the other side of the common, and deserted by her friend in her quest for refreshments, Susannah found herself — to her combined delight and mortification — standing close to where Rob was watching with two middle-aged adults – his parents, she presumed. She hadn't sought him out, and she hoped he didn't think so. She couldn't move away – Al and Amelia were coming back to this spot, and there was no chance of finding each other again if they got split up now, plus it was crowded out here, and dark, away from the fire. She wasn't sure at first if he'd seen her in the flickering firelight, but suddenly he was next to her. She was quite genuinely afraid she might get so dizzy she'd fall forward into the fire if it weren't for the rope that encircled it – to keep those who weren't officious Rotarians at a safe distance. She'd never, *never* felt like this before.

'Hi.' He spoke first.

'Hi.'

'This is amazing,' Rob offered, gesturing towards the fire.

She nodded and her answer was full of genuine enthusiasm. 'I love it. I think it's my favourite night of the year in the village. Everyone's here.'

'Have you always lived here?'

'Yup. All my life. So this is, like, the sixteenth or seventeenth Bonfire Night I've been to. I'm pretty sure they had me out here when I was a baby.'

'Is it always this big?'

'Think so. Don't know. When you're a kid, things seem bigger, don't they?'

He smiled. 'Where's your friend?'

'Amelia?' Susannah's heart sank, and she felt a sharp stab of disappointment. It was Amelia he was interested in. That figured. Amelia was the flirty one, attracting boys like moths to a flame. Not awkward and shy. She shuffled from foot to foot, realizing that her toes were cold. 'She's gone with my brother to buy drinks and stuff. She'll be back in a minute.'

'Shame.'

She looked at him, and his eyes were sparkling before he looked away. He was almost smiling.

An uncomfortable silence ensued. Susannah trawled her mind for something interesting to say. She was really, really bad at this. The tension was unbearable. Any second now, she just knew, he was going to nod at her and go back to his parents. When she spoke, words tumbled awkwardly out of her mouth. 'We're . . . a bunch of us . . . we're going to the funfair after we watch the fireworks. Wanna come? I mean, if you like . . .'

'Sure.' Rob shrugged, as if he was easy either way.

When the others came back, Amelia smirked at her. Susannah narrowed her eyes and pursed her lips in warning, and Amelia raised a finger to her lips in a shushing motion, winking at her. Alastair chatted easily to Rob, oblivious to the scene.

Susannah still felt utterly breathless and self-conscious as the fireworks began to explode in Technicolor above their heads. The lump came into her throat. Everyone put their heads back to watch, and all around them were the gasps and aaahs of children. It felt like he was so close to her, in the cold and the dark. And she liked how it felt to have him next to her.

When she put her hand down to her side, her coat sleeve brushed against his, and then she felt his hand slide slowly into hers, until their fingers were laced. He squeezed once, but his gaze never left the sky.

Present Day

August

So often in recent years it seemed as though England was teasing its people with a handful of hot days in May, prompting a hysterical rush of toenail painting, leg waxing, and strappy top buying, only to turn on the grey rain and chilly breezes in July, but this year, the summer proper was really delivering. The English Riviera was booked up for August, and the tabloids carried pictures every day of Hyde Park full of bikini-clad sunbathers. Doug had had three weekends out on the boat, and gone mahogany in the sun. Susannah had managed to dodge one, claiming a backlog of work that needed to be cleared, but all five of them had been down there last weekend, Daisy sulking because she wasn't with Seth, lying on her stomach all day, slathering herself in Piz Buin, with Fin leaning precariously off the rails while his father barked instructions at him. She wished she loved to sail as much as Doug did, but truthfully, Rosie was the only willing and vaguely useful crew member he had.

The sun was still shining hot, and the air was thick and heavy when Susannah finished work and emerged, blinking mole-like, from her darker, air-conditioned office. She peeled off the cotton cardigan she wore over her coral-pink shift dress to combat the electrical chill of the air conditioning, and headed to the underground. The discernible spring in her step was probably due to the fact that she wasn't heading straight home this evening, though Douglas had offered to barbecue and open a bottle of rosé, and had acted quite shirtily when she'd reminded him of her plans. Nor was she, like most of the people who milled sweatily around her, off to the pub to enjoy the August evening with a Pimm's or three. She had a long-standing date to keep, and she was as excited about it as she had been about anything in a while. She was meeting Amelia for an evening at the Porchester Spa in Queensway – they went three or four times a year and had been going, pregnancy permitting, since 1993, their first year in London, when they'd discovered it almost by accident.

A truly old-fashioned Victorian municipal bathing house that had first opened in 1929, they'd paid their first, speculative visit one winter's Tuesday night, after a colleague of Amelia's had told her it was as cheap as chips. Which it had been. It was still much cheaper than the other spas that had sprung up in the intervening decades all over the city – cheaper still since they'd become members (they'd bought each other a membership for Christmas, both of them thinking they'd had the best, most original idea ever for a present). But that wasn't what kept them going. They had more money these days, and had tried others – the Bliss Spa and The Sanctuary and, once, when Susannah had received an unexpected bonus at work, the spa at The Berkeley. But in other places, they'd felt out of place and constrained – silly sometimes. Nothing else did the trick the way the Porchester Spa did. Amelia said it was because it was the only one still populated by fat white middle-aged women who didn't care, and that they kept going because it made them feel svelte and young. Susannah thought it was just a little more romantic than that. She loved the space – the high ceilings and the original Victorian tiles. She loved that they'd been coming here for so long together. They'd made plans and whispered secrets to each other in here for years, lying side by side in the wet steam, or the dry heat. Squealed together in the ice-cold plunge pool. They'd been here to celebrate promotions, and console broken hearts, and to bitch and moan about bosses, babies and bank managers. They'd been here for Amelia's hen night, obsessing over the details of the impending big day, and, not quite a year afterwards, for her first outing post-Elizabeth, when her engorged breasts had leaked on to the scratchy white towel and she'd cried over her poochy stomach and the way her baby's head smelt. They never brought other people here – it was *their* place – and it was almost sacred to Susannah. The management had given the place a big facelift a couple of years ago, and she'd been worried they would have destroyed what was special about it, but they hadn't. Most of the staff had been there as long as she'd been going, and they were as much a part of the experience, with their gruffness and frowns, as the surroundings and the treatments themselves.

This ritual was part of what connected the two of them after all these years. Their lives had taken such different directions. When she'd been young, she'd imagined that they'd do the same things at the same time, always. College, university, careers, marriage, babies, careers again. They'd dreamed subtle variations of the same dreams. And so it had seemed to go, at first. They'd ended up at different universities – Susannah studying Law at Bristol, and Amelia French at Manchester – but they'd both put in the effort required to stay good friends. They'd spent weekends on each other's floors and gone on holiday together, and ended up each Christmas Day and New Year's Eve in the Coach and Horses in the village. They'd still been close enough after they graduated to eschew their uni mates and live together in Clapham, in a two-double-bed, third-floor flat with a lascivious landlord and a view over the rooftops to the common. She'd met Sean. Amelia had met Jonathan. They'd married within the same thrilling twelve months – meeting in their lunch hours to compare John Lewis wedding lists and lace swatches.

It was only as their respective honeymoons ended that their paths began to seriously diverge. Amelia had fallen pregnant quickly, with Elizabeth, and then there had been Victoria two years later, and Sam, her last, a neat and tidy two years after that. She'd given up work after Victoria. She and Jonathan had moved out of Zone 1 – to Richmond, and a terraced house with a garden they filled with climbing frames and sandpits. Susannah had stayed at work, through the collapse of her marriage. She'd found refuge in work at first, then she'd rediscovered her passion for what she did, it having been sidelined by her marriage to Sean. She moved on from the law firm where she'd been since her year at law school in Chester. Her ambition had shifted slightly – making partner wasn't so crucial. She took a job as legal counsel in a firm of architects. And then she'd found Douglas.

Amelia always said she started shopping in the Boden catalogue around the time Susannah started shopping in Nicole Farhi. They would meet for lunch so that they could tell each other they envied each other's lives, each claiming it made them feel better to do so. Amelia said she longed for 'dry clean only' clothing and her own bank account. Susannah looked into the buggy and dreamed of a baby possetting down her Jaeger jacket. Amelia told bitchy stories about the mummies in her book club, and Susannah carped about her bosses and the undeniable existence of the glass ceiling.

But Susannah was never entirely convinced by Amelia's tales of fear and loathing in South-West

London. Amelia didn't compromise – she never really had. She was doing exactly what she had always wanted, always planned. She loved her life. She gave marriage and motherhood the same energy and drive she'd given work. Susannah always imagined that the other mothers in the nursery school might have hated her, though she was hard to hate. Her kids were always immaculate, always well mannered. She never bought a cake when she could make one, and she could always make one. No distressing of store-bought mince pies for Amelia.

At first, Susannah had been shocked when Amelia told her she'd asked Jonathan to move out. But she quickly came to see it as another facet of her best friend's bright, fierce nature. She would not stay in a marriage that had become, if not unhappy, then significantly less happy than it had once been. Not for convention, nor for her children, and not for herself. There was no one else. She always said that eventually there would have been, for Jonathan or for her, and that this would have been significantly more damaging to both of them and, above all, for the kids. Better to get out when you still had love for each other, she said. When you stood the best chance of building something new and civilized between the two of you, that protected your children and made a world for them that was workable, and while the possibilities of glittering, shiny futures with other people were still real.

She said she'd watched her own parents coexist for

long enough to know that it wasn't the answer. 'My parents thought everything was okay because there was no shouting in my house. They never understood that the silence was far worse.' They'd waited until she'd left home to finally separate, both certain that was the right thing for their daughter. She didn't agree that it was right for any of them. Her dad had moved, first to a flat nearer his work, and then to Spain, once he'd retired, where he now lived in an apartment in a gated community on the Costa Brava with a middle-aged bottle blonde called Sandra who Amelia neither knew nor cared to. He played golf every day – Sandra played, too, with a set of pink clubs he'd bought her for a first anniversary present. Amelia always said after she'd seen him – which she did rarely, and actually quite grudgingly – that she couldn't relate this new guy to the man she'd grown up living alongside. Mum hadn't met anyone else. She still lived in the house Amelia had grown up in – rattling around, Amelia called it.

Amelia was a wonderful 'manager', and she'd managed this latest change wonderfully, as ever. Jonathan had moved out. The kids were fine. Genuinely fine, not just appearing so, Susannah believed. Amelia had never looked better than she looked these days. If Susannah had been waiting for a meltdown, she should have known better.

Susannah's own life seemed to her, sometimes, to be in stark contrast. It was a series of compromises. Connected episodes of not quite being happy enough.

She sometimes wished she had Amelia's courage, although what exactly she should be brave about, she wasn't sure.

She greeted the receptionist, who'd worked here for years, and went to the changing room, undressing quickly, pulling a cotton robe on, and putting her clothes in a locker.

Amelia was there before her, as usual – in the first, least steamy steam room – their habitual meeting place. She'd stripped naked – always the same unselfconscious girl, even three kids later – and covered the top of herself with an old blue and white striped cotton sarong she'd had for ever. Susannah remembered her coming out of the sea in Mykonos a hundred years ago in a string bikini, nut brown and super skinny, and wrapping herself in it. Her hair was pulled back and she had some sort of thick greyish gunk all over her face.

She hadn't seen Amelia since Alex and Chloe's wedding, though they'd spoken many times on the phone. It was unusual for them not to speak three or four times a week. It was unusual, come to think of it, that they hadn't seen each other for this long. And this, as she might have expected, was Amelia's conversational opener.

'So, have you been avoiding me? I haven't seen you for weeks. The kids think you've emigrated!'

'I've been busy. Besides, you've been away.'

Amelia and the kids had spent ten days on a Sunsail holiday in Crete. Amelia had spent the whole time sending Susannah hilarious texts about her ineptitude and phone photos of the kids expertly sailing Lasers around an azure bay.

Amelia stared at her hard, then shook her head. 'I've been back a week. You've been avoiding me.'

'I was waiting for the tan to fade a bit.'

'No. Avoidance. You always do this when things are off with you.'

'Nothing's "off".' She'd told Amelia about the wedding. About the fight with Douglas.

But not about Rob.

There was no point dissembling now. Amelia was like her conscience. It had been that way between them for years now. But there was nothing to tell, anyway. A chance encounter with an old boyfriend, that was all. Why did it feel like a big deal?

She picked up the tube of face mask from the floor by Amelia's lounger, and squeezed a dollop on to her fingers, before rubbing it slowly on to her cheeks. 'I saw Rob.'

'Get out!' Amelia sat up sharply, and the sarong fell away, momentarily revealing her right nipple.

'At the church. He was there with Lois.'

'Blimey.' Amelia nodded. 'Of course she was there. How long's it been?'

'Years.'

'How did he look?'

'He looked . . . like Rob. He looked great. He called me Susie.' She shouldn't have said that.

79

Amelia's stare sharpened. 'What's that face mean?'

'What face?'

'That face. You don't need a mirror to see what face you're making.'

'Nor do you.'

'So, what's he up to these days? Still in the RAF? Is he married? Kids?'

'I don't know.' Susannah shrugged.

'You didn't talk to him?' Amelia asked incredulously.

'Not really. Alastair rescued me. I'd already had the waterworks, in the church. I think he thought it wasn't a good idea . . .'

'So, it was just a "hi, bye" thing?'

Susannah nodded slowly. 'Hi, bye. Pretty much . . .'

'But . . . ?'

'There's a "but"?'

'Your face says there's a "but" . . .'

'My face says, "Aah – this mask stings!"'

'It would do – it's for my skin type, not yours. You'll probably get a rash. That'll teach you to help yourself. But what about the "but"?'

'But he looked good.'

'He always did.'

1987

After Bonfire Night, when Rob had held her hand in the darkness, the two of them had become inseparable, almost overnight. It was as if the invisible dam between them had burst, and they really couldn't get enough of each other. His coach always left school first, and he would walk, once he was back in the village, across the common to her stop to wait for her, then walk her home, the two of them dropping Amelia off at the rectory on their way past. Amelia teased them mercilessly, but they didn't care. Sometimes he took her to his house, sometimes they studied together at hers. At the weekends, Mum wouldn't let her go out until she'd finished her homework, so she'd get up at 7 a.m. on Saturday and race through it so that she could escape. Mum and Dad started muttering about 'A' levels and UCCA forms, but she kept her marks up.

After a few weeks of long phone calls, and short lunchtimes holding hands, Susannah was in love. She never said so, not to Amelia, or to Mum, or Alastair. She was afraid they'd laugh, afraid they'd denigrate or belittle what she felt — she had so little experience —

how could she know? But she knew. With all the vehemence and absolute certainty that a sixteen-year-old can feel, she knew.

She just wanted to be with him. She wanted to be with him every minute. When she wasn't with him, it felt like she was just waiting for him. There weren't many places they could be together, and in almost none of them was it possible to be alone. Their respective homes, the lounge at college, with its drinks machine and institutional furniture, the local cinema, parties held at the houses of friends . . . there were always throngs of people around them. They went for long walks through the cold, wintry lanes surrounding the village.

They hadn't shared their first kiss until almost three weeks after that first night, Rob confessing himself as inexperienced as her. They'd been in the kitchen at her parents' house, and the air had been heavy with intention all evening. He'd caught her, at last, when she turned to take coffee mugs out of the cupboard behind him, his hands on her waist, his face leaning into hers, the slight shadow of stubble grazing her cheek a little before their lips met.

Practice had made perfect. And they'd had lots of practice. Not going further than kissing, not at first. But the kissing . . . By the time the DJ at the Christmas sixth form disco played that year's big hit – the Pet Shop Boys' version of 'You Were Always On My Mind' (the one that so offended Mum, a major Elvis aficionado) – it felt like they'd been together always. Or maybe it was just that Susannah felt like life hadn't started until he'd held her hand in the firelight.

Present Day

Susannah was amazed by how vivid the long-buried memories of Rob were. She remembered songs and weather and gifts and moments she hadn't thought about for years. She and Amelia fell easily into a nostalgic mood, as they often did in this venue of their youth, chatting and laughing for a while about the 'old' days. Shared history was a great thing. *Smash Hits* and Chelsea Girl and Kajagoogoo and Frankie Goes to Hollywood. They'd both had enormous white T-shirts with RELAX in foot-high fluorescent letters stamped across the front. Slow dancing to Kool & The Gang. Two fat old ladies of the kind they treasured most shushed at them from across the room, through the steam, and they giggled, feeling, for a moment, as far from forty as it was possible for them to feel.

But a conversation about their own adolescence led inevitably to one about the teenagers in their lives now. Elizabeth was driving Amelia crazy. She complained that she was monosyllabic, sullen, uncommunicative. Daisy seemed the same way to Susannah. Both girls had boyfriends now, apparently. Amelia's method was to let Nick, as Elizabeth's gangly, spotty youth was called, spend as much time as he wanted at the house

– 'where I can keep an eye on them'. Susannah acknowledged that she'd never met Seth, so had no idea whether he was gangly or spotty, though it seemed unlikely – Daisy was a pretty girl (a lot like her mother, though it pained her slightly to admit it). If Susannah ever demurred – after all, Daisy wasn't hers, and she didn't even have her full time – Amelia would assert that Susannah's job was even tougher for both of those reasons. 'Unconditional love is sometimes the only thing that stops me from killing her. God knows what holds you back . . .'

Victoria was railing against the house rules. Susannah harrumphed. 'No rules in my house, so there's nothing to moan about . . .' And the boys were just noise makers and laundry producers. Susannah loved Amelia for letting her pretend it was the same for her.

The kids didn't really know each other. They should do. But they didn't. They'd met a few times, over the years, but they'd never really got past the shy and awkward stage, and Susannah had eventually given up. She knew Amelia didn't really like Douglas. She'd wondered, briefly, when Amelia had said she was going to take the kids on a sailing holiday, whether they'd get them all out on the boat, but she didn't know how that would work, and she suspected that Douglas would be irritable at having so many people to marshal.

And then the two of them came back, at last, to each other, and the present. And back, inevitably, to the subject of Rob.

'So, are you going to get in touch with him? Get some answers to those questions?'

'What questions? Who said anything about questions?'

Amelia just looked at her, one eyebrow arched meaningfully. 'Really?'

'Okay. So, maybe I'm curious. I may have a question or two.'

'One or two, yes.' Amelia was smiling now. She looked like she'd got a joke Susannah hadn't understood.

It was vaguely irritating, even from this person she loved so. 'No. I'm not going to get in touch. Why would I do that?'

'You tell me.' Amelia shrugged.

'No.' She shook her head. 'I'm not going to. Absolutely not. It's all ancient history. Water under the bridge.'

'And other clichés.'

'They're called clichés because they're true, you know. Besides, life is quite complicated enough . . .'

'And just not quite happy enough either . . .' This last line Amelia said so quietly that she wasn't even sure Susannah heard it. If she did, she didn't acknowledge it.

Susannah was absolutely right – Amelia didn't love Douglas. Certainly not like Susannah claimed she did. Or used to – not so much recently. Not in any way, in fact. She didn't actually like him much either. She couldn't see – even looking as objectively as she could – what Suze saw in him. He was always grumpy, it seemed to her. Controlling, too. Amelia had nothing against an age difference, but Douglas had seemed middle-aged the first time she'd met him eight years ago. Suze didn't seem to have much fun with him. And Suze could have a lot of fun. It wasn't an obvious characteristic, but Amelia had known her a long time, and she knew she could. If she was with the people who could bring it out of her. That wasn't Douglas. He had been weird, too, about his kids, back in the beginning, when he'd first started seeing her, and Amelia had never really forgotten. Susannah knew, of course. She hadn't tried to hide it much in the early years. But it was easier not to go there these days. She couldn't resist her digs and occasional comments, but she tried not to cross the line too often. She hadn't asked, for years now, about kids, or marriage . . . She *did* love Susannah.

They were dressing now, smoother, softer, and more relaxed than they had been a few hours earlier. The place closed at 10 p.m. – they were always the last two out, and Susannah reckoned that if she treated herself and grabbed a taxi home, she could be in bed by 10.45, asleep by 11, before the delicious soporific wooziness wore off.

Standing in just their bras and knickers, Susannah noticed that Amelia looked thinner than normal.

'You lost weight?' Susannah narrowed her eyes and looked Amelia up and down appraisingly.

Amelia shrugged. 'A bit.'

'More than a bit, I think. How much?'

Amelia had the answer at her fingertips. 'About a stone since spring.'

'Wow.' That was a lot. Amelia didn't weigh much more than nine stone in the first place. She never had, apart from when she'd been carrying the babies. Even then she'd carried them like footballs and been back in her normal clothes in time for the christenings.

'How have you done that? You never said you were dieting . . .'

Amelia pulled her skinny jeans on. They hung low on her hips, and when she turned round the denim wasn't tight around her bum, like it normally would have been. The jeans were almost saggy. Funny how the weight loss showed much more when she was dressed than when she was naked. She tightened her belt buckle. 'I haven't been trying.'

That made no sense. A stone was a lot. 'Are you okay?'

Amelia stood still, and stopped buttoning her shirt. 'I don't know.'

Susannah felt a stab of panic, and put her hand out to clutch at her friend's arm. 'Meels?'

Amelia shook her off. 'No big deal. Don't get all dramatic on me, Susannah. I've lost some weight, that's all. Without trying.'

It didn't sound like all . . .

'And?'

'And I've been having these night sweats. Real wake-up-to-wet-sheets stuff.'

Susannah didn't know what that might mean. 'Do you feel okay?'

'I don't feel ill. I mean, I'm achy. Like when you've got flu, you know – across my shoulders. But no. Not ill.'

'And?'

'And what?'

'And your appointment with the doctor is when . . . ?'

'See? This is why I don't tell you things.'

'Bollocks. You *do* tell me things. And this *is* why you do.'

'So you can nag me?'

'I'm not nagging. When?'

'Next week.'

It alarmed Susannah even more that Amelia had already made an appointment. That meant she thought something was wrong – she hated doctors almost as much as Susannah did.

'Is that soon enough?'

'That's the best the NHS can do.'

That much was true. Actually, based on Susannah's experience, that was pretty fast. 'Why are we just having this conversation now? We've been here, talking about me, for hours . . . and you've said nothing . . .'

'There's nothing to say. I'm going to the doctor.'

'You'll call me. As soon as you've been.'

'I'll call you. If you promise you won't nag. And you'll stay off Wikipedia – no Googling symptoms. I know you. I don't want any helpful lay diagnosis, thanks very much.'

'Can't promise that.'

Susannah hugged her friend tighter than normal as they parted ways on the corner.

Amelia felt suddenly very slight in her arms. 'Get off.'

'Shan't.' One last squeeze, and she released her with a gentle shove. 'And eat a bar of Dairy Milk, for God's sake, will you? I can't get naked with you again if you're going to go all Carol Vorderman on me.'

'Carol Vorderman.' Amelia was walking away now, laughing and shaking her head. 'I can't be Kate Moss. I've got to be Carol Bloody Vorderman . . .'

September

Three weeks after their evening at the Porchester Spa, Susannah felt her blood pressure going up just walking into the small waiting area in the hospital she and Amelia were directed to. Amelia had asked her to come, and she wouldn't have dreamed of being anywhere else, but she hated it nonetheless. She wasn't good at hospitals. She didn't like the way they smelt. There were several other groups of people in this 'oncology' waiting area, and Susannah tried not to look at them. Some of these people were ill. Some may be dying. It was creepy. This was not a mature word, she realized, but it was exactly the right word for how this felt. And now Amelia, sitting beside her, sipping a latte from a paper cup, might be ill. Might be . . . she didn't even want to say the word in her head. She had a bad feeling. Her pulse was racing and she wished she'd eaten breakfast.

She tried to remember the last time she'd been in a hospital. It was a pretty charmed life, she realized. She'd never spent a night in one. She'd broken her collarbone when she was about ten, but that had just been a couple of visits to Outpatients, and her memory of it was vague – most prevalent was the recollection of her irritation at not getting a proper plaster to compensate her for the pain of the injury. Alastair had had his tonsils removed the same year, and she remembered sitting on his bed, a happy visitor, sharing the medicinal ice cream, but it was only the memory of the ice cream – chocolate and strawberry – that she could summon up. Neither Mum nor Dad had ever been admitted for anything serious. They were in their sixties and neither of them took so much as a blood pressure tablet. No one close to her had died in hospital, except her grandparents, and she'd been young – if she'd visited them, she certainly didn't recall the experience. It was frightening, when you came to think about it, how little her life had been touched by tragedy. It made you wonder what fate might be storing up for you . . . you see . . . that was exactly the kind of morbid thought process that dogged her when she had to spend time in a hospital, and precisely why she wished herself anywhere else but here right now. She flicked through the *Country Life* on her lap – it was two years old – the best the dog-eared pile of magazines in the corner could offer. She tried wondering who was living in the five-million-quid Cotswold stone pile that had been up for sale in April 2008, but it wasn't easy to distract herself.

She hadn't come with her friend last week. Amelia said she didn't need anyone for the tests, just for the results.

'I'm not sure I'm the right person to be here with you, you know, Meels. I've got chronic white coat syndrome, and it isn't even my appointment.'

Amelia smiled, and didn't look up from her ancient copy of *Good Housekeeping*. 'You're exactly the right person. I know you're a big baby about this stuff. World's most useless birthing partner. But you're going to have to get over that. Buck up, buttercup. Your job is to cheer me up. Make me laugh.'

This seemed like a tall order. She was tearful already and they hadn't even heard anything bad.

'See – the last three times I was in one of these places was also your fault.'

Amelia nudged her. 'You're comparing a labour ward with an oncology department?!'

'Blood, gore, screaming and guys in white coats. Seems pretty similar to me.'

Amelia smacked her arm now. 'There's no blood and gore in here. And I did not scream.'

She hadn't, actually. She'd been almost silent and totally stoic, and although Susannah might not have said so, she had been utterly in awe of her friend. Jonathan, on the other hand . . .

A middle-aged nurse with a clipboard appeared and called Amelia's name without looking up.

Susannah squeezed Amelia's hand lightly and stood up. 'Come on. Let's go . . . unless you want me to stay here . . .'

Amelia glared, then grimaced.

'Guess not.'

Mr Swift was sitting behind his desk looking at some papers when they went in, but he came across the room to shake their hands, and then, when he'd directed them to two chairs, sat on the edge of his desk, only a couple of feet away. He was young, and quite handsome in a clean-cut sort of way, as Amelia had said (implying that clean-cut was not her type at all). No white coat – just a check shirt and a pair of chinos.

'How have you been, Amelia?'

She shrugged a little. 'The same as before. Just more scared. Let's get it over with – you've got the results, right?'

He seemed to take a deep breath, then he smiled broadly at her. 'Okay. I remember. Straight talking.'

Poor sod – goodness knows what Amelia'd said to him last week.

'So, here it is . . . with both barrels, as requested. It is cancer.' He allowed no pause.

94

That was far too straight for Susannah. She felt dizzy.

'You've got Hodgkin's lymphoma. It's a cancer of the lymph nodes. That's what the lumps in your shoulder are. The blood tests and MRI scan and X-rays you had last week have confirmed it.'

Susannah looked at Amelia. She didn't realize how many tests her friend had been through last week. She had watched enough *ER* and *Grey's Anatomy* to know what MRI scans were. She wished she'd been here, hospital phobia notwithstanding.

Amelia was nodding slowly. 'I knew it. It's almost a relief, in a funny way, to hear you say it. I knew it was something serious.'

'And it is serious. Of course. I'd never describe it any other way. But I have lots of good news – and I'm not just sugar-coating. This is one we're pretty damn good at these days. Caught early, and treated properly, there is a ninety per cent survival rate at five years.'

'Did we catch it early?'

He nodded. 'I think so. You're what we call Stage One. That is really good news – what it means at this point is that only a single lymph node region – the supraclavicular region – is affected.' He gestured at Amelia's shoulders. 'The scans and X-rays showed no spread.'

'And can you treat it properly?'

'Absolutely.'

'But it means chemotherapy, right?'

The consultant nodded. 'That's the gold standard for a case like this. We'd put you on a course called

ABVD chemotherapy. The name comes from the four drugs in the cocktail, if you like. Full names: adriamycin, bleomycin, vinblastine and dacarbazine.'

'Can I have an umbrella and a maraschino cherry with that? I bet everyone says that, don't they? Boom, boom.'

'You can have whatever you like, honey.' Susannah watched her friend intently, biting her own bottom lip. She would not cry. She couldn't. Not if Amelia wasn't going to.

'How long will I have to do the chemo?'

'I'd like to do six to eight months. Really make sure. Then, if all has gone well, we'll see you every six months after that.'

That amount of time was a blow, Susannah knew. She saw Amelia look down at her hands for a moment, taking it in.

Amelia blew her cheeks out, and then exhaled slowly, before she looked back up. 'And I'll lose my hair?' She put both hands on her head. 'I can't believe that's the first thing I'm worrying about . . .'

He nodded. 'It's the first thing a lot of people think about. And yes, most likely you will. There are certain regimens these days that don't lead to hair loss, but in most cases it does go, and you should obviously be prepared for that. It starts after the first couple of treatments, and we'd want you to expect it. Most women get it cut short first, so the change isn't so dramatic. Mainly you'll feel tired – particularly in the first couple of days after each treatment. You'll probably experience some nausea, but that's one thing we are making great headway with – we have good anti-emetics to help with that. And you'll be immune suppressed while you're receiving the chemo, so you'll need to be very careful about infections.'

'Better get rid of the kids, then. They're germ magnets.'

Mr Swift smiled. 'That shouldn't be necessary. You'll just need to be more vigilant. And if they had flu, or something, I might consider shipping them out – to Granny, or maybe to your friend here . . .'

Was it possible he was fishing for information? There was something in the way he said 'friend'. Was he wondering why there was no husband here with Amelia? Susannah wasn't sure where the Hippocratic oath might stand on flirting with a woman you've just diagnosed with cancer. But it was just something men did around Amelia. She'd seen it often enough over the years. Just never in an oncology department . . .

'I'll make sure she's careful,' Susannah said.

There was a brief silence. If Amelia had picked up on anything, she wasn't responding.

'Amelia – do you have any more questions?'

She shook her head. 'I think it'll just take me a while to get used to this.'

'Of course. You can always ring me. If you think of anything at all. We'll set up the first session before you leave today. Go from there, shall we?'

97

She nodded. She looked smaller, diminished by all this news.

'And Amelia . . . I truly believe we're going to have a positive outcome. You're young, you're strong, and otherwise healthy. The odds are absolutely in your favour.'

Outside, Susannah put her arms around Amelia. 'I'm so sorry, Meels.'

Amelia shook her off, not particularly gently. 'What are you sorry for? You heard him. Ninety per cent after five years. If you believe that statistic that says we're all going to get cancer at some point or another, I've just got a lucky break.'

'That's one way to look at it, I suppose.'

'That's *the* way, Susannah.'

It was an order, not a request. Amelia was back, for now at least. It never took long.

'Are you going to tell everyone?'

'Not right away.'

'But you've got to tell Jonathan, surely?'

'Yes, of course. I'll tell him, and I'll tell Mum, and Dad, I guess, if I can catch him off the golf course. That's it. For now.'

'What about the kids?' Elizabeth was fifteen, and Victoria thirteen. They'd know something was wrong. Samuel too. Children weren't daft. Or blind.

'Not yet.' Amelia sounded emphatic. 'Not until I have to.'

'Are you sure about that?'

98

Amelia fixed Susannah with a stare that brooked no argument. 'Yes.'

In the car, driving home, Amelia put the radio on, and sang along, too loud and out of tune. She'd always done that. Susannah had been listening to her for ever.

One night just after Jonathan had moved out, three glasses of red wine later, Amelia had waved her glass in Susannah's face, trying to explain why she'd asked him to leave. 'He used to love it when I sang along to the radio. You know – *love* it. Now he shushes me, the minute I start. It really bugs him.'

It had seemed a fatuous reason at first, to Susannah. But she'd come to understand it. Susannah still loved it, that Amelia sang. Maybe today more than any other day she remembered. Amelia didn't want to talk about it any more now – that much was clear. Susannah knew it wasn't so much denial as just a stubborn refusal to entertain despair or fear. She was as brave as hell. She always had been.

'Did you think he was flirting with me back there – Swift?!' Amelia fired the question sideways at her between choruses, with a wink.

'Of course he was.' Susannah winked back. 'Poor devil doesn't know he's not your type.'

'My type could change, I suppose. I could develop a Dr Kildare kind of a thing . . .'

Susannah listened to her friend murder a Christina Aguilera ballad and remembered her labouring with

Elizabeth, fifteen years ago. Amelia had decreed that Susannah be there. She didn't want her mum – she said she'd make too much fuss – but she needed a woman there, she claimed. She thought there was a good chance that Jonathan would fall to pieces when the going got tough, and she wanted someone she knew wouldn't. Then she'd winked and said that she wasn't actually one hundred per cent sure about Susannah, but that Susannah was the only woman she could possibly imagine seeing her legs akimbo with no knickers on, so Susannah it must be. Susannah had agreed, on the strict understanding that she'd be nowhere near what she euphemistically referred to as the 'business end'. But when it came down to it, of course, watching had been irresistible. It had been as amazing as everyone always said it was. Gross. But amazing. And the most staggering thing had been Amelia herself. She was right when she claimed she hadn't screamed. She'd made everyone in the room laugh. Almost to the end.

Susannah was grateful for the dark emptiness of the house when she got home, having dropped Amelia off with a last hug, and a promise to call her tomorrow. She kicked her shoes off by the front door and went to the sideboard in the living room, pouring herself a glass of cognac – the first bottle at hand that didn't require the complication of a mixer or an ice cube. She slumped into the deep sofa without putting on the light, and then began to cry. This was frightening, and the strain of being okay all day for Amelia had been more exhausting than she'd realized. It was a relief to stop pretending.

Death – and tragedy – had stayed far away from Susannah and, somewhere at the back of her mind, she'd always wondered where it would rear its head. Maybe it was here, and now. God – Amelia would be furious if she could hear what she was thinking. As she sat in the dark, taking gulps of the alcohol, she played scenarios through her mind – her and the kids all in black in a graveyard; Amelia, pale and wan on her deathbed; having conversations like the ones Debra Winger has in *Terms of Endearment*. All the while, she sobbed softly and hiccuped, self-indulgently wallowing in the possibilities the future held.

The last time she'd been this frightened . . . it was over Rob. In 1990, when he'd been in the Gulf. She'd lain in bed so many nights wondering where he was, what was happening to him, gripped with a self-perpetuating terror, playing out disastrous scenarios in her sleepless mind.

And here he was again, insinuating himself, almost by stealth, into her present life. She'd gone years without thinking about him, and now here he was, a starring role in all her silent thoughts.

That's where she was when Douglas came home. With the lights in the front room out, he went through first to the kitchen, and she heard him open cupboard doors and uncork a bottle of wine. He wandered leisurely back along the corridor, and flicked on the overhead light, reaching at the same time for the remote control on top of the television. She squinted against the sudden light.

'Christ – you scared me to death.'

'Sorry.' She put her hand across her eyes to shield them.

'What are you doing, sitting here in the dark?' He sat down beside her, leaning in to kiss her cheek, then stopped. 'Have you been crying?'

She nodded and sniffed.

Douglas put his arm around her shoulder. 'What's wrong?'

For a moment she couldn't speak.

He leant back. 'Please, Susannah – what's wrong? You're scaring me . . .'

'It's Amelia.' She saw something of relief in him, just for a second, that the cause was not closer to home, before he rearranged his features carefully, and listened to her as she spilt out the events of her day. For her, this was as close to home as it came. Amelia was one of the people she'd loved longest and best in her life. Amelia *was* her family.

He made all the right noises, speaking in the platitudes and clichés people use about illness. Then he made dinner.

It wasn't his fault, she told herself, that he couldn't quite get it right these days.

*

Just before Susannah went to bed, at 11 p.m., Amelia called her mobile phone. As usual, she didn't introduce herself – she went straight to the heart of the matter.

'You've *got* to call Jonathan.'

'It's . . . What time is it . . . ? It's late, Meels.'

'So, call him in the morning.'

'Why am I calling him in the first place?'

'Because he's gone nuts.'

'You told him?'

'Yeah. I called him this afternoon, after you dropped me off. I told him what Mr Swift told us, told him it wasn't a big deal, just that I might need him to take the kids a bit more, you know, once the treatment starts . . .'

'And . . .' Susannah could easily imagine Amelia blindsiding Jonathan with this information. Her delivery would have seemed bizarrely matter-of-fact, she presumed. She felt sorry for him, poor sod. Not for the first time, actually.

'And he freaked out. I think he was actually crying. He went very quiet for a minute, and then there was this snuffling going on in the background. And then he started talking nonsense.'

'What do you mean, nonsense?'

'He wants to move back in.'

'What?!'

'Exactly. That's what he says. Straight away. Where did that come from?'

Susannah suspected she knew exactly where that

came from, but she didn't dare say so. 'What did you say?'

'I asked him what Jess would think of that.'

Susannah knew Jess was the woman Jonathan had been seeing for the last few months. Ouch.

'And then he went off into this ridiculous monologue. Said Jess wasn't as important. That I was the mother of his kids . . . blah, blah, blah . . . And then he started saying how sorry he was that things had gone wrong.'

'Poor bugger.'

'Why poor bugger?'

'Come on, Amelia, you just ring him up, announce you have cancer, and expect him to have a coherent, measured response on the tip of his tongue?'

'I didn't expect this.'

'More fool you, then. Look, I hate to be the voice of reason here, but you're asking for it. I've been drinking, and it's late, and you're making me be a part of this. You're so much into the straight talking, I'm going to talk straight to you.' She'd known this point would come. It was the cognac that made it come this soon. 'This is a *big deal*. You're going to carry on pretending it's not, that's fine. But you can't expect all of us who love you to agree. And he's one of the people who love you, however inconvenient it is for you to acknowledge that. So am I, for the record. We care, and we're scared – and, frankly, we're the normal ones in this little scenario you've got going here . . .'

Amelia was silent. For a second, Susannah thought she might have hung up.

But then she spoke. 'Tell me how you really feel, why don't you?'

They both laughed. That was classic Amelia. It didn't mean she had taken on board what Susannah said, but it didn't mean she hadn't either.

'So? Do you want him to move back in?'

'I can't believe you're even asking me that.'

Amelia had asked Jonathan to move out three years ago. He'd been renting a flat in Chiswick, a few miles from their home, ever since. Their divorce had been final for about a year. He'd been seeing Jess for maybe six months.

Susannah sighed. She knew she'd relent eventually and agree to ring Jonathan, and she was tired. 'What exactly do you want me to say to him?'

'I want you to make him understand that I can't have him acting like that. I don't need it. Don't want it. Won't have it. So, will you talk to him?'

'If you think it would help, of course I will.'

'I know it will help. He loves you and he'll listen to you.'

'What about you?'

'I just love you. I don't listen to anyone. You know that.'

Susannah had always loved Jonathan, too. They'd been friends for a long, long time. She'd known him longer than he'd known Amelia, in fact. She was there the first time the two of them met, part of a big gang in a crowded, smoky pub on Clapham Common. You could see the sparks flying, even through the smoke and the haze of drunkenness.

Jonathan was always the quieter, more shy one. Amelia, when she'd had a couple of drinks, could best be described as predatory. Susannah used to tell her she behaved like a man. She wasn't exactly a slut – at least, her best friend would never have described her that way. There wasn't a very long list of conquests (although it was always much, much longer than Susannah's). It was just that she went after what she wanted. With gusto, appetite and enthusiasm. And without a great deal of considered thought, usually. What was unusual about that night, Susannah remembered, was that Jonathan *didn't* get dragged back to her flat after the pub. They exchanged numbers: they 'dated'. It was a couple of weeks – three or four, maybe – before Susannah woke up and found his coat on the banister. That was the giveaway.

When she and Amelia had shared their second home together, the flat on Latchmere Road, she'd called Jonathan 'the squatter'. He was always there, sprawled on the sofa on Sunday morning, using the hot water and dry towels on a Monday morning. If he hadn't been Jonathan, she might have resented him. But he was always the most charming man she'd ever known, and she'd found it almost impossible to be cross with him. He had always accepted the totality of their friendship – he sometimes called them his 'wifelets', even though doing so inevitably ended up in him getting pummelled with a sofa cushion. Besides, it hadn't been very long before he'd been joined by Sean, and the foursome that had been so much fun, back in those days, had been born.

And so, she called him. Right now, she reasoned, she needed him as much as he might need her. They both loved Amelia, and if they were going to be strong for her, they'd need to get strength from each other.

They met two days later, after work, in a pub near Susannah's office on Adam Street – Jonathan worked as a reasonably successful stockbroker near Fleet Street. She was there first, and she was halfway down the first glass of white wine from the bottle she'd ordered before he arrived. She stood up to greet him, and he folded her into a long, close hug that made her feel strangely emotional. She missed Jonathan and Amelia. She missed her friend. It wasn't that Amelia had asked her to take sides (there were no sides, anyway – there'd been no war). It was just that life galloped on apace. She saw Amelia. She saw the kids. She didn't see him.

His hair was longer. He pulled at the curls on his neck self-consciously. 'Trying it longer,' he offered, by way of explanation. 'Apparently it makes me look younger. Grows like weeds, too. This is just a missed trim or two.'

It did make him look younger, although he'd never really looked his age. He had a full face, and it was still barely lined. Susannah supposed it was Jess who liked it longer. According to Elizabeth, Jess was 'disgustingly much younger' than her dad, although Amelia had said she thought Jess was in her early thirties. Teenagers were judgmental little beings, when it came to their parents. Susannah couldn't imagine him with someone else. It jarred, just a little, that he didn't mention Jess – if it was Jess who liked his hair longer. As if the secret was hanging in the air between them. A silly secret that wasn't one really. It was as if he felt guilty, though God knows he needn't.

She busied herself pouring him a glass of wine from her bottle, and he took off his jacket, and then sat down opposite her.

'Cheers.' She raised her glass, and clinked it against his.

'Here's to Amelia.' He put the glass down without drinking.

She saw now that his hand was shaking a little. 'She's going to be okay, Jonathan.'

'How do you know?' He ran his fingers through his hair.

'I don't *know*. They're not in the business of giving guarantees. But she has amazing odds. They caught it early, they're treating it aggressively. She told you all this, right? Ninety per cent survival at five years. She says she told you when you spoke.'

He nodded. 'She told me. Did she tell you what I said?'

'Of course.'

'So, you've been sent to talk sense into me, have you?'

'I haven't been "sent" anywhere.'

'Liar. I haven't seen you in months and months.' His tone was reproachful.

'I'm sorry. I know.'

'You don't have to be sorry. I miss you, Susannah, that's all.'

He looked sad. 'I miss everything, actually. Still.'

'I know you do.'

They sat for a moment without speaking.

'So, how's it going with Jess, then?'

He snorted. 'You know about that, too, do you?'

'No secrets. You know the drill.'

'Does that mean Amelia tells you everything?'

She nodded.

'What does she think about it?'

Amelia hadn't exactly said. Susannah shrugged. 'What does she expect? That you'll stay single for ever?'

He smiled. It wasn't the answer he might have hoped for. It wasn't, strictly, an answer to his question, but he knew Susannah of old, and he knew that was the best he'd get. 'It's fine.'

She arched an eyebrow. 'World's most damned affirmative word.'

'It's fine. What can I tell you, Suze? It's nothing really. I'm not in love.'

'Are you "not in love" in a 10cc way?'

He laughed. 'No, I'm not in love in a "don't really give you much thought when we're not together" way. She's a nice girl. I'm flattered, I suppose, in a sad middle-aged divorcee kind of a way. That's about it. Sex, and someone to be with on Sunday nights.'

Susannah felt a sudden rush of sympathy for Jess, although they'd never met. She first knew about her because Victoria had spilt the beans, and Victoria only knew about her because she'd confronted her dad a few weeks ago with a lipstick she'd found in the bathroom. 'Not your shade, I don't think, Dad!' She'd been very pleased with her humour.

He shook his head. 'I'm sorry – that makes me sound like a complete shit. She's a nice girl.'

'You said that already. You're making her sound like a *Blue Peter* presenter.'

'She is. Nice, not a presenter. But I'm a million miles away from being ready for something serious. I've told her. She knows. I wouldn't lead her on or anything. She says she's happy with a fling.'

Susannah raised an eyebrow again, and Jonathan raised a hand. 'I know, I know. I shouldn't believe her entirely.'

'No.' Susannah didn't know every woman in the world personally, but a straw poll of the several hundred she did know would reveal that no matter what percentage of women claimed that to be the case, only a tiny fraction actually meant it . . .

Hadn't she told Douglas she was happy not to get married, when he gave her the patented 'I've tried it, you've tried it, it doesn't work for either of us, clearly – can't we just stay as we are' speech, all those years ago? She might even have meant it, at the very beginning. But not for long, of course.

'And I don't. I'll be careful, I promise. I won't let it go on too long if I think she's too into it. But I'm lonely, Susannah. You can understand that, surely? I went from a house full of noisy kids, and a wife I slept with every night, to an empty flat. It wasn't my decision, if you recall.'

'I know. You don't have to get defensive with me, Jon. I was there, remember?'

He rubbed the back of his neck. 'Anyway . . . that stuff doesn't seem to matter much now.'

'No.' She looked down at her hands on the stem of the glass.

'So, how is she doing?'

'Exactly as we'd expect. She's being practical, strong, determined.'

'And you believe her?'

'Well, you know her better than me, I suppose . . .'

'Not sure that's true.'

'Well, pretty damn well, at least. I think it's real. I haven't seen any chinks yet. And, believe me, I'm watching.'

'I just want to do something.'

'And you can. You can stop with the drama. She

won't accept it from either of us. And God help her mum, if she starts. She wants no fuss. She just wants help, when the time comes, with the practical stuff. The kids, the house. All of that.'

'Of course. Anything.'

'Anything – but not moving back in. You've got to drop all that, Jon. That isn't going to happen.'

'I know. I shouldn't have said it. I was just . . . shocked.'

Susannah put a hand on his shoulder. 'I know. She's a stranger to breaking things gently. I've heard her reaction to a new haircut I've had often enough to know that. She pulls no punches.'

'Why do we both love her so much? She's actually pretty dreadful.' He laughed ruefully.

'You still do, huh?'

'More than I even knew, I think, until she called and told me this.'

His eyes filled with tears, and she took his hand, saying nothing, because at that moment there was nothing to say.

Douglas had asked her to marry him once. Not in the beginning. In the beginning he'd said he didn't want to get married again. To be fair, he'd been consistent. To be accurate, he'd waited until she was in love with him before he said it. It was one of the things she always wondered whether he'd done deliberately – like the way he always apologized when she was exhausted. He said he had three children, and he didn't want to have any more. Not even with her. That if she wanted to be with him, she'd need to be okay with that. Then he'd left her alone, to decide, and after two miserable weeks without him, she'd reasoned she could live with anything, as long as she had him. She'd gone to him. He'd held her and kissed her and said it again, and she'd stayed.

The proposal had come about three years after that, if you could really call it a proposal. They'd had a fight – about the kids, about his inability to commit to her – a big, angry, fight that seemed, at the time, insurmountably vast. She'd stormed out, and stayed at Amelia's for a few nights, and he'd come to her there.

'We can get married, if that's what you really want.' Those had been his exact words. No ring, no bended knee, no flowers and certainly no violins.

But she'd gone home with him anyway.

1988

Rob had never asked her to marry him, of course. They'd been far too young. It would have been mad to even have contemplated it. But that didn't mean she hadn't. She was a young girl, and young girls did that. She'd spent hours daydreaming about it. Doodling Mrs Rossi, Mr and Mrs R Rossi, Susannah Rossi on her notes when she was supposed to be revising.

Rob passed his driving test three weeks after his seventeenth birthday. He and Frank had been practising three-point turns and parallel parking between white lines in the car park at Tesco's out of hours every evening. He read from *The Highway Code* interminably, while they sat on the sofa in her house or his house, his free arm around her shoulder and her head on his chest. Sometimes she tested him, calling out road signs and having him draw them in the air with a finger, and sometimes – mostly – she just tried to distract him, planting tiny kisses across his neck and up to his earlobes until he groaned and put the book down to kiss her back.

Frank insured his son to drive his car, and let him borrow it after he came home from work, and at the weekends. With the car, and the freedom of the road, came a new freedom for the two of them. Finally, at last, they could be on their own. At Rob's house, Frank and Lois asked that they stayed downstairs, but largely left them alone. Still, though, they were almost always there, in the next room. Their voices carried. At Susannah's it was even harder. If it wasn't Mum coming in all the time on some pretext or another, it was Alastair or Alex. In the car, it was just the two of them.

Her mum and dad thought she was 'too obsessed' with Rob. They'd had rows about it – the first real rows of Susannah's adolescence, of her whole life actually. At least, she rowed with Mum, in Dad's vaguely embarrassed presence. Mum was convinced that Rob was, if not exactly a bad influence, then the first teetering domino in an inevitable tumble towards all the things she feared most as a mother – drink and drugs and failed exams and sex before marriage and pregnancy and STDs. Her sexist double standard infuriated Susannah – she had never ranted at Alastair this way – and her mistrust hurt her more than she wanted to admit. It was unfamiliar and uncomfortable to her to suddenly feel that her mum didn't get her at all. That the gap between them was so much wider than it had ever been and than she had ever imagined it could be. She felt defensive, and she felt compelled to be secretive, and she didn't like how either of those things made her feel. And she judged her mum, holding her more responsible for this new, unpleasant atmosphere at home. Judged her as harshly as she felt she was being judged herself. For the first time in her life, she saw her mum as a silly woman.

One Friday night, Mum tried to stop her from going out to meet Rob. It was summer – it didn't get dark until late. Kids from their year at school – just too young for the pub, way too old for the playground – all congregated on the common. Susannah had wanted to skip dinner, but Mum had put her foot down, and so she said she'd meet Rob after she'd eaten. Mum started nagging her about eating too fast. She was spoiling for a row – at least, that was how it felt to Susannah. Alastair shot her a sympathetic look, and Alex put his head down nervously, shovelling his food in, but Susannah took the bait.

'Why are you having a go at me?'

'I'm not. I just think it isn't too much to ask for you to sit with your family and eat nicely. It took me an hour to make this dinner, and I don't want it wolfed down in five minutes, that's all.'

Susannah hated it when Mum tried to make her feel guilty. 'That's not all, though, is it, Mum?'

'What do you mean?'

'I mean you don't want me to be out with Rob.'

'Who said anything about Rob?' Mum looked around the table at the others, her arms open in incredulity. 'Did I say anything about Rob?'

'Rosemary.' Dad spoke quietly, but his note of warning was incendiary to his wife.

'Don't you "Rosemary" me, Clive. The girl is obsessed.

You know I'm right.' This was a phrase she used often.

After this the row followed its usual script for a while. Rowing by numbers. These days, it usually ended with someone flouncing out. This evening it was Rosemary, who took a Silk Cut from the pack she kept in the biscuit barrel into the garden. Since she only ever smoked, as she always said, when stressed or upset, the action of removing the cigarette from its open hiding place was a statement as much as anything else. Designed to maximize Susannah's guilt.

But she only really felt guilty about her dad. She knew he tried to be a buffer. She knew it was he who would have to go out into the garden and listen to the rest of whatever Mum had to say.

Sometimes she could hear them talking about her, when they thought she was asleep in bed. Her dad was usually defending her. He was good at calming her mum down. Once, she'd heard him, exasperated, asking Rosemary whether she'd completely forgotten what the two of them were like when they were young. Her mum had been quiet for just a moment, then she'd heard her laugh, and it sounded nice. 'Don't you know that's why I worry so much . . . ?'

Now he was finishing his meal.

'Sorry.' She looked down at her plate.

Her father put down his fork and laid his hand over hers, squeezing her fingers.

'But she isn't right, Dad. Not about this. She isn't.'

He gave a wry smile that silently agreed with her.

'She'll calm down. I'll talk to her. You go, love. The boys will do the dishes.'

Alex groaned. 'For a change.'

Dad shot her brother a withering glance. 'You go and have fun.'

She and Rob talked. A lot. More than they did anything else, though her parents, and certainly Amelia, might not have believed it. Rob would park somewhere, the radio on quietly, and they would climb into the back seat, curl up into each other and talk softly, for hours and hours. Susannah didn't think she had ever known another human being as well as she knew Rob. That she ever could or would. Or might want to.

They talked about their childhoods, and their parents, their beliefs, their fears. About where they'd been and where they wanted to go. He talked a lot about joining the air force. He made her understand why he wanted it so much. He'd been offered a scholarship at Biggin Hill after his 'O' levels, and the RAF were paying his way through 'A' levels. He wasn't going to university – he would go, the September after their final college exams, to Cranwell, in Leicestershire, to do his officer cadet course. Eighteen weeks of pretty intensive training, by the sound of it. And then he'd be in the Air Force. For six years at least, but he said he couldn't imagine doing anything else. He wanted to fly. He wanted to belong to something. He wanted his life to be organized and planned and, to some extent, controlled by other people.

She understood him, she thought, but she didn't really understand it. It was nothing she wanted, and nothing she'd ever really thought about, not before him. She couldn't imagine herself in that life. Everything she'd been working towards was taking her in another, opposite direction. And she didn't like to look forward. Everything was going to change. What had so recently been exciting was now fraught with fear and tinged with sadness. She didn't want to be apart from him. In fact, she couldn't imagine it.

Rob always saw it differently. He said, without irony or even sadness, but with a matter-of-factness that was disarming and hard to answer, that she could do much better than him. He held her face in his hands, and stared into her eyes, and said that she was only his for a while anyway, and that it wasn't his going to Cranwell that would split them up. 'You're destined for greater things, Susannah Hammond. I see it in you. You're so clever, so bright. So beautiful. So special. I'm not any of those things. Except when I'm flying, maybe. Down here, I'm ordinary. I'm going to be just a memory for you. A sweet one, I hope. Happy. But just a part of your past. I might be good enough for now, but I'm not good enough for you for ever. Not for you.'

It made her cross and it made her sad, when he said things like that. She knew she was clever. But those other things, the other things he saw in her – she felt those things, but she only felt them when she was with him.

He wouldn't talk about the future beyond their exams. And when he couldn't rationalize her out of talking about it, he kissed her to make her be quiet. And that usually worked.

There was something really old-fashioned about Rob, and it was part of what she loved about him. They never had sex in the back of Frank's car, even though with the car came the first real chance they had to do it, and even though both of them wanted to so much sometimes that it was almost physically painful, and even though they got wonderfully, tantalizingly close so often. Mostly it was Rob. There were many occasions when Susannah was too drunk and dazed, with what she didn't realize at the time was a very adult lust for him, to have stopped him.

'It should be in a bed, if it happens. A big, white, clean bed. Not in a hurry, not with us being afraid someone is coming in to catch us, or that a policeman is about to tap on the window. Not with my trousers around my ankles and your sweater around your neck. Just us, just the two of us. I've got too much respect for you, Susie. Frankly, too much for my dad, too. This is his car, and he trusts me.

'And if you think I'm scared, you're right. Of course I am. If you think I don't want to, you're crazy. There is nothing – absolutely nothing – I can think of that I want to do more. If you think –'

She kissed his mouth while he spoke, until he stopped. 'Do you want to keep telling me what you

think I think, or do you want me to tell you? I think
. . . you're the best man I know. I think I love you.
Actually, I know I do . . . and I don't mind waiting.
Because it's going to happen, Rob. I know that one
day it's going to happen. And it's going to be worth
the wait . . .'

Present Day

Susannah kicked the door closed behind her, and went straight to the kitchen with the two heavy shopping bags she had carried home. She should put things in the refrigerator first, she knew, but her feet hurt in the three-inch heels she'd worn and her suit felt too tight – she wanted nothing more than to change into the fancy cashmere-blend lounging pyjamas Mum had given her for her birthday, and just slob out in front of *Holby City*, or whatever was on. Doug was away overnight, with work, and she'd been planning an orgy of finger food and soap operas all day, relieved at the thought of his absence. Maybe a long, bubbly bath and definitely a blissfully early night. It was exactly what she needed – a bit of space and a bit of selfishness. She'd blown off the rest of the afternoon at work – the meeting at Canary Wharf she'd been to after lunch had ended at 3 p.m., and she had just not gone back. She'd called Amelia, but she was tired, she said, and planning to go straight to bed. Poor thing. She said she wasn't sleeping properly, for the first time in her adult life, and she looked like she wasn't, too. Dark circles had appeared under her eyes. She was so indignant about the insomnia that she made Susannah laugh. By contrast, she was no stranger to 2 a.m. They had always been different that way. Susannah remembered watching, with something like irritation, as Amelia slept sitting up, her head leaning against her rucksack, on a bumpy, noisy train somewhere in Europe, while she sat there, wide awake and lonely.

There were a hundred things she should go back to work to do, but not this afternoon . . . She'd called her assistant, Megan, and established that there was nothing that couldn't wait until the morning. Now, slipping out of her shoes and putting her jacket on the back of a chair, Susannah climbed the stairs in her stockinged feet, pulling her silk blouse out of her skirt.

She was halfway up when she heard the noise coming from above, along the landing, and instantly a jolt of pure adrenalin ran through her. Someone was in the house. She stood, frozen on the stairs, her mind racing with what she should do. Who the hell was here? The door hadn't been unlocked. It was broad daylight outside – she could hear cars passing in the street, and a child's voice laughing. There was no sign of anyone here in the hall, on the stairs. Through the open door to the sitting room she could see the television, the i-Pod dock, with Doug's i-Touch still in it. She could see her handbag, on the pew in the hallway. Her phone was in it.

'Who's there?' Probably not the smartest choice, but it was instinct.

'Shit.'

She recognized Daisy's voice immediately, and the worst of her fears immediately subsided.

'Daisy?' What on earth was Daisy doing here on a Wednesday afternoon? She called her name again, hearing her own irritation in her voice this time.

There was no response, but now Susannah continued up the stairs. The door to the bedroom Daisy shared with Rose was wide open, but Daisy wasn't in there. Across the landing, Fin's bedroom was empty, too. The door to the master bedroom was the only one closed.

'Daisy?' She turned the handle, and pushed the door ajar, mystified and tense.

'Don't come in!'

But she was already in.

Daisy was in her bed. She had the sheet held up tight against her, but beneath it she was clearly naked, or, at the very least, topless. The curve of her youthful breasts escaped the cotton cover. Her hair was all messy, like it had been backcombed, and her cheeks were bright red. Next to the bed Daisy's boyfriend, Seth, was hurriedly pulling on boxer shorts, breathing fast. She'd never seen him without clothes on. Let's face it, she and Doug had barely seen him dressed either – Daisy was never keen to bring him round or even to discuss him – and his muscled, hairless back, the underwear coming up over a smooth, high behind, was somehow shocking to her. She was amazed, in the moment, that she noticed how he looked, that she registered him on that basic level. The sexuality in the room at that moment was palpable, and she felt like a voyeur. These two beautiful young people had been, up until a minute or so ago, making love in here – that much was perfectly obvious. In the middle of the day, in her bed, under her sheets. Where she slept with Doug, Daisy's father.

Christ.

The two of them – she and Doug – hadn't had sex, here or anywhere else, in a couple of weeks, she realized. And then, it had been in the dark. With older, less lovely bodies, and probably considerably less enthusiasm, and athleticism.

She was furious, yes. What on earth was Daisy thinking of? It was utterly unacceptable, and it was revolting. But there was definitely something else. Something much worse, and much less expected. Was she jealous? Not of Seth. Of course not. She knew she was old enough to be the kid's mother. But of the two of them, so desperate to have each other that they'd sneak around, come here in the afternoon? That they were so young, and so beautiful, and so in love, or lust, or on heat, or whatever it was that had brought them here this afternoon, to do this extraordinary thing?

She tried to push those uncomfortable, inappropriate thoughts to one side. Tried to think like a parent. 'What the hell is going on here?' She heard her own voice, shrill and shocked.

'I'm sorry, Susannah . . . I . . .'

She put a hand up to stop Daisy's sputtering. She didn't know which one of them was more in shock. She just wanted to get out of the room. 'Actually, forget the explanation. I think I can see exactly what's going on here – it seems pretty obvious. I don't need to have it spelt out to me.'

Backing out of the door, concentrating on controlling her breathing, Susannah looked hard at the lines in the sand-coloured carpet, like a ploughed field, willing herself to stay calm. What she most wanted to do, at this precise moment, was to stride across the room and smack Daisy hard in her face.

But she kept her tone as even as she could, and her voice quiet and calm. 'Seth – I think it would be a great idea if you'd get dressed now, and just go, please.'

She didn't look at either of them. She closed the door behind them, and went downstairs, straight into the sitting room, where she poured herself a stiff measure of bourbon, and drained her glass. She refilled her glass and went to sit at the kitchen table. It was still and silent in the house. She could see through the house to the front door, and she waited . . .

It took Seth about three minutes to finish dressing, come down, and let himself out of the front door, which he closed quietly behind him without a backward glance. He couldn't get away quick enough. She didn't blame him.

It took Daisy about five minutes after that to appear in the kitchen. Susannah had thought it might take longer. She wouldn't even have been surprised if Daisy had gone straight to her room, and she'd heard the familiar slam of the door. But she came down to face the music. Susannah had to give her points for that, at least, although she was still extremely angry. She had put her jeans and sweatshirt back on, and pulled her tousled hair back into a loose ponytail, but her cheeks were still red, grazed by kissing, and with embarrassment. Susannah's own face was hot, too, she knew.

Without saying anything, Daisy pulled out the chair opposite Susannah and sat down. Susannah couldn't bear to look at her for a moment, but when she brought her eyes up to meet Daisy's, Daisy's face crumpled into sudden, unexpected tears. Susannah didn't remember the last time she'd seen Daisy cry. Had she ever seen her cry?

'Susannah, I'm so, so sorry.' The words were hard to hear through the sobbing.

'What were you thinking, Daisy?'

'We . . . we weren't thinking . . . we weren't thinking at all. We just . . . we wanted to be alone so . . . so . . . much, you know. Just be on our own. I didn't plan it, Susannah . . . I didn't . . . honestly. I just thought we'd come here . . . you know . . . while you and Dad were at work . . . and that we could . . . you know . . . that we could just be together. It just . . . it just happened. Honestly . . .' Her breathing was shallow and uncontrolled. She'd worked herself up into a complete state.

'It just happened in my bed?'

'I couldn't . . . we couldn't . . . not where Rose and I . . . or Fin . . .'

'So, you knew it was wrong to do it there, but somehow my room, your *father's* room – *that* seemed okay?'

Daisy hung her head. 'No.'

'Damn right, Daisy. None of it's okay. You were in my house without permission. I presume you're bunking off school. You scared the shit out of me, for starters. I thought . . . I don't know what I thought . . . I can't *believe* you've done this, you stupid, careless, thoughtless girl.'

Daisy bowed her head at the words, as though they were blows being rained down on her. She looked about ten years old, sitting there in her school sweatshirt, with her hair all over the place. She wiped at her snotty nose and her eyes with her sleeves.

The tears finally undid Susannah. She'd never seen Daisy so vulnerable. She might have expected rage, or defiance, or attitude. But she hadn't expected this. She couldn't quite believe she was doing it, but Susannah slowly pushed the chair back from the table, and walked round to Daisy. She stood next to her for a moment, then put an arm around Daisy's shoulder. As soon as she did, Daisy leant into her, putting both arms awkwardly around Susannah's legs, and sobbed anew into her skirt. Susannah could see no point right now in doing anything but holding her while she cried.

Daisy cried for maybe four or five minutes, while

Susannah found herself murmuring softly to her, as though she was a baby. Gradually, her breathing slowed and her shoulders stopped heaving. Gently Susannah pulled herself away from the girl, and went to put the kettle on. She took two of the Penguin Classics mugs from the hooks under the cabinet and put a tea bag in each, adding a spoonful of sugar to both. She put a box of tissues from the window sill on the table, and Daisy took one and blew her nose noisily.

Neither of them spoke until the tea was made. It seemed like they were both listening intently to the kettle as it boiled in the stillness.

'Come and sit down with me.' Susannah led Daisy into the sitting room, carrying the two mugs. She undid the top two buttons of her pencil skirt, before sitting down on the floor. Daisy slid to the ground next to her, close but not touching, and picked up her mug of tea from the coffee table, nursing it against her chest, her hands still covered by the sweatshirt.

'So, do you want to tell me what happened?' The anger was gone. She didn't honestly expect that Daisy would want to, but Daisy started talking, stopping to take small sips of her tea, and to sniff.

'I really love Seth, Susannah. I know you probably don't believe that – you probably think we're too young to even know what that means.'

Rob's face flashed into Susannah's mind. The shy smile. The first time he said the words to her. Daisy was wrong. 'I don't think that, Daisy.'

Daisy harrumphed, just a little.

How old and desiccated I must seem to her, Susannah thought.

'Well, everyone else does. You've heard how Dad talks about him. Mum won't let him come in the house, and she gets really uptight when I go out with him. She hasn't given him a chance at all.'

'And we haven't either, right?'

Daisy gave a little smile. 'Not much of one, no.'

'You haven't done a lot to encourage us, Daisy. You've kept him pretty much under wraps. I didn't know it had got so serious.'

'It hadn't. I mean, this afternoon – it was the first time. Honest.'

'Did you . . . I mean were you . . . ?' Susannah was a little surprised at the parental question that sprang to her lips.

'Careful?'

Susannah nodded.

'We were. He had . . . things . . . you know.' She caught herself sounding childish and forced herself to use the word. 'Condoms. He had some with him.'

'So, he'd planned it, even if you hadn't.'

Maybe Daisy hadn't thought of it that way. It stopped her from talking for a moment. 'I think he loves me, Susannah. He says he does.'

'Has he had other girlfriends?'

'A few, I think. But he said it was his first time, too.'

'And do you believe him?'

'Yeah.' Daisy nodded slowly, and even smiled. 'I think so.'

She remembered Amelia, all those years ago on the bus, talking about her first time with Tristan, the boy on the Amalfi Coast. She was amazed to realize that she remembered his name. How perfect it had been. She thought about her own first time for a moment, and then pushed the moment away. Far from perfect, as it turned out. Had it been perfect for Seth and Daisy? It would always be connected to this now. To being caught. To the excruciating scene. Seth dressing with his back to the bed.

This was what Douglas meant. She wasn't Daisy's mother. She might be angry about the bed, about the violation of trust, but she couldn't feel the mother's indignation she was sure she should. She realized she wasn't overwhelmed by this. Or hurt, or confused about how to handle it. She found she was thinking clearly.

'Have you talked to your mum or your dad about this?'

'No way.' Daisy shook her head vociferously. 'I can't. And you can't either. You have to promise you won't tell him, Susannah. Please. Please.'

'Because?'

'Because – Dad's Dad. I couldn't talk to him about stuff like this. And he'd go mad if you told him, too.'

Susannah could never have talked to her dad either. If he knew anything about that part of her life, he knew it from Mum, and not from her. 'And your mum?'

'No. Mum still treats me like I'm ten. She doesn't want to think I'm getting older – I think that just makes her feel older. And that's her biggest fear. If she keeps me a kid, she doesn't have to admit she's getting older. It isn't just boys and sex. She doesn't want me to have driving lessons. She won't talk about university either.'

Poor kid. What she was saying made sense. Sylvie was one of those women for whom ageing was an agony – you could tell just from looking at her. She wore her hair too long, her clothes too young. She was too thin, and always at a yoga or a pilates class. The pursuit of youth. It had occasionally given Susannah a flicker of pleasure, knowing that what most aggravated Sylvie about her was the one thing she was powerless to change –Susannah was ten years younger. But she'd never considered the impact all of that might have had on her elder daughter.

Daisy had never, in the seven years since they'd known each other, talked to her like this. It was both strange and somehow a huge relief to be sitting here on the rug speaking this way. For the first time, she could see a place for herself in Daisy's life. She didn't have to judge. She didn't have to lay down rules. She had to listen, and she had to treat Daisy like she was sixteen, going on seventeen. Because someone had to.

At last it was the weekend, and Susannah was at her parents' home. Mum had issued a three-line whip for lunch. She'd popped in to see Amelia's mum on the way this morning, for a coffee. She couldn't get used to the fact that Amelia's dad wasn't there any more. They'd finally divorced ten years earlier. Her mum had redecorated much of the house – a more feminine style – with pastels, florals and lace trim proliferating. It didn't really suit the style of the house, but it was very her. Mrs Lloyd, still handsome, still well dressed, had started crying as soon as she'd seen her – but balled-up tissues in each hand, and red-rimmed eyes told Susannah she was crying a lot, and not just because she was there. Amelia had driven down a couple of days earlier, she knew, and told her about the cancer.

She stayed for half an hour, sitting in the kitchen that was, these days, a Cath Kidston showroom, drinking chamomile tea, telling her it would be okay, promising to keep an eye on Amelia, and to call her if she thought Amelia needed her.

'Because she won't say so herself. You know her better than most, and you know I'm right.'

Her own mum knew about Amelia, too. Susannah had told her on the phone the week they'd heard the diagnosis together, swearing her to secrecy, but knowing that Mum would turn the air at St Gabriel's thick with prayers while she dusted. Which couldn't hurt. She'd hugged her extra tight when she'd arrived.

Douglas wasn't here with her today either. He was with the kids. Of course. Sunday lunchtime. They'd gone down to the harbour, to clear the boat out for the winter, before it was taken into dry dock, and God knows she hadn't wanted to do that any more than the three kids had. She hadn't especially wanted to come, but she hadn't had a great reason not to. And she thought it would be good to see Al. The sun had been shining earlier and she'd thought that the drive, at least, would be good.

Alastair had volunteered himself and her to wash up after lunch, which meant he had an agenda. He never volunteered to wash up. In the kitchen, while she ran a sink of hot, soapy water, the two of them made small talk about work, weather and politics. They were almost finished – and she'd almost got away with it – when he raised the subject of Douglas.

'So . . . he's not here . . . *again.*'

'Nope. Kids.' She kept her tone light.

'I'm beginning to think he's your imaginary live-in significant other.'

She flicked him with the corner of the tea towel.

'Although, presumably, if you were going to make one up, he'd be younger. And hunkier. And child-less . . .'

'Ouch. Now you're just mean.'

'Come on, Susannah – he never shows up for these things. What's that all about? Does he hate us? Because if he does, I just want to go on the record as saying I don't think he knows me well enough to hate me. Let him decide that after a few more Sunday lunches . . . hey?'

She started to say something about the children, but Alastair wasn't in the mood, and he interrupted her crossly. 'That's bullshit. He could bring the kids, for God's sake. We don't bite. Mum would love it. My kids would love it. Those kids are like his human shield. Besides, it isn't really about us. I can take the fact that he obviously doesn't want to be with us.'

She started to demur, but he fixed her with a hard, cynical stare. 'But why doesn't he want to be with *you*? Everyone else might be happy to let it ride, but you're not fooling me. It's not right, Suze. Either you guys are a family, or you're not.'

Susannah leant back against the kitchen counter. 'You're a nosy bugger, you know that?'

'I know. And you're my sister. Know that?' He leant beside her, so close their hips were touching.

'I know.' She leant her head against his shoulder.

'I don't like it, that's all, Susannah. I'm not trying to interfere, I just want you to know – I'm trying to look out for you.'

'I do know, and I'm glad you are. And when I need to talk, I promise, you'll be the first person I call. Today – I don't want to talk about it. There's just too much else going on in my head. Stuff I can't talk about now.' She didn't want to tell him about Amelia, not today. 'Is that okay?'

He put his head down on top of hers. 'That's okay.'

Al was too close to the mark, as usual. She loved him for it, but she wished he wouldn't.

She would see the kids tonight. They wouldn't go back to Sylvie until after school on Monday. She wanted to see Daisy – to make sure she was alright. She'd taken her to the GP last week, to get her put on the pill. Neither Douglas nor Sylvie knew. Daisy had asked her not to tell them, and she was happy enough to go along with that for now – Daisy was right when she said Douglas would be angry. He'd be furious. She was sixteen – she didn't need a parent's permission. She didn't need Susannah to go with her either, but she'd asked if she would, and Susannah, touched, and feeling a slightly surprising protectiveness, had readily agreed. Daisy had been so nervous, sitting in the grey waiting room. Susannah hadn't gone in with her – she'd waited outside. Afterwards they'd gone out for a pizza – they'd never done that before – and chatted more easily than Susannah could ever remember.

Over ice cream, Daisy had thanked her. 'You're cool, Susannah – you've been so cool about this. I'm still so sorry . . . about what happened. I can't believe I did that. But I'm so . . . I'm so grateful for everything you've done for me, since. I didn't deserve it. You could have behaved really differently, and I'm so glad you didn't. I feel relieved to have someone to talk to about this stuff. I told Seth, and he thinks you're amazing, too.'

Susannah was moved by Daisy's speech – probably

the longest one she'd ever heard her give, even as she acknowledged to herself that it shouldn't have been her that Daisy took into her confidence.

It was amazing, she'd thought earlier, sitting around the reproduction mahogany dining table, how much Douglas *wasn't* missed at these family occasions. He was more often absent than present. Even Chloe, a novice by his standards, and a foreigner, seemed a better fit here. Did I do that, she wondered? Did I exact revenge for him making me keep the kids at arm's length by doing that with my own family? Who exactly hasn't put any time or effort into this relationship? Him, them or me? She didn't know the answer to that one.

Lunch was . . . nice. It usually was. And she was usually surprised that it was, which said more about her, she thought, than about lunch. They were her parents. The kids ran around squawking and dancing, and Mum overcooked the vegetables to a grey mush like she always did, but she beamed so with the pleasure of having 'everyone' under her roof that it was easy to forgive her (and just to make a mental note to find that day's vitamin C some other way).

Outside her mum's house on a foggy Sunday afternoon, Susannah wrapped her coat around her tightly and pulled the collar up to shield the back of her neck from the chill wind. It was getting cold out here. Alastair and his crew had left a half-hour or so ago, anxious to get the kids in the bath and into bed. Alex and Chloe were staying the night so they could meet up with some of Alex's local friends they hadn't seen since the wedding. Lunch had been the first time they'd all (almost all) been together since the wedding. Cue around 1,000 photographs, and a premiere screening of the wedding video. She'd been sent a website link by the wedding photographer, as was the modern way, but she hadn't got around to pushing the slide-show button and seeing them all. They were lovely – much lovelier than you might have imagined if you'd seen how uptight and anxious the guy had been on the day. Some of them were downright arty – Chloe photographed in the bedroom, through her veil, and what looked like precious little else bar her underwear, and some actually pretty nice shots of the wedding party's shoes arranged alongside their bouquets on the stairs in Mum's house.

The video had been shot by a friend of Chloe's, to save money, and was less artistic, but infinitely more informative, catching people's asides and expressions throughout the day. Susannah was in the background at one point, watching as the newly-weds danced their first dance to Louis Armstrong. She looked sad and distracted, standing watching them. She saw Alastair watching her watch herself, and poked her tongue out at him. No one else seemed to notice. Mum, it seemed, was mainly interested in how the flowers had looked.

And now, lunch was over, and she was going to see

Lois. She hadn't told them – her own family. She'd sat for a while with her dad in the conservatory, talking about David Cameron. Then she'd kissed Mum and Dad and left, but rather than driving to the motorway, and thence home, she'd gone just a mile or so, then stopped and parked outside Lois and Frank's house.

She'd called in the week. She found their number, and just dialled it one lunchtime from her desk, her heart pounding. Lois had sounded warm and friendly, just like she had at the wedding. If she was shocked to hear from her, she didn't say so. Susannah felt more shocked than Lois had sounded, and she was the one who had dialled the number. They exchanged small talk and pleasantries for a minute or two, and then Susannah said she was coming down that weekend for lunch at her Mum's and that she'd love to stop in for a cup of tea, if that worked for Lois. She hadn't known she was going to do that until she heard her voice. Lois said that would be a delight. They didn't have many visitors, these days, she said, and she knew Frank would love to see her. At the end, she added, almost as an afterthought, that Rob wouldn't be there. Maybe she thought it was Rob Susannah wanted to see. Maybe it was. But Susannah said she was coming to see them and rang off, still quite surprised at what she'd done, and why.

She told herself she was doing the right thing. That too much time had passed. She'd known them well – they'd been close. It was nice of her – overdue, but nice, to go and visit Frank, ill now, and, she imagined, mostly confined to home. It was the decent thing to do.

She knew, though, that it was significant that she didn't tell Amelia. They spoke a lot that week – Amelia had her chemo dates, and Susannah had promised she'd be with her. She'd hardly touched her holiday allowance this year, and she had plenty of days still to take. But she didn't mention going to tea with Lois once. Amelia wouldn't have believed the explanation she was trying hard to believe herself.

God, this house was full of memories. She parked on the street, and walked down the drive. Hadn't the front door been blue? She'd always loved it here. From the first time she'd been invited in. Walking across the threshold had always been like walking into another world – one that was warm and welcoming and embracing.

Frank was Italian – the fourth son of Italian immigrants from Naples, who'd come to England in the 1920s, settling at first into an Italian community in London. He'd moved out of the city when he'd met Lois in the 1960s. She'd grown up a few miles from here. And they'd lived in this house since the year Rob was 16 – more than 20 years. Frank (Francesco – though he always joked that no one had ever really called him that, except his grandmother) didn't sound at all Italian, but everything else about him screamed it. He had told great stories. His grandparents had lost family in the eruption of Vesuvius in 1906 (who even knew there'd been one . . . ?) and most of his male cousins had ended up in New York, in Little Italy. His own parents hadn't wanted to go that far from their homeland – hopeful, perhaps, that one day they'd return, though they never had.

The house was furnished with dark, ornate wooden pieces that were slightly too large for the rooms, and full of small oil paintings of the Amalfi Coast. An old-fashioned picture of the Virgin Mary hung in one corner, with Frank's rosary hanging over it. Large photographs in gilt frames lined the walls – young Lois and Frank on their wedding day, Rob as a naked baby lying on a sheepskin rug, and as a small boy in shorts and braces. Nothing much had changed since she was here last, it seemed. Rob had always hated those photographs.

She sat at the same round kitchen table that she'd sat at hundreds of times before. They'd eaten here, she and Rob, sat holding hands unseen beneath it, pretending to listen, and longing to be alone. They'd done homework here, night after night, studying for their 'A' levels, fuelled by huge quantities of the delicious cannolis Frank made from an old recipe his parents had handed down to him. She remembered him folding the thinly rolled dough around the squat wooden sticks made especially for the purpose that he'd inherited from his family, lining them up ten at a time in a wire tray and then plunging them into a large pot of boiling lard – always lard, Frank insisted – on the hob. Sitting here, she remembered the sound and the smell of them frying in the fat. And she could still taste the cannoli cream he'd piped into the cooled tubes from a big white piping bag – thick and flavoured with cinnamon and chocolate chips and ricotta. He'd pipe standing beside the table, and then hand them straight to Rob and Susannah, so they could eat them while the shell was still crisp.

He always did most of the cooking. Susannah remembered trying to imagine her own father standing over the pans on the stove – tasting a sauce from a wooden spoon and deciding whether to add more rosemary or more basil. Her mum would have a heart attack if he'd done so much as open the fridge, much less take ingredients out and do something with them. Washing up was his limit, and that was restricted to high days and holidays. Were these the same doilies Lois had always had? Susannah fingered the delicate white crochet nervously.

Lois wasn't Italian, but she'd embraced life as Frank's wife. She once said to Susannah that her own life had been so bland before he came. That the day she met him she'd known life would be more fun if she went through it with him. At the time, Susannah recalled feeling the exact same way about Rob, and loving Lois all the more for having that in common with her.

Susannah remembered a lot of laughter. It wasn't that her own parents weren't happy. They always had been, she imagined – and they certainly still were. It was just that the Rossi family was a rich, dark chocolate gelato, compared with her own family's Lyons vanilla ice cream.

Until she walked back through the door, she'd forgotten just how much she'd loved not just Rob, but being a part of this family. Today, though not much else seemed to have changed, there were no cannolis. There was a plate of cakes and biscuits, but they were all store-bought.

Frank shocked her. She didn't know much about the illness that had struck him, except that it was horrid, and she hadn't known what to expect when she saw him. She might not have recognized him if she'd passed him on the street. He looked so old. He'd been a big man – broad-shouldered and muscular – but now he was too thin, and most of the muscles had wasted away. He wasn't in a wheelchair – she thought perhaps he might have been – but he struggled to get out of the armchair and hug her hello, and through the open door to the dining room, where there had once been a walnut table and sideboard, she saw a single bed with a blue candlewick bedspread on it. She supposed stairs were too much for him. He didn't so much shake, as sort of strike out periodically with particularly his left arm and leg. When he said her name, his voice was slow and slurred, almost like he was drunk. It made her want to cry. Rob must hate this. They'd always been so close, so similar.

Lois busied herself boiling the kettle and chattering away. By contrast to her husband, she seemed unchanged. A little rounder, perhaps, but the same energetic whirlwind – warm and welcoming – that Susannah remembered. On the wall between the two windows in the kitchen was a picture of Rob in full dress uniform, taken years ago, flanked by his parents, both looking giddy with pride.

Lois nodded towards the picture when she saw her looking. 'That's my boy. The uniform suits him, doesn't it?'

Susannah nodded in agreement and smiled. It always had. She thought referring to the picture was Lois trying to put her at her ease.

Lois had a lot of questions. Was she married? Had she had children? Was she working? Where was she living? Susannah relaxed and let herself be grilled, wondering why it felt faintly embarrassing to admit that she was neither married, nor a mother. Lois smiled – was there a little sympathy in her expression? – and brushed it off easily, claiming marriage was an old-fashioned institution these days, and that stepchildren were a great responsibility and joy. Susannah wasn't convinced she actually believed either statement, but it was sweet of Lois to try. Frank sat quietly while the two women talked. She thought, at one point, that he'd nodded off, but then he opened his eyes and smiled at her.

She had questions of her own. 'And Rob? Is he married?'

'No.' Lois shook her head. 'Like you. Not married. So my dream of grandchildren is still just that – a dream.'

'I expect that's the life he's led?'

Lois shrugged. That wasn't it. Most men in the services managed to meet girls, have families.

'He never found anyone he loved as much as he'd loved you.' It was the longest sentence Frank had uttered since she arrived. He sounded more like his old self as he said it.

'Frank!' Lois admonished him gently, putting one hand over his on the table and squeezing his fingers.

'Well, it's true. I'm too old and too ill to mess around any more. You know it's the truth. She was the love of his life.'

Lois looked at Susannah apologetically. 'I'm sorry, love.'

'I never did know what happened to you two young people. I know that's what you were – young. I know it doesn't always last. But it's lasted for Lois and me, and we were no more than your age when we started up, and I'd have put a bet on you two. I really would.'

'Stop it, Frank. Please. You're making her uncomfortable.' Lois almost squirmed with embarrassment.

'It's fine. Really.' Susannah laughed it off. So, he'd never told them what had happened. He couldn't have done.

'No, it's not.' Lois was agitated. 'It's years ago. You've finally come to see us, and now you'll probably never come back again, if he's going to be raking all this up again. And it's been so lovely to see you again, dear. Really, it has.' Her voice was tremulous now. She leant forward and took both Susannah's hands in hers. 'You were always such a lovely girl.'

Susannah nodded, not knowing what to say.

At the door, Lois hugged her. 'Sorry about Frank. Speaking to you like that. It's part of what's wrong with him. Doctor calls it disinhibition. I call it a bloody nightmare. You never know what he might say.'

Susannah laughed. 'That must make life difficult.'

'You've no idea, love.' Of course she hadn't. What a stupid thing to say. As if that was the worst of it.

'It must be very hard.'

'What is really hard is watching how much he hates it. You remember – how he was? He was always so strong and . . .'

'I know.' Susannah didn't know what else to say.

Lois seemed to shake herself out of it. 'But he's here. And while he's here, and I can take care of him, we'll be fine. I'll be fine.'

'He's lucky to have you.'

'I'm the lucky one, Susannah. I've had him.'

God. There it was. A simple declaration.

Lois looked into her face. 'Are you happy, sweetheart?'

It was a strange, unexpected question, but then Lois had always had an unusual directness about her.

147

Susannah nodded, and tried speaking, but her throat was suddenly constricted, and no words came out. She nodded again, vigorously, horribly afraid that she might cry.

'I hope so. You should be happy.' Lois kissed her cheek one last time, and waved goodbye, entreating her to return whenever she wanted to.

1989

They'd planned a holiday – to celebrate the end of 'A' levels, and their eighteenth birthdays. Susannah had officially become an adult earlier, in February, but Rob and Amelia had summer birthdays. They'd all been working to earn money, except Rob, who'd been away. And they all felt an impending sense of everything changing . . . They'd decided to spend some of what they'd saved on a few days away at the end of August. They'd either celebrate or commiserate – away from their parents, and their homes, and their rules.

To celebrate her eighteenth birthday in the winter, Mum and Dad had taken her and her brothers, along with Rob and Amelia, for dinner at a Mexican restaurant in Covent Garden. She hadn't wanted a party – just this – just the people she loved most. It felt completely grown-up – having Rob there with her parents. It had seemed so weird, ordering a drink in front of her mum and dad, although they'd been letting her have a glass of wine with dinner since she was sixteen or so. Dad – who was proud, and excited – made an embarrassing fuss about it, loudly telling the waiter it was her first drink as an eighteen-year-old. Alastair, Dad and Rob had drunk beer, with Dad muttering about the wedge of lime that came shoved in the neck of the bottle, but Amelia had insisted Mum and Susannah choose something more exotic than wine or beer, off the cocktail menu – so she'd asked for a Margarita, and drunk it all, feeling she should finish her first cocktail, though she hated the acrid taste of the salt around the rim of the glass, and hadn't much loved, either, the strong, sharp taste of the tequila and Cointreau in the drink itself.

Mum and Dad had taken Alex home after dinner. The four of them – Alastair and Amelia, Susannah and Rob – agreed to have one more drink and follow on the next train. Alastair – who'd come home from Exeter for the weekend – seemed absurdly pleased to be with Amelia, though Susannah was completely sure he stood no chance at all with her. Amelia had once confessed she could never go for him.

With a sibling's mock indignation, Susannah had asked why not.

'I never fancy anyone who is so clearly interested in me,' Amelia had laughed. 'Where's the fun in that?'

They'd gone to the Punch & Judy pub, and had two more, then walked down to the river, although it was so cold your breath came in clouds and your feet felt like they might shatter in your shoes if you stepped too heavily. She remembered thinking that – freezing or not – if this was drunk, drunk was good. She felt a little dizzy, a little dreamy, and so, so happy.

Rob had given her a necklace, then, by the river. An

art deco-style rose gold locket, engraved with a pattern of flowers, with a tiny picture of the two of them, no more than an inch in diameter inside. His fingers had fumbled, numb and icy, chilly against the skin under her hair, as he'd fastened it around her neck.

And Amelia had kissed Alastair in the moonlight, even though she could never fancy him. Back when kisses didn't really mean much.

They couldn't get away for long now – just a few days, not even a full week – after the results came out in the middle of August, and their respective fates were decided. God forbid any of them ended up in the clearing system, but you never knew, and they needed to be home until then. They began as a four-some: Susannah, Amelia, Rob and Matt – a guy from school, who'd started hanging around with them a lot in the last year. Then Alastair, home from Exeter for the summer, and at a loose end, butted into a planning session in the Hammond family kitchen and invited himself along.

It had been a strange, bittersweet summer. The huge relief they all felt at being finished with exams and liberated from college was tempered by fear of the unknown, and a definite air of melancholy that this stage of their lives was coming to an end. The weather was customarily lousy. They were all working at dull jobs to earn money for university – all except Rob, who was off for a seemingly endless six weeks with the RAF as part of his sponsorship, getting his private pilot's licence before he started at Cranwell in September. Susannah missed him horribly. She felt disconnected from him, too, a little. He clearly loved what he was doing, and he didn't sound like he was missing her nearly as much as she was pining for him. She was a little bored, and a little in limbo and, if she was honest, just a little resentful about it.

The girls took the bus to town every morning. Susannah was working in Marks & Spencer, stacking the shelves and working the tills in the food department. Amelia — as always the cooler one, who didn't really need to work in the first place — had a job in Top Shop three doors down (which she'd started after two sun-soaked weeks in Corfu with her parents). Alastair was doing day shifts in the pub in the village, and working some evenings washing up in the French restaurant on the high street. Matt was packing boxes in a factory.

They rented two relatively cheap caravans on a site near Minehead in Somerset, and drove down one Monday morning in two cars — Frank's dad lent Rob his, and Amelia borrowed her mum's runaround. The sun came out halfway down the M4, and by the time they arrived at the site, it was almost hot. Amelia and Susannah were to share a two-bed van and the boys were next door, with a pull-out sofa in the living room for Alastair. At least, that was what they had all told their parents. Susannah wasn't actually sure what might happen.

Amelia had asked her, on the bus home from work one day before they left, slightly incredulous that it hadn't happened yet, whether she would sleep with Rob ('at long last', as she put it) on the holiday. Susannah wasn't sure. Everything was about to change. She wanted to, of course she wanted to. She wondered why it felt such a bigger step to her than it seemed to other people, and she wondered if Rob assumed it would happen. He hadn't said so, either before he left or when they'd spoken on the phone.

It was exhilarating to be so free – they were all a little giddy with it. Alastair had been away from home for a year already, but for the rest of them, it was their first real taste of self-determination and liberation, and a very welcome respite from a summer of drudgery. Rob, fresh back from his flying course, was high with the excitement and triumph of his first solo flight. He seemed pleased to see her, but they hadn't been alone at all – he'd only arrived home quite late the night before they left. They spent the rest of the afternoon exploring the small town and the harbour, shopping for food and beer in the Spar near the seafront. It was still warm well into the evening. The caravans came with little lean-to gazebos and small charcoal grills, and on their first night they drank beers and cooked sausages which they ate with baked beans, sitting in deck chairs, laughing and joking. Alastair had started calling Rob 'Biggles', and hummed the theme tune to *The Dam Busters* whenever Rob walked past him. Amelia was flirting as usual, with Matt and Alastair indiscriminately, and Susannah was just happy – happy to be here with Rob, her brother and her best friend. She liked Matt, too, though she didn't know him very well. He'd applied to Bristol as well, to read History. Susannah would be reading Law, so they'd be together next year – it would be nice to have a friend there.

Later, Susannah and Rob went for a walk along the cliff-top near the site, leaving the others playing poker in the van. He put his arm around her shoulder, pulling her close.

She held on around his waist, feeling at home there. 'It's so good to see you. I missed you.'

'I missed you, too.'

'Did you?'

'Course I did. Why ask me that?'

'You sounded so happy, that's all. I felt miserable and you didn't sound that way at all.'

'Don't be daft, Susie. I thought about you all the time.'

'Good.' She squeezed his non-existent love handles. 'That's what I like to hear. Pining.'

'Pining! Don't push your luck . . .' In a deft movement, Rob hooked one of his legs behind hers and felled her, slowing her fall to the ground with his strong arms, and cushioning her. He straddled her on the grass, and forced her arms above her head with one hand, tickling her under the arms and across the belly with the other, until she begged him to stop, and then he kissed her, gently at first, but soon his mouth was hard, more urgent against hers, and for a few moments they lay in each other's arms, their legs entwined, oblivious to anything beyond each other. Then a middle-aged man with a bulldog on a lead walked past, about ten feet away. He let the dog come almost right up to them and sniff at their feet, and they sat up, breathless and a little embarrassed, as he finally pulled at the lead and walked off.

When he was out of earshot, Rob laughed ruefully. 'Story of our lives. Always getting interrupted.'

She leant into him. 'What about here? The caravan . . . we could . . . here . . .' She felt shy saying exactly what she meant.

He looked at her, searching her face for her intentions. 'Do you want to . . . ?'

'D'you?'

'I'd be lying if I said I hadn't thought about it. The whole time I was away from you.'

'Apart from when you were flying, of course.'

'Of course. Very distracting, that would be . . . But on the ground . . . all the damn time. Had some very nice dreams about it, too, actually. But it's up to you. It has to be right for you.'

At that moment, Susannah thought she knew. She put her hand in his and nodded decisively. 'I want to.'

Rob lifted her hand to his mouth and kissed it tenderly. 'Are you sure?'

'Yes!' She was almost shouting. 'Stop!'

They walked slowly, hand in hand, back to the site without talking much. She was unbelievably nervous suddenly. They'd done stuff before – lots of stuff. But this was different. This was huge. He'd never seen her naked. She knew she was putting too much pressure on herself, and she was afraid she might ruin it by doing the same thing to him. She kept thinking about Amelia's 'perfect' first time with that boy on holiday. That's what she wanted. If Amelia could have that with a guy she hardly knew, she and Rob – they should definitely achieve 'perfect', shouldn't they? This wasn't exactly the big white bed Rob had spoken about, but it was a double bed (barely), in a room with a door that locked. There was no one around to 'catch them' or even to disapprove. What else was there to wait for? It felt like it was time.

The coals on the barbecue were glowing embers by the time they returned. The others had disappeared, leaving a box of empty beer bottles. Rob opened the door to the girls' caravan, and held it while she climbed the steps inside.

Amelia was obviously in bed already. The door to her room, barely six feet from the door to Susannah's in the back portion of the caravan, was closed. At first, Susannah was relieved. She didn't want to have to explain anything to her friend tonight, or to be watched going into her room with Rob. But it very quickly became apparent that Amelia wasn't asleep, and she wasn't alone. Rob started to speak but Susannah heard something, and held a finger up to her lips to quieten him. At first it was only Amelia's low, rhythmic moans that Susannah could hear, and they froze her to the spot. Then she heard a male voice – a groan at first, a whispered 'yes', then another, then something more guttural. The thin walls of the caravan rippled. With a sickening feeling, Susannah realized that it was Alastair's voice she was listening to. Her brother was making love to her best friend barely two feet away from where she was standing.

She couldn't get out of the caravan fast enough. Rob followed her. She sat down hard in a deck chair without speaking, and he pulled over a coolbox and sat beside her.

'What the hell is she playing at?'

'I didn't know things were happening between them. How long was I gone on that course, anyway?' Rob was trying to make light of it.

But Susannah couldn't. 'Things weren't happening. Nothing. Nothing I know of, at least.' For the first time, Susannah wondered if Amelia had been sneaking around with Al behind her back. She shook her head. She couldn't have been. They'd been together every day. She'd have noticed . . . something.

'So, they're fast movers.'

She snorted. It was embarrassing – she didn't even know why. She and Rob had been together for ages, and they hadn't slept together. Amelia and Alastair weren't even in a relationship, but they were already in bed. Her hands formed fists, and she banged them on her knees.

'Why are you so angry?'

'I'm furious. Amelia knows he has a thing for her. He always has had. She shouldn't be doing this.'

'How do you know she hasn't got a thing for him?'

'Because I know. This is Amelia we're talking about – she doesn't internalize a damn thing. If she felt it, believe me, I'd know about it. She doesn't like him – not that way.'

'But surely that's Al's problem. He's what – nearly twenty? He knows her – he must know what he's getting into, mustn't he?'

'But it's not fair.'

'It's nothing to do with us, though, Susie.'

She rounded on him. 'It's everything to do with us.'

'I don't see how.'

'He's my brother. She's my friend. This won't work out.'

'How do you know?'

'I just know. And then everything will be weird.'

'Does it have to be?'

'It will be.' She was so mad she was crying now. 'And what about you and me? We can't do it now. She's ruined it.'

'I don't see how.'

'Because she turned our caravan into a knocking shop, that's why. It's like a bloody brothel. She's cheapened it. She's ruined everything.'

Rob was laughing now, and that made her madder. 'What's so funny?'

'Sounds like an excuse to me . . .'

She hit him, hard, in the chest. Once, twice, and then in a series of flapping slaps, until he took her hands and held them away from his body. 'Oy! Stop it.'

The rigidity went out of her arms, and she crumpled against him. 'Don't you know what I mean? Don't you get it at all?'

'I get it. I think you're being a bit over the top, but I get it. He's your brother, you're protective of him, you're mad at Amelia for doing something that might hurt him, you're mad at her for turning the van into a . . . what was it – a "knocking shop"?' He giggled again.

She looked up at his face, half laughing and half crying now. 'Don't laugh at me.'

'I love you, you daft cow.'

They sat that way for a few minutes. 'I'll kill her.'

'Kill her in the morning, will you?'

'How about my place?' He winked, and pointed his thumb behind him.

'Haven't got a toothbrush. It's in there . . .' She gestured behind her.

'I'll let you use mine.'

'Just to sleep?'

'Just to sleep. Don't worry. I'll keep taking the bromide.' He kissed her on the forehead.

'What's that?'

'Bromide. It's a drug. They used to put it in soldiers'

tea, in the Second World War, allegedly – it diminishes libido. Stopped them all going mad with sexual desire while they were supposed to be concentrating on fighting.'

'Can you get me some?'

It wasn't the night they'd hoped for, but in its own way it was amazing. They were lying in a bed together for the first time, in just their underwear, their bodies touching all the way down. There was a reverence in the way Rob touched her, once they were like this, that made her feel unbelievable. He knew the mood was destroyed for her, and his touch was relatively chaste, but she could feel everything he felt for her in it, and in his eyes on her in the semi-darkness. She felt every breath, her head on his chest as it rose and fell. Her leg across his lap, her knee bent up, and his arm around her waist, gently stroking her back and side. Extraordinary. Falling asleep together. It was such an intimate thing to do. In the morning, lying beside him, watching him sleep, his eyelids flickering in dreams, Susannah wasn't sure that it wasn't enough, for now.

She was still furious with Amelia. Amelia knew it, too, when she sheepishly stepped out of the caravan several hours after Matt, Rob and Susannah had been up, Alastair trailing behind her, both of them unable to meet Susannah's eyes. Amelia had a towel over her shoulder, and her washbag under her arm, and announced to no one in particular that she was going to shower in the block two or three hundred yards behind them.

Susannah followed her. 'What the hell do you think you're playing at?'

Amelia rolled her eyes. 'I knew you'd be like this.'

'Like what?'

'All judgmental.'

'Is that what you think I am?'

'Aren't you?'

'I think you made a big mistake last night.'

'Why?'

'Because you don't like him. How many times have you said so to me? That you don't fancy him. That you're not interested in guys that are interested in you. He's the ultimate guy interested in you. He's been interested in you since you were both kids. How could you do this to him?'

'We did it to each other, actually. And it was nice.' Amelia was trying not to laugh.

Susannah punched her, hard, in the arm, but then she was laughing, too. 'I'm still angry with you. Just because I'm laughing doesn't mean I'm not.'

'Don't be. It's none of your business, Suze. I love you, but you can be a nosy old cow. We don't all want to do things the way you and Rob do. We're not all so serious.'

'Is that what Al says?'

'I presumed you'd noticed that we weren't talking much.'

Susannah wrinkled her nose with distaste. 'That's

what I mean. You don't know what he's thinking. For all you know, he's sitting back there thinking he's just embarked on a relationship – a relationship with a girl he's had a thing for for a million years. You're over here thinking you're on to a good little holiday fling.'

'You don't know what he's thinking.'

'And nor do you!' Susannah's voice was high and shrill now.

They'd reached the showers, Susannah having followed her friend round the brown fence that separated the sexes, and Amelia had turned the water on. She held one hand under the flow until it got hot, and then peeled off her T-shirt and tracksuit bottoms, hanging them on pegs. Underneath she was naked. Susannah had seen her naked countless times before, but she'd never seen her naked after she'd spent the night shagging her brother, and she turned away, newly embarrassed. Amelia put her towel on Susannah's shoulders and stood under the water, running her fingers through her hair as it got wet.

'I can't believe you. You're really shameless, you know that?'

Amelia was lathering her hair now. 'Look, Suze. We had fun. That's all. He's not an idiot. There were no declarations. There won't be. He's going back to Exeter. I'm going to university. It's fun. Not everything has to mean something. We're not all you. I promise, promise, promise not to hurt him. Okay? But I'm not going to stop just because you want me to.'

She didn't either. Rob and Susannah spent the next three nights in the boys' caravan with Matt, while Alastair and Amelia 'shacked up', as Matt put it, in the girls'. An uneasy truce, brokered by an appeasing Alastair and a calming Rob, broke out in the camp. But it had ruined things for Susannah.

Present Day

Susannah smiled as they passed the turning for Mine-head. The early autumn sunshine was bright, after a few days of grey rain, and the foliage was beautiful. Tonight she'd be sleeping at Babington House, in a luxury double in the Stable Block — not in a slightly mildewed caravan — beneath 600 thread count cotton sheets, instead of a scratchy nylon sleeping bag. It would cost more — quite a lot more, she suspected — for this one night at the hotel than both caravans had cost for the best part of a week. What a difference a couple of decades made. She wondered ruefully whether she'd have half as much fun, but she already knew the answer, really.

She'd booked the night for her and Douglas — it was a belated birthday gift for him. He was notoriously difficult to shop for, and she'd felt slightly inspired by the idea. They'd been once before, a couple of summers ago, for the wedding of a partner at Doug's firm, and they'd been meaning to come back for ages. It had been one of the things they hadn't got round to. One of a long list of things.

They'd have dinner this evening in the relaxed and stylish dining room. Before, she'd tried to interest him in a treatment in the famous Cowshed spa, but Douglas was not a treatment kind of a guy. He'd packed a stack of paper in with his change of clothes and toiletries, and told her she should go – that he'd be busy most of the afternoon. She bit back irritation. One weekend without any work, for God's sake. It didn't seem a lot to ask. Then it occurred to her that perhaps he was hiding behind the paper.

She left him in the beautiful, airy room, and crept downstairs in a voluminous white robe. There was a time, she vaguely remembered, when a hotel bed in the middle of the afternoon would have proved irresistible to both of them, and they'd have rolled around in it for hours, sating themselves before dinner – and then, probably, afterwards as well. Douglas hadn't so much as looked tempted. And she'd thought of Rob. What he'd promised to do to her in a double bed, one day. One day that had never come.

So, a massage seemed like a good option. She tried, as the young masseuse expertly pummelled and kneaded the knots away from her neck and shoulders, to think about nothingness, but it was impossible. She thought about Rob, and the holiday all those years ago. She thought about Douglas, sitting upstairs, and she thought about Amelia, her poor friend, facing a ghastly journey that, she knew, already exhausted both of them even though they had barely started. She thought about how much the room, and the dinner and the massage, were all going to cost, and about whether or not she and Douglas were going to have sex this evening. They should, shouldn't they? You came to a country house hotel with that in mind. It would be a problem if they didn't, wouldn't it? Amelia would definitely say so.

At dinner, Douglas, who didn't seem any more relaxed by his afternoon with legal documents than she was after her massage, ordered chicken with a pungent garlic sauce. It felt like a sign. Then he had a cheese plate and a glass of port. Which seemed more like an open invitation to indigestion and possibly a migraine than a prelude to lovemaking. She was making too much of this, she knew. Putting too much pressure on herself, and probably on him too. But she couldn't relax. She compared everything that he said and did with everything that she wished he would say and do, and, each time, found him wanting.

Conversation didn't flow. It was as if they were in a maze, and every route they took led to a thick hedge of potential misunderstanding. The kids, Amelia's illness, even a summer holiday. They were on the cusp of scratchiness with each other, and she kept making about-turns in the chat, trying to avert a crisis. Everything felt forced and disjointed. She tried flirting, but he seemed oblivious, and she seemed ridiculous, even to herself. By sharp contrast, the couple at the table next to them had clearly spent the afternoon in bed. They sat perilously close at their table, hand in hand.

He fed her from his fork, and she looked at him as if she'd much rather be eating him. He kept bending his head to whisper things in her ear, and Susannah just bet she knew what he was saying. Douglas noticed them, too, but threw them a glance of distaste rather than the wistful envy Susannah felt must be etched on her own face.

They hadn't always been like this, had they? She knew they hadn't. The question was, could they ever get it back again . . . ? Whatever 'it' had been.

Upstairs in their room, the housekeeper had turned the bed down. Susannah felt a sense of doom about the evening. Sex didn't start once you got into bed. At least, good sex didn't. It should have started at dinner. Maybe they'd take a bath in the beautiful and vast tub . . . maybe . . . maybe . . .

But Douglas had brushed his teeth and was climbing into bed. When she joined him, she made one last attempt at intimacy. She raised herself on her elbow and kissed him, although he smelt garlicky, but their noses bumped awkwardly against each other, as though they hadn't known each other eight minutes, let alone eight years, and Douglas's glasses got smudged. He took them off, folding them neatly on the bedside table, and then turned back to her, returning the kiss, a hand on her breast. She tried to feel lustful, but before she had a chance, his hand was under her nightdress, far too soon, and his probing fingers found her dry and unyielding. He made a small noise – disappointment, irritation? – then kissed her perfunctorily.

'I expect I'm tired.' She offered excuses – too tired, indeed, to tell him what she really felt.

'Yes. Me, too. Tired and full.' He seemed satisfied. 'Lovely dinner. Maybe in the morning . . .'

Lying beside him, twelve inches and a thousand miles away, with her nightie pulled back, and her arms by her sides, Susannah listened to his breathing become slower and deeper. Sadness washed over her, and she felt a tear escape from the corner of her eye and trickle down the side of her face into her ear.

But in the morning, when Susannah opened her eyes more refreshed from her sleep than she had thought she might be, the space Doug had occupied was empty, and she heard the sound of the shower running.

1990

Iraq invaded Kuwait in August 1990. When news of the invasion broke, Susannah was on a cheap camping holiday with Amelia on Mykonos. She saw it on the front of a two-day-old *Daily Mail* in a café by the harbour. She didn't immediately connect it to Rob. Rob was on one of a succession of different training courses, having graduated from Cranwell. And he connected it to himself immediately.

She'd gone to his graduating ceremony earlier in the year with Frank and Lois. She'd taken the train home from university the night before, loaded with laundry, and stayed at Mum and Dad's. Then the three of them had driven up in Frank's car. No parents could have been prouder. They knew an inordinate amount about Cranwell – their knowledge of the course Rob had been on, and of the traditions and rituals of the establishment, was almost encyclopedic. 'There's a carpet, you know, Susannah, that cadets can't walk on until they graduate!'

There'd been a dinner, and a ball that evening after the graduation ceremony. Frank and Lois had left her there – they were going to stay in a bed and breakfast in town and take her back down the next morning.

Susannah had hired a ball dress – a tight black strap-less bodice with a voluminous white satin short skirt. She felt unlike herself in it. The dinner was vaguely civilized, but the ball was anything but. Whatever Cinderella fantasies Susannah may have entertained were quickly supplanted by drunken graduating officers and their even more drunken girlfriends. The music was too loud. Rob seemed different.

She had thought, wondered, before she came, whether this night might be *the* night. But she knew early on that it wouldn't be. It wasn't right. He'd been drinking. He had a swagger about him she didn't remember and didn't much care for. She began to wonder why she'd bothered to come, and to wish she hadn't said she would stay. Maybe, she thought, watching him down two pints in quick succession, their time had passed. Maybe they were moving in different directions.

She stayed in his narrow single bed that night. He slept, snoring, on the floor next to her, too drunk to even try anything except a slurred apology and a sloppy kiss. The next morning, when Frank picked her up, Lois pinched her cheek and winked at her. 'You kids have a good time, did you?' She really hadn't.

When she told Amelia about it, her friend laughed it off. 'You're such a Pollyanna, Suze, you know that? Of course he got drunk. He'd just been through, what was it . . . ? Four months, more even, of pure hell. Did you *not* see *An Officer and a Gentleman?*'

'There were no gentlemen there as far as I noticed. Him included.'

'Ah, go on. You said he gave you the bed and took the floor . . .'

She didn't see him again, after that, until Easter, when they were both home for a few days. Their timing wasn't great. When she was free, he was away, and on the rare occasions when he was around, she always seemed to be somewhere else. It frustrated them both, though she thought it was slightly worse for him than for her, and she felt bad about it. And then, back home, where everything had begun, confoundingly, things were lovely again. He apologized for what he called 'the Cranwell debacle'. He said he'd been tired, and triumphant and too susceptible to peer pressure. She said sorry right back. She'd been a prude, she said. She hadn't fully appreciated how hard it had been for him.

They had a few gorgeous days together and it felt like the old days again. His swagger was gone, and by the time she went back to college, and he went off to the next course, her doubts had disappeared, and she believed, again, that they could make it. That they would make it.

By the time she and Amelia were back from Mykonos that September, with their Sun-In streaks and their hard-won tans, the military PR machine was in full swing, but it was still difficult for Susannah to engage seriously with the idea that it might somehow directly affect her. She couldn't believe Britain would go to war, and she certainly couldn't – or wouldn't – believe that, if they did, Rob would have to go, too. She went back to university in October, and normal service was resumed.

When Rob first told her he was shipping out to the Gulf, it seemed surreal to her. Men didn't 'go to war' – it was the stuff of film, and books. Too young to have anything but the vaguest memory of the Falklands – Prince Andrew in his helicopter and crowds waving flags at Portsmouth Harbour as ships came in – Susannah couldn't conceive of it. Couldn't grasp that Rob was flying out – deployed – with his kit in a pack, to fight in a war.

For Amelia, it might have seemed impossibly romantic and thrillingly dramatic. For her fellow undergraduates, it barely registered, apparently, except as fodder for a bar debate over Western intervention – protecting oil supplies under the cover of defending freedom – a political issue for those proactive or pretentious enough to want to discuss one over their pints.

For Susannah, it was terrifying.

Years later, flying through Atlanta, the big US hub for United Airlines, just after 9/11 had started the Second Gulf War, she'd been moved to tears watching soldiers in their desert camouflage uniforms, changing planes on their way to and from the fighting, children staring and old men nodding their respect. The feeling never really went away.

Rob could be killed. That was her constant, stark thought at first. For weeks and weeks it hit her, the simple anxiety, as she went about her own unchanged daily routine, sitting in lectures, cycling through town, in the cinema, in the shower. He could be killed. He could already be dead.

She worried that she'd wasted their time together. The Minehead holiday, the Cranwell ball – not seeing him the whole summer after their few golden days together at Easter. It all felt pointless and silly to her now.

Thin blue aerogrammes arrived from him every few days. At first, she was happy to receive them. They felt like tissuey proof that he was still alive – nonsense, she knew, as they took at least a week to arrive, which meant you could get a letter from someone already six days dead. You could hear that news and still get a letter from the dead. And she wouldn't even hear the news. It would be Frank and Lois who would get a phone call, or a knock on the door. They would have to walk across the common, once they'd found the strength to think straight, and tell her own parents. Her dad would have to drive to Bristol, find her, pull her out of a lecture hall, or wake her up in her room. In her dreams she imagined his mouth shaping the words.

But then the tone of the letters changed. So did the length.

In the early letters, Rob's messy handwriting covered every inch of the available space with information –

about his mates, the food, how hot it was. How he loved her, how he lay in his cot at night and dreamed of her.

The letters reconnected them. It was like the old days again — the days of first being together — they were sharing their thoughts and dreams again.

Thank you for your letters. The funny thing is that you're so far away, and I can't see you, or touch you, but when I read them I feel so close to you. It sounds weird to say you can be lonely here — when you can never be alone, and something is always happening. But I get so lonely. I can hear your voice in my head, when I read them, you know. Your laugh. And it helps.

The letters were all she had. Phone calls were impossible. At the beginning she called Frank and Lois often — they were more likely than she was to have heard his voice, know his news.

One night, she called later than usual. She'd been in the library, working on an essay, and she felt a sudden urge, walking back to her hall, to hear that he was okay. It was almost too late to call, but she knew Lois wouldn't mind. But they didn't answer immediately — she was about to put the receiver down when she heard Lois's voice, which sounded strange. She felt a flutter of panic in the pit of her stomach.

'He's had a bad time, we think. He cried, tonight, when he called . . .' Lois was tearful herself. She couldn't speak.

Susannah heard Frank tell her to go and sit down, to drink her tea, before his deep voice came on the phone. 'Susannah? Frank. I'm sorry about that. She's a bit upset.'

'What's happened?'

'We don't know. He can't really say.'

'Is he okay?'

'He's fine. I think Lois was right – he's had a bad day is all, love.'

It was after that day his letters changed. He never said why, or what had happened. He just wrote less, and less often. All the humour had seeped away from what he wrote. There was less and less of Rob on the page. Susannah felt an inexorable shift – he was sliding away from her. Her powerlessness and frustration chewed at her all day and she began to dread the aerogrammes in her pigeon hole.

She once read them straight away, leaning against the wall in the post room, desperate to hear him the only way she could. But now she put them in her bag, sometimes not reading them for hours, or until the next day.

She played scenarios over in her head all the time, instead of sleeping – Rob killed or injured, or simply rendered unrecognizable by emotional trauma. When she did sleep it was fitful and interrupted by bad dreams. Once, a low-flying plane passed over the halls of residence and she sat bolt upright in shock and panic.

Rob's face silently regarded her from the bedside table.

1991

Susannah's cashpoint card popped out of the machine, followed by four crisp five-pound notes. She always felt relieved, especially this late in the term, when it spat money at her. The grant covered tuition and board, but the rest came from Dad, and it was running out fast. She couldn't ask him for more. He was keeping Alastair, too. She'd lined up a job at WHSmith for the holidays, and she'd save what she could, but she wasn't earning now. Tucking the money into her denim wallet, she stepped aside to let the next kid in line get to the machine for the moment of truth. Twenty pounds. She'd try to make that last until Sunday. It was Friday night. She had meal tickets for halls, so it was basically beer money, although she needed new shampoo and couldn't do without conditioner, and some of her mates had been talking about going to see a film on Saturday afternoon. She had already bought her five-quid ticket to the bop tomorrow night.

She needed cheering up. She'd had another letter from Rob this morning. Funny seeing his handwriting on an envelope in her pigeon hole. Funny how so recently it thrilled her, and she'd rip the missive open and read it right there and then. If you'd told her even a few months ago how fast the chasm would open up, and how vast it would become, she wouldn't have believed you. It couldn't happen, she'd have said.

But it had happened. Something. She couldn't articulate what. It was subtle and secret, but it had happened. It wasn't only her, she told herself. A girl along her corridor – Maria – she'd been engaged when she arrived in her first term at uni, to a policeman in Croydon she'd been going out with since she was sixteen. She had a tiny diamond ring on her left hand, and she'd shyly shown it off the first time they'd met. They were going to get married the year she graduated, she said. He would come up every other weekend, and she'd go home for holidays . . . They had it all planned out. Susannah remembered how excruciating it had been the first time he'd come. He'd sat in the bar looking like an alien. She'd gone home the next weekend, to break it off.

Everything was different here. Different and fantastic and all-consuming.

She'd been terrified, at first, of course. Everyone was, though some hid it better than others. Mum and Dad had delivered her to Bristol, with two suitcases, a large cardboard box from Waitrose, a yucca plant and a duvet. Dad had driven her mad, going on and trying to arrange the plant and hang her Robert Doisneau posters for her. He'd kept hugging her and saying he couldn't believe his little girl was leaving home.

They'd taken her to a Berni Inn for lunch, and then they'd driven off, and she hadn't known whether she was more relieved or bereft to see the car disappear round the corner. She'd never been anywhere before where she didn't know anyone. There were a couple of kids from college here – Matt, of course, and some girls she frankly hadn't been that close to – but she had no idea where their rooms were, and this place seemed huge, much bigger now she was here than it had appeared when she visited. She'd found the phone room nearest her room – more of a cupboard, really, at the end of the corridor next to the stairs – and tried calling Amelia on the number she'd left at home yesterday, but whoever answered hadn't known who Amelia was, and she hadn't got a room number for her yet. There hadn't been anything else to do but go back to her room, move all the posters to where she wanted them, and line up her photographs. She had a picture of her and Rob, taken in the summer. He was behind her, with his big arms around her waist. It was taken just before he left. She had her head back, against his shoulder. She kept that one by her bed. That first night, when she'd changed into her pyjamas and brushed her teeth in the sink in her room (wondering all the while how she would ever bring herself to shower in the mixed stalls), she'd felt tearful, and ridiculously lonely, running one finger tenderly across the image of his face.

The first couple of days were a blur of finding her

way around, and getting organized. She signed up for hockey trials, had her first tutorials, nervously looking around at her fellows, and her first lectures, given in an enormous, echoey hall, and lay nervously in bed at night listening to the soundtrack of music, shouting and laughter coming from the other rooms. Looking at Rob.

Matt found her on the second day. He was the first person to knock on her bedroom door, and she was profoundly grateful when she opened it and saw him. She hugged him warmly. He dragged her to the bar with him, incredulous that she hadn't been. He seemed to know everyone there already, and the middle-aged bartender greeted him like a long-lost son. Her request for a diet Coke was denied with a smile, and a pint of beer put down in front of her like a challenge.

And that was how it all started to work. Matt's very new friends embraced her with the same instant intensity they had presumably shown towards him. Girls confessed crushes and guys talked about which teams they were trying out for. Everyone seemed to be yelling, and laughing, and soon Susannah was, too. They were all in this new, strange boat together, and the obvious thing to do was drink and smoke. Susannah had never been a big drinker at college. There'd been the odd party where someone brought beers, or broke into the absent parents' drinks cabinet and stole the vodka. She associated it with the 'cooler kids' while, at the same time, objectively recognizing that there was nothing really cool about throwing up in someone's flower beds or having to do a Monday morning trigonometry test with a hangover. On the rare occasions when she had more than one drink, she hadn't liked the sensation of being out of control, but here, in this new arena, the sensation was helpful. She *was* out of control, after all – why not embrace it?

Tonight, though, more than a year since that first heady term at uni, Susannah was drunk. Not so drunk she didn't know what she was doing, but drunk enough to think that doing it was okay. Not so drunk that afterwards she would be able to say that it wasn't her fault. She was absolutely here, in this moment.

The big crowd of earlier in the evening had dissipated, as sometimes happened – some had gone clubbing, and some home, to whatever essay crisis awaited them back in their room. Ten minutes ago, there had been perhaps twenty people around – laughing, chatting. And now there were just the two of them.

Just her and Matt, back in Matt's room. She hadn't been here before. Her room had become one of those rooms where people congregated, and Matt was one of the crowd who was often there, but this was the first time she'd been in his. It was closer. He'd suggested it. It wasn't as messy as most guys' rooms, she reflected vaguely, thinking of the guys on her corridor, who lived like pigs, wading through dirty laundry until they ran out of clothes, and drinking black tea from stained mugs.

There wasn't too much personal stuff in evidence – that was the standard undergrad male – girls needed an estate car to transport the pantechnicon of their stuff at the beginning of each term, but boys seemed to be able to manage on the train with a duffel bag. She saw just a few photographs stuck on the ubiquitous corkboard, and a plain, utilitarian duvet cover on the bed. His toiletries were lined up a bit too neatly on the narrow shelf above the sink in the corner, and there was a single U2 poster hanging on the wall. A few dirty clothes were strewn across the floor, but not many, and Matt immediately scooped them up and shoved them into the wardrobe. He had a kettle and a box of English Breakfast tea bags. Most guys she knew had optics.

Matt had been a good friend. He knew her from home, and it gave them a private shorthand. He knew Rob, he knew Alastair. When they were out in a big group, he always looked out for her – wouldn't let her walk home alone, that kind of thing. She'd written to Rob about him, and how great he was. She thought she was lucky to have him. He was pretty cute – plenty of girls flirted with him, but he never seemed very interested. He hadn't had a girlfriend at college either. There'd been a time when she thought he fancied Amelia, but the Minehead debacle might well have cured him of that.

She never knew, afterwards, what had started it: what had changed the mood. She'd gone back there with him because she was suddenly tired. Because she didn't feel like being on her own. Because Matt was their friend, hers and Rob's, and she thought he missed him, like she did. And because in her drunkenness she felt very fond of him. It had never entered her head that there would be anything else.

But now suddenly he was kissing her, and it felt good, and she wanted to kiss him back. She was turned on. This was a different Matt. He had his hands in her hair, holding her face still. He planted a deluge of small, gentle kisses on her cheeks, her eyelids, her forehead, her lips. And then something began to stir between them, seriously, and he was kissing her deeply, hungrily. The mood shifted heavily. His arms went around her back at first, holding her close, but soon, as she responded to his kisses, and pressed herself into him, his hands were on her breasts, pulling impatiently at the buttons of her cardigan.

And then she was pushing his hands away. But not because she wanted to stop. She could do the buttons more quickly herself. He undid her bra and peeled it off her shoulders slowly, staring down at her.

They were skin to skin, her hands at her sides. His fingers stroked her shoulder blades, her collarbone, tantalizingly. He broke away from kissing her mouth to suck at her nipples, and she arched her back, her fists clenched.

All the time, as he sucked and licked and kissed her, he was murmuring her name. 'Oh my God,' he whispered. 'Susannah – I can't believe you're here.'

Afterwards she wondered why his words hadn't broken the spell. She'd been too far gone. No one had touched her like this in months. She'd been so worried and so lonely . . . so very lonely.

And this felt so good. She didn't know how they got naked, but suddenly her jeans and her knickers were gone. And his were, too. This was the point of no return.

His fingers explored her warm wetness and she felt him, hard in her hands. 'Susannah – can I . . . can we . . . ?'

She must have nodded. Maybe she spoke. She saw him, in the moonlight from the window, pull something out of his bedside drawer. Heard the wrapper rip and watched him pull the condom on and then, his hands under her behind, tilting her upwards, he was inside her, more quickly and easily than she might have expected.

She had the sudden thought that this wasn't his first time – he'd done this before, even though she'd never known him to have a girlfriend. Did he know it was hers? Probably not. Everyone assumed she and Rob had slept together. Something that felt like sadness penetrated the pit of her stomach. *It should have been Rob.*

She waited, her hands hovering above his shoulders, waiting to brace herself, for it to start hurting. But it didn't.

Matt raised himself on his elbows and began pumping into her, his eyes never leaving her face. She closed her eyes, to shut out the thought that had exploded in her brain. *It shouldn't have been him. It should have been Rob.*

Most of the pleasure, the delicious sensations of a few minutes ago, had evaporated with the first thought of Rob that had invaded her brain. She was detached from this now. She wanted him to stop.

But in the end, it was over quickly. He came in about three minutes. He reared up and the veins in his neck stood out. With a grunt of satisfaction he dropped down heavily, forcing the breath from her in a whoosh. He was kissing her neck, still murmuring her name. If it had taken any longer, she might have stopped him. Waves of revulsion – not for Matt, for herself – were starting to wash over her. But it was too late. He was done.

In a few minutes more, he rolled off her and she turned her back to him so he couldn't see her face. He spooned her, his breath still coming fast, and put one arm across her proprietorially. She lay there until it seemed like he'd fallen asleep. Then she wriggled out of his grasp, and sat clutching her knees and looking at him.

Amelia's mum used to tell them – far more often than either of them wanted to hear it, and often at completely inappropriate moments, when she was obviously struck by the opportunity – that their virginity was a 'precious gift', not to be given away lightly. They'd giggled and pretended to gag, and tried to make her talk about . . . anything else. Now it felt like she was right. Mrs Lloyd would most definitely not approve of this. She'd given it away. Not just lightly, but drunkenly.

She thought of Lois and her own mother. And then she thought about Rob. Guilt slapped her hard around the face, and a single tear escaped her eye and rolled down her cheek. She was afraid that if she started crying she might not be able to stop, or control herself, and that her crying would wake Matt.

She needed to get out.

Matt was sleeping soundly, it seemed. Crawling around the floor as quietly as she could, careful not to wake him up, she collected her clothes, and dressed quickly. Then she slipped out of the door and crept back to her room, desperately hoping she wouldn't bump into anyone. She had just reached her own floor, and her own corridor, before the vomit rose in her throat. She got to the toilet in time, sinking to the floor beside the bowl. Her head was killing her now – sharp stabbing pains seared her temples.

It was the worst hangover of her life. Her head pounded, her stomach ached from throwing up, her throat was sore, and her heart palpitated.

Later, much later in the day, back in her room, as she lay as still and quietly as she could in her narrow bed, waiting for time to pass so that she might stop feeling so disgusting, Matt knocked at the door. He stood on the other side, knocking gently, and saying her name, for five or ten minutes, but she didn't answer. Eventually he went away.

She couldn't believe what she'd done. Nothing about it was right. The only thing she could take comfort in was that Matt had used a condom. At least she couldn't get pregnant . . . at least she hadn't been that bloody stupid.

It was around 6 p.m. the next afternoon that she crawled from her bed to the desk and wrote to Rob. By then it was the only thing she could think of, the need to explain herself to him.

Dear Rob

I've done something horrible, and I can't bear to tell you, but I know it would be much worse if I didn't tell you. I'd rather tell you in person, but who knows when we'll see each other again, so I'm writing this letter – the hardest letter I've ever written.

I slept with Matt last night. I was drunk and I was sad and lonely, and it just happened. And I know that sounds so pathetic, and it is. I don't have any excuses.

I hate that I did it. I thought of you the whole time, and the minute it was over I felt sick. I would do anything to take it back, but I can't.

But I can't not be honest with you, Rob. We've always told each other the truth and so I have to about this one, awful thing.

Please forgive me. Please tell me that you have. I can't bear it if you don't.

It is you who I love. It is you who I want to be with. I hate that I can't be with you. I want you every day. Please believe me.

Susie

She cried the whole time she was writing. Then she pulled on her jeans and a sweatshirt, grabbed her towel and washbag, and went down to the postbox to post the letter before she changed her mind, still moving gingerly. Then she went straight to the shower, and scrubbed herself hard under the hottest water she could stand on her skin. She was dry, dressed and back in her room, risking a piece of dry toast, before she began to wish she hadn't mailed the letter, but it was too late by then, of course.

Saudi Arabia

The letter took six days to arrive. Mail was given out in the morning, in the mess hall. Your name was called, and your letter, or parcel or package, was unceremoniously thrown at you. Rob heard his name often – his mum and dad wrote all the time. Mum wrote long chatty letters, with stories and cartoons she cut out from the newspapers, and socks, and Juicy Fruit chewing gum. Dad scribbled brief notes on the end of Mum's letters, always signing off with *io ti amo, figlio*.

Susannah wrote, too. Not quite as often as Mum, but something came once a week, usually – even if it was sometimes a postcard with a quick message. When he saw her handwriting on the envelope, he smiled to himself, and tucked the letter into his pocket to read by himself. Being alone was one of the hardest things to achieve here. There was always someone around, always noise.

It was still chilly in the mornings. There was a definite nip in the air sometimes, although the sun was bright and strong – by lunchtime it would feel warm. Squinting in the sunlight, Rob found a box to sit on and pulled out the letter.

After he'd read it, he sat for a while, staring out beyond the fence with the barbed wire, looking towards the desert that stretched away into the horizon. Then he slowly folded the letter neatly into four, and put it back into his pocket.

1993

Almost from the first moment Susannah met Sean, in a wine bar in Battersea, just before Christmas 1993, she thought she was getting something right at last. It was as though the last years, in personal terms, she'd been travelling up the wrong track. Now she'd corrected the path she was taking. This was the right time. The right place. This was the right guy. Everyone was pleased about it. Mum and Dad liked him. He was already mates with Alastair, so he'd passed that particular test before he even knew he was taking it. Amelia liked him, but didn't fancy him, so that was okay, too. It was simple and straightforward and easy.

Sean was lots of things Rob had never been. He was a strawberry blond, for a start, with blue-green eyes. Not nearly as tall as Rob had been, he had just a few inches on Susannah. He was thin – almost wiry. And he was funny. Rob could be funny, but overall he was a serious, sometimes intense guy. Sean seemed, the first time she met him, and for a long time afterwards . . . just light.

That, as much as the sparkling blue eyes, was what had worked for her, that first night. He was the first guy in a very long time that she could imagine being in a relationship with.

She hadn't gone out with anyone at all in the previous eighteen months, except in big groups, and Amelia said that didn't count. Susannah had chosen Chester for her year of law school, after she graduated. A lot of her friends headed to Guildford, close to London, and Mum wanted her to go, too – she'd have been less than an hour from home – but she preferred to be somewhere far away. She'd never been to Chester, before she chose it, but in the end she loved the town, and it had been a good year – flying by and over almost before it had begun. She'd shared a surprisingly un-grotty terraced house with three students who'd been on her course at Bristol – two guys, Conrad and Ben, and a girl she'd never known well but had always liked, Robyn. Robyn was sporty – probably the main reason they'd never been close as undergrads. She ran long distances and trained almost every day. Conrad and Ben were easy-going and a good laugh, but serious students, too. It was a fast-paced year of baked beans on toast, quiet nights in the pub and bloody hard work. She'd found jobs in shops and restaurants in Chester during the Christmas and Easter holidays, not keen to come home to the village. For all sorts of reasons.

Amelia was back from her third year in France, and was finishing her own degree at Manchester, which was a doable and affordable train journey – they saw more of each other that year than they had in the previous couple. And that summer, when they'd both finished, Amelia graduating with a 2.1, they took the InterRail trip they'd talked about so often as young teenagers, travelling widely in France, where Amelia's fluency made life easy, and then through Switzerland, Italy and Spain, too. It had been everything Susannah had imagined it would be. It felt, when they got home, that they were back to where they'd been before Minehead, and Cranwell. They felt close again, and Susannah knew she never wanted to go back to those estranged days. Amelia was her best friend, and she loved her. She understood herself better when she saw herself reflected back at her from Amelia. They talked about another trip, further afield – Thailand, maybe, or India. But real life beckoned Susannah much more forcefully than it did Amelia, who would have happily kept on travelling for a few more years. She found herself quite ambitious after her years of studying, applying to the best firms.

Susannah was taken on by a big City law firm – one of her top three choices – for her articles, and Amelia got a job she found interesting enough to stay around for at a translating agency with a group of young, like-minded colleagues, all still vaguely uncommitted to their adult lives. The two of them rented at first – a small, ground-floor, two-bedroom, one-bathroom flat together – Susannah paying two thirds of the rent to reflect the difference in their salaries, and therefore getting the bigger bedroom and the double bed.

Amelia petitioned hard for it, claiming that a double bed was wasted on Susannah, and that she'd get much more use out of it, but Susannah refused to give in. She had a feeling, she laughed, that her luck was about to change . . . A few months later, the argument was resolved, when Amelia's father, horrified by a visit to the small flat, pretty much insisted on paying the deposit and half the mortgage on a bigger and nicer place within reach of Clapham Common.

Susannah could have had no idea, though, when she first came to London, how relentlessly the law firm would extract their pound of flesh from the small army of articled clerks they took on that, and every, September. By November, she was regularly working fourteen-hour days. Sometimes they worked into the early hours, coming home in company taxis only to shower, before heading straight back in.

Amelia petulantly, and sometimes only half jokingly, claimed to feel like a neglected wife, tutting at her and claiming the long hours were all about machismo and hot air. Her hours were pretty lax – 9.30 a.m. until 5.30 p.m. with a lunch break of 90 minutes, so far as Susannah could gather. On those mornings, when she heard Susannah come in and jump into the shower while stripping off yesterday's clothes, Amelia would get up and make her tea and a fried egg sandwich, and sit with her, her dressing gown wrapped tightly around her, nursing her own mug, while Susannah ate, and moaned, unconvincingly, about work. One evening

Susannah came home at 7 p.m., and brought flowers, like an errant husband.

She loved the work, truthfully, and she loved the environment. She liked the discipline of what she was able to do, exercising her intellect and utilizing all the work she'd done at university and law school. She saw a clear path here. She'd work hard, she'd progress. Associate, partner . . . She liked earning her own money, too. It wasn't a huge amount, but compared with student days, she felt wealthy. She had money for rent and food, a pension, and there was still disposable income – more than she'd ever had before – left over at the end of the month. Spending it was fun. She really felt like a grown-up, for the first time. She cut her shoulder-length hair into a bob with a thick fringe, and had subtle highlights put into it, drying it straight and smooth. She started shopping for work clothes at places like Jigsaw and Hobbs, and then (as Amelia put it, it was the fashion equivalent of going from dope to cocaine – inevitable, really) a beautiful black wool gabardine trouser suit at Joseph, knowing with a frisson of almost shameful excitement that she'd never be able to tell her mum how much it had cost, even forty per cent off in the end of season sale.

She'd been wearing the suit in the wine bar the night she met Sean. That and her new hair and her new confidence.

Alastair worked with a guy called Hugh, who lived with Sean, who was an old school friend from home.

So his provenance was secure – he was vouched for. Susannah was at the bar with Amelia and a couple of other girls from the firm who lived nearby. Amelia had invited three colleagues from the agency – and Jonathan, of course, who was omnipresent now. It was a big gathering that night – everyone in a festive mood – offices were closing tomorrow or the next day, and frankly could have closed the day before for all the work that was being done, even at Susannah's uptight firm. Christmas was coming, and the wine was flowing, barely soaked up by the fancy bar snacks.

Susannah was pleased, these days, to see that Alastair and Amelia had recovered the easy teasing bantering relationship of their youth. Maybe Al had been right when he said she was the one, of the three of them, with the biggest problem. They greeted each other with a huge bear hug. Alastair was head over heels these days with a secretary from his office – Kathryn – who was, he said, coming later. Everyone was coupling up, he said, and he wasn't going to sit out.

Susannah had met Hugh a couple of times – at dinner parties at Alastair's flat, and tagging along to corporate softball tournaments on Clapham Common the previous summer – and liked him, although she had never considered him romantically, and she was pretty sure he didn't see her that way either. He was a lot like her brother, and she found him easy, unthreatening company. She was talking to him about her articles when Sean came into the bar, straight over to them, loosening his brightly coloured tie with his finger and undoing his top button.

'I'm Sean Dexter,' he said, straight away, offering his hand formally, and fixing her with an unwavering stare that might have been disconcerting if it wasn't so very nice to be in its beam.

She shook his hand, and he held hers for just a few seconds longer than he needed to.

'Susannah. Susannah Hammond.'

'This is Alastair's sister,' Hugh offered, though neither of them was really listening to him by then.

The attraction was instantaneous and, as Susannah related to Amelia the next day, instantly sexual, even if, in her case, it was fuelled by a couple of glasses of wine. His eyes had an enticing sparkle to them that she found almost irresistible. She knew, almost immediately, that she was going to sleep with him. And that really never happened to her. Everything about Sean and that first encounter swept her away just a little. She didn't know, that first night – couldn't have done – that she was going to marry him.

It didn't happen that first night, of course. Nothing happened. That wasn't her style – Matt, and what had happened in her that wretched evening at university, had made her forever wary of decisions made under the influence. And it seemed it wasn't his style either. He kissed her cheek softly, smiling at her almost regretfully as she left with Amelia and the other girls. She had written her numbers on his card, and he waved it at her as she climbed into the taxi, nodding his promise to use it.

He'd called her, the next day, at work, and they'd flirted down the line for a while. He was flying to Chicago that night with his cousins to spend Christmas with family who lived there. He wouldn't be back until the 2nd of January, he said, but could he please see her on the 3rd if she was free? It amused her that he added the 'if she was free'. There was something sincere and earnest about his request, and of course she acquiesced.

Two days later, on Christmas Eve, Alastair picked her and Amelia up from their flat to drive them home for the festivities. He was the only one with a car, a new Renault Clio. It was freezing cold and damp, and they ran out when they saw him, double-locking the door to the flat, keen to get back into the warm as fast as possible.

'Susannah's in love,' Amelia had blurted out, after planting a big smacking kiss on his cheeks as he put their cases in the boot.

They climbed in. Susannah punched Amelia's arm, but only playfully.

'Hallelujah.' Alastair took both hands off the steering wheel for a moment, and raised them heavenward. 'Is it possible? Can it be? The long drought's over?'

'Shut up, both of you. I liked it better when you weren't talking to each other.' Susannah tried to sound stern, although she didn't pull it off, even to her own ears. She'd known Amelia would do this. 'You make me sound like a bloody nun.'

'You've certainly been doing a passable impression of a novitiate over the past few years, unless you have a secret double life neither of us know about, which I highly doubt,' Alastair laughed. 'Who is the poor unsuspecting guy?'

'Like I'd tell you?'

'He's called Sean. He was in the bar, you know, the other night? The blond one – cheeky chappy looking . . .' Amelia offered helpfully.

'Hugh's flatmate?!' exclaimed Alastair.

'Cheeky chappy?! That's a bit harsh, isn't it?'

'You know what I mean – you like that clean-cut, wholesome type. Think so, Al. Is that right, Susannah?'

Susannah nodded. 'Don't want to talk about it. Nothing to talk about.'

'Not true!' Amelia shouted accusatorially. 'He's away for Christmas but he's fixed to see her the day he gets back . . . jet lag notwithstanding. Can't wait another minute, obviously . . .'

'Do shut up. Or I won't go out with him.'

'Thus cutting off your nose to spite your face . . .'

'Thus not giving you anything to wind me up about.'

'You know we'd find something else.'

'You're bastards.'

'What about you, Meels?' Alastair asked, looking at her in the rear-view mirror. She was sitting in the middle of the back seat, all the way forward with her knees hunched up, her face resting on her hands. 'Who've you got dangling on your hook these days? Jonathan still in the picture?'

'Yes – that's right. Start on her. She's a much easier target than me. And what about you? We can talk about Jonathan and Kathryn all the way home . . .'

Alastair and Amelia cheerfully continued the thrust and parry of their conversation, laughing and joking – and Susannah sat back in the front seat with her eyes closed and let their voices wash over her. She was happy. She felt so . . . normal. Almost just like them. Yes, there was a guy, and although it was ludicrous to start talking about love, or a future, it felt like it might, just might be the start of something. And it was time, after all.

The happy mood lasted all through Christmas. Everyone noticed.

True to his word, Sean had picked her up from work on the 3rd of January and taken her to dinner at Joe Allen's, where they ate steak frites, drank a full-bodied red and talked for hours, knees bumping under the table, 'accidentally on purpose', as Mum would have said. She knew nothing about him, she realized, except for the very basic facts and provisional thumbs up Alastair had been able to provide when he'd stopped making fun of her, and Sean seemed keen to fill in the blanks for her. He was great, easy company – he had a great delivery, everything he said was peppered with jokes – and if the conversation was slightly more about him than about her, she really didn't mind. She laughed a lot, and felt far more comfortable than she might have imagined she would. He was one of four kids – with an English father, a cardiologist at Birmingham City Hospital, and an Irish mother, a former children's nurse. Still married after forty years, and still in love, he said (looking at her significantly, she thought). He'd been raised in a middle-class suburb of Birmingham, the spoilt only brother of three sisters – his father still called him the Sun God, apparently – and studied Economics at St Andrews university. Two of his sisters were married, and he had two nephews, who he adored – although most of the family was still in the Midlands, and he didn't get to see them as much as he would have liked. He made it sound rather like Birmingham was somewhere just inside the Arctic Circle. One sister – Becky – was doing a PhD on James Joyce at Goldsmiths College in London. At twenty-nine, he was six years older than Susannah was, more established in his career and his life in London. He was a bond trader, he told her. A good one. Things were good. He'd made enough money to buy his first house at twenty-three, though he still shared it with mates.

On the 7th, after daily phone calls and one delivery of a dozen American Beauty red roses that got both the long-married receptionists at her firm completely overexcited, he'd taken her to the theatre, to see *Miss Saigon*. And a week later, he took her to bed.

It seemed like time, although Amelia had laughed at her afterwards and said if she'd done it Susannah would have called her a slut. He swept her off her feet – there was no other way to describe it, however hackneyed the expression. He'd taken her for drinks and for dinner at Claridge's, and then afterwards, he'd produced a room key and laid it on the table in front of her, saying that the room was hers for the night, and that he'd only share it with her at her invitation. That he'd never done anything remotely like this for anyone else, with anyone else. That he wanted to be with her, and that if she wanted to be with him, too, then he wanted the first time to be somewhere wonderful – away from flatmates and alarm clocks and everyday things – but that if she wasn't ready, he would wait until she was. That he'd wait a long time, because he had a feeling, already, that she might be someone worth waiting for.

It was a good speech. It had seemed almost impossibly romantic to Susannah. The gesture had both touched her, and excited her. It felt like something that should be happening to someone else – to Amelia even. Not to her. So she'd nodded, shyly, and they'd walked hand in hand across the extraordinary marble-tiled lobby to the lifts, and then to a beautiful room on the third floor with a view across Mayfair.

She didn't know then – how could she have done? – that hotel sex was almost always way above average. There was something about the anonymity and the unfamiliar surroundings and the cool, clean sheets on the bed you'd never have to remake. And if Sean had known it at that point and had used it to his advantage, who could blame him? She was halfway to swooning and collapsing at the knees just from the romance of the offer, and the rest was just as unexpected and just as delightful. That was the word that sprang to mind the next morning as she lay in a fragrant frothy cloud of Floris bubbles in an enormous bathtub, blowing gently at them in her hands to watch them fall like snow all around her, and listened to a butler serving breakfast in the bedroom next door. She remembered Amelia's 'perfect' from all those years ago, and wondered how it might compare. This had been pretty good. Delightful, in fact.

Susannah believed herself to be absolutely in love with Sean. She felt like he ticked all the boxes for her. She believed in their shared values and their shared vision for the future. She wanted to make a life with him. She had been swept away that first night and she stayed swept on the tide of new feelings for weeks on end. She hadn't done anything wrong, anything to spoil it. It was fresh and new and simple.

Four months later they were engaged. Sean did that properly, too, of course. He drove down to Mum and Dad's one evening when she'd been at the Porchester Spa with Amelia, and thus was safely out of the way, and solemnly asked her father for his permission –

which was granted, Sean having made a very favourable impression on them both during several visits in the last few months. He'd even gone to church. There was a ring – a sparkling oval emerald encircled by a row of small round diamonds, from Garrard – and there was a bended knee. And an instant, tearful yes.

And eight months after they'd first met, on a mild and sunny August afternoon in 1994, they were married in Susannah's mum's beloved St Gabriel's church.

Planning the wedding had been more fun than she would have expected, although four months turned out not to be very long at all. Susannah bought a large lever arch file, and kept meticulous notes and records of everything. Sean's parents – who she thought she liked a lot when she met them for the first time, a week after the two of them got engaged, when she and Sean took the train to Birmingham for the weekend – offered to pay for half the cost of the wedding, after which Dad seemed relieved and more relaxed about everything. Susannah had wondered if his earlier tension was because he didn't think she and Sean knew each other well enough, and was relieved to discover his anxiety was of a more prosaic, practical nature. Mum was beside herself, and prone to sudden unexplained bouts of crying that came and went swiftly and could be provoked by anything from fabric samples to cake brochures. If she thought it was too quick to be getting married, she never said so. And

Sean's mum had held her hand tightly on the drive from the train station to their home, and said that she and Sean's father had known, 'just known', only weeks after meeting, that they were right for each other, and that it was clear from everything Sean had told her on the phone about Susannah that he was sure, too. She still had an Irish lilt in her voice and it made everything sound lovely, most especially that.

Susannah had worn a dress from an expensive bridal shop in Bath, a long lean ivory sheath covered with Chantilly lace, with a wide apricot sash. Amelia and Kathryn had been her bridesmaid and matron of honour – Kathryn was now married to Alastair since a whirlwind engagement and wedding after a May visit to Marrakech – 'not too hideous' (as Amelia graciously put it) in apricot organza. She'd carried a bouquet of tightly packed peach and cream tea roses tied with a satin ribbon. Sean, his best man, Hugh, and the ushers (who included Alastair and Alex) wore traditional morning dress, with embroidered waistcoats to match the bride's dress made by Favourbrook, the exclusive tailor in Jermyn Street. Dad wore a navy suit. The men all wore an apricot tea rosebud in their buttonholes.

They chose 'Jerusalem' and 'Love Divine, All Loves Excelling' as the hymns. Sean wanted 'Immortal, Invisible, God Only Wise', but Susannah's mum said the organist always had trouble with it.

They'd held a reception in a nearby small country house hotel, where Hugh's best man speech recalled the evening the two of them had first met, and how he instantly knew his friend was off the market the moment he saw him talking to Susannah. Sean nodded as his friend spoke, and grasped her hand. Susannah's dad had welled up and had stopped for a moment to recover his composure when he'd spoken about his dreams for his only daughter, of whom he was, he said, inordinately proud. A DJ played 'I'll Be There' by Mariah Carey as they danced for the first time as man and wife, and they cut a three-tier fruit cake decorated with sugar roses – guess which colour? Alex got drunk on his own allotted alcohol supplemented with surreptitious gulps from other people's glasses and threw up not quite as surreptitiously in an urn flanking the front door of the hotel.

'Do you ever think he might be too perfect?' Amelia had asked, late in the evening, as the two of them sat outside on a teak bench, sharing a glass of champagne, the buzz of the party still going on inside.

'What do you mean?'

Amelia shrugged. 'I don't know. Nothing. Don't listen to me. Drunk cow.'

'You mean *something*, Meels. You always do.'

But she'd refused to elaborate. Gone off on a monologue about hats guests had worn. Susannah had let it go. Maybe she was just drunk.

When she'd hugged her, just before Susannah and Sean had left their reception, she'd looked at her intently. 'Be happy, Susannah.'

'I will,' she'd answered, completely confident that she would be.

They honeymooned in the Seychelles, where they made love every night and most mornings, in a room on stilts over water more turquoise than she'd ever seen, and learnt to scuba dive, which Sean loved and Susannah merely tolerated – and was sometimes very frightened by – because she loved Sean and wanted to be with him every minute. And came back two weeks later to a large pile of boxes from John Lewis full of Le Creuset cookware, Waterford crystal glasses and 400 thread count bed linen from their wedding list. Which they then moved into their new house, a three-bedroom terrace in Battersea they'd completed on just before the wedding, Sean having waited until he proposed to make the move he'd spoken of on their first date.

They'd gone back to work – Susannah to her final year of articles – and spent weekends painting and decorating the house in modern shades and fabrics, with silver framed pictures of themselves on almost every available surface downstairs, and throwing three course dinner parties for their friends, at which they got out their wedding albums and talked about their wonderful day, throwing each other misty-eyed smiles across the room.

That year they went to seven more weddings – the hit movie of the year, *Four Weddings and a Funeral*, felt more like a fly-on-the-wall documentary than a romcom to her – including Amelia's, when she married Jonathan at St Gabriel's in September.

She thought she'd got it right. Maybe it had always just been somebody else's blueprint for how her life should be.

1997

But the end – when it came – came from him, and not her.

She had always believed she'd never have left him. But not necessarily because she still loved him, or because she'd made vows for life. She would have stayed.

Things changed. When he made his speech, Sean said it was she who'd changed, but she didn't think it was just her. It was everything.

It was as if they'd gone through the motions of this perfect, right thing. The courtship, the engagement, the wedding, the honeymoon, their first home together. They'd done it all right. And then everything stopped, the circus left town, and it was the two of them, just the two of them.

And it wasn't, she thought, because they'd married too quickly, and didn't know each other well enough to make the adjustments married life required. There was no toilet seat or nail biting issue. No gambling addiction. Nothing so obvious.

Just a slow, aching realization that there wasn't that much between them. Everything that had seemed so right on paper seemed suddenly insubstantial in real life. A shared vision for the future didn't mean much when you faced each other across the breakfast table on a Sunday morning and couldn't really think of what to say, preferring instead to read every article in *The Sunday Times* until it was time to meet friends for lunch at the pub and concentrate again on projecting the image of perfect, and perfectly happy, newly-weds that everyone else was also concentrating on.

The hotel sex from Claridge's became Saturday night with the lights off sex before the year was even over. Susannah wondered if she was bad at it, but Sean wouldn't talk about it, brushing her questions away.

Years later, when Susannah saw *The Truman Show*, she thought that her life then had been just like that.

She might have thought it was normal if she hadn't had the example of Amelia and Jonathan. They weren't like the others. They didn't care what anyone thought. They fought and bickered about extraordinarily trivial things through dinner and then you'd find them outside on the patio twenty minutes later, snogging the faces off each other like a pair of teenagers. Susannah envied them the ups and downs.

But her downs were coming. Sean left her thirty months later, four months after Susannah miscarried her first pregnancy, and six months shy of their third wedding anniversary.

Afterwards she realized that she wasn't as shocked as she thought she was.

He left her for a woman called Miriam. He was, at

least, honest enough to confess to that straight away, and not to pretend he thought it was her fault. Or worse, that he needed to be alone – the classic 'it's me, not you' speech that was never, ever true as far as Susannah could see. For Sean, there was someone else. He did seem genuinely distressed to have discovered that not only was he not in love with his wife – or at least, not, as he put it, 'the way I'm supposed to be' – but that he was, actually, in love with someone else, and he thought she was the one. It had all been too quick, after all, he said, the two of them, and that was his fault, he said – he took full responsibility. He thought it had been time. But he'd been wrong, and he saw that now, and could he please have a divorce? She could stay in the house. Until it was sold, at least.

How could she be too angry when she realized he was saying exactly what she'd said to herself? That it had been time. It was almost, but not quite, a relief when he said it.

She mostly felt humiliated. Telling people was somehow more painful than hearing it herself had been. She and Sean had mostly done a terrific job playing their parts, she realized. Mum and Dad were as shocked as she'd ever seen them. That was the worst – driving home to tell them.

Mum had opened the door, still in her apron. The smell of her roast lamb wafted as far as the hallway, and Susannah could see the dining-room table set with the Sunday lunch china and glasses. She hadn't said, when she invited herself over, that Sean wouldn't be with her. She hadn't wanted to get into it over the phone. Mum peered over Susannah's shoulder, back at the car, looking for Sean. Disappointment registered on her face when she saw that Susannah was alone. She didn't seem to notice the dark circles and rheumy eyes of her daughter's sleeplessness and crying jag.

Dad did. Dad always took in every detail of her face. 'Something's wrong.' His voice was calm and gentle.

She nodded, grateful for his perception.

She'd sat on the edge of her chair opposite the two of them on the sofa, and stared at her hands while she spoke. She heard her voice, speaking in short staccato sentences, tightly controlled. She heard a sob catch in her mum's throat, and when she looked up, her dad had taken her hand and was holding it tightly between his own. Mum had stood up then, and come over to her to hug her. Dad had stood behind the chair, awkwardly trying to enclose them both in his embrace. Afterwards Mum sat down heavily on the sofa again, pulling a handkerchief out of the sleeve of her pullover, and started talking, to herself as much as to either of them, while she sniffed and dabbed at her eyes. About Sean, and how she hadn't suspected a thing, and about how awful Susannah must feel, and then, finally, about how she was going to tell her friends up at St Gabriel's.

Eventually, she excused herself and went into the garden, leaving Susannah and her dad alone in the living room. She came over to sit beside him. He put his arm around her shoulders and she sank into his familiar embrace. He stroked her hair gently.

'She's not still smoking, surely?'

Dad smiled wryly. 'No. The cigarettes are gone, thank God. But she still goes out there, just like she always did. Calms her down.'

'I'm sorry, Dad. I'm so sorry.' Now that Mum had done her sobbing, Susannah's tears came again. She felt tremendously guilty about the wedding. And she felt like a failure.

Dad turned her round to face him, holding both her shoulders. 'Don't you dare say that, Susannah. You have absolutely nothing to be sorry for . . .'

'But the wedding . . . and everything. I've let you down.'

Dad's eyes filled with tears. The only other time she'd ever seen him cry was when Alex was born. She almost couldn't bear it, if Dad cried. 'You've let no one down. You've been let down. In the very worst way. My poor, darling girl. Don't you ever be sorry. I just need you to promise me that you won't let this change who you are. Because you're wonderful, my lovely girl. If he didn't see what he had, then he's a fool. But some day soon, I promise you, someone will. Someone who might deserve you.'

He'd pulled her close then, and held her for the

longest time, and she tried to believe what he was telling her. Until Alex came home from football practice.

Amelia was the only person who didn't seem surprised.

Sean and Miriam had been married for ten years or so now. He hadn't rushed so headlong into his second marriage, it seemed. They had two kids – a girl and a boy – and they lived in Connecticut. Miriam was American, and resolutely determined, it seemed, to be civilized. This mainly entailed sending a Christmas card every year with a saccharine sweet photograph of the children – both with Sean's blue eyes and strawberry-blond hair – stuck on the front, wishing Susannah 'Happy Holidays and a Peaceful New Year'. Every year she gazed at her ex-husband's children and felt like Sean was laughing at her – although, in reality, of course, he wasn't. He wasn't interested enough in her to laugh, or even know what there might be to laugh about.

Amelia always sniggered at the card, which helped enormously.

Present Day

October

Douglas had been in Chichester all weekend, oversee-
ing his beloved boat into dry dock. Fin had gone
unwillingly with him. Fin liked the sailing well enough,
and he was pretty good at it, considering his slight
weight and height, and even slighter attention span,
but he wasn't interested in the hard work that went
along with it. Rosie had gone with her mother to visit
some cousins or other in Suffolk. Sylvie's explanation
had been garbled and late, as ever. So Susannah and
Daisy had spent Sunday together. In the morning,
she'd read the paper from cover to cover while Daisy
claimed to be doing homework in her room, with
Green Day blasting. In the afternoon, at her suggestion, Susannah had taken her to Jigsaw and let her
choose a whole new outfit for herself. She'd sat in one
of the baroque velvet chairs, moaning that it was so
dark she could barely see, while Daisy had paraded a
series of options in front of her. She looked so grown-
up, skinny as you like in the drainpipe jeans. Her long
wavy hair suited the bohemian clothes that seemed
to be in fashion this autumn – and she looked, to

Susannah, like a model. Daisy had fun with it, peeping seductively out from behind the curtain, then sashaying up and down the carpet in front of the changing rooms. Susannah felt a flash of something like maternal pride as she watched other women look at her with envy. Daisy looked good in everything. She settled on a pair of cords, a blouse with a small print and a long, thick sweater. She hugged herself with delight as Susannah paid the bill and tried not to look shocked, and then hugged Susannah outside on the street, squealing her delight.

Susannah had been carried away by something, and they'd marched arm in arm to L.K. Bennett to buy a pair of glossy brown ankle boots to go with the clothes.

'This is so much fun,' Daisy had noted, a child's happy face above the young woman's body, and Susannah had nodded her agreement.

Later, over a coffee and a piece of cake, she'd asked Daisy how Seth was, and been touched by Daisy's answers. She clearly believed herself to be in love with the boy. Her eyes shone, and the dimple she had always had in her left cheek deepened as she smiled at the thought of him. It was infectious, and it made Susannah feel 105 years old.

She tried to talk to Douglas about it that night, after he got home. He'd squabbled with Sylvie, dropping Fin off – Susannah didn't know what about – and he was crabby and cold. She ran him a hot bath, and poured him a whisky. Then she sat on the edge of the bath and scrubbed his back for him as the steam rose and he sipped his drink.

'You haven't done that for ages.'

'Is it nice?'

'It's very nice. Thanks.' He put a hand up to where hers was on his shoulder and covered it with his own.

She kissed the top of his head, gently. 'I had a great time with Daisy today.'

'You did?' He'd put his head back, and his eyes were closed.

'We went to Hampstead. Shopping. Had a coffee. Just girlie stuff.'

'That's nice.' He sounded non-committal. Disinterested, even.

But she was so pleased, she didn't want to let it go. 'I bought her some clothes, and she was so pleased, Doug. And she's gorgeous in them. You should see her. She's really beautiful.'

She did look like Sylvie. Susannah wondered whether that ever bothered Douglas. There was definitely some disconnect between him and his elder daughter. It may just be the usual adolescent stuff, but sometimes she wondered. And just occasionally she wished she knew Sylvie. She didn't want to be friends. But it might, sometimes, be good to be able to talk to her – about the kids. Douglas didn't seem to want to talk much tonight.

'And we talked,' she persisted.

'Oh yes?'

'Yes. We did.'

'What about?'

'Life, the universe and everything. A bit, anyway. We talked about Seth.'

He bristled at the name.

'She really loves him, you know.'

'She's too young to know what she's talking about.'

'She isn't. I'm not saying anything ridiculous – that they'll end up together, or anything like that. I just think she's very serious about him. He's her first love, Douglas.'

Douglas snorted derisively.

'Come on.' She tried to jolly him out of it. 'You're not so old you don't remember how strong those feelings are, do you?'

He sat forward now, and splashed his face with bath water. 'Hormones and rebellion.'

'It's more than that, Douglas.' Surely he didn't mean that.

'And I don't think it's helpful to have you believing every word she says about it.'

Just like that, she felt the tide turn. 'I didn't say that.'

'You're encouraging it, basically, aren't you, by even listening?'

She couldn't have disagreed more. She frowned, not sure what to say next.

'Are you trying to make me the bad guy, is that what you're doing?'

'Not at all. You're overreacting.'

'But you go shopping with her, and buy her God

knows what, and she pours her heart out to you, and then the next time she wants to stay out or go to some party held God knows where by God knows who, she'll look to you . . . and I'll be the monster if I say no. Which I will do, because I'm her father, and I know what's best for her.' Douglas stood up crossly, sending a tidal wave of bath water across the tiled floor. He grabbed a towel from the rail and stood rubbing himself vigorously. His penis bounced ridiculously.

She looked away, feeling anger rising in her now. These days, it came quickly. 'Where is this coming from? I'm just telling you about your daughter. I'm just telling you that we had a nice day, that she's happy, that I think she's in a good place. You should be pleased, you silly bugger. And instead, you're getting angry with me. What the hell for?'

'I don't like you being her friend. It undermines me, Susannah. Surely you can see that. We're not supposed to be their friends.'

'What am I supposed to be, then, Douglas?'

The question hung unanswered in the air, its rhetorical answer floating beyond it in the steamy atmosphere as Susannah walked out without another word into the cooler, clearer air of the bedroom.

On the Friday morning of Amelia's first chemotherapy session, Susannah sat in her car outside her friend's house, unable to park, and honked until Amelia came rushing out, hurriedly pulling on a coat and fishing in her capacious bag for a front-door key to lock up with. 'Alright. Keep your hair on.' She didn't apparently realize the irony of her rejoinder.

'Don't want to be late. I'm in charge of the Chemo Express, and we're bloody well going to run to time, if it kills me.'

'Or me.'

For a moment, Susannah thought her friend was serious, but when she looked over, Amelia was smiling.

'Black humour. I intend to rely on it a lot in the next few months, so you had better get over it.'

'Okay, okay. *You* keep *your* hair on. While you can.'

'Ha, ha. That's better. Touché.' She laughed. 'Speaking of which, I was Googling wigs last night. We're definitely going to need a sense of humour for that part. You definitely get what you pay for, in wig world. And you pay a lot . . . if you don't want to look like a drag queen. Has to be human hair, I reckon.'

'As opposed to what?'

'Fake hair, you daft bugger.'

'Like dolls have, you mean?'

'Exactly. I found this place in Shoreditch that's supposed to be really good – we have to go . . . You'll come, will you?'

'Only if I can get one, too . . . I always fancied a short bob – like the one Julia Roberts wears in *Pretty Woman*.'

'Like you need one. If you were any kind of a friend

you'd chop off that mane of yours and we could have that made into a wig for me.'

'Not a chance. I've always thought that the artful scarf was the way to go myself . . . so don't go getting any ideas about a sympathy shave. I'll drive you the length and breadth, but that's not going to happen. Apart from anything else, I just know I haven't got the head shape for it.'

'What about me?'

'I think you've got a beautiful head, Meels. You're going to be gorgeous bald. And it goes from all over, doesn't it? Just think of the money you'll save not having to wax . . .'

'Oh God.' Amelia was grimacing. 'I never thought about that. How's that for a silver lining?' She giggled. 'Gave up waxing when Jonathan moved out, anyhow. It's been rather liberating, growing a pelt for winter.'

'That smacks of defeatism, doesn't it? Wasn't it part of the plan – finding someone else?'

'I'm not you, Susannah. You're the serial monogamist who's terrified of being alone.'

'Ouch.' She was thinking of Douglas and what an arse he'd been the other night.

'Sorry. That was harsh. But you know what I mean. I'll wax, when the time comes, believe me.'

Susannah did.

At Amelia's suggestion, and to her relief, Susannah explored the gift shop, and the coffee place, and bought magazines and coffee while Amelia went upstairs to oncology and was 'hooked up'. When Susannah found her, armed with large lattes and a stack of magazines and newspapers, she was sitting, still fully dressed, in a high-backed, upholstered chair. She had her head back and her eyes closed. There was a thin tube going into her arm, taped around a cannula that had obviously been inserted into a vein, connected to a drip that stood beside the chair on a sort of metal coat stand. A utilitarian curtain separated them from the other patients sharing the space. She had this weird thing on her head, a bit like an old-fashioned hairdryer.

'God, I wish I had my camera!'

'Don't you dare!'

'Does it hurt?'

Amelia opened her eyes and smiled faintly. 'What? The drip or having to wear this on my head?'

'Both, since you ask . . . what's that for, anyhow?'

'They think it slows down hair loss.'

Susannah nodded.

'And no – it doesn't hurt. I wouldn't have it done for fun, but no, it doesn't, really. Just feels a bit weird. And cold – a bit cold. But this is the easy part, really, I think. It's how I'll feel after this, when the stuff kicks in – that's what's going to be tough. It's freaking me out a bit, to be honest, thinking about what I'm putting into myself.'

Susannah had wanted to go and stay in her house, but Amelia said her mum was going to come up to stay for a few nights this first time, while they all waited to see how horrid it was. She'd collect Victoria and Sam from school, she said, and feed them their tea and help with their homework. Amelia loved her mum, but as an adult herself she'd found her increasingly irritating to be around – knowing she needed help must have taken some adjustment. Susannah couldn't imagine how Mrs Lloyd felt, knowing her only child had to go through all this. She was glad Amelia had let her come. Turns out, she hadn't needed to call her – she'd promised herself she would, if Amelia couldn't, or wouldn't. Amelia was still doing the tough-guy thing, but there was no doubt the penny had dropped at least part of the way. Jonathan's reaction, and her mum's – they'd forced her, Susannah supposed, to confront it to a degree.

She'd been there with her when Amelia had told the kids. She'd listened to reason at last – let herself be convinced that the children needed to know *before* the side effects of the treatment threw them in at the deep end. Susannah had gone round one evening last week after work, and Amelia had sat them all down in the sitting room, delivering the news more bluntly than Susannah might have recommended, or chosen for herself. They'd all burst into tears immediately, long before Amelia had finished her speech about success rates and early detection. It was such a heinous word. Even children knew to be paralysed with fear when they heard it. Elizabeth had run out of the room, as was her teenage way, to shed her tears in private with a Snow Patrol soundtrack, and so Susannah and Amelia had taken a sobbing youngster each on to their laps, staring wide-eyed at each other over the children's heaving shoulders. When Susannah's own eyes had filled with tears, Amelia had wagged an admonishing finger at her from around Victoria's waist.

'So, I'm coffeed up and I have trashy mags. How long's this going to take?'

'This bit – an hour or so, the nurse said. Then we can pretty much go. They've given me a prescription for the anti-nausea medicine – we can fill it in the pharmacy downstairs before we leave.'

'Then?'

'Then we go home and see what happens. Maybe nothing this time. Mr Swift says I'll get more and more tired as this goes on, but this time I might feel okay. I'm not going to wake up bald tomorrow or anything. It's more gradual than that. Like I say, we'll just see what happens. I haven't got any big plans to go climbing Everest or anything . . . And then I guess we come back next time and do it all over again.'

Susannah nodded quietly. It seemed, to her, like an unremittingly grim plan.

'At least, I shouldn't say "we". There's no need for you to come every time. Really.'

'Who else would bring you?'

'Mum. Jonathan. And I could actually come all by myself, you know.'

'No way is that happening.' Susannah shook her head. 'That would be horrid.'

'But you have to work.'

'It's two hours, every couple of weeks. They can manage without me. Despite what I may have said in the past, I'm not completely indispensable, you know.'

Amelia put out her hand, the one that wasn't connected to the drip, and squeezed Susannah's in her lap. 'You are to me. Thank you, Susannah. Really.'

Susannah squeezed back. This was unusually soppy for Amelia, and she found it disconcerting. 'You're welcome.'

'There should be friendship vows. Did you ever think that? When you get married, you promise all that stuff – in sickness and in health, for richer and for poorer . . . But you do that when you're friends, too, don't you? The thick and thin stuff.'

'Are you stoned already? Are you sure they're putting the right stuff in?'

'I'm just thinking, that's all.' She paused. 'You're the best friend I ever had.' Amelia's eyes filled with sudden tears.

Susannah couldn't bear it. This was the most frightening moment so far. 'Stop it. Right now. Please, Meels. Don't cry.' She put an arm around her friend's shoulder. 'You're going to be fine. You've been saying it yourself. Mr Swift said it. Just fine. But I won't be, if you carry on like this.'

Amelia released her friend's hand, sniffed violently

227

and ran her fingers under her lower lashes impatiently, wiping away the tears that threatened to spill over and down on to her cheeks. 'Sorry. Momentary lapse. Won't happen again. It's the needles. Did I mention that I hate needles?'

'I know you do.' Keen to distract her, Susannah opened the current *OK!* magazine at the pages detailing the OTT wedding of a soap celebrity star. 'Look at this – proof positive that money doesn't buy you class, even if it buys you a five-thousand-quid dress. Blimey. Check out those knockers!'

Amelia gave the proffered page a brief glance. 'Actually, I've got real-life gossip. I've been saving it for now. Figured it would help the time pass a little quicker. Besides, it wasn't gossip of the phone variety – I needed to see the whites of your eyes when I told you this . . .'

'What?' Had she relented and let Jonathan move back in? Susannah felt a flash of excitement. She hoped so. She closed the magazine and waited.

'Rob Rossi.' Amelia was, indeed, staring at the whites of her eyes as she said the name.

'What about him?' Susannah felt her heart beat dangerously fast in her chest, and heard her voice, a little higher than normal. She sounded brittle, even to herself.

'He just got married.'

The beating stopped. For a moment, Susannah thought she might not be able to exhale. 'What?'

'Married. He got married. A couple of weeks ago.' Amelia was watching her closely.

'Who?' She couldn't manage more than a one-word question.

'We don't know her – she's not local. Mum says she thinks she's in the RAF, too. That must be how they met. She's much younger than him, apparently. That's all I know, pretty much.'

'Who told you?'

'Mum. Of course. You know how she likes to be in the loop. She heard it from someone else in the village. It was abroad – the ceremony – Cyprus or somewhere like that, I think. Or was it Vegas? Can't remember. Somewhere abroad. Lois and Frank didn't even go, I heard. Not that it would have been easy for Frank to go, I suppose, if he's sick. They sort of just did it, apparently – I don't know whether it was a spur of the moment thing, or whether they planned to keep it a secret. I'd kill my lot, if they did that to me . . . Anyhow, they drove down – the two of them, after the event – and told his parents. Someone saw Rob in the village, asked Lois about it, and she told them, in the butcher's. It was a friend of Mum's in the queue behind her, listening to all this, who told Mum. Who told me. Last night, when she arrived. I mean, she was just doing her usual litany of village news, you know, the births, deaths, weddings, who's building a two-storey extension or a conservatory – that sort of stuff. The crucial updates! In between wailing and gnashing her teeth about all this . . . you know.' Amelia gestured towards the drip.

Susannah knew she was supposed to say something. She couldn't.

Married. He was *just* married.

He'd married since he'd seen her. Had he already decided, was he engaged, when they'd met? What was it? Four months ago? Four months ago, had he been with this person, this much younger woman? Had he known, when he'd stood and smiled at her, and said her name – Susie – that he was going to marry her?

'So?' Amelia was still watching her face.

'So, what?'

'So, how does that make you feel?'

It made her feel like she'd been physically assaulted. It was like a swift, sudden, unexpected punch in the pit of her stomach. Something was very, very wrong. It shouldn't do this to her. She didn't answer Amelia.

'So, I guess "hit by a tank" would be your answer, if you were actually forming words at this point . . . ?'

She moved her mouth, by force of will. She could feel her cheeks pinking up. 'No! You're *so* dramatic. I mean, I'm surprised, that's all. I just saw Lois last month, and she didn't say anything about a wedding . . .'

'You saw Lois?' Amelia sounded incredulous. 'You didn't tell me that!'

'Well, yes, I did see Lois – it was no big deal. I didn't *not* tell you. Don't make that face. I was home, for lunch with Mum and Dad, I'd seen her at the wedding,

I'd been feeling bad because I never said anything, or wrote, or anything, about Frank. I just went for tea.' She was ranting, she knew.

Amelia nodded. 'You went for tea. Okay. Nothing weird there. You went for tea with your old ex-boyfriend's parents, out of the blue, just after you'd seen him for the first time in a gazillion years. Perfectly normal behaviour.'

'You're making it sound weird. It wasn't strange.'

'Okay.' Amelia drew out the word into two slow syllables, the implication that she thought it was utterly strange very clear.

Susannah ignored her. 'And she didn't say anything, that's all.' She thought of Frank, and what he'd said, and Lois shushing him.

She hadn't told Amelia how much daydreaming she'd been doing about Rob these last few months. Not just going over the past, not just remembering things they'd done, things he'd said, how he'd been then. Present-tense daydreaming. How he was now. How they might be. On the underground. At work. In the shower. Lying next to Doug in bed, in the dark. Barbara Cartland-esque, heart-pounding, Fabio-type daydreaming. Acting out scenes between them in her imagination. She couldn't tell Amelia – she'd die of embarrassment. It made her sound foolish. The daydreams had been precious and delightful to her, and to Amelia they'd seem ridiculous. She'd say she was in denial. She'd say she was hiding from her real problems. She'd try and make her face them. That's what she always did.

And she didn't want to.

She couldn't believe he was married. Her chest ached. 'Hit by a tank' was closer than Amelia knew.

Afterwards, she took Amelia home, where her mother was waiting for them, and helped cook egg and chips for the kids. She could see that Amelia was tired, and she tried to get her to go up to bed, but Amelia was determined to keep things as normal as possible. She sat at the kitchen table nursing a mug of some herbal tea that smelt like cat wee while Susannah served the food and the two of them helped Sam with his homework – or tried to. They both reached a point with the maths where Victoria had to be recruited to explain something they couldn't remember how to do.

'We used to be clever, you know, didn't we, Suze?'

Sam rolled his eyes indulgently. 'You used to be young, too, Mum. Nothing lasts for ever.'

Amelia laughed and slapped him playfully. 'Cheeky beggar.'

Susannah stayed until Sam was in bed. She folded his uniform and laid it over the chair in his room, balling his dirty socks up and throwing them in the hamper.

'Go home, Suze,' Amelia said at last, watching her from the landing. 'You're not planning on tucking me in, too, are you?'

'I was thinking of it.'

'Stop fussing. Vic and Libby will be up for hours yet. And Mum's here, if I need anything. Which I won't.'

'Are you sure?'

'I love you for being here, and I really love you for cooking. But yes, I'm sure. I'm going to curl up and watch crap TV. So far so fine. I promise. Mum'll make sure I get plenty of rest . . .'

At home, there was evidence of Doug – his shoes and jacket – but no sign of him. Doubtless he was at the top of the house. The kids were there, too – their coats and backpacks were strewn on the chair nearest the front door. This was to be a full weekend – Friday night until Monday morning. Sometimes they were delivered home to Sylvie by their dad on Sunday evenings, but this time Sylvie was going to be at a yoga retreat in the Cotswolds, and they were staying all weekend. Doug had a conference next week, too – he'd reminded her earlier in the week – so Susannah would have to take them to school on Monday morning. She wouldn't mind a yoga retreat, she thought sniffily. Actually – she caught herself – she'd *hate* a yoga retreat.

Daisy's stuff hadn't exploded all over the downstairs: Susannah remembered that she was sleeping over with her friend Natalie. There was some concert or other they had tickets to, and Natalie's mum had said she'd keep her overnight rather than drag both of them out to pick her up in the small hours. Fin was asleep with his hand down the front of his pyjamas and his pillow over his face, as usual. Susannah lifted it off. She knew he was too old to suffocate, but she didn't like it anyway.

She was on her way to the top of the house to find Doug when she heard something. She was pretty sure it was the sound of Rosie crying. She knocked quietly, but there was no answer, so she gently opened the door and poked her head round. Rosie was lying in her bed, still fully dressed, staring at the ceiling, emitting what were by now quite loud, snotty sobs. She took no notice, at first, when Susannah went in. She'd lost all her colour, Susannah realized, and her eyes suddenly looked sunken in grey shadows. Wondering if she was sickening for something, and thinking, just briefly, how typical it would be of Sylvie to swan off for two days of downward dogs knowingly leaving a sick child with her for the weekend, Susannah went to her, put her palm under Rosie's thick fringe, checking for a fever. Rosie felt clammy and cool, not feverish.

'What's wrong, sweetheart?'

Rosie didn't answer, turning her head into her pillow.

Susannah sat down on the bed, feeling Rosie's legs under the duvet beside her. Lying here, she seemed smaller and less substantial than she did sprawled on the sofa downstairs, where Susannah was used to seeing her these days.

'Don't want to tell me?' She felt a familiar ache in her ribcage. She should know. The ache was followed immediately, as it always was, by a small stab of irritation at

Doug. He had fostered these sterile, frustrating little relationships. And now Rosie was crying in her bed and neither her mother nor her father was here to help her – just this distant, awkward woman who'd known her and not known her all these years.

'Do you want me to get your dad?'

Rosie shook her head vigorously.

She patted Rosie's gently heaving form gingerly. 'Okay. I'm going to go, Rosie. I'm going to go, but I won't be far away. If you want to talk to me, come and find me. Okay?' She stood up, feeling bizarrely embarrassed by Rosie's tears and her own inadequacy, and took two steps towards the door.

'Susannah?' Rosie had half sat up, and was holding her arms out towards her.

'Oh, love . . .' Susannah could have cried herself, but she went back to the bed and sat down, almost falling backwards as Rosie launched herself at her. She put her arms around the child and smoothed her hair, thinking of Amelia, crying in the hospital chair, and of Daisy a few weeks earlier, sitting at the kitchen table red-eyed, and suddenly felt very tired.

Rosie's story spilt out of her slowly and, at first, made little sense. Susannah had to concentrate hard – she was drained herself by the day she'd spent with Amelia. She listened, asked questions, and began to piece together what was going on. And as she understood, she began to get very, very angry. Rosie was being bullied at school. Not physically. No one was hitting her. (Susannah couldn't help but think that would be easier to deal with.) Evidently there was a small but toxic group of girls who were targeting her every day, singling her out in the big class. She was fat, they said. Roly-poly Rosie. Fat and ugly and stupid. Rosie hadn't been invited to a birthday party all term, she said. And only one last year. And all the girls in the class had been invited to that, so it didn't count. Her distress and confusion as to what she had done to deserve this was heartbreaking to Susannah, who hadn't heard a word about this up until now.

'Have you told your mum?'

Rosie nodded, and sobbed and sniffed.

'What did she say?'

'She . . . she said . . . she said I had to fight . . . my own battles. She said what doesn't kill you makes you stronger.'

Jesus. What a stupid woman Sylvie was.

'Has she telephoned your teacher? Or been in to see her?'

'She said it . . . would . . . only make things . . . worse . . .'

Susannah bit back her anger, and held Rosie in her arms, smoothing her hair and whispering that it was okay. Eventually, Rosie lay back, calmer, and Susannah pulled her duvet up around her, drying her cheek with the back of her hand.

'Let me tell you a few things, Rosie. Firstly, you are not fat, or ugly or stupid. You're none of those things, do you hear me? Anyone who says so is an idiot. You're a sweet, pretty, perfectly normal, smart kid. Secondly, I am afraid that I don't agree with your mum. I don't think your dad will either. Some things, I know, you have to sort out on your own – if this was a fight with a friend, or if we were only talking about one girl, or something like that. But this is bullying, Rosie. This is nasty, mean girls in a gang deliberately trying to make someone else feel rubbish, because that's the only way they can feel good about themselves. It's bullying, and it needs to be stopped. And we're going to help you. Okay?'

Rosie nodded.

'We're going to put a stop to it.'

She'd stopped crying now. She looked sleepy.

'I'm sorry, sweetheart. I'm sorry we didn't know. You could have told us, you know? You could have told me.'

When she'd settled Rosie down, Susannah went to find Doug in his study.

'Didn't hear you come in. How was it?'

She sat down heavily on the footstool, and laid her head on his lap.

He stroked her hair. 'That good, huh?'

'Did you know Rosie was being bullied?'

'No. Bullied? Who told you that?'

'She did. Just now. She's downstairs, crying in her room. You didn't notice anything this evening?' She couldn't help the trickle of resentment in her voice.

'No! She seemed fine. We had a pizza. They ate

theirs in front of some show they apparently "had to" see. She went to bed fine. What's going on?'

Susannah retold the story she'd extracted from Rosie, including Sylvie's solution. 'I'm sorry, Doug, but that woman really is the most unspeakable, insufferable, ridiculous idiot.'

Doug laughed. 'She speaks well of you, though.'

Susannah slapped his thigh. 'Don't laugh – this is serious.'

'What do you think we should do, then?'

'Well, it's obvious – we've got to speak to her teacher. On Monday.'

'I'm away on Monday. Remember?'

She'd forgotten.

On Monday morning, Susannah walked to school early with the kids. Daisy hung back on the corner, waiting for her mates. Fin disappeared to join a game of football on the playing field, slinging his backpack on to the muddy ground. His shirt was already untucked, and one shoelace was undone. Susannah walked with Rosie to her classroom. The teacher was sitting at her desk with the door closed, reading something. 'Wait here, Rosie,' Susannah said, and knocked, opening the door as she did so.

The teacher was obviously irritated to be disturbed. She stood up and pulled primly at her twinset, before fixing Susannah with a rictus smile. She was pretty in a haughty sort of way, and young. Not a mother,

Susannah guessed. And not all that sympathetic, by the look of her.

She took a deep breath. 'You're Rosie's teacher, I believe.'

'Miss Norton, yes.' She extended a hand. 'And you are . . . ?'

Susannah hadn't been to parents' evening, of course. Sylvie and Douglas always went together to those things.

And she was?

Who was she?

She was Rosie's father's live-in girlfriend.

And right now, she was all Rosie had.

She hesitated for only a moment. 'I'm Rosie's stepmother, Susannah Hammond.' She saw Miss Norton's glance take in her ringless left hand. She drew herself up erect. 'And there's a problem in your classroom . . .'

Sylvie rang that night, just as Susannah was about to climb into a hot bath. Work had been stressful – everyone wanting something from her. And the house had been its usual Monday mess when she got home – she'd spent an hour just moving things from where they were (floor, sofa, kitchen) to where they should be (kids' rooms, cupboards, fridge) and feeding the voracious washing machine another load of towels and sheets. Then she'd found herself too tired to cook anything for dinner, so she'd eaten a bowl of Honey Nut Cheerios and a slightly overripe banana in front of *Have I Got News for You* and then come upstairs to fill the tub.

'Doug's not here, I'm afraid. He's away at a conference.'

'I wanted to talk to you.'

That never happened. Susannah felt herself tense up.

Sylvie carried on. 'You went into school today and spoke with Rosie's teacher.'

'Miss Norton. Yes.'

'She called me this afternoon and told me what had gone on. Did Douglas know you were planning to do that?'

'Yes. Of course. He would have gone himself, but he had to leave early this morning – the conference is at Gleneagles. In Scotland. And nothing "went on", as you put it. There was a situation which needed to be addressed and I brought it to her attention.'

'You had no right.'

'Pardon me?' Susannah was shocked. And she was tired. Premenstrual, too, she realized. Sylvie had picked the wrong night.

'She's not your child, you know.'

'I'm well aware of that, Sylvie. Just as you were well aware, I gather, of what was going on at school.'

'Of course I was.' Sylvie was all righteous indignation.

'But you hadn't done anything about it?' Susannah had little patience for her.

'I had given Rosie the tools to deal with it herself, which is how I thought it needed to be sorted out.'

Susannah detested that kind of language. 'The tools'. She couldn't keep the sarcasm out of her voice. 'Well, the tools weren't doing the job, Sylvie. I found her sobbing in her bed on Friday night. You weren't here. Something needed to be done.'

'Not that. Not by you. I won't have it.'

Susannah almost laughed. She pictured Sylvie fulminating – the yoga retreat hadn't done a lot for her chi. 'Sylvie, I'm not going to have this conversation. I'm tired, and I'm going to take a bath now. You should be thanking me, not having a go at me, but since there is no chance of that happening, you'll excuse me.' And then she hung up.

It felt great. She caught a glimpse of her naked self, hair piled on top of her head, in the bathroom mirror, and gave herself a reflective high five. 'Let's hope she never finds Daisy's little pink pills and traces them back to me,' she offered out loud to herself, giggling just a bit as she sank gratefully into the bubbles.

Rob

Rob had been thirty-seven years old when he met Helena. Thirty-seven years old, and Susannah was still, up until that point, his longest relationship to date. And probably the most mature, too.

There'd been women, of course, although not as many as most of his friends had had. The longest gap

– that had come after Susannah. It was two years after her letter arrived before he'd even been with another girl. That letter, and everything else that was happening to him, had precipitated a period in his life when he was as off the rails as it was possible to be when you were an officer in the RAF. Always conscientious on duty, he'd drunk too much, and smoked too much when he was off duty – things he'd never really done before. Everyone else did. You had to, over there. Fear and boredom were a dangerous combination. If he was escaping from more than everyone else, he never talked about it. He told his mum he and Susannah were over, for good this time, on the phone, and said he didn't want to talk about it. She never pushed. No one else asked. He tore up the pictures he had of her – one strip of passport-booth pictures of the two of them taken at Waterloo station, laughing and kissing, and several of Susannah alone that had been taped above his bunk – and threw them away, fighting the temptation to keep just one. Everything else that connected the two of them was either in his head or in a small cardboard box in the loft at his parents' house, and he did his best not to think about either store of memories at all, although sometimes, late at night, when he was really tired, it was hard to keep her face out of his mind.

He was relieved of his virginity on his twenty-first birthday, by the sister of a mate of his from the regiment, after a drunken night in a bar and a garbled confession that she'd always fancied him like mad, but he remembered very little about it – except that, the next morning, she smelt smoky and wasn't as pretty as he had thought the night before.

Then, over the next seventeen years, there had been a dozen different postings, several different ranks and a few girls. He was a good-looking guy, who knew how to be charming without being in the least oily, and women liked him. Some were in the regiment – he lived, wherever he was stationed, in the Officers' Mess, and there were always younger female officers up for a bit of fun, although you had to be careful. Some were sisters, friends of friends – he met them on skiing holidays, or at parties, in pubs. Set-ups, sometimes. Random, mostly.

He never fell in love. In lust, maybe. And he was fond of some. The relationships sometimes lasted a few months, and they were mostly a lot of fun. He'd gone out with one corporal for almost a year, although she was in the Falklands for six months, and he was in Scotland, so it hadn't really counted. He wasn't sure anyone had really fallen in love with him either. He didn't give much thought to whether he was unlovable.

Most of his mates married, in time. The rules had been changed so officers could marry other ranks, and some did. Pilots often married what were jokingly called 'trophy wives' – good-looking, glamorous civvies. He was one of the older guys in the mess, although divorced men often moved back. He was a best man twice, and an usher several times. But he never got close himself. He never looked at a woman and thought that he wanted to go through life with her by his side. There were periods when he didn't want to be tied down, and periods where he saw his mates going through messy relationships, and couldn't see the point – especially when young men in his regiment came to him asking for leave to go home to sort out bad marriages. And there was no one who moved him that way.

Until Helena. She was different. He was different, too. Timing was everything, didn't they say? He was beginning to be tired of his life. There were things he began to want that he hadn't craved before. He wanted a home away from the mess. A house. He wanted children. He saw his mates with their kids hoisted on their shoulders, and began, at last, to feel like something was missing.

And then there she was. In the right place at the right time. They met in Germany. The first time he saw her, she wasn't in uniform – he thought she must be one of the civilian teachers on the base – she was wearing tight white jeans and a T-shirt. Her blonde hair had been longer then, and it had been tied in a high ponytail that swung as she walked – and it was a great walk – past him one sunny afternoon. He'd felt a jolt of lust – it had been a while – and an appreciation of her leggy prettiness, but thought nothing more of it. The second time, she'd been in uniform, and it was the walk that he recognized, even though the high-heeled sandals had given way to standard-issue black boots, and the ponytail was subdued into a bun. It had taken a few more smiles to engage her, and a week or two to persuade her into conversation, but something about her had made him persevere.

Helena, for all the blonde slightness, turned out to be as tough as old boots, and absolutely not interested in being a notch on the bedpost of a senior officer, even one with rather amazing dark brown eyes.

Raised by a strong, capable single mother in a small flat above a bakery in Cardiff, she'd joined the RAF because it was a way out. A route to a life different from the one she'd had. She had a stronger sense of who she was than anyone Rob had ever met before, and sometimes the age gap between them felt like it should be the other way around.

Her mum, Helen, had been only fifteen when she'd fallen pregnant with Helena. She'd married her boyfriend – three years older than her, but not as bright – the same month she turned sixteen (pushed into it by her parents), and three months before Helena was born. She added the 'a' to her own name when she went to register the birth a couple of weeks later. She wanted something extra for her daughter.

Helena's father had stayed until she was four. She hadn't seen him much since then – he'd paid token visits for the first couple of years, though he'd never paid child support – and she barely remembered him.

Helen was a good looking woman who'd never had much fun before she became a mother. There'd been a number of 'uncles' in Helena's childhood, some of whom she'd hated, and some of whom she'd regarded with fondness. But they never lasted long, her mother's relationships. The two of them were the unit, and Helen hadn't ever let anyone get very close again.

She could be terrifyingly formidable, Helena's mum, but she loved Helena fiercely, and she'd raised her to be independent and self-sufficient.

It was that which had most attracted Rob to her when they began to get to know each other over their months in Germany. He liked her honesty and her straightforwardness. She seemed simple, uncomplicated. Most girls didn't. She was fun, too. She laughed easily and often, and about silly things. He began to feel lighter and freer when he was with her and, at the same time, more grounded than he had done in ages. She was sexy, too, in a way that wasn't obvious, but which, once you were tuned into it, was enthralling. She did the seducing, in the end, their first time.

By the time he recognized – somewhat surprised at himself – that he had fallen in love with her, she was way ahead of him.

He hadn't already decided to marry her when he saw Susannah at Alex's wedding in the summer. But somehow, seeing her again made him think about it. Susannah was lost to him – just as lost as she'd been all those long years – he didn't see anything in her face, or in her eyes, that told him otherwise, and living without her was by now an old habit. It didn't stab him with pain, but seeing her was like feeling an old injury that ached in the rain – sore, but bearable. But it reminded him of how he *could* feel. Of what he'd wanted to have with her, all those years ago, and of what it might be possible to have with Helena now.

And still, he never proposed to her. It had been a mutual decision. A 'we should probably think about getting married' conversation they had in bed one night in late summer, after they'd been seeing each other for about a year and a half, rather than a bended-knee, ring-box affair. He wasn't afraid any more. Or maybe it was just that he was more afraid of the alternative. Since his father had been diagnosed with motor neurone disease, life had been scary. Coming out of the RAF and into a world he had not experienced his entire adult life was disorientating. Helena represented stability and continuity to him, and those two things suddenly became what mattered most.

They'd married in Cyprus, on a hotel terrace at sundown with two witnesses from the hotel staff in attendance. Rob hadn't wanted to tell his parents – they were busy with their own issues – so Helena agreed not to tell Helen, although she knew she'd get it in the neck for it.

If someone had asked Rob how often he thought about Susannah, he would answer, if he were being honest, that in the beginning, after her letter, it had been every painful, waking moment. Then at night, before he fell asleep. Still painful, but gradually less often. In the years between the two women he had loved in his life, she sprang to life in his imagination at odd and sometimes inappropriate times – when he made love to a girl, or saw a film they'd seen together. Always when he went home. When he ate cannolis. And then, after Helena, less and less. Except at the moment when he took his marriage vows, and put the slender gold band on her ring finger. At that moment – and it terrified him so much he shook as he did it, and everyone saw, though no one understood – he remembered sliding his fingers into Susannah's the last time he'd been with her, when he'd told her he'd never love anyone else the way he loved her.

He went home alone to tell his parents. He'd sat at the table and told them he'd married a girl he'd been seeing, and that he was sorry he hadn't told them. And Lois had swallowed back tears that were both happy and sad, and hugged him, and Frank's eyes had filled with tears that Rob's mum said came more and more easily, and slapped his back too hard. And then Lois had told him Susannah had been to see them, and for some reason it made him feel instantly queasy.

December

Christmas. God, she'd loved it when she was a kid. What kid didn't? These days, though, it always made Susannah think of that Dickens line – the one about it being the best and the worst of times. She and Douglas – as a couple they'd certainly had good ones and bad ones. Good ones alone, bad ones with his kids. And, in the last couple of years, the novel twist of bad ones alone, when the children were with their mother.

It hadn't started that way. They'd been on their own the first year, and very much in their honeymoon period – Doug had spent Christmas Eve with Daisy, Rosie and Fin at Sylvie's house, at her request, and Susannah had spent the same day at her own childhood home, not even minding that he was with his ex-wife, believing that the next day would obliterate it all. She still loved going to midnight mass at St Gabriel's, with the life-size nativity scene she remembered once being bigger than she was. Christmas Day had been gloriously unconventional – they'd stayed in bed, dozing and romping, until noon, then cooked shrimp with chillis and drunk champagne, some from glasses, and some off each other's bare skin. She'd made herself the gift – buying fire-engine-red underwear for the first and last time in her life, and accessorizing the lacy bra and thong with an elf's hat, complete with jingle bells, and a giant red bow.

The second year they'd had the children, of course. And that year she'd spent Christmas Eve fully dressed, stuffing her first 12 lb turkey, and wrapping rashers of bacon around chipolatas. The next day, a sullen Daisy said, during lunch, that nothing tasted like it did at her mother's. She then added that it didn't matter, since Sylvie had promised to cook a 'proper' dinner for them tomorrow, negating all Susannah's effort, and causing her to bite her lip, followed by the top off all the chocolate liqueurs and to drain them during the Miss Marple Christmas special. The third year they'd gone home to Susannah's parents, and Douglas had gone to the pub with Alastair, Alex and Dad for the traditional Christmas morning pint. Doug had wanted to go home straight after lunch. He had never felt entirely comfortable at her parents' home, she knew. They had never said a word, to her or to him, about the age difference between the two of them, but it clearly bothered him enormously, and came home to roost during family occasions. At least, she thought that was what it was. In year four Daisy stayed in bed until lunch was on the table, eating in her pyjamas, and Rosie and Fin complained throughout lunch, that it was really, *really* boring to have Christmas in England – in the third year, Sylvie had been going out with an airline pilot, and he'd flown them all to the Bahamas for Christmas. Five – they'd spent with Amelia and Jonathan and their kids, which had sent Douglas into a rare, maudlin guilty mood that lasted for days – as though he somehow blamed her for the fact that he'd had to watch Elizabeth, Victoria and Samuel open presents and load batteries into toys while his own kids were miles away. But in year six the guilt was forgotten, and it was Susannah who spent three hours on her knees building a Lego Taj Mahal with Fin. And so on . . .

She'd actually come to rather dread the whole holiday now, in stark contrast to the feverish anticipation and groundswell of good feeling with which she had always greeted it in her previous lives. Divorce had a way, she reasoned, of ruining all the good days – Christmas and birthdays and summer holidays. Once you were divorced, all those occasions were fraught – the biggest mines in the minefield that is the life of a family torn apart by parents who don't love each other any more. It didn't seem to make a real difference whether or not she made a Herculean effort to go all Nigella, or approached the day with all the preparation and excitement a Hassidic Jew might display. She never managed to make a magical day happen for any of them.

This year – number 9: was it really that many? – it was Sylvie's turn to have the children for Christmas. Susannah and Douglas would be alone at home. She thought about booking them into a country house hotel, but then decided to stay at home. An elegant, adult Christmas with long walks, log fires and lacy lingerie would have felt strange. They were not in a good place, and it had nothing to do with geography. She wanted them to be on their own, not surrounded by people, let alone strangers. Susannah was determined to try and make their couple of days together work. Too many days didn't, lately.

She and Amelia had been talking about it a couple of weeks ago, during Amelia's chemo session. Amelia was letting Jonathan stay overnight on Christmas Eve. Susannah raised an eyebrow.

The two of them were shopping for wigs, in a shop Amelia had found on the internet. It was run by a dead ringer for Kenneth Williams (except that he was completely bald, the irony of which made them giggly from the start) with an obsequious and oily manner Amelia described later as very 'suits you, sir'.

Amelia had declared her intention to buy several wigs, determined not to try and make her hair look real. 'If I have to wear one, I'm going to have fun doing it.' She looked like a human condom in the wig cap Kenneth — whose real name was an only slightly less comic Jeremy — fitted for her first. 'What was that you were saying about me having a great-shaped head for baldness, Suze?'

Jeremy brought out a seemingly endless supply of wigs in every shade and style imaginable, and endeared himself to them by apparently not minding how many they tried on. So they were Charlie's Angels, twin Purdeys, The Supremes . . . Jeremy told them they both looked good in everything. This, Amelia assured Susannah, as he went out back and Susannah tried a Mary Quant, was not true.

In between fits of laughter, they talked about Jonathan.

'Don't give me that face. It makes sense. It all

happens in the first hour – you know that – those three can rip a thousand square feet of wrapping paper off in about six and a half minutes. Then, once they get halfway through their Cadbury's stocking, before breakfast, it's all about the crowd control and the noise level. Mum's coming, too. She's doing a Delia – goose-fat roast potatoes, and all that. I couldn't face cooking that much right now. Don't even know if I'll feel like eating it. So I figure it's not the day to play the martyr, and I said yes to both of them.'

'Just the day to play happy families, huh?!'

'Oh, why not? We were once. We can do it for a day. Especially if we get Mum enough Harvey's Bristol Cream in.'

'I agree.' Susannah nodded. 'I think it sounds nice.'

'What about you? Can't remember – is it your turn to have *les enfants terribles*?'

'Nope.' She shook her head. 'They're with their mother.'

'The divinely insane Sylvie? Lucky devils. So you're just the two of you. Wanna bring Douglas round to ours? The more the merrier . . .'

'Yeah – I still remember how much joy he injected into proceedings the last time we spent Christmas with you. He was a regular laugh a minute.'

'Go on. Come. We could ignore the rest of them and lock ourselves into my bedroom with a bottle of Baileys. I'll even let you watch Christmas *Top of the Pops*, like we used to . . .'

Christmas *Top of the Pops* had been banned in Susannah's childhood home. Between midnight mass at St Gabriel's, Christmas morning service at St Gabriel's, egg-nog with the neighbours, and the compulsory Christmas game of charades, there was never time to watch anyhow. After the age of thirteen or so, Susannah would beg off to go round to Amelia's to watch in her bedroom. She could never hear Frankie Goes to Hollywood's 'The Power Of Love' or Band Aid's 'Do They Know It's Christmas?' without thinking of lying on the double bed in Amelia's pink and green bedroom eating Terry's Chocolate Orange segments until they felt sick. At that age, it had seemed a bonus that Amelia's mother was watching her video of *It's a Wonderful Life* and crying softly in the TV room after three schooners of sherry, while her father shut himself in his study and played golf on his mini executive desktop set.

'Tempting, but no. I think Doug and I could use a bit of time on our own. No work, no family.'

'No best friend battling cancer?' Amelia made a puppy-dog face.

'No, no one, irrespective of battling.' Susannah laughed. 'Just the two of us.'

It had been a strange time – and yes, Amelia had been a part of it. It had been enormously unsettling learning that her friend was ill. Rob was in the mix, too – she knew she'd been distracted by the idea of him, had wallowed in memories of the past. That wasn't Douglas's fault. Then there was Daisy, and

Rosie. Life had been . . . complicated. She wanted to slow it all down. Climb off the ride for a while.

She hoped they would talk. She hoped they'd make love, and find some of the intimacy that had been missing lately. She wanted to feel close to Doug again. She wanted to stop thinking about Rob. It made her feel ridiculous. And sad.

Sylvie didn't call until the evening of the 23rd. Susannah was unpacking the food shopping she'd just done. Sylvie still, after all these years, never really spoke to her. When Susannah answered the phone, Sylvie said hello – always guarded, and vaguely brittle – and then immediately asked for Doug. She never said who was calling, although Susannah always knew. She'd tried, once or twice, in the early days, to chat to her, about the children, but she'd never got very far. Sylvie's voice had expressed resentment and disdain, and Susannah knew that she'd complained to Doug about her. Anyone would have thought Susannah was the catalyst for the end of their marriage. Maybe Sylvie had respun the web of history and actually thought she was.

But she bloody well wasn't. They'd split up long before Susannah had met him, and the divorce and custody arrangements were already signed when they'd started going out. Amelia always said she couldn't believe the cheek of the woman – that Sylvie ought to kiss her hand for taking care of her kids for her.

This evening when Sylvie rang, she didn't bother to

try and talk to her, she just called Doug, laid the receiver down on the hall table, and went back to the kitchen, but from there she could still hear Doug's quiet, tense responses to his ex-wife. For reasons she had never completely understood, he always seemed slightly afraid of Sylvie, as if his main aim was to stop her from flipping out. She wanted to swap weekends, she said. And so did the kids. She knew appealing to Doug's vanity was the way to smooth her path towards getting exactly what she wanted. If Doug thought the kids wanted to be with him . . . Susannah could tell from his responses what Sylvie was saying.

He asked her before he said yes. She heard him, her heart sinking, tell Sylvie he'd call her back once he'd talked it over with her. She wondered if Sylvie was as aware as she herself was that he didn't mean a bit of it. How was she supposed to say no?

She opened the fridge again, irritated, and looked at all the little delicacies she'd just unpacked. Foie gras, smoked salmon, smoked duck breast. Not enough to feed five of them, even if they wouldn't turn their noses up at every delicious morsel. A collection of little plates, to be eaten in bed, in the bath, curled up in front of the fire, or even the television, not around a full table of paper hat wearers feigning gaiety. Susannah sat down heavily on a stool at the breakfast bar and grabbed a notepad and pen. She'd already written a few things on the list before Douglas came in. Turkey, potatoes, Brussels sprouts, crackers,

Pringles . . . The thought of battling her way round Sainsbury's on Christmas Eve was exhausting, but it was too late to do anything online. She knew from Amelia that those delivery slots had been booked out for weeks and weeks. Like the 'no make-up' make-up look, no-stress, fuss-free Christmas entertaining involved a great deal of stress and fuss . . . you just had to have it in October.

This was messing it all up. She felt the Christmas she'd imagined receding. She'd told Mum she'd come over for lunch tomorrow. She'd accepted for herself, though she hadn't told Douglas she was going yet. She knew he wouldn't have done any gift shopping – he never did it until the last minute. Probably because it was a good excuse to dip out of the whole family thing. Alastair and Kathryn were with her family this year, but Alex and Chloe were going to be there – they were flying to Canada on Boxing Day for a week's skiing with Chloe's lot. She'd bought and wrapped gifts, and she was feeling vaguely festive about the whole trip. She'd play Christmas CDs in the car and get herself in the right mood to make Christmas Day with Doug work.

And she'd thought she might call Lois. It wasn't a complete thought, just a vague idea, and not necessarily a good one at that. But she might.

Douglas came in from the hall with both hands raised in his 'what can I do?' gesture. Probably her least favourite of his mannerisms.

'What's the story?' She tried to keep her voice even and calm.

He shrugged helplessly. 'Some friends of hers have asked her if she wants to go skiing. She can get on a flight to Geneva that leaves tomorrow afternoon.'

Susannah nodded slowly. 'And the kids are okay with that, are they?'

He smiled. 'She says the kids would rather be here. She's never said something like that before.'

Susannah snorted before she could stop herself. 'She's never wanted to dump them with less than twenty-four hours' notice on Christmas Eve before.'

'Don't be like that.' His voice was imploring. 'Maybe it's true. You said yourself you've been getting on better with Daisy lately. Rosie, too.'

'Don't be like what?' She didn't want to bring the girls into it. That was beside the point.

'So hard and cynical.'

His words stung. 'I'll tell you what, Doug. I'll try and be less hard and cynical if you try and be less pathetic and gullible. How's that?' Her voice sounded mean and shrill. She was spoiling for a fight now.

'Gullible?'

'Yeah. Gullible. You think this skiing holiday just came up out of the blue, do you? Like people just decide to go skiing in the most popular week of the year . . .'

He interrupted her angrily. 'Of course not. I'm not an idiot, Susannah.'

She wasn't so sure about that.

'She said someone else had to drop out, and there's a place in a chalet.'

'Great. So, she just rings you up and dumps them, and you just let her. What if we were going somewhere?'

'But we're not,' he whined. 'We were just going to be here on our own.'

'On our own, Doug. That was the point.' She let the point hang in the air for a moment, hoping he'd pick it up.

But he didn't.

'I think we need that, don't you?'

He sidestepped an answer to that one, and went back to his original, entrenched position.

'What am I supposed to do, Susannah? Put yourself in my shoes.'

Too late for that. He'd spent years making sure she stayed out of his shoes. He had no right to chop and change to suit himself. 'Say no. You could say no.' How many times had they had this conversation? How many more times could she keep having it?

'I can't do that. They're my kids.'

'And they're her kids, too.' They're not mine. They're not even close to being mine.

'I don't want to do that. I really don't know why you're making such a big deal about this. You don't even like Christmas much.'

God – the arrogance. She used to love Christmas.

Like lightning, the certainty that she didn't want to

have this argument with Douglas tonight struck her, and with it, the rage seeped away instantly. She turned to the fridge so he couldn't see her face, suddenly afraid that she might cry. 'Fine. You're right. I'm not into Christmas. I'm making a fuss. They'll come. Of course they will. Sylvie will ski, we'll cook. It'll be fine.'

'Fine. I hate that word.'

'It's the best word I can manage this evening, I'm afraid, Doug.'

His voice, when he spoke again, sounded relieved, and conciliatory. 'I'll do the shopping.'

Damn right he would. The cooking, too, though she didn't say so now. 'You'll have to – I'm going to Mum's tomorrow.'

'You didn't tell me.'

Was that resentment in his tone? Was he kidding?

She bit down hard on her lip. 'Last-minute thing.' Her voice dripped with sarcasm. Ouch. But he had that coming.

'Fine. Was I invited?' His voice was testy again.

'You're always fucking invited, Doug.'

He always cringed when she swore at him, almost as though she'd physically hurt him.

She almost enjoyed watching him. 'For God's sake. You just never come. And now, tomorrow, you can't anyway, can you?'

The next morning, after an uneasy peace had settled at home, and they'd got through the night without fighting any more, thanks to a long bubble bath and a good film, Susannah found herself driving to her parents' house the long way round the common – the way that took her past Lois and Frank's house. She came off the main road one exit earlier, watching the car move, curious, as though it was steering itself. She hadn't called, but she couldn't resist this. There was no plan. As she approached, she saw the car a short way in front of her – a blue Ford – pull into their driveway. Without thinking, she stopped, too, a couple of hundred yards away, slamming her brakes on and turning on to the grass verge opposite The Cricketers, feeling like she was spying.

Because she was.

It was Rob. She knew she'd hoped it would be, and it was. Almost like she'd summoned him up by thinking so hard. He climbed out, wearing a navy down vest over a check shirt, and stretched his arms high above his head, arching his back, as though he was stiff from a long drive. Then the passenger door opened and a tall, slender woman climbed out. Although Susannah couldn't see very clearly, she looked a few years younger than Rob from this distance. She had dark blonde hair, cut in a short and wispy style, modern, and she was wearing a navy pea coat over skinny jeans, with a vivid pink woollen scarf wrapped several times around her neck. She said something to him, leaning over the top of the car. He answered, smiling back at her. Then she opened the rear door and pulled out a small brown overnight bag and a large red and white striped gift bag full of wrapped presents. Rob walked round to take the duffel from her, and she reached up to kiss his cheek quickly. He ushered her in front of him, and locked the car before he followed her. Lois had opened the front door before they got to it – wearing a red sweater and an apron – she must have been looking for the car from the front window, eagerly waiting for them. When they got to the door, she opened her arms wide to embrace each of them in turn, and Susannah saw that she was chatting expansively the whole time. She was happy to see them.

Her jealousy shocked her. And that was what it was. A shot of adrenalin-filled envy. A few nights earlier, she'd been at Fin's school Christmas concert. She'd sat in the row, at the end, with Rosie, while Douglas and Sylvie had both gone forward with cameras and beams of pride, and she'd watched as they both kissed and hugged Fin. And hadn't felt so much as a flicker of jealousy. Nothing even remotely resembling what she felt now as she watched Rob and his wife. Susannah shook her head. There was something very wrong with this picture.

The door closed behind the three of them, and Susannah sat, both hands still on the steering wheel of her own car, waiting for her heart to start beating normally again. That had to be his wife. The two of them were home for Christmas. Of course they were. She felt oddly guilty for her voyeurism. She drove off, but she didn't go straight to her Mum's. She needed a few minutes – she drove aimlessly round the village for a few more minutes, trying not to hear Amelia's voice in her head, before she parked her car behind Alex's, rearranged her features into a bright, happy countenance and rang the doorbell.

Chloe refused a glass of egg-nog. That wasn't strange in itself. Egg-nog was a bizarre and very English concoction, and Susannah only drank it herself out of politeness and for the sake of tradition. It was odder that she refused a glass of wine with lunch. Mum had gone to town, stuffing a pork loin with pistachios and cherries. This was her version of the fatted calf for Alex – she said she'd already told their dad he'd get a turkey crown and only one kind of potato tomorrow, and Dad had uncorked both red and white for the occasion without prompting, neither bottle from his extensive supermarket under-five-pounds selection.

Dad tried several times to push a glass on Chloe, saying it would be hours until she'd drive, and it couldn't hurt, and it was Christmas – all the stock reasons . . .

Eventually, Susannah saw a brief glimpse pass between Alex and Chloe, and instantly knew what was coming.

When their mum came back into the room, Alex put a hand over Chloe's on the table. 'Mum, Dad, Sis . . . we've got something to tell you all, actually.'

'Yes, love . . .' Mum was trembling with anticipation immediately. Only good news was delivered at a Christmas table with a stuffed pork loin and two kinds of wine on it.

'Chloe's . . . pregnant.'

Mum's hand flew to her mouth, and her eyes filled with instant tears. 'Oh my darlings. My darlings. How wonderful.' She flew round the table to embrace Chloe, while Dad pumped Alex's hand vigorously.

Susannah sat stunned in the midst of the chaos, her glass in her hand.

Until Alex prompted her with a nudge to the shoulders. 'Well, Sis . . . what do you think?'

She nodded and smiled. 'It's great news. Great, great news. Congratulations.'

Alex was beaming. 'It's way sooner than we thought. I mean, I know we haven't even been married a year yet. We certainly weren't planning . . . But you know what they say . . . and once we'd had a while to get used to the idea, we were both really stoked.'

Mum was pressing them for details. Chloe wasn't twelve weeks yet – she was ten – but they'd given her an early scan before the trip. She wouldn't be skiing, she said, so they'd have to tell everyone there, and they'd been unsure about telling Alex's family before they went . . . but then Dad had pushed the wine.

'Sorry. Stupid me. Wasn't thinking,' Dad coloured up.

'No, no.' Chloe put her arm around her father-in-law.

'I was secretly dying to tell you. I mean, they say twelve weeks, just to be safe, but I want to tell everyone . . .'

Mum looked briefly at Susannah. Chloe didn't know.

Susannah had been thirteen weeks pregnant when she'd lost her baby. The twelve-week rule hadn't worked for her. She'd had the scan, seen the heartbeat. She lost it anyway. Those things didn't give you insurance, and nor should they give you too much peace of mind. At the time, she remembered wondering, almost abstractly, whether she'd relaxed too much. It wasn't as if she'd started smoking and drinking and doing high-impact aerobics. It was just that she'd started taking it for granted.

At the time, it honestly, honestly hadn't felt like the end of the world. She knew it wasn't fashionable to say so. It certainly hadn't felt like losing a baby. She'd woken up one morning with a familiar ache dragging her belly, seen spots of blood in her knickers. By lunchtime she'd lost quite a lot of blood – enough to soak two or three pads – and passed something that looked to her, however much she stared at it, like a clot or a piece of liver. Not a baby. She didn't need a D and C – she wasn't admitted. It was all very straightforward and quick. The doctor and her nurse were very gentle and kind to her, and she was sent home with an A4 sheet of information, and a brief explanation. The main text of which was that there was no explanation. It struck her as very primitive, in the midst of all the technical equipment of the casualty department. 'It just happens sometimes, and we don't always know why.' Really?

She'd cried a bit – mostly when she told her mum. And Mum cried. She'd felt slightly embarrassed about having to tell other people. It felt like failure, however much she knew it wasn't her fault. But, at the time, she'd genuinely believed she'd conceive again. Quickly, easily. And that the next time, everything would be okay.

Amelia had been incredible. Elizabeth had been a cherubic toddler when it had happened. She came round to see her the first day, parking a sleeping Libby in her buggy in the front hall of Susannah and Sean's home without comment. Then, when Libby had woken and demanded attention, she'd picked her up and put her in Susannah's stiff arms. Libby immediately reached for the flat gold disk Susannah wore at the base of her throat, pulling at the chain and talking her still almost incomprehensible talk. At first Susannah hadn't wanted to hold her, but Amelia had stood there, the two women almost touching, until Susannah's arms had softened, and until she had looked into her god-daughter's chubby face, and then at Amelia's, both their eyes full of tears.

Amelia had nodded, then kissed her cheek. 'So, we're all okay here, then?'

It was funny peculiar – definitely not ha, ha – how she was so much sadder now, all these years later, about the miscarriage, than she had been then. It had become sadder with each passing year, directly proportional to that dreadful line on the graph delineating her diminishing fertility. Now, as she faced her forties, still childless, at the table beside her newly married, much younger brother, and his fecund young wife, it seemed almost tragic. But she smiled quickly at Mum, and shook her head briefly, but forcefully, to signal that her story was *not* to intrude into this moment, which belonged rightly to Chloe and Alex.

Later, in the kitchen, while they were drying the dishes, Mum had given her a long hug. 'Are you okay, love?'

'I'm fine.'

'Really?' Mum peered at her.

Susannah nodded, then carefully, deliberately folded the tea towel she'd been using.

'Do you ever think about trying, you know, for a baby, with Douglas?' She'd never asked her that before. Certainly never suggested it.

For the first time, it occurred to Susannah that maybe her mum hadn't ever wanted her to stay with Douglas. It seemed obvious, the moment she thought it. 'I'm over forty, Mum.'

'Not yet, you're not.'

'I would be, though. If I got pregnant tonight.' And she didn't even say how unlikely that was. 'I'd be forty when the baby was born. Nearly sixty by the time he or she went to college.'

'Darling – it's the twenty-first century. Forty now

isn't what forty was when . . . when I was forty. Women are having babies much later than they used to.' Mum was staring at her intently.

Susannah didn't want to talk to her, not today, about the state of her relationship with Douglas. She didn't want her to know that she and Doug were as far away as they had ever been – further, maybe – from having a baby. Although now, it seemed possible that Mum might actually be relieved . . .

But Mum's concern would be oppressive at this point. And it would seem cruel, when Alex and Chloe had just made her day – her Christmas, her year – to deliver news that would worry her. 'You're right, I know. Maybe next year . . .'

'Don't leave it too long, my sweetheart, will you?'

She shook her head. 'I know.'

Her mum held her face in her hands for a moment, and looked into her eyes. 'I want you to have what your brothers have. You deserve it, too, Susannah.'

Susannah nodded. 'I'd like that.'

That was, it seemed, enough for now. Mum squeezed her shoulder, smiled contentedly, and carried the plate of mince pies she'd laid out through to the living room.

Parenting 'lite'. She couldn't blame Mum – she'd cooked, and she had the house full, and it was a happy day. If she felt a little that her problems were being skirted round, given a cursory kitchen airing, before the fun could begin again, she could hardly blame her mum today. And wasn't that what she wanted anyway?

Chloe didn't know – about the miscarriage – because Alex didn't. Nor Alastair. She hadn't told either of them.

Sometimes she wished she hadn't even told Mum.

Back in London, on Christmas morning, Daisy and her dad got into the festive spirit by having a screaming row. She wanted Seth to come over for lunch, and waited until breakfast time to ask. Douglas, rendered immeasurably grumpier than usual by an early start to get the turkey into the oven – Susannah having taken a certain perverse pleasure in rolling over at 7 a.m. and going back to sleep for another hour, holding him to his promise to prepare the meal – said he didn't want Seth to come.

Daisy offered the incendiary, 'Mum said he could.'

'Your mum's not here, is she? This is a family day. You're seeing too much of him anyway. You're way too young to get so serious.' He looked over at Susannah. 'Back me up here, Susannah.'

Daisy had looked at her imploringly.

Susannah smiled at her, and her answer was truthful – that it got up Douglas's nose was an added bonus. 'I don't mind if he's here.' Douglas glared at her, and she shrugged. What was it Amelia had said about the more the merrier? Couldn't get much less merry . . . 'I really don't. If that's what Daisy wants. Sorry. But doesn't his family expect him to be with them?'

Daisy threw her a grateful smile and shrugged. 'It's no big deal at their house. He's got, like, a thousand cousins – big family – all shouting and screaming all the time, and they'll all be there – he says his mum'll barely notice whether he's there or not. And he wants to be with me.'

Susannah remembered that feeling.

She remembered a Christmas Day when she just wanted to be with Rob. There'd been no question, of course, of skipping out on the family lunch in her house. That could never happen. But Mum had let her go at around 4 p.m. She was used, after all, to letting her go to Amelia's to watch TV and compare presents. Dad always fell asleep on the sofa with a paper hat across his eyes after lunch, and once the dishes were done, Mum just wanted to put her feet up, too. Alex had Scalextric that year, and Alastair had promised to help him put it together. She'd run all the way. Frank had cut big slices of raisiny, lemony cake from a vast cylindrical panettone, and served them with tea. Lois had given her a small bottle of Anaïs Anaïs. After the cake, Frank and Lois had gone for a walk around the village. Frank claimed he needed to walk off all the food, but Lois winked at her as they left, and Susannah had known they were giving them some space. They were much more likely to do that than Mum had ever been. Mum was forever coming in with a drink, or a question, or in search of something she claimed to have left in whichever room – downstairs, always downstairs – she and Rob were in. Lois had once squeezed her arm, and said she trusted them both, and wasn't averse to a closed door. Much later, Rob had walked her home, and they'd stood for ages at the end of her drive, kissing and kissing in the cold air, until Dad came out in his slippers and called her in.

In the end, Doug relented sulkily, and Seth came after lunch. After a brief and tense conversation, in which Seth avoided eye contact with Susannah and gave monosyllabic responses to her questions, shuffling uncomfortably from one foot to the other as Douglas barely acknowledged his presence, Daisy dragged him upstairs into her room.

They were washing up in the kitchen. Susannah had relented. There were twice the number of pans, bowls and utensils there would have been if she'd cooked – how did men manage to do that?

'I really don't think she should be doing that,' Douglas offered, after they'd gone, as though he expected Susannah to do something about it.

'They've left the door open,' Rosie added, having just been upstairs. She was sitting at the kitchen table, busy separating all the strawberry delights from the family-size tin of Quality Street Mum had given her yesterday.

'I'm sure it's fine. They're not exactly going to start having sex on Christmas afternoon, with us downstairs, are they?'

'Ew. Gross.' Rosie gathered her booty and left the room, her nose wrinkled in pre-teen distaste.

Douglas looked at her as if she'd just spoken Esperanto. 'Sex?' He sounded horrified.

Susannah couldn't help laughing. 'Don't make that face. You look like Rosie. She's nearly seventeen years old, Doug.'

'She's a child.'

'You may think so, but she certainly doesn't.'

'What do you mean?'

This was dangerous territory. She didn't want to have this conversation with Douglas. Not today. And especially not with Seth upstairs, in right-hook distance.

She still hadn't told him about the incident with Daisy. Nor about the subsequent visit to the doctor, nor the pink package of pills she knew Daisy was now taking. Daisy had begged her not to. That wouldn't have stopped her, if she'd thought he might take it well, or if she thought he needed to know. Deserved to know. But she suspected he wouldn't take it well, and so she'd said nothing.

She didn't think Daisy had told her mother either. After the Rosie incident, she didn't doubt she'd hear about it, if Sylvie knew. She was defiant, though. Rosie was feeling better – whatever that poker-faced, mealy-mouthed teacher had thought of Susannah, she'd obviously dealt with the problem for now.

Dishes done, Doug fell heavily asleep on the sofa in front of *Chitty Chitty Bang Bang*, adding his intermittent snoring to the already cacophonous soundtrack. As she crept away to boil the kettle for a cup of tea, Susannah heard muffled giggles coming from the top of the stairs. She almost hoped they *were* at it. Someone in this house should be getting some for Christmas.

Rob and Helena were making love silently – or, at least, as quietly as they could – under the old-fashioned sheets and blankets on the guest bed in his parents' house. Helena swung one strong, lean leg across Rob's lap and straddled him, rearing up and throwing off the covers. She looked fantastic from where he was lying, her breasts with their tiny brown nipples jutting forward, the muscles of her stomach strong and defined.

She pushed her short hair back from her forehead, and it spiked with sweat. She exhaled loudly, not moving for a moment. 'Christ! It's so hot in here. Like a sauna. How many layers are on this bed anyway?'

'Sssh.' Rob was laughing at her. 'Mum likes a warm house and a well-dressed bed.' He stroked her skin, pushing himself upwards at her. 'Don't stop. Please, don't stop . . .'

She leant forward and kissed him deeply, pushing herself back hard against him, reestablishing their rhythm of a few moments earlier. 'Okay. Since you asked so nicely. I . . . won't . . . stop . . .'

She was sexy as hell when she was like this. Dominant and confident and strong. Earlier, when she'd reached for him under the covers, he'd paused, wondering if he dare make love under his parents' roof – he never had before. She'd giggled when he told her that, and then kissed him from the base of his throat down his chest and down further, way down under the candlewick and duvet and flannel, kissing until his objections faded away.

Afterwards, they whispered to each other about the day. Rob hadn't admitted how nervous he'd been. This was the first time they'd met Helena. He'd brought his wife home to meet his parents – all the wrong way round. He knew how much he'd hurt his mother by getting married without her there, and he was sorry. He'd told Helena all about them, about the house, and their marriage, and Dad's illness. He realized, when they drove up to the house, that he hadn't told them much about Helena.

But Mum had treated her as if she'd known her for ever. There was no awkwardness. She'd opened her arms wide, like she always did, and held Helena tight. Told her she was beautiful, far more beautiful than in the pictures Rob had sent of her. And so skinny. Too skinny, she'd clucked. She needed feeding up.

Mum had gone crazy in the kitchen, baking and cooking for them. He almost wished she hadn't – she looked so exhausted – but it had clearly given her such pleasure to do it for them. The tree was up and dressed, exactly as it had been when he was a boy, with its garish, multicoloured lights and 1970s tinsel.

His dad had been in his chair by the gas fire. It was obviously a struggle for him to stand, but he did when

274

Helena came in, though it took a while. He'd kissed her hand, like he always used to do with women, but his arm shook, and the gesture cost him, Rob could see. Helena put an arm gently around his shoulders and kissed him on the cheek, and Rob found the sight of the two of them together almost unbearably poignant. He looked at his mother, and saw her wipe away a tear, so he put an arm around her.

'He'll hate that she only sees him this way.'

'I told, her, Ma. I told her all about him. I haven't forgotten.'

'She's a beautiful girl, Rob.'

He nodded. She was. She was sitting now, on a footstool she'd pulled up so it was beside Frank. She was resting her face in her hands, and her elbows were on her knees, and she was talking softly to him.

'He seems worse.'

Lois shrugged. 'You think so? I see him every day, so I see everything and nothing, if you know what I mean.'

'He's shakier. He can barely stand, and I bet he can't walk far.' Rob hated the thought of his mother buckling under the weight of his father as she helped him to the bed next door. They were getting close, he knew, to a time when she wouldn't be able to cope alone here with him. He didn't know how he was going to handle that. It wouldn't be easy – Mum was determined to care for him herself.

She nodded. 'You're right.'

'What does the doctor say?'

Lois made a clicking sound with her tongue against her teeth. 'What *can* the doctor say?'

Later, after they'd eaten as much of what Lois put in front of them as they could manage, Helena helped her wash up in the kitchen. From his seat beside his father, Rob could hear the two of them chatting happily. Lois was telling stories about him, he knew, but he didn't mind. He loved his mum for her easy, embracing style. Helena was laughing and exclaiming. Later, she'd promised to bring out the photograph albums, and Helena had winked mischievously at him above his mother's head.

His dad's voice was so much quieter than the booming one he remembered from his childhood. It was one of the things he missed the most. He couldn't remember the last time he'd heard his father sing, and he used to sing all the time when Rob was a boy. Now, he had to lean in to catch words, and sometimes Frank had to repeat himself, something he obviously found frustrating.

'She's a looker.'

'That's what Mum says.'

'She's right. She's sweet, too, son. Much more important.'

Rob nodded. 'Like a meringue. Tough on the outside, sweet and soft inside.'

Frank laughed and raised a hand. 'I saw no tough.'

'You should see her in fatigues, ordering blokes around.'

'And you're happy together, the two of you?'

'I think we are. Yes.'

His father looked at him strangely.

Neither of them wanted to tell his parents that she was leaving in January. Not tonight, they'd agreed. They didn't even talk much about it themselves. They saw it differently. Helena was excited. She saw it as her job – the thing she'd been training for. She was gung-ho to get out there. Rob knew better. But when he tried to talk to her about the realities of the situation she was about to find herself in – a combat zone, a real war, with real dangers and real crises – Helena almost brushed him off. It was the only real source of tension between them – this difference between her expectations and his knowledge. They'd declared an amnesty over Christmas. Helena's mother, Helen, couldn't acknowledge it. And Frank and Lois didn't need to know.

Not yet, at least.

January

When she was young, Susannah had made New Year's resolutions religiously, writing them out on the pages of a new diary the week before school started. Save money, get more sleep, be nicer to Mum, lose 5 lbs. She'd loved the start of a new year almost as much as September and the start of term. It always felt like anything was possible. She thought about resolutions as she walked to the underground on the 4th of January, her first day back at work. What would this year's be?

Pull yourself together.
Stop daydreaming about your past, and someone else's husband.
Lose 5 lbs.
Stop accepting the status quo.
Heal Amelia.
Be happier.
Get pregnant.
Run away.

She didn't feel exhilarated so much as exhausted, before she'd even begun. Going back to work was a relief. Christmas week hadn't panned out the way she'd planned. Sylvie had only got back on the 2nd of January, so they'd had Rosie and Fin for New Year's Eve. Another row – Daisy had wanted to go to someone's holiday house in Abersoch, with a load of mates. Doug had said no the moment he'd heard Seth was going, and much door slamming and silent treatment had ensued. In the end Daisy had flounced out at around 6 p.m. on New Year's Eve, saying she was going to stay at her friend Alice's, although Susannah wasn't sure she believed her. Doug didn't check up on her either – demonstrating the kind of inconsistent lack of follow-through that Amelia swore was the beginning of the end of the world in parenting terms.

Amelia and Jonathan had come round for drinks, bringing their two youngest, Elizabeth having been invited to her first formal New Year's Eve party. The kids sat stupefied in front of Harry Potter, while Jonathan and Douglas made their most valiant attempt at amiable small talk.

The women escaped to the kitchen at the earliest opportunity, claiming canapé duty, but once there they both sat at the table with their champagne while Amelia told Susannah about Elizabeth. 'You should have seen her, Suze. She looked about twenty-five. She was wearing my shoes, and my earrings, my Chanel perfume. She was beautiful.'

Susannah clinked glasses with her. 'Shouldn't surprise you. You're beautiful.'

Amelia rubbed her head ruefully. She wasn't wearing the wigs they'd bought together – not yet – but she'd had her hair cropped very close. Because it was so blonde you couldn't see how thin it was until you were up very close to it.

Susannah tried to tell her she looked elfin – like Mia Farrow in the Polanski years.

But Amelia wasn't buying it. 'Maybe once.'

'You still are, you self-pitying marc. Drink with me. Come on. Drink to the all-clear.'

'Bloody hell, yes. I'll drink to that . . .' She downed

the last of her glass, the fingers on both hands crossed and her eyes closed, and then held it out for more. 'Fill me up. Douglas only poured me half a glass first time round. He does know it's chemo – not rehab – I'm in, does he?' She was obviously feeling good. She hadn't had a treatment since just before Christmas.

There was a pattern now. Treatment. Three really crappy days. Three not quite so crappy but still really tired days, a good five or six days. Treatment. This was a good day. But it wasn't just that. She looked good, too. Her eyes were bright, and her colour was up.

'You're practically twinkling. Something's up. What gives?'

For a moment Amelia looked like she was going to withhold information, but then she remembered that she was Amelia. Leaning forward as though there were other people in the room who might overhear her, she almost whispered, 'I slept with J yesterday.'

Susannah leant, too. It was lean-worthy information. 'You did what?' Was everyone she knew having sex except her?

'Actually, there was no sleeping.' She was giggling lasciviously, suddenly more like her old self than Susannah could remember her being for the longest time. 'I should say, to be absolutely accurate, that I had spectacular, orgasmic, very yummy indeed sex with J yesterday afternoon while my mother took the kids to the IMAX to see something or other in 3D. Twice.'

'Blimey.' It had been a while since Susannah had

done it twice. Years, in fact, now she was forced to think of it.

'Blimey indeed.' Amelia looked absurdly pleased with herself.

'What brought that on?'

'Christmas spirit?' Amelia laughed. 'Oh, I don't know. Christmas was part of it, though I hadn't been on the Baileys. He's been around a lot. He's been great with the kids . . . and me. I haven't been a real ray of sunshine. You know that as well as anyone. He's just . . . he's been a real brick.'

'So, you were paying him back? Reward sex?'

'No! It wasn't like that.'

'What was it like, then? Explain it to me.'

'Only if you tell me why you suddenly sound pissed off with me.'

'I'm not pissed off, Meels. It's none of my business.'

'We both know that isn't true.' Amelia smiled.

'I just don't want you to mess him around. You don't know what a mess he's been. You *know* it will mean something different to him than it means to you.'

'I don't *know*. Not any more.'

'What are you saying?'

Amelia shook her head. 'I'm not sure what I'm saying, Suze. Things are different, you know. This illness – it makes you think. Re-evaluate. It makes things that did seem huge, and really important, seem like nonsense. Does that make sense?'

Susannah nodded.

'So, on Christmas Eve, we were all in the kitchen. All five of us. Can't remember where Mum was. Jonathan was making the brandy butter. He always used to do that, do you remember? And he hasn't made it, the last three years. And he's making it, and there's never much brandy in the bottle. There never was much brandy left in the bottle – it's one of those little half-bottles of Courvoisier – not any of the years we cooked a Christmas lunch. And we're having the same conversation we always used to have. Like, who drinks the brandy, because neither of us do – we don't go near it, in fact, except every Christmas Eve, to make the brandy butter. The same talk we had every year. So we're laughing, and it just felt so familiar and so comfortable. And I see the kids' faces, and they're loving it. Sam is just beaming.'

Amelia's eyes had tears in them now, and Susannah reached over and touched her hand.

'And then later, at bedtime. Mum's in the guest room, so Sam is on the sofa in the study and Jonathan's got his bed, and I've gone downstairs to get a glass of water, and when I come back up, he's standing in the doorway of Victoria's room, and the light from the hall is shining on her face, and he's just staring at her.

'He kissed me goodnight. On the landing. Just on the cheek. And it felt . . . it felt right. Does that make any sense at all?'

'It makes such sense to me, you have no idea. It's all the other stuff that never made any sense, Meels.'

Amelia pursed her lips and nodded her head.

'So, this is going somewhere?'

'I don't know. I don't want to make those kinds of decisions while I'm still sick.'

'Why not? What you described to me – none of that was because you're ill. All of it was because you all miss him.'

'But maybe I just miss him because I'm sick. I feel so vulnerable, Susannah. You've no idea how vulnerable.'

'Of course you do.'

'But that's not enough, is it? Just because in those moments I can't remember why I didn't want to be married to him any more, and just because I feel so alone – those aren't good enough reasons, are they?'

'You're asking the wrong person.'

'I'm asking the person who knows me best.'

Susannah shrugged. 'I can't tell you what to do, Meels. I don't want either of you to get hurt.'

'I know. I don't want that either.'

'Just be careful, will you? Be careful for both of you.'

'Promise.'

January quickly settled into its cold, relentless routine. She went to work. She took down the tree and put the decorations away. She went to the hospital with Amelia and read a James Patterson thriller to her while she sat with her eyes closed. She refereed between

Douglas and Daisy. She didn't think any more about her resolutions.

And then, early in the month – out of the blue – Rob telephoned her. She'd given her mobile phone number to Lois when she'd seen her that time – shyly passing her a business card from her wallet when she'd asked her about work. His mother must have given it to him.

He called on a Monday afternoon. She had just left work, and was walking down the busy street towards the underground – at first she didn't recognize his voice, couldn't hear what he was saying. The sales were on and the pavements were crowded.

She stopped, and ducked off the main street, into a doorway, putting a finger in her ear to block out the passing traffic. 'Hello? Who is this?'

'Rob. It's Rob. I'm sorry. Susannah?'

Not Susie. 'Yes. It's me.'

'Is this a bad time? You sounded like you were in a crowd. I could call back . . .'

He was almost shouting, but it was quieter here now, and she heard him clearly.

'No. It's okay. I . . . I can hear you now. Rob. Hi.'

He spoke fast, sounded nervous. 'Look, I hope this doesn't feel like a real intrusion – I got your number off Mum. And the idea of calling, I suppose, really. She said – she said you'd been to see them, how nice it had been to catch up, how good it had been to see you . . . And I mean, I'd been meaning, really, thinking

284

of . . . well, when we saw you last summer . . . So . . . I've called. I would have emailed – it's much easier to ignore an email, I know, than a call, but I didn't have an address . . .'

'Rob! I'm happy to hear from you.' She was. Ludicrously, amazingly happy to hear from him.

'Good.'

They were silent for a moment.

'You still there?'

He laughed. 'Yes. Still here.'

'And where is here exactly?'

'London. Piccadilly, to be precise. Where are you?'

'Walking towards the Embankment. I've finished for the day – I was on my way home.'

'Sorry. I've interrupted you.'

'No. Not at all. What are you doing in London?'

'Working.'

Lois hadn't said anything about where he was posted.

'Susie – I wondered if you fancied getting together for a coffee, or maybe lunch or something. One of these days.'

'I'd like that.'

'Fantastic. I'd like that, too, very much.'

Again, silence. But this time she knew he was still on the line.

'What days – I mean, are there good days for you? You probably don't have your diary with you, right now.'

She didn't know, then or afterwards, what made her say it. 'I'm free right now, actually. I mean . . . if you don't have to be anywhere else.'

As soon as the words were out, she regretted saying them. How ridiculous did that make her sound? Right now, for God's sake. Who did that? Go twenty years without spending any time together, and then suggest meeting five minutes in.

'We could do that. I'm just about finished here. Yes, let's do that. That'd be great.'

He was probably just being kind.

He suggested a pub somewhere between the two of them and then rang off, agreeing to see her there in twenty minutes or so.

Susannah retraced her steps, went back into her building and took the elevator to her floor, going straight to the ladies' loo, which was mercifully deserted. She stood with both her hands on the edge of a sink, and stared at her reflection in the mirror for a moment, then began to panic. Her hair was a mess, most of her make-up had faded until she looked tired and grey, and there was the beginning of a run in her tights. She had been planning to go home and soak in the tub. Not meet the 'great love of her life' in a pub for a drink.

When had he started to be called that? She peered at herself. What the hell had got into her? He was married. Not just married. He was a newly-wed, with a pretty, tall, slim, blonde wife. And she knew that because she'd spied on them. Great. She ran a sink of cold water, and splashed her face, then delved in her handbag for a new pair of tights and her make-up bag.

Ten minutes later, spritzed with perfume, glossed, brushed and de-laddered, she caught a cab, feeling as sick and excited and confused as she could remember ever feeling before.

It was quiet in the pub – a cold, damp, windy Monday night in January. A couple of regulars sat at the bar, chatting to the bar staff, and a small group of middle-aged office workers had taken over a couple of tables at the back. It was an old-fashioned place – so much more a pub than a wine bar. The kind of place where you'd ask for red or white, not Merlot or Chardonnay. Susannah was contemplating a whisky.

Rob was sitting in a small nook behind the door, already nursing a pint of beer. He stood up when she came in. For a split second they stood facing each other, a couple of feet apart. He opened his arms, like his mother had done all those months ago on the common, and Susannah stepped into them, and back in time as his arms closed around her, and her head nestled, just for a moment, in the spot on his neck that was so familiar to her it felt like coming home. She felt little and precious in his embrace, and it felt wonderful.

For the first five minutes, they busied themselves getting her a drink, hanging her coat on the hooks behind his head, talking about the weather. She kept looking at him, not quite believing they were here together.

Then her drink was in front of her, and they began to talk. She asked him how he came to be in London.

'I'm not in the RAF any more. I'm a consultant now.' Rob drew inverted commas in the air when he said 'consultant', and made a face, as though the new job title still amused and bemused him.

'Wow.'

'I came out at thirty-eight. In 2009. It's the first time, apart from after a short commission – six years in – that you can come out with a decent pension and a lump sum. A lot of the guys do it.'

'I didn't know you'd done that.'

'Why would you?' He smiled.

'But why? I always thought you loved it.'

Rob shook his head. Susannah thought she'd been too nosy. How the hell did she know he loved it? She needed to remind herself that she didn't know this man. She knew the boy he'd been, but she didn't know him.

'Sorry.' She stopped herself.

'No. Please. It's just funny. We haven't talked in – what? – twenty years – and you're just like you always were. Straight to the heart of the matter.'

'Sorry.'

'Don't be. It's nice . . . familiar. Too many people pussyfoot around.'

She felt suddenly shy.

'And you're right, anyway. I did love it. I was one of your actual career soldiers, for years. Decades, I suppose.'

288

'So, what changed? I mean – if you don't mind me asking? I'm asking too many questions, I know. Lawyers.'

Rob shook his head. 'That's right. You're a lawyer.'

'Don't hate me. We're not all bad.'

'I don't hate you. And I don't mind you asking questions.' He shrugged. 'Dad. Dad changed. He was diagnosed two years before I came out. It's terminal, the disease, and it usually kills you within three to five years. And it's bad. It gets really bad. I knew Mum would need me. I was still getting postings – that's the job. Six, nine months. Anywhere in the world. The Gulf wasn't out of the question. Or Afghanistan – not entirely, although not many of my lot deployed to the fighting there. You don't nip back from these places. When you're gone, you're gone. And I didn't want to be away when she needed me. I didn't want her worrying about me as well as Dad, either. And she always did – worry herself sick if I was anywhere she thought was dangerous, even though I'd mostly been teaching and training in the last few years. She still worries. You remember what she's like?'

Susannah nodded. She remembered. 'So, you gave up doing what you loved?'

'He's my dad, Susie. You'd have done the same, if you needed to.'

Would she? Susannah couldn't imagine her dad ill in the way Frank was. Ill and waiting to get worse. Waiting to die.

All her memories of her dad were somehow physical.

Dad swinging her above his head until she giggled insensibly and begged to be put down. Dad holding her bike saddle, running alongside her until he let go, and she heard his voice receding behind her, shouting encouragement and triumph. Dad's arms around her. Dad digging in the garden. Her dad. And Mum. She wasn't sure how Mum would cope. Mum was the noisier parent, and maybe the busier one, but she wasn't the stronger one. Or the wiser one. Susannah shivered at the fleeting idea of a world without Dad's counsel, and his gentle smile.

'I bet he was really angry when you told him.'

Rob laughed. 'He certainly would have been. Really, really angry. If he'd known the real reason.'

'What did you tell him, then?'

'The truth. Part of it, at least. That I'd had enough. That I was tired. That I'd had enough of this war. We've been at it now for what – nine years? We're not getting anywhere.'

'And he bought that?'

'He did, mostly the part about being tired of it. He'd said several times over the years that it is no life for an older man. I think he wanted me to have a family, you know – kids – some stability . . .' Rob's voice trailed off.

Susannah wasn't ready to talk about his wife yet. 'And how is Frank now?'

Rob rubbed his forehead. 'When was it that you saw him?'

'September, I think it was.'

He shook his head. 'He's gone quite a long way downhill since then. It's weird – for months he seems unchanged, and then there's a sudden acceleration, he deteriorates. And then maybe it stops again. Maybe not, I suppose. Eventually, it won't stop, of course.'

'Is he in a wheelchair now? I was sort of surprised he wasn't when I saw him in the autumn.'

Rob nodded. 'Yeah. That happened right before Christmas. Most of his strength is gone now. That and the shakes make standing up really difficult, without help. And Mum isn't up to it, not really. And walking – that's impossible now.'

'God. How bloody awful.'

'It's wretched, Susie. Really hard to watch, to be honest. His speech is much worse, too. He has a lot of trouble getting his words out. And he hates it. That's worse, for Mum, I think. She'd resigned herself to the wheelchair, but I think him not being able to communicate – that's been incredibly hard for her. She's lonely, basically.'

'Of course.'

'She was so pleased when you went to see her, Susie. She always loved you.'

'Did she?'

'Yeah. You set the bar very high, she said. She never really stopped being fed up with me about it.'

'Fed up with *you*?'

'Yeah. Thought I shouldn't have let you go.' He looked suddenly shy.

The conversation dried up. They just looked at each other.

Then Susannah forced herself to say it. There was nothing else to say. 'So . . . you're married now!'

'You know?'

'Please! I certainly hope you weren't trying to keep it a secret – not in our village!'

'Not a secret, no. I just didn't know everyone knew.'

'So . . . who is she? Tell me all about her . . .' She couldn't believe how light her voice sounded, but Susannah couldn't say she'd already seen her.

Rob smiled shyly, and it stung just a little bit. 'Her name is Helena. She's in the RAF. That's how we met.'

'New spin on the office romance, I guess?'

'I suppose. She's a fair bit younger than me.'

Susannah nodded. She almost wanted Rob to tell her how much he loved his wife, how he'd never been happier. But he didn't.

'You must have been engaged, when I saw you in the summer . . .' She couldn't help it.

He shook his head. 'No. We weren't. It wasn't exactly planned. Not at that point.'

'Where is she now?'

'Afghanistan.'

'Oh God.' She hadn't expected him to say that. Stupid, really.

'She left just after New Year.'

'How long will she be there?'

'Six months, most likely. It could be a bit longer.'

'How scary.'

Rob shrugged. 'It can be. But it's the job. It's what we all train for. It sounds like a cliché, but it's true – you'd be frustrated if you didn't get to go. She wanted to go.'

'And you?'

He shook his head. 'That I don't miss. You don't feel that same way the second time, or the third. Not when you know what's coming. You think the training's prepared you, but nothing can, not really – not for some of it. I feel like I've done my share.'

'It must be weird, being the one left behind after all those years of being the one doing it. Can you speak to her and stuff?'

He gave her a strange look. 'Yes. It isn't like it used to be.' In our day, he meant. 'Mobile phones, and Skype cameras and the internet . . . lots of ways to stay in touch.'

'So, is she okay?'

'She's fine. Least she was yesterday,' he joked.

Susannah cringed.

'Sorry. I didn't mean it to sound that way. She's okay. She's in a place that's relatively safe right now. She's going to be fine.'

'Okay. Good. But you must miss her.'

He nodded, but didn't speak. She fingered the beer mat beneath her glass, twisting it to the left and the right, and watching the liquid swirl gently up the sides of the tumbler.

'What about you, Susannah? You're not married any more, Mum says.'

'To Sean? God, no. We've been divorced . . . oh, a really long time now.'

'I'm sorry.'

'It's okay. He left me.' She didn't really know why she said that.

'Idiot.'

That was why.

'He's married to someone else now. Miriam. And they have kids. He lives in America.'

Rob nodded slowly.

'I saw the two of you, you know.'

'What?'

'I saw you and him. In . . . 1993, 1994, I think. I was in London.'

'What do you mean?'

Rob took a deep breath. 'I came to look for you. I was on leave. I'd been wanting to, for ages. To come and see you. We never . . . we didn't end it well.'

'That was my fault.'

'Mine, too.' His eyes bored into hers. 'And I wanted to see you. I tracked down your address. Went to your flat. I was going to wait for you. Stupid plan. I don't know what I was expecting. I sound like some crazy stalker, I know.'

'I never knew.'

'Of course not. I'd almost thought better of it before you showed up. Then you came home, but you weren't alone. You were with him. The two of you pitched up, carrying a bunch of Sainsbury's bags, chatting away. You looked really happy – really together.'

'Why didn't you come and say hello?'

Rob raised his eyebrow sardonically at her. 'And the point of that would have been?'

God. She didn't know where to begin. She didn't know how to answer. Would it have made any difference at all, would it have changed things?

Probably not. It would just have been an embarrassing, stilted encounter. She'd never told Sean much about Rob. She'd always been ashamed of what she'd done, and she hadn't wanted to carry her past into their future – she'd made a concerted effort *not* to do that. He'd done the only sensible thing, sloping away into the night.

She looked down at her hands.

'Lousy timing, I guess.'

She guessed so. They'd always had it. Never quite had a clear run.

'There's someone else, though, right?'

'Yes.'

He looked at her expectantly, and she shrugged. 'Douglas.'

'But you're not married?'

'No. Tried that. Didn't work out for me.' Doug's line. Why the hell would she say that? It always sounded crappy when he said it – always mock jovially – and it sounded the same way coming from her.

'And no kids.'

'He has three. Two girls and a boy.'

'So, you're a stepmother? How's that?'

She grimaced. 'Like being a real mother, except everyone resents you more for everything you do . . .'

'Wow. You make it sound so great.' His eyes were laughing.

'Don't take any notice of me. I sound bitter and jaded, don't I? How attractive.'

'It's funny to me that you don't have any of your own.' His turn to be up front.

'Because?'

'You always said you wanted some.'

'Did I?'

He looked at her quizzically. 'You don't remember?'

Of course she did. He was her past, sitting here in front of her in her present. Making her remember. She shrugged again and answered obliquely because she knew that would stop him questioning further. 'It hasn't happened, that's all.'

'Shame.' Such a Rob-ism that she had to smile.

'What about you? You said Helena was younger than you. Besides, who cares how old a guy is, right? Charlie Chaplin and all that . . . you'll have some, I suppose?'

'I don't know. We're not long married. And she's got years to make up her mind. She's ambitious, too, for her career. She wants to outrank me.'

'How close is she to that?'

Rob smiled. 'Not that close yet. I came out a squadron leader. She's a pilot officer. She's got a couple to go . . . Besides, you tend not to think about kids while your wife is on active duty. They'd take a bit of a dim view of that sort of thing at the moment.'

She nodded. 'One day, though? You'd be a great dad.'

'Would I? Isn't that one of those things people say?'

'I think you would. I used to think you would anyway. Have you changed much?'

'We all change, don't we?'

'We change . . . and we stay the same . . .'

'See – you were always the philosophical one. No change there!'

Outside, later, it was colder than ever. They stood facing each other. Susannah's long woollen scarf lay loosely around her neck. Still looking at her, Rob took both ends and wrapped them once more around, moving close enough to her that she could feel his warm breath on her face. He didn't let go straight away, his hands at her throat. It was proprietary, and it was kind, and it was like an electric shock. She stepped back, involuntarily, and pulled on her gloves efficiently, shivering after the pub's warm interior.

'So, can we do this again, Susie? I've really enjoyed seeing you.'

'I don't know,' she hesitated.

'What don't you know?'

'Whether we should.'

'Are we doing anything wrong?' He put his hands out.

Not yet. But she wasn't sure how long it might stay that way. The magnetic thing that had always been there – from the first day in the English class, and the Bonfire Night on the common . . . it was still there.

It was way, way too complicated.

'Go on, Susie. Please. I've . . . I've missed you.'

In the immortal words of Jerry Maguire, he had her at 'Susie'. And she'd missed him, too. Seeing him again, talking to him – it was always going to have done one of two things to her. She'd half hoped (or had she, really?) that it would have laid the ghost of him to rest at long last. That he would have seemed nice, sweet, kind. But that the encounter would have put him back in his rightful place in her mind – a piece of her past.

It had done the second thing. What was it the Japanese admiral had said just after the Pearl Harbor attacks? Something about awakening a sleeping giant?

Douglas was sitting at the kitchen table when she got home, and she heard another male voice from the side of the table she couldn't see from the hall. She took her coat off and hung it in the cupboard, slowly, taking a minute to calm herself down. She looked at her face in the hall mirror, but she didn't look any different, except that, maybe, her eyes were brighter. But she felt utterly transformed. Smoothing down her skirt and tucking her hair behind her ears, she walked towards the kitchen. It was Alastair, sitting nursing a bottle of beer, his suit jacket on the back of the chair and his tie loosened.

'Hi, Sis.'

Shit. She'd forgotten. He was in town for a few meetings, and he'd called at the weekend to ask if he could stay the night. She'd agreed, of course – it was always nice to see him. And then she'd forgotten, when Rob called.

'God. I'm so sorry. I forgot you were coming.' She went cross-eyed at him. 'One of those days at work, I'm afraid.' She almost felt her cheeks redden. The first lie she'd told because of Rob. Even now she wondered whether there'd be more.

'No worries. Doug was home by the time I got here. I wasn't left out on the doorstep with my overnight bag.'

Susannah smiled gratefully at Doug. 'Good. Good.'

'Did you get supper?' Douglas looked at her empty-handedness, with something like the beginnings of exasperation in his voice and on his face.

She'd said she would, this morning. She hadn't done that either. She shrugged. 'Indian?'

'Indian works for me.' If Alastair was aware of the tension, he was covering very well. 'Kathryn doesn't like curry, as you know, so it'd be a treat . . .' He was smiling broadly at her, but there was curiosity in his face, too.

She knew this wasn't like her.

'We'll need to pick it up, though.' Doug interrupted her thoughts. 'Not have it delivered. We're out of milk and bread, too.'

She nodded. 'Great. Fine. I'll go.'

'Can't I go? You just got in.'

'No. Of course not. It's fine. I'll go. I took a cab home, so I haven't walked far or anything . . .'

'I'll come with you, then.'

'That'd be nice.'

Douglas didn't offer – just asked for a chicken tikka and a garlic naan bread – and went upstairs to change.

Alastair watched his retreating back, but Susannah couldn't read his face.

On the way, they talked about Christmas – his in Cambridgeshire, hers at the house. His mother-in-law was a handful, and he made her laugh with a Christmas morning story about bread sauce and a Kathryn so incandescent with rage that she'd had to go to the spare room and bite a pillow so hard she'd torn the embroidery and had then sat up Christmas evening repairing it with one of those hotel kits. She told him about Daisy and Seth, and the row, and he shook his head, and said he was in no hurry for the girls to grow up. They both marvelled at the news that their baby brother was to have a baby of his own. Al chatted easily about work, and his hopes for the meetings he had coming up. She offered a few details of work.

In the restaurant, they sat in the foyer and drank a beer while they waited for the food.

'How's Amelia?' Alastair's face was grave, and the sparkle had gone completely from his eye.

'Mum told you?'

'You should have told me.'

'Amelia doesn't want any fuss.'

'And would I have made any?'

'I don't know. I never quite know, when it comes to you and Amelia.'

He shook his head ruefully. 'You've never really believed I'm not still carrying a torch for her, have you?'

'Well, are you?'

'I'm married. To the most fantastic, gorgeous, sexy-as-hell woman who knows me inside out and loves me anyway. We have three kids together.'

'And . . .'

He laughed out loud, throwing his head back. 'You don't give up.' Then, 'And I'll always, always, always have a soft spot for Miss Amelia Lloyd.'

'I know.'

He nudged her. 'One that I'd never in a million years do anything about.'

'I know that, too.'

'Anyone ever tell you you're a know-it-all?'

'You.'

Alastair shrugged. 'She was the first girl I loved, I think. You don't ever really forget that, do you, Sis? You know that more than most, I think.'

'Now who's a know-it-all?' She wasn't ready to talk about it, not even to him.

His face was serious again. 'So, how is she?'

'Tough as old boots. Self-possessed and strong. Brave as hell. Scared to death. Nearly as scared as me.'

Alastair laid an arm around her shoulders. 'She'll be okay.'

'Everyone says so.'

'You okay?' He was talking about Amelia, she knew, but he was also asking about Douglas.

She smiled. 'I'm fine.' It was easier, right now.

'Tell her . . . tell her I'm on her team, will you?'

'Like she hasn't always known that?!'

It was funny – Susannah had lived in London for years, ever since she'd finished law school. And over those years she'd done all the things a visitor would do – most of it with Doug's kids. They'd taken them on the London Eye – where, on learning that the cabin took a sedate twenty-five minutes to complete a circuit rather than a hair-raising, roller-coaster-style ninety seconds, Fin had lain spreadeagled on the floor of their pod, moaning that this was the most boring ride he'd ever been on in his life, to the bemusement of the coach party of Dutch tourists accompanying them. He'd displayed a similar ennui at London Zoo. He liked HMS Belfast, but that bored the girls to tears. They liked Hamleys, but that gave Douglas and

Susannah a simultaneous headache. She'd seen the Crown Jewels, the Tower of London, the Houses of Parliament and the Cabinet War Rooms (twice). She'd been dragged, eyes mostly closed, around the London Dungeon and she'd bruised her coccyx ice skating at Somerset House at Christmas.

She knew the city well. She knew if a minicab driver was taking a longer route on purpose, and she knew the best places to park if you were shopping on Oxford Street. She had favourite restaurants and cinemas and delicatessens.

With Rob, though, she started to see a different London. After that first drink, he'd sent an email to the work address she gave him. He wasn't taking no for an answer, he said. He didn't have many friends in the city – she *had* to see him again. They started to meet for lunch, after work, on Saturday afternoons when Doug was at home with the kids.

She hadn't realized how easily she could extricate herself from her daily life – and how little, apparently, she would be missed when she did. It seemed to her that she'd extricated herself emotionally a while back – the physical stuff was much easier.

It would only have been lying if she'd had to answer questions about it. And she didn't.

During the week, her day was her own. If Megan noticed anything different about her, she didn't say so to her face, and Susannah would never have been aware of what she might be saying behind her back.

She might have stopped eating so many lunches at her desk, but so what?

And in the evenings, during the week, she and Doug were well past the 'when are you coming home, honey, and what would you like for dinner?' stage – an extra hour or two never even raised an eyebrow in a house where two lawyers lived.

Weekends were easy, too, when the kids were there. She'd often 'escaped' in the past, sometimes just walking round the corner to sit with a large coffee and the *Guardian* for a couple of hours, or shopping, or having lunch with Amelia . . .

But now, instead, she met Rob. She met him for lunch, after work, and on Saturdays. At first a couple of times a week, then every other day. Sometimes every day. One morning, as she applied make-up in the mirror in the bathroom, Susannah looked at herself and smiled at the recollection that this was exactly how it had felt the first time. She remembered her mum shaking her head, complaining that she was obsessed, that it was unhealthy. She was as sceptical about that diagnosis now as she had been then. This wasn't bad for her, this was good. This was doing her more good than anything had in a long time.

They never went to his house, or to hers. She never suggested he meet Douglas. She never really talked about Douglas much. And Rob didn't ask. She presumed her freedom and her availability were as eloquent a statement about the nature and state of their relationship as any she might have made.

The only days that were sacrosanct were the appointments with Amelia. She never missed one. But she didn't talk to Amelia about Rob. She didn't want to talk to anyone about it. It was her delicious, blissful secret, and she wanted to keep it.

She was having so much fun. Breathless, wide-eyed, sparkling fun. She realized it had been a long time since she had. They talked a lot, and they laughed. She felt young again. It was cold – far too cold to spend much time outside. Their London was, now, a London of museums. Warm, cheap and anonymous, they made the perfect place to meet. They tried the London Aquarium one day, but it was full of school trips, barking teachers and squealing children, and, even though it wasn't actually cold, it felt like it was. The museums were a much better bet. The National Portrait Gallery on St Martin's Place, Tate Modern on the river, The Courtauld at Somerset House, the British Museum. Sometimes they wandered, vaguely interested by an exhibit or a painting; sometimes they found a bench facing a beautiful picture or an interesting sculpture and sat there for an hour. Sometimes they just went to the coffee shop and talked over endless cups of tea that sat and grew cold. Sometimes they didn't talk that much. They looked at each other for long, lovely minutes, taking in every detail of each other's faces. Rob paid her compliments. When she dressed in the mornings, now, she looked at herself through his eyes, choosing things she thought he'd like. She caught herself choosing matching sets of underwear, pulling lacy panties and balcony bras from the back of the drawer for the first time in a long while. It made her feel pretty. He made her feel pretty.

They filled in the gaps of their missing years for each other. It had been a long time. He talked to her about all the places where he'd been posted – the Falklands, Scotland, Germany, twice to the USA, a spell back at Cranwell where he'd trained twenty years earlier.

He'd become a great skier, an accomplished horse rider, and done skydives, and bungee jumps. He'd been on every continent except Antarctica, but he wasn't ruling that out. He talked enthusiastically about everything he'd seen and done, and Susannah could have listened for hours, except that he reciprocated every question she asked, anxious not to monopolize the conversation. His physicality was exciting to her. He was a much bigger man than Douglas – broader, more muscled. She felt slight beside him. She watched his mouth while he talked, the way his full lips moved across his teeth. The smile that had always melted her still did.

One night, over a bottle of wine in a hotel bar just off Bloomsbury Square where they went sometimes after they'd trawled round the British Museum, he told her – unprompted – some of what he'd seen in the First Gulf War. The memories were extraordinarily vivid and still painful to recount. He spoke slowly, and without really looking at her. The regiment had been first responders to the scene when an American missile had been fired into a crowded shopping area, missing its more legitimate military target. They'd arrived within minutes, while survivors were still staggering out into the streets, bleeding and burning. It was the first time he'd seen dead bodies, and some of those had been women and children maimed so severely they were almost unrecognizable to the family members who scrambled hysterically through the rubble, screaming the names of loved ones and holding their heads in shock and disbelief. He said he truly believed that he and his buddies had gone into the situation boys and come out men, growing up overnight. His eyes welled with tears in the retelling, and she squeezed his hand, knowing instinctively when exactly that had been, remembering Lois's tearful voice on the phone. Hating that he hadn't been able to tell her, to talk to her then, when it had been fresh.

But sometimes, most of the time, things were much lighter and more frivolous between them. One of their quickly established routines was to fire staccato questions at each other. They'd missed so much – they both wanted to catch up.

'Favourite film?'

'*The English Patient*. You?'

'Haven't seen it. Can't stand Ralph Fiennes. *Léon.*'

'Got a thing for Natalie Portman, have we? You and the rest of the male population . . .'

'Not in that! She was just a kid . . . Now . . . in *Star Wars* . . . you're talking. Mind you, I always had a thing for Princess Leia, too. Me and the rest of the male population.'

She remembered. 'Favourite song?'

'"Stairway To Heaven". Led Zeppelin. Hands down.'

'Saddo. I knew you were going to say that. In fact, there are as yet undiscovered tribes in the heart of the Peruvian Jungle . . .' his voice joined hers as she finished the sentence and they spoke in unison, '. . . who *knew* that you were going to say that.'

It was a line from *The Young Ones*. They used to say it all the time.

Susannah clapped her hands delightedly.

'How dare you dis the Zeppelin? What's yours, come on . . . ?'

She'd been laughing, unable to think of one.

'I bet it's The Fray or Snow Patrol or Coldplay or Keane, isn't it? Come on, admit it. You're a soft rock girl, aren't you? Probably loved the Corrs, too . . .'

'Cheeky sod. U2.'

'Which one?'

'I don't know . . . any one . . . they're all brilliant. *The Joshua Tree* best album, hands down . . .' She never heard a song from that album without thinking of him. The album had come out in 1987, and had been, pretty much, the soundtrack of their time together. She remembered a night at his house, when they'd been playing it, and Frank and Lois had been out on one of their tactful walks. She'd taken her bra off before she went round, and his face, when his hands had snaked up her sweater, at the back, and realized . . . his eyelids drooping heavily with lust, his gratifying groan of desire. She remembered tingling with wanting him. She blushed. She saw on his face that he remembered, too, but he concentrated on the game.

'Half a point.' He paused, and his eyes burnt into hers. 'Bloody hell, Susannah.' Then he shook himself out of it. 'Best song on the album . . . ?'

'"One".'

'That's *Achtung Baby*.'

'Smart-arse. It's still my favourite. Still their best . . .'

He held his hand flat and waved it side to side. 'Maybe. "With Or Without You"?'

'Maybe. Favourite composer?'

'May I refer you back to my answer on Led Zeppelin?'

'Come on. I'm talking classical music now. You listen to that?'

'I'm not a total philistine, if that's what you're suggesting. I may have a bit of Mendelssohn knocking about somewhere. You? Still a Rachmaninov girl?'

She was impressed. With the Mendelssohn, and the Rachmaninov reference. Dad's favourite, she'd always loved his music. She still did.

'You're impressed, aren't you? Admit it.'

She held her hands up in surrender. 'I admit it. But then, I always was. Does your dad still play Italian opera too loud?'

Rob smiled. 'Absolutely. Rossini, Verdi and Puccini are still top of the hit parade at Mum and Dad's house.'

'Did he ever get you to like it?'

Rob shook his head vigorously. 'Not a chance. Tolerate it, maybe. Like it – never!'

When they were young, Frank would sometimes put on an aria or a chorus and translate for them as it played, standing in the living room, acting out the stories melodramatically, his voice and his face full of emotion. They were a tough crowd, she remembered. But then it had never really seemed as though he was doing it for them – he used to get lost in the tale he was retelling, his eyes half closed in pleasure or vicarious sadness.

And now, on one of their outings, wandering through the Poetry and Dream rooms at the Tate Modern, Rob slipped his hand into hers, just as he had done that first night all those years ago. It felt as exciting and as thrilling and as right as it had done then. Not just lust, though there was plenty of that still left behind. She was feeling things again that she had thought were part of her past, not her present or her future. There was affection. And memory. And trust. And there was magic. That was the only word for it, she realized. It was like a chemical reaction with a celestial effect. Magic. After that, they held hands every time they were together. Susannah told herself that's all it was, all it would be, as though telling herself would make it so.

One evening, a few weeks after Rob had come back into her life, Douglas came up behind her while she was washing an omelette pan. He snaked his arms around her waist and rested his chin on her shoulder. 'You seem happy lately.'

She closed her eyes and bit her lip, waiting for guilt to wash over her. But it didn't. There was no room in her, she realized. 'I am.'

'I'm glad.' He held her for a moment, then kissed the side of her neck and went back to the television, leaving her bracing her hands against the sink.

She realized she felt nothing physical from his touch. Rob just had to touch her fleetingly, accidentally even, and it was like his skin burnt into hers, and a sensation dropped through her thighs and into her knees, making her feel trembly. Douglas had held her and kissed her, and she'd felt nothing.

No magic.

She'd never thought before, about whether she was a good person or not. These days it was a question she asked herself quite often, and one she couldn't quite answer.

February

Susannah woke up with a start at four thirty on the morning of her fortieth birthday. For nearly an hour she lay in bed, listening to Douglas breathing in and out, and hearing the central heating crank into action, willing herself back to sleep. But her brain was too busy, and eventually she gave up, slipping her feet into her slippers and sloping down to the kitchen to make a cup of tea. She put on Radio 4 and listened to the shipping forecast while the kettle boiled.

She sat at the kitchen table and pulled her Black-Berry out of her handbag. The red light flashed. A text. It was Rob. He'd texted ten minutes earlier.

Happy Birthday. Are you celebrating?

He just remembered. She hadn't said a word.
She pushed the reply button and texted back.

Can you meet today? Call me if you're awake.

Within a minute the phone vibrated in her hand, and she answered it before it rang.
'You're up early.'
'Can't sleep. What's your excuse?'
'Twenty years of military life. Happy birthday, Susie.'

'Thank you.'

'So, how do you feel?'

How did she feel? No one else had asked her. There was all the usual fortieth birthday nonsense. Life begins. And in a way, it had.

A couple of months ago, she'd have had a different answer. A couple of months ago, she was acutely aware that the threescore years and ten were more than halfway through, and that she wasn't where she had expected to be. Where she wanted to be.

That feeling had gone, though. And he was the reason.

She had nothing to show for the feeling. She knew that. He was married to Helena. She was living with Douglas. No one knew. There was nothing to know, for God's sake. They hadn't so much as kissed. A bit of teenage hand holding, that was all. Talking. But she knew. She knew.

'I feel great. Happy.' Thanks to you, she thought.

'Good. Just checking. Didn't have you down as the type to go mad over a birthday, but you never know . . . So, the text sounded like you have time to meet, today?' He sounded tentative.

Douglas had booked a table for dinner. He'd told her a couple of days ago. He'd raised her birthday before Christmas, but she'd said then, genuinely, that she didn't want any fuss. It was no big deal, she said. He'd nodded, and said nothing more about it, until he'd mentioned the restaurant. Just the two of them, he said, at the Oxo Brasserie at Gabriel's Wharf.

'I could meet you for a drink.'

'This evening?'

'Around six?'

'Perfect.'

'I . . . I have to be somewhere, later . . .'

'I'm sure. That's fine. Of course. I didn't think you'd be able to have a drink at all.'

'I really want to see you.'

'I want to see you, too.'

Amelia rang a little later.

'Happy birthday, Suze. Welcome to your fifth decade.'

'Great. Thanks.'

'So, strip off yet, in front of the mirror? Watching everything start falling . . . ?'

'No!'

'That's what I'll be doing.' Amelia would be forty in August. 'But not for . . . oh, six whole months.'

'Please. Spare me the gloating.'

'So . . . is Douglas around?'

'He's in the shower, I think.' Susannah heard the water running.

'Okay, so you know tonight's a surprise party, right?'

'God, no,' Susannah groaned. 'Please tell me you're kidding.'

'I kid you not. It's quite sweet actually. Even if it denotes a total lack of understanding of you . . . you're

314

not a surprise party kind of a girl. Even Sam would know not to surprise you.'

'Douglas did this?'

'Yup. He's arranged everything.'

'Christ.'

'Okay, so you're going to need to work on your surprise face, clearly. I'm only on the phone and I can see the expression . . .'

'Thanks for the heads-up, Meels.'

'Like I'd let you show up at a surprise party without warning you. I figured this way you'd have time to get your hair done, and wear something sparkly . . .'

'Don't know about that. But thanks anyway. You'll be there?'

'Me and the wig. Jonathan's coming with me.'

Susannah let that pass. She didn't really know what the state of play was, and she didn't ask. 'Who else will be there? Do you know?'

'Well, I didn't write the guest list, obviously, but I think there are going to be about thirty people. Something like that. Al and Kathryn, Alex and Chloe, your mum and dad . . .'

'Mum and Dad!'

'Yes – amazing, huh? I was shocked, too. Your mum and dad . . . and, you know, the usual suspects. Some from work . . . you know . . .'

'Bloody hell.'

'Okay. Still not quite there with the attitude.'

'I just don't want it, Meels.'

'I know. I'd have tried to tell him that, if he'd asked me before he arranged it all, but he didn't. He only called when it was all sorted.'

She'd taken the day off, and resisted the attempts of several people, including Douglas and Amelia, to meet for lunch. She'd have met Rob, but she knew he had a full day of meetings. She took her breakfast back to bed and watched *This Morning*, opened her cards and read magazines. With Amelia's words ringing in her ears, she stripped off in front of the bathroom mirror to see whether gravity had sped up overnight, decided that it wasn't any worse today than it had been yesterday, and lolled in a deep fragrant bubble bath for an hour. Then she spent the rest of the afternoon getting ready to go out. She told herself she wanted to look her best for the surprise party that was no longer a surprise, but it was her drink beforehand with Rob that she was thinking about. She had her hair blown into smooth waves at the salon round the corner, and her finger and toenails painted at the new nail place that had opened up a few doors down. She put on a new black shift dress she'd bought in the sales, with crystals sewn into the neckline, and high heels with a diamanté toe, and ordered a minicab to take her to the bar where Rob had asked her to meet him, rather than walk to the underground station. She figured she deserved it today.

He stood up as she walked towards him, looking gratifyingly impressed. He was dressed up, too, and she was touched. When she reached him, he took both her hands in his own. 'You look unbelievably beautiful, Susie.'

Wow. 'You don't look so bad yourself.' She knew they were grinning at each other, but she didn't care.

There was a bottle of champagne on the small table, and two tall flutes.

He poured two glasses, and, handing one to her, raised his own in a toast. 'Happy Birthday, Susie.' He pulled a small brown cardboard box out of his jacket pocket. 'I got you something.'

'Thank you. This is so nice. All of it. I feel spoilt.' Susannah took the box, and kissed him on the cheek. 'You didn't need to. Really.'

'I know. I wanted to. Spoil you a bit.'

'What is it?'

He laughed. 'It's not a car. Open it. Find out.'

Susannah took the lid off the box. On a bed of crumpled white tissue paper lay a locket. She recognized it straight away. It was the little rose gold locket he'd given her for her eighteenth birthday. She'd left it in his room at Cranwell after the strange, uncomfortable evening at his graduation ball – and she'd never asked to have it back.

He'd kept it all these years.

Her eyes were full of tears when she looked up at him. 'You kept it? I can't believe you did that.'

He smiled. 'Cost me a lot of money, you know.'

She laughed, but what she wanted to do was cry.

Looking back down at the small piece of jewellery, she ran her fingernail down the edge and eased the locket open. The photograph was the same. Their faces stared up at her, frozen in time, in a smile of joy. She remembered exactly how that had felt.

'I can't believe you kept it.'

She stayed too long, in the bar with Rob. Time passed too fast. In the end, it was Rob who reminded her she was supposed to be somewhere else. She looked at her watch. It was 7.25 p.m. She was supposed to be at the restaurant in five minutes, and it would take at least fifteen, she reckoned. She had to get across the river. Susannah didn't want to go.

'D'you want to come with me?' She wasn't entirely serious. 'It's a surprise party.'

'Aren't you supposed to be surprised by a surprise party?' Rob was smiling.

'Amelia told me. She knew I'd hate walking in without warning.'

'Good for Amelia. So . . . if I came with you, I'd be the surprise, would I . . . ?'

'Yeah. You certainly would!'

'I think I'll let you go alone, if that's okay with you.'

Susannah shrugged exaggeratedly. 'Party pooper.'

'Don't want to share you, that's all.' His face was suddenly serious, and she knew exactly what he meant.

He walked her to the front of the bar and helped her into her coat. Outside on the street it was freezing.

He put his hand out to hail her a taxi. Their breath came in puffs of white. Pulling the collar close around her ears, he held on to the lapels, and pulled her towards him to kiss her once on the lips, but when he moved away, he didn't get more than a few inches from her face. Their eyes were wide open. The next kiss was inevitable, although it took a few long seconds for him to move back in. His lips touched her mouth again, but this time he couldn't break the contact. He couldn't keep the kiss a kiss between friends – there was much, much more in it. And she didn't want him to, not any more.

If the black cab hadn't pulled up at that moment, she would never have left.

Fifteen minutes later, as she emerged from the lift on to the top floor of the building, it wasn't hard to act surprised when she walked into the private room. She was in a kind of shock from Rob's kiss, all the way to the Oxo Tower. She felt wired, and alive, and startled, and it had nothing to do with her friends and family applauding and whooping at her.

Amelia had one of her new wigs on. It was an Anna Wintour-esque sharp brunette bob, and it made her look fierce. Or maybe that was just the expression on her face. 'Where've you been? I've tried calling you.'

'Sorry.' Susannah waved her narrow clutch bag. 'No room for a phone.'

'So, where were you?'

'I'm not that late, am I?'

'I suppose not,' Amelia grudgingly agreed, but she still eyed her friend suspiciously.

The trouble with having a friend like Amelia, someone who'd known you so well for so long, was that lying to them, even by omission, became very difficult after a certain point. Amelia knew something was up, but she didn't know what, and it was driving her crazy. Not knowing, but also not being trusted. It worked both ways, though – Susannah knew exactly how to distract her.

'Loving the wig. Very scary editor of *Vogue*.'

'Do you think?' Amelia preened a little.

'I do.'

'You look gorgeous. New dress . . . ?'

'New dress.' Susannah twirled a little. As she swung round, she saw Jonathan watching them from across the room where he was half engaged in a conversation with Susannah's dad. He was smiling, and when he caught her eye, he winked.

'How's J?'

'He's home. Not now, obviously. Now he's over there, talking to your father. But he's come home.'

Susannah threw her arms around Amelia, who put one hand on her head. 'Watch the wig, will you?'

'Oh, thank God. I'm so glad. So, so glad, Meels.' She was crying – sudden, happy-sad tears.

Amelia smiled, mystified. 'Me, too. What's with the waterworks?'

'Ignore me. I'm a bit emotional this evening, that's all. When did this happen? Tell me, tell me . . .'

'This week. I sat the kids down and told them I was thinking about asking him to come home, permanently. Asked them for their vote.'

'Let me guess how that went?'

'Unanimous, actually.'

'*Quelle surprise.*'

'Elizabeth did surprise me, actually. She asked me if I was sure it was because of her dad, not because of the cancer.'

'Smart girl that one.'

'Like her Auntie Susannah.'

'And are you? You weren't sure, at New Year.'

Amelia was looking across the room at him, and Susannah knew the answer from the expression on her face.

'Okay. Enough, you two . . .' Jonathan was walking over to them, with the same inane grin Amelia was wearing and his hand cupping one ear. 'My ears are more than burning.' He put a casual arm around both their shoulders. 'What's she saying about me, Suze?'

'She's just telling me that everything is back as it should be.'

'Except my hair.' Amelia straightened the wig unnecessarily.

Jonathan reached out and stroked her cheek, and she caught his hand and brought it to her mouth, kissing it, her eyes never leaving his.

'And that'll be next. I'm really happy for you two. This is a good thing. Thank God.'

Susannah's mum and dad were there, and Alastair, with a glamorous and smiling Kathryn – who told her excitedly that they were celebrating Valentine's Day late, having left the kids with her mum and booked a night in the Covent Garden Hotel, where they'd stayed the night they got married, before they flew off on their honeymoon. Alexander and Chloe were there, too, her normally washboard tummy beginning to swell slightly beneath a definitely bigger cleavage. The rest of the list, she guessed, had been cobbled together by Doug with Megan's help – a somewhat bizarre smattering of colleagues and friends as old as their relationship, most of her university friends having failed to make the transition from her marriage to Sean to this new partnership. It was hard to concentrate on everyone else and their jovial party small talk – her mind was so much preoccupied with Rob, and what had just happened between them. She couldn't believe everyone couldn't tell, just by looking at her. She felt as if her cheeks were pink. She was officially hot and bothered. She wondered briefly where the kids were – why Doug hadn't brought them. She'd barely spoken to him – he'd greeted her with a kiss when she first came in but the two of them had been absorbed by the guests, at either end of the long space, and she hadn't had a chance to ask him. She supposed

Rosie and Fin wouldn't have been interested, but Daisy might have loved this – a smart adult London party. If she'd known, if she'd had a hand in organizing everything, she would have included her. And let her bring Seth. She'd worked out, lately, that the more you treated Daisy like a grown-up, the more like a grown-up Daisy behaved. Not rocket science, Susannah knew, but a lesson Doug had apparently yet to learn.

Doug now tapped a fork against his glass to call the room to order. God, Susannah thought, he's going to make a speech. It seemed profoundly un-Douglas-like. She tried to insinuate herself into the crowd, as though that would help, but miraculously people evaporated so she was alone, centre stage.

'Sorry to interrupt, everyone. Come here, will you, Susannah?'

He held out his hand to her, and she went across the room and took it. He pulled her to stand alongside him.

'We're all here, as you know, to help celebrate a certain, significant birthday with Susannah. One that ends with a zero, and that's all I'm saying.'

A ripple of polite laughter went round the room.

'She's still a way behind me, so I'm not sure why the need for all the discretion, but I understand that's what ladies like.'

She'd never said that. She tried not to squirm. This wasn't her style. She didn't like being the centre of attention – she never really had. And tonight, she felt like a fraud, standing beside him. She hoped he would be quick.

'But that's not the only reason I decided to get everyone together this evening.'

Amelia raised an eyebrow at Susannah in a silent question. Susannah shrugged, and smiled weakly. She had no idea where this was going. At least – and she was almost queasy now – she hoped she didn't . . .

'As you know, Susannah has shared my life for almost ten years now. That's quite an apprenticeship. And lately I've been thinking that it's about time the two of us made it official. What better night than tonight for me to ask her, in front of all her family and friends, to marry me, and be my wife?'

Susannah had never fainted. She didn't really believe in it – it seemed so Southern Belle, to swoon at such a time. But she actually thought she might now. She couldn't believe what she was hearing. Could there, in fact, be a worse night? She could still feel the imprint of Rob's lips on hers. She could smell him on her.

What the hell was Doug playing at? This had come from a million trillion miles away, and it had just hit her full force. The very idea couldn't have been further from her mind, her imagination or her dreams, and he had given no indication, in recent days or weeks, that it was anywhere near his either. It didn't make sense. They hadn't been getting on. Things were rocky. Things were uncertain. Why would he do this to her now?

In front of all these people.

Susannah was vaguely surprised to discover that anger was rising like bile in her throat. How dare he put her in this position? This proposal was a proverbial finger in the dyke. A single grand gesture when a hundred small and simple ones were missing from their everyday lives.

She realized that it was silent in the room. She looked at everyone's expression, and it seemed to her, for a moment, that she was looking through a kaleidoscope – the faces swam and floated in front of her eyes. She focused in on Amelia, her face full of concern. She was clearly horrified at what he'd done. Susannah was glad she wasn't the only one.

'So . . . Susannah . . .' Douglas was prompting her.

'I'm . . . I mean . . . wow . . . wow.' She could feel her cheeks redden.

'Is that a yes?'

This was excruciating. Of course it bloody wasn't. How could she say no in front of all these people? But how could she say yes, when she didn't mean it?

Just when it began to become unbearable, to be standing there and saying nothing with everyone's eyes on her, Amelia, wig swinging, stepped into the middle of the room, her glass held aloft. 'Okay, everyone. Let's let them have their moment, shall we? Talk among yourselves. Give them a sec.'

Jonathan stepped in, right behind her, turning to the people on his left. And then her dad, holding her mum's hand. And Alastair, full of vocal bonhomie. All moving into the empty space and making more noise than was natural. All rescuing her from this untenable moment. The two of them were absorbed into the room again. She'd never been so grateful to anyone for anything.

But he was still here. Still looking at her expectantly.

'Doug. You really sprang this on me.'

'I wanted to do something romantic.' He looked, just for a second, like a petulant child.

'Do you think this was the right place, the right moment?'

He shrugged. 'I thought it would be.'

'Really? Really?' She reached for his hand.

He pulled away.

Susannah felt people's eyes on them. 'Can we do this later? At home? When it's just the two of us. Wouldn't that be better?'

'It's a simple enough question, Susannah.'

And it was a simple enough answer, she realized. It was going to be a no. She just didn't want to give it to him here and now.

'Do you really think this is the right thing for us right now?'

His eyes were cold. 'I don't know. I thought so. Clearly you don't.'

'Not here, Doug. Please,' she implored him.

'Okay.' He held up two palms in surrender. 'Okay, then. Not here. We'll talk, later.'

She nodded.

'Happy Birthday, Susannah.' His voice was hard, and angry.

She bit back her own rage. He had no right to be angry with her.

Did he?

As soon as she could, she walked as casually as she was able to manage towards the Ladies. Amelia followed her. Fortunately there was no one else there.

Amelia pulled her into a cubicle, locking the door behind the two of them, put the seat of the toilet down, and pushed Susannah down on to it. 'Are you okay?'

Susannah pushed an index finger into the corner of each of her eyes, shaking her head. 'Not really. Is everyone out there gossiping about us?'

'Yup. Wouldn't you be? Jonathan and Alastair are doing their best to change the subject all over the place. But most people know if you don't say yes straight away, you ain't ever saying it. But most people, I'm guessing, also think it was pretty daft of him to ask you like that. Who are they, anyway? I don't know half of them. But what an idiot! What on earth possessed him? Did you have any idea that was coming?'

'None.' She shook her head. 'If I'd had the slightest inkling, I'd have headed him off at the pass. The truth is, Meels, I don't think we've ever been further away from it than we are right now.'

'Which begs the question . . .'

She smiled. 'Why did he do it?'

Amelia shook her head. 'No. What are you still doing there?'

It was almost midnight before everyone left. Her mum had squeezed her tight when she said goodbye. 'A birthday and a proposal, all in one night, hey?'

Susannah knew her mum wanted to know what she was going to say, but she couldn't talk to her about it now. She thought something in her dad's face expressed his reservations, but he said nothing, just kissing her gently on the cheek. 'Happy Birthday, my little girl.'

Kathryn and Alastair had left an hour or so earlier – Kathryn was desperate, it seemed, to get to her mini second honeymoon. Susannah was glad she didn't have to deal with Alastair's perceptive comments and pointed questions. She didn't have the energy. And anyway, she had Doug to deal with. She was glad, now, that he hadn't brought the kids.

Doug didn't speak much in the cab until they were about halfway home. Then he spoke, but he wasn't looking at her – he stared out of the window at the lights flashing by, with his arms folded. 'I hadn't planned that. The proposal part. It was "spontaneous", in fact.' He laughed, but it was a small, choked laugh with no humour in it.

She didn't know whether that made it better or worse. She thought of Rob's 'not exactly planned' wedding to Helena. What was everyone thinking? Spontaneity seemed like a dreadful idea to her right now.

'What made you do it?'

He snorted gently. 'Hmm. Beginning to wonder now.' He didn't sound mad any more. He sounded sad, and tired.

She didn't know what to say.

A minute, maybe two, later, he spoke again.

'I thought it would make you happy, Susannah. I thought it might be what you wanted. You know — what was missing. You've seemed happier lately. So, I told myself that you still loved me. That maybe just this was missing. That this would fix things.'

'So, you think things need fixing?'

Now he looked at her, his eyebrows knitted. 'Of course. I'm not stupid, Susannah. Slower than you, maybe. A bit more ostrich-like. But not entirely clueless.'

Except that he had no clue about her.

'You're so quiet.'

'I don't know what to say, Doug. You took me completely by surprise.'

'I know. I shouldn't have done it. I see that. It was stupid to do it in front of everyone. Unfair. I'm sorry.'

She reached out a hand, and he took it.

'You don't have to be sorry.'

His face had diffused her anger — his face and her guilty conscience, and her profound desire not to have this conversation now.

He smiled a weak smile, his lips pressed together. 'So. Will you think about it?'

And she lied to him. Not for the first time. She'd

lied about where she was – the night Al had come round. Was she getting good at this? She nodded her head. 'I'll think about it.'

He wanted to make love when they got home. She had washed and moisturized her face carefully, and brushed her teeth, staying in the bathroom for longer than she needed to, but he was still awake when she slid into bed beside him. He turned on to his side and began to kiss her shoulder, pulling gently on the satin strap of her nightdress, sliding his hand in at the side to gently stroke her breast. It was always how he started.

She couldn't do it. Just as gently, she put her own hand on his and stopped him without words, rolling over so her back was to him, feeling suddenly sad as she felt his stiffness against her subside, and his breathing slow.

In the morning, Douglas had gone before she was awake. She'd forgotten he had a business trip to Paris – some big merger was happening, and he'd be gone a few days. She felt bad that she hadn't woken up before he left – said something to clear the air. She didn't know what. He hadn't left a note.

But Rob had left a text on her phone.

I can't stop thinking about you. Call me when you can.

March

Walking through the doors of the hospital had, by now, become a horribly familiar routine for both of them. Coffees, magazines, drips – the sights and smells of the place. Susannah dreaded it. It had to be a hundred times worse for Amelia. She was really tired now. She'd lost even more weight and teetered on the edge of being emaciated. Her hair was all gone and, on days like today, she eschewed the wig, tying a brightly coloured scarf around her head. Her mother had arrived, just after the first session of chemotherapy, with a stack of the iconic shallow orange boxes from Hermès which contained her collection of silk twill scarves – Amelia's father had given her one every Christmas from the year he could afford such a luxury until the year before he left her, although she always seemed to have known, or guessed, that he sent his secretaries out in their lunch hours to buy them, and she hadn't worn one since he'd gone. The vivid hues of the scarf made her pale skin seem even more pallid. Her lips were dry and beginning to crack. She looked as ill as she had ever done throughout the whole process, and Susannah wondered if she could take another month or two of this. She had always known chemotherapy worked, in an almost medieval, crude way, by killing everything along with the cancer, erasing you slowly, until it almost killed you. Today, Amelia looked exactly like that. And Susannah ached for her, as she had done every day like this one since the diagnosis.

But, by God, she was crabby, too. Susannah wondered whether Jonathan was regretting moving back home. He had once, famously, said – after she'd asked him to leave – of loving Amelia that it was like eating raw cake mix. You loved it and you kept eating it, even though you knew it was going to give you stomach ache.

Today, Susannah thought of that and smiled. Displaying the kind of short, rude grumpiness that only an old best friend could tolerate, Amelia had griped and moaned through the journey to the hospital, complained about the wait, and was now sitting in the high-backed chair with a face like thunder.

Susannah instinctively knew it wasn't a good day to talk about Rob, although she needed to talk about him – and if not to Amelia, she didn't know who else – but it seemed that Rob was the first, and only, item on Amelia's time-killing agenda.

She'd been afraid to see him, after the kiss on her birthday. She'd texted him back. She'd typed an excuse at first – a fabricated business trip – then pushed the erase button and started again. She needed some time, she said. At least a few days.

> **I'm a bit afraid of what will happen when we see each other again. We've taken the lid off Pandora's box, Rob.**

His reply came back within a minute or two.

Nothing will happen that you don't want to happen. I want to be near you, Susie. Your terms. Entirely.

'You're seeing him, aren't you?'

Susannah shrugged. 'I've seen him. We've had a drink. We've talked.'

'More than once?'

She nodded. 'A few times.' How many hours was it? If you laid them end to end, how far would they reach?

'That's where you were the other night, isn't it? When you were late for your party?'

'Yes. And I wasn't late. So?'

'So?' Amelia raised her eyebrows.

'Yes. So, what? Can't we be friends?'

'And is that what you are? Is that all you are?'

Susannah thought about the kiss.

'Exactly.' Amelia interpreted her brief silence with pinpoint accuracy. 'Has he met Doug? Does Doug know you're seeing him?'

Susannah shook her head.

'Well, God knows I never thought I'd feel sorry for Doug, but I think I'm starting to. He asked you to marry him, and you'd been in the pub with your boyfriend.'

'It isn't like that.'

333

'What is it like, then? Make me understand. Explain it to me.'

'Stop being so aggressive. I can't talk to you when you're like this.'

Amelia sniffed. But when she spoke again, her tone was softer, and her eyes were more wide and imploring than narrow and accusatory. 'What are you doing, Suze? What do you think you're playing at? This isn't right, and you know it. You wouldn't be being so damn secretive, sneaking around everywhere, lying, if you didn't know it was wrong.'

'Why is it so wrong, Meels? We aren't doing anything wrong.'

That wasn't true. And Amelia knew it as well as she did.

'Oh, don't give me that crap,' she spat at her – so, imploring wasn't going to last. She smiled sarcastically. 'Really. You should know me well enough by now to know that I'm not going to buy it. You're forty years old. We're not kids any more. Of course it's wrong. Wake up, will you? He is married to someone else. He's another woman's husband, Susannah. Just because she's umpteen thousand miles away doesn't mean she doesn't exist, doesn't mean she isn't real. Whether you want to pretend that's the case or not. And just because you're not sleeping with him doesn't mean it isn't wrong. And if you don't think that's just a matter of time, then you're even more gone than I thought you were. And don't tell yourself that it's not you doing it to her. Because it is – it is both of you.'

'I'm not pretending anything, believe me.'

'Really? What would you call it? Because I'd call it pathetic, I think.'

'I really don't think you're in any position to preach to me about right and wrong, Amelia.'

'Someone has to. Might as well be me.'

'Well, not you. Not today. Not now. Okay? Don't you dare judge me. You've got no idea what my life has been like. What it's like now he is back in it.'

'I can't believe you're saying that to me. No idea? I've known you for thirty years, Suze. Thirty years. I've watched you make mistakes – big ones – Rob, Sean, Douglas. And I've never interfered, have I? But you've got to stop painting yourself as some kind of victim. You're a volunteer. You're making victims of everyone else.'

'Who? Who am I making a victim of?'

'Douglas, for a start.'

'You don't even like Douglas.'

'What's that got to do with it? Doesn't matter if I like him or not. I don't think anyone deserves to be cheated on, Susannah. Not just Douglas. Rob's wife.'

'I'm not cheating.'

Susannah's voice had risen higher now, and other patients on the ward were starting to listen. A nurse had stopped a few feet away, pretending to check something, but riveted by the quarrel.

Amelia's voice was lower, a hiss. 'Don't fool yourself, Suze. You will. You will. Don't expect me to condone what you're doing. Don't expect me to wait around to pick up the pieces when it all falls apart.'

Susannah stood up, her knees shaking. 'I can't stay here and listen to this any more.'

Amelia sat back in her chair, a stubborn expression settling on her features. 'So, go.'

Bluff called, Susannah wavered. This was a chemotherapy ward. Poison was coursing this very moment from a drip in her best, oldest friend's arm into her veins, beginning its sickening, destructive journey around her body. She'd promised she'd be here.

'Go. I don't want you here. I don't want to look at you right now. I don't even know you.'

Amelia left her no choice.

She turned and walked away before she started to cry.

Before she was out of earshot, she heard Amelia's voice. 'Your life has been what you've let it be, Susannah.'

April

She couldn't eat and she couldn't sleep. She couldn't concentrate. She could barely talk. She needed to be somewhere else. Her anxiety focused on a triptych now, not just two men. She'd never fought like this with Amelia. She hated it.

When she ran away, Susannah left both of the men in her life a note. Douglas's was written on a sheet of paper she pulled from the printer at the computer in the dining room.

I've gone away by myself for a few days. Sorry to be dramatic, but I need to think, and I can't do that while I'm here with you. Please leave me alone while I do this.

Susannah

Rob's was a text to his phone.

Dear Rob - I don't think I can do this. I'm so confused. Everything is wrong. I need to clear my head. I'll call you when I get back. Susie

It took Susannah a moment to realize where she was when she woke up to bright sunshine. London had been grey and chilly – classic spring weather – but it was instantly different here. It had been very late, and pitch black outside, when she'd arrived last night. The easyJet plane had been late – no surprise – and it had taken a frustratingly long time to pick up the hire car she'd pre-booked online at a surprisingly crowded Toulouse Airport. She wasn't the only escaping English person in town, it seemed. Mum's idiosyncratic directions (heavy on local landmarks, but light on road numbers, and almost totally devoid of left and right, this not being Mum's strong suit) from the airport to the house had required all her concentration – easier said than done while driving on the opposite side of the road in a left-hand-drive car on unfamiliar French roads in the dark. She'd been too tired when she arrived to do anything except drink a large glass of water, pull off her jeans, and fall into bed.

It was such a relief, this morning, to be here. Alone. And far away. She'd never actually been here before, though she'd sat through a thousand photographs of her parents here. But all around her were familiar objects – Mum and Dad had furnished the barn with pieces from the family home, and she recognized pictures and photographs, as well as the big bed she had just slept in, from her childhood home. The walls were painted her mum's favourite shade of yellow – finally at home here in the sunny South of France. Anxious to be outside, she put on her jeans – still crumpled on the floor from last night – and pushed her feet into a pair of wellington boots she saw near the door, grabbing a fleece from a hook, and went to explore. Mum and Dad's home was a small barn conversion on an old farm in a tiny hamlet a few miles outside the town of Samatan. Nearby were a renovated farmhouse and a little cottage – also owned, she knew from Mum, by English people. There hadn't been any lights on when she'd arrived last night, and she rather hoped they were unoccupied right now – she wanted total seclusion, not neighbours, however friendly they might be. The barn had perhaps an acre of ground – a gravel area immediately adjacent to the house, and then a gently sloping lawn with some shrubbery and a few established trees. An old wooden fence separated the property from fields that ran as far as the eye could see. She knew from Mum that they were sunflower fields and that in a couple of months they'd be a mass of the tall, iconic yellow flowers. In the far distance, all along the horizon line, she could see the snow-capped Pyrenees. And beyond that, a cloudless, cobalt-blue sky.

She had no idea what time it was, but the sun was already warm. She took the fleece off and tied it around her waist, then walked down as far as the fence, revelling in the silence. She could almost feel her thoughts slowing down, untangling themselves, with each fall of her foot on the grass.

Things had become so messy. Douglas and the kids, and Rob.

And Amelia.

The fight with her best friend disturbed her more than she might have expected. It was like everything Meels had said had held up a mirror to her very soul – she was right. With Amelia she couldn't hide and she couldn't lie. Amelia had a treatment today. It would be the first one she wasn't around for, and she felt lousy to be missing it. Amelia had made it pretty clear, the last time they'd seen each other, that she wasn't flavour of the month, but Susannah knew she'd still expect her to show up as usual. She hadn't even been brave enough to call Amelia and let her know she wouldn't be there. She'd texted Jonathan.

> **Running away. Expect you know why. Such a bloody mess. Sorry. Will you tell Amelia? And go with her to Tuesday's appointment?**

He'd replied almost straight away.

> **She told me. Don't worry - she'll calm down. I'll go with her. Breathe, Susannah. Relax. It'll be okay. We love you. J**

Susannah wished she was as sure as he was that everything would work out. She and Amelia had disagreed before. Loads of times. Theirs was not a relationship based on seeing everything exactly the same way. She wouldn't have wanted a best friend like that. They'd fallen out before, too. About small things – like cleaning out the refrigerator, when they lived together. And big things – like Alastair, all those years ago, and about Amelia leaving Jonathan.

This felt worse than all of those times. She was afraid there might not be a way back to the way they had always been.

Right now, though, Amelia was just one of the things in her life that she felt frightened about and uncertain of. Everything was shifting. This was too hard.

She'd called home the day before she'd come out here. She didn't even really know why, but she suspected that she wanted to hear the voice of unconditional love. She wouldn't tell them what was going on – she couldn't. But she'd hear their voices. Dad had answered. Mum was out, he said, at St Gabriel's. It was Saturday, and there was a wedding later that day. Normally he asked her how she was, and then passed the phone straight to Susannah's mother. This time, hearing his familiar, calm voice, she started to cry softly into the receiver.

'What's wrong sweetheart?' Her dad sounded alarmed.

She sighed. 'Everything.'

'Ah . . .'

She'd run away from home one summer afternoon, when she was about twelve, over some long-forgotten and probably imagined injustice. She'd taken her bike, flouncing out of the kitchen door dramatically with some spare clothes stuffed in her green Army Surplus shoulder bag, throwing a mouthful of vitriol back at her mum. Dad had just been pulling into the driveway after work, but she'd ignored him pointedly, and pedalled off furiously. Just round the corner, she never knew how or why, she came off the bike spectacularly, flying over the handlebars and landing on the road a few feet in front. She'd cut her head, an angry inch-long gash just above the right eyebrow, and grazed her elbows and knees. One knee was particularly bad – black grit from the road was embedded in the streaks of blood, and it stung badly. She'd been stunned, embarrassed and hurt, and she'd sat where she landed, too shaky to stand up, crying hot angry tears, and letting the blood run unchecked in rivulets down her arms and legs. She tasted it, too, trickling down her cheek into the corner of her mouth from the cut on her face.

Dad had come round the corner five minutes later, before anyone else saw her. He was still wearing his suit, but he'd picked her up and moved her to the side of the road. She'd bled on his white shirt and blue tie, where he held her. They sat there for a while, on the pavement, with her snivelling and relating her tale of woe, while he dabbed at her wounds with his red spotted handkerchief. All she'd wanted, she remembered, was to be listened to, to be understood. Right then, and even sometimes now, it had seemed as if Mum didn't listen often, or well. And didn't understand, when she did listen. That afternoon, it felt like Dad did.

After a few minutes, he helped her back to the house, and she sat on the low brick wall outside the back door while he went in and spoke to her mum. Mum had come out then, with her striped apron still tied around her, and taken her inside. She never knew what he'd said to her, but she wasn't told off that day.

And now it had been his idea that she should go to the house in France. There was no one there, he said. Within ten minutes he'd found a flight on the internet.

'Perfect place for thinking, if that's what you need to do, darling. Always clears my head.'

She wondered what he needed to clear his head of.

He took control, once she'd agreed, just as he'd done when she was a child. She remembered that problem solving had always been his thing. Two hours after she made the phone call, they met at a service station and drank a cup of coffee together at a melamine table.

'Does Mum know?'

He nodded.

She felt so pathetic.

He put his hand on hers. 'We're both worried about you, love. You don't have to tell me, Susannah. I think I might already know. So far as I'm aware, no one gets this emotional over work, so it doesn't take a genius to guess it's trouble at home.'

She looked down at her hands.

'And I hate to see you so unhappy. After you called me, while I was driving here, I was trying to remember the last time I saw you really happy. Saw you with the sparkle in your eye that you always had when you were a little girl. It frightened me when I couldn't remember. That's a rotten realization for a parent to come to. Makes you feel guilty, because you haven't seen it before, and makes you feel unutterably sad, because it's all you really want – for your kids to be happy.'

'I'm sorry, Dad.'

'That's a ridiculous thing to say, silly girl – don't do that.' He squeezed her fingers tightly. 'You mustn't be sorry. You must be happy. That's what matters. Go to the house. Stay. Stay as long as you want. Figure out what it's going to take to make you happy. Then come home and do it.'

'You make it sound so simple.'

'And it can be. You young people always make it so damn complicated.'

'What if making yourself happy makes other people unhappy, Dad?'

He stared out at the car park for a moment, as though he was thinking. When he looked back at her, he smiled gently. 'What if not being happy yourself makes it impossible to make anyone else happy?'

'That isn't an answer.'

'I haven't got all the answers, sweetheart – just the keys.' He pulled a red key fob out of his jacket pocket and laid it on the table beside their hands.

Susannah looked at the dry skin, the age spots across his knuckles.

'I'm just a parent. Life isn't black and white, Susannah. It's grey – a million shades of grey. But it seems to me that if you're going to get anywhere, you have to answer my question to you first, before any of the others.'

She leant down and kissed the top of his hand.

*

For the first day or two, she just slept. She couldn't believe how tired she was. The moment she relaxed, and forced herself to release the tension she'd been carrying in her neck and her shoulders, the exhaustion set in. She woke up late, walked in the garden, drank tea on the terrace, and then just went back to bed. The sun was setting before she woke up again. She didn't know it was possible to sleep for so long.

On the second morning, fighting the urge to curl up again after she woke up at eleven, she made herself shower and dress, throwing back the sheets on her bed, and opening the windows wide to air the room. She wanted to do something. She opened the neat blue binder Mum kept on top of the refrigerator, full of information for guests about shops, restaurants and things to do locally, and read about the nearest town, deciding that, after lunch, she'd go.

It was evidently market day in the town of Samatan. It took her ages to find a place to park. People were milling around, chatting and shopping. The whole square was taken up with market stalls. She used her schoolgirl French and an eager smile to buy some fruit and vegetables at one stall, and then some extraordinarily pungent cheese and plump dark olives at another. It wasn't fair that people said the French were unfriendly and uncooperative, she decided. That was Paris, maybe. Here, they listened to her strangle their beautiful language and did their best to give her what she thought she'd asked for. Her parents used the big

Leclerc supermarket nearby to stock up, and there was enough in the store cupboards to keep her going – this was just playing at shopping, and it was fun, she realized. The anonymity was comforting. She felt like Juliette Binoche – if Juliette Binoche couldn't really speak French. She wandered around, wondering if she blended in. The large corrugated-iron warehouse at one end of the car park was full of livestock. There were sheep and cows and pigs and chickens. Children played with them, poking their fingers through the cages and chattering happily. The noise and the smell were almost overwhelming. One man in a peaked cap had some small rabbits she really hoped weren't supposed to be eaten, and another had a litter of chocolate-brown Labrador pups. She stood and watched them wrestle and roll. He passed her one, when he saw her looking at them, and she held the tiny creature for a few minutes. He nuzzled into her hand, and curled along the crook of her arm. The farmer said something to her that she didn't understand, so she handed the puppy back, smiling apologetically and bowing, for some reason.

It was late afternoon as Susannah pulled into the driveway, and the sun shone, low and strong, in her eyes as she made the right turn off the road and swung her car into the gravel driveway. She shoved her foot down hard on the brake when she realized there was another car where hers had been parked earlier – a red Fiat with English plates. Someone must have come

346

to open up one of the other two properties. Susannah felt a flicker of resentment – she wished they hadn't come, and she wondered why the hell they'd had to park outside the barn. It must be someone who wasn't familiar with the place.

She climbed out, and took her string shopping bags out of the boot of the car, trying not to mind. It had been a good afternoon. She'd forgotten everything for just a while.

And then she saw him.

He'd walked down to the fence where she'd stood on her first morning here. His hands were in his pockets as he watched her and he looked, for a moment, like a nervous little boy. He was lit from behind and so she couldn't see his face, but she recognized instantly the shape and the demeanour of the man with whom she was, once more, crazily, amazingly in love.

She took the first few steps in his direction in slow motion, held back by a hundred questions. But then she dropped the bags she was holding, and ran at full pelt towards him, her heart racing. He took his hands out of his pockets and held his arms out to catch her as she launched herself headlong at him. They stood, for the longest time, still in each other's arms in the late afternoon sunshine, holding tight.

She'd never been so aware of the physicality of another human being in her life. Every one of her senses was full of him – how he felt in her arms, how he smelt.

He put his forehead against hers, and for a heart-stopping moment, their eyes inches apart, they felt their breath mingle, their noses fitting together. The first touch of his mouth on hers was so gentle it almost tickled her lips. The tiny kisses he planted grew firmer and stronger, and then they were finally kissing hard, breathless and full of longing.

First kisses. He'd been the first boy to kiss her. All those years ago. And now this was another first kiss, every bit as extraordinary, twice as meaningful. She kissed him back with all that she was.

Eventually, she pulled back to look at his face. He hadn't shaved, and for the first time she saw that his beard was flecked with grey. He looked exhausted.

'How?' She couldn't believe that he was here.

Rob shrugged. 'Your dad. I practically begged him to tell me where you were. I promised him I wouldn't upset you – he wouldn't tell me until I promised him that. I said I just had to find out that you were okay. I know you asked me to leave you alone, Susie, but I couldn't.

'Then I just drove. I took a ferry last night, and then I just drove straight through.'

More than once, he'd asked himself what the hell he was doing. He'd never in his life felt so conflicted. Never liked himself less, never felt so alive. He wondered what he would do if Helena wasn't far away. He hadn't had to tell lies to do this. They'd spoken on the phone the day before. It would be a few days before they would again. He hadn't had to explain an absence or make up a story. Her absence gave him freedom. Would he have told lies? Would he have invented fishing buddies or some conference?

He was afraid that at this moment there wasn't a thing he wouldn't do to be with Susannah. And it was the power of his feelings that terrified him.

More than once, on the drive to Dover, once his car was locked into the lines for the ferry, when he wound down the window and told the customs guy what the purpose of his trip was, and when he stood on the deck of the ferry among the school kids, the chilly wind making his ears ache, he wondered what the devil he was playing at.

He wasn't the type. To lie and cheat. He'd grown up with two parents who'd loved each other long and well. He'd loved with an open heart. He'd waited, waited a long time, to meet and marry Helena. He'd never even come close before. He'd married her believing she was right for him, and he for her, and that they'd be happy together, for ever, like Frank and Lois. He'd meant every word he'd ever said to her, and he was horrified by the idea that might change.

He hadn't spent every day of the last however many years dreaming of Susannah, any more than she had of him. He wasn't sure how to explain it, even to himself, and he knew he wouldn't be able to articulate it. But he couldn't resist it, God help him.

349

He didn't even know what he expected to happen when he got there. He hadn't rehearsed any scene in his mind. No speech. No gesture. He just knew that when he saw her, running towards him across the grass, a girl again, her face incredulously happy to see him, the sunlight turning everything around her into an orange aura, he felt a surge of joy that nothing in his life up until that point had ever produced, and in the moment when he felt it, he couldn't apologize for it.

'You're crazy.'

'No. I *was* crazy. I was crazy worried about you. I was crazy frustrated that I couldn't see you. I would have stopped at a hotel or somewhere if I thought I'd have been able to sleep, but I wouldn't have.

'But I'm not crazy now. I think I may be saner this minute than I've been in a long, long time, Susie.' He pulled her back into his embrace. 'And thirstier. And smellier, I expect. And hungrier . . . pretty hungry right about now.'

They both laughed.

'You didn't eat, you idiot?'

'I ate a fairly unpleasant burger, on the ferry,' he looked at his watch, 'about twenty-four hours ago, it feels like . . .'

She slapped his chest. 'You need to eat . . .'

He caught her arms on him, and pulled her hands up to his face. 'I need you.'

She looked at his lovely face. 'I can't believe you did

this. I can't believe you came all this way. No one ever did anything like that for me before.'

His eyes bored into her. 'No one ever loved you the way I love you, Susie.'

In that moment, she knew he was right. Not Sean. Nor Douglas, who apparently had made little effort to find out where she was, and hadn't come after her. Who was happy to give her all the space she wanted.

It was Rob.

He was the one.

Rob took a hot shower while she cooked something for them both. She loved him being here. She could hear the water running, and loud splashes as water ran off him. She lit the fire she'd laid earlier that day, and the dry wood crackled and sparked in the grate. She found a few white candles in a drawer in the kitchen and she lit the table with them, laying two places side by side, although she didn't feel remotely hungry – she was full. Full of him. It occurred to her, as she uncorked a bottle of red and checked on the pasta dish she'd made, that they'd never had this – never been in this simple domestic setting together. This was a first.

When he appeared, his hair was wet, still dripping on to the shoulders of his check shirt. 'God, that feels better.'

She passed him a glass of wine.

He took it, winking at her before drinking deeply. 'Something smells good.'

'I should think anything would smell good to you at this point.'

He caught her around the waist and pulled her to him, kissing the side of her neck. 'You certainly do.'

'Ew. So cheesy. That kind of line work for you?'

He laughed. 'Sometimes.'

Later, when he'd eaten everything on his plate, and half of her virtually untouched meal, he led her over to the fireplace. They hadn't talked much while they ate. It was as if there was so much to say that it was easier to be quiet. There was something enormous happening, and it almost commanded silence. Susannah wondered how much Rob was thinking about Helena. Rob wondered how he so successfully compartmentalized his life – as though the simple act of crossing the Channel made him a different person. Made him free. There was no room in this moment, in this evening, for anything but Susie – his Susie. Being this close to each other was enough, for now. He put a couple more logs on the fire she'd built earlier in the grate, and the two of them sat down facing each other on the thick wool rug. They couldn't get close enough that way. Uncurling her, Rob put her legs over his, grabbing her behind and pulling her almost into his lap, then stretched his own legs out behind her. Gathering all her hair into his hand, he pulled her head gently around to kiss her mouth. Susannah felt light-headed. Kissing was all they were doing, and already she was more dazed than she'd been in a long, long time.

'I used to dream about being somewhere with you, just like this, Susie. When we were kids. When we couldn't seem to find a place to be alone, or a time. Do you remember that? Somewhere just like this. With a glass of wine and a fireplace. Somewhere stupid-romantic.'

'You mean you didn't find that caravan romantic?'

'Christ – that caravan. I haven't thought about that in forever. Bloody Amelia. No. Not that romantic, no. Not exactly what I'd had in mind.'

'I know. Do you remember, you used to talk about us in a big, white, clean bed?'

'Never got there, though, did we?'

She remembered. Everything. She remembered Lois catching them, flushed and breathless, when they were supposed to be doing homework in the conservatory. She remembered kissing themselves weak-kneed, standing up against walls, and being interrupted at parties. Lying, cross and frustrated, on the narrow, thin mattress in the caravan. Wanting him. She didn't really know what it was she wanted from him, wanted him to do to her, in those days. They'd been learning together. She knew now.

She kissed him back, her mouth wet and open and increasingly urgent. 'What would you have done, back then, if we'd had a place like this?' She was daring him.

'I'd have kissed you just like this . . .'

'And . . . ?'

'And I'd probably have seen if I could have got away

with undoing some of these buttons.' His hands were on her shirt.

She ached to feel his hands on her bare flesh. 'I bet you could have. You were always pretty good at that sort of thing.'

He laughed a deep throaty laugh, but then he was suddenly very serious. His mouth dropped to the hollow at the base of her throat, and his fingers started to work at the buttons, slowly, but very deliberately. She moved her own hands to his shirt, and they matched each other button for button, until all the buttons were undone. Susannah pushed the shirt back from his shoulders, and he moved his hands away from her for a moment to let it fall to the ground behind him. She kissed a small trail of kisses across his chest, and stroked him with her fingers. He was both familiar and strange – it was utterly intoxicating that he could be both things at once. He was Rob, as he had always been, in some ways. But he was different – thicker, and more muscled, too. He'd been a teenager, the last time they'd seen and held each other this way. And this was the body of a man.

Susannah felt a sudden pang of anxiety and self-consciousness. Her body was different, too. Softer, less pert than he might remember. She sucked in her stomach involuntarily as he pushed her shirt back.

'Don't.' His voice was harsh. 'Don't do that.'

She exhaled.

'You're lovely. Lovelier than ever before.'

She looked him straight in the eye without blinking as she reached behind her back, and undid her bra, but his glance dropped as he brought his hands up to cup her breasts before the fabric even fell away from them. And she didn't feel shy any more. His fingers and his mouth worked at her until she felt dizzy with lust.

He lifted her off his lap and the two of them stretched their denim-clad legs out, and lay down beside each other, her flat on her back, and Rob up on one elbow, leaning in to kiss her, his free hand stroking her, pulling at the waistband of her jeans. Susannah threw one leg across Rob's and pushed at him. He grabbed her bum and pulled her in. When that wasn't enough, they both kicked impatiently out of their jeans. They reached into each other's underwear, greedily. Susannah felt herself pulsing. She couldn't believe how turned on she was. He was rock hard in her hands, and his breath was coming in great rasping gusts. Was this happening? Was it really happening?

She didn't know which one of them pulled back first. Maybe it was both of them. They sprang apart, and lay on their backs, catching their breath.

He spoke first. 'We can't.'

'I know.'

'I want to.'

'God. Me, too.'

'Remind me why we can't?'

She could hear the wry smile, though she wasn't

looking at his face. 'Because we're both "good". Too bloody good.'

'Still? I'm not sure.'

'Yes, you are. We both stopped, Rob. For the same reasons. Because you're married and I'm . . . with someone . . . and because all those years ago, we didn't, because it wasn't right – and it still isn't.'

He turned to look at her face while she spoke.

'I want it to happen when it's right. Not just between the two of us – because I think we're there. When it's right in the world. I know that probably sounds ridiculous . . .'

'No, it doesn't. You sound like Susie.'

'Queen of excuses, right?' She turned to face him.

'No.' He shook her gently. 'You weren't a tease then, Susie, and you're not now. Listen. I've never wanted to make love to you, or to anyone else, for that matter, as much as I want to right here and right now. And, God knows, when I was seventeen I used to think I was going to die if I couldn't. Die, or burst, or something. But I agree with you. It isn't right yet.'

And it was all in the word *yet*, wasn't it? All the promises. Yet. When would it be right? When he'd left Helena, when she'd left Douglas. When they'd told the truth to the people around them. Then they'd be free. Yet. The word was full of her future. Susannah knew tonight wasn't the time to have the big, tough discussions. Not the time for deadlines and ultimatums and concrete plans.

'Yet' was enough, for now.

She kissed his forehead, and sat up to lean back against the sofa. It was incredibly hard not to touch him. In the firelight, she could see his chest rise and fall. He pulled himself round and sat beside her, a few inches apart from her. He reached behind her, pulling a throw around her shoulders. Their breathing steadied, and slowed. She felt very calm. Then he took her hand in both of his, and held it gently. She smiled at him.

He held her glance for the longest time. 'So, twenty years have passed, and we're basically back where we started.'

'How do you mean?'

'I've got a stonking hard-on and nowhere to go with it.'

She smacked his arm. 'So base. So, what now? Wanna watch TV? Think there's a boxed set of 24 round here I've been meaning to catch. Or there's bound to be Scrabble. My parents are Scrabble nuts.'

Rob laughed and lifted her hand to his mouth to kiss it. 'I want to fall asleep with you, in a bed. I want to lie down with my arms around you and fall asleep and sleep for hours and hours. Can we do that, Susie?'

'We can do that. I'd love to do that.'

It felt chilly, away from the fire, in the guest bedroom. Susannah pulled a couple of T-shirts out of a drawer, and threw one at Rob, then pulled back the duvet and climbed in.

'Brrr.' She shivered. 'I'm not taking off my socks.'

'Good. They're the only thing keeping my lust in check.'

'Spoons?'

'Spoons.' She lay facing the wall, and he slid across the bed to hold her, one arm under her neck, and the other around her waist, resting on her stomach. His breathing slowed, and she thought he was asleep, but just before she surrendered herself she heard him say, 'I love you,' very quietly into her hair.

Susannah slept for ten hours, but Rob was still, apparently, deeply asleep when she awoke. She lay and watched him, the rise and fall of his chest, his lips pursed slightly. She laid her own arm against his: her skin looked milky white against his olive colouring. She'd always loved that. She remembered looking down at their clasped hands, when they'd been seventeen, and loving how it looked, dreaming stupid schoolgirl dreams of olive-skinned babies.

They hadn't spent a whole night alone together in the same bed since they were eighteen years old, in the caravan.

Not wanting the night to end, she snuggled down beside him again. When she opened her eyes what felt like a few minutes later, but must have been longer, he was gone. She found him in the kitchen, still in his T-shirt and boxer shorts, scrambling eggs. When he saw her, he came over and, taking her face in his hands, kissed her deeply.

'Good morning.'

'Morning, Susie. You slept well.'

'You, too.'

'I liked the way you felt, lying beside me.'

Mum had placed a teak bench outside, facing the amazing view, where the morning sun would hit it, and after they ate their eggs, Rob wrapped the blanket from last night around Susannah's shoulders and they took mugs of coffee out there. Susannah stared at the mountains in the distance, her knees hugged to her chest.

'Are you okay?' he asked her, stroking her thigh gently.

'I don't remember why it all went so wrong. I mean, I do remember. I remember what I did. I just don't remember why any more. This – you and me – this feels so right, Rob. It just seems stupid – so stupid – that we had it before, and we let it go. We wasted so much time. I'm sorry.' She was close to tears.

'Hey. Don't. There's no point in that, Susie. It's the past, and that's where it belongs. This is us now. We're here.'

'But where's here, Rob? We're hiding out. We're playing house. This isn't real life.'

'It feels real to me.'

'But it isn't.' Susannah persisted. 'I have Douglas at

home, waiting for me, wondering what the hell is going on with me. You've got Helena. She doesn't know she needs to be wondering, too – but we both know it won't stay that way.'

He didn't reply.

'What are we going to do?'

'I don't know', he admitted. 'It's crazy. In some ways, lots of ways, this feels like the simplest thing in the world. You and me. In others, it's as complicated as it gets.'

They sat quietly for a moment, watching clouds drift across the horizon.

Then Rob turned to her, and took both her hands in his. 'I don't know everything, Susie. But I know this. We are supposed to be together. The rest, I think, is just stuff we have to sort out. Isn't that the most important thing – figuring out what we both want? Both need?'

'Just sort it out. You make it sound easy.'

'I didn't say that. But I love you, Susie. You make me happy. This is what I want.' He kissed her mouth, gently. 'Can we do something?'

'What?'

'Can we just play house a while longer? Can we not talk about all of that? It doesn't belong here. Just for a while?'

And it was so easy, when he kissed her, and the sun warmed her face, to agree.

Mum's binder recommended a restaurant in the

town, and they decided to take a chance on getting a table that evening. It was a weeknight, out of tourist season, although it was still warm and lovely. Susannah thought it was more likely to be closed than full. It was funny how nothing much mattered here. Eat out, or not. Get up, or not. Just being together – that was all that mattered. She thought for a moment about life at home with Douglas. Ruled by the diary. Complex arrangements, deadlines, schedules. It seemed a thousand miles away, and she pushed the thought of it, and of him, away. The tension had gone, from her neck and her shoulders, without her even thinking about it. When she'd looked in the bathroom mirror after she'd showered, her skin looked clear and brighter – her eyes somehow less lined. Left to dry naturally, her hair curled, more like it had been when she was a teenager. She looked less polished, younger. Rob said he liked her that way.

She'd left her BlackBerry in the car, gone cold turkey that first night when she'd arrived. She'd stopped reaching for it now. When she'd checked it this morning there was a text from Jonathan, letting her know that Amelia was okay after the chemo. A few from work, but Megan said there was nothing that needed immediate attention. Nothing from Doug.

They were wrong about it being a quiet night. Something was going on in the town. They parked where Susannah had parked the day before, and strolled hand in hand through the gathering crowd. The main square was full of long trestle tables laid with checked tablecloths, and brightly coloured bunting was strung between lamp posts. Music was playing in several different bars, and everyone, it seemed, had their doors flung open for the evening. People milled around, chatting and laughing, and they nodded at Susannah and Rob as they made their way to the restaurant.

Rob had a little more French than Susannah, and after a nodding, smiling exchange with the proprietor, established that it was a fête evening – that the restaurant was closed but the kitchen was open. They may eat at the trestle tables with everyone else. Every restaurant in town, it seemed, was serving the same way. The menus were all slightly different, but all relied heavily on foie gras and duck, the local specialities. They paid their twenty euros each, which bought them a pink ticket and a bottle of red wine, the cork already removed, and took two free seats at the end of a long table occupied by a big extended family with several children, including a newborn, who was wrapped in blankets and lying in a pram, seemingly oblivious to the din. Rob poured them both a plastic glass of wine, and they toasted, then he kissed her, across the table. Susannah saw that the young mother with the toddler on her lap was smiling at her, nodding as though she understood something. She smiled back.

'I want babies.' She said it to herself almost as much as to him.

'Right now? Do you want that one?' Rob pointed at the baby in the pram. 'I reckon if you could distract the mother, I could get that one.'

She smiled. 'In January – the first time we saw each other – I brushed you off when you asked me about kids. I pretended I didn't remember that I always wanted them. It was too hard to admit that I'd let myself make such a cock-up. Get to be forty and not have had them. I did want them. I still do. I'm just afraid it's too late.'

'It's not.'

'I lost a baby. When I was married to Sean.'

'I didn't know.'

'Of course you didn't. How could you have done?'

'I'm sorry.'

'He or she would be . . . I don't know . . . fourteen now. Something like that.' She shook her head wistfully. 'It's an extraordinary thought. Already a teenager. Where did all that time go? What about you?'

'No babies. Not that I know of.'

'But you and Helena . . . I mean she wants them, wanted them . . .'

That's why it was too difficult. She didn't even know what tense to use about his wife.

His face darkened. 'Susie.'

'I know. I'm sorry.'

'I just feel . . . I know it sounds ridiculous. I'm a

raging hypocrite. But . . . talking about her . . . it feels disloyal . . .'

Susannah looked down. She felt suddenly ashamed.

He lifted her chin with his index finger. 'Can we do what we said . . . can we let it all fade away . . . just for now? I'm a coward, I'm a bastard, I'm whatever else you can think of. You can't call me worse than I've called myself. But not tonight.'

After dinner, they wandered down to the other end of the square, in the direction everyone else was heading, to where a band was playing on a temporary stage. It was dark now, and the sky was incredibly clear and starlit. Everyone, it seemed, was dancing, except for the old widows in black who sat on metal chairs around the edges, watching. Parents swayed together with toddlers on their hips, and youths jumped and flailed out of time in big, happy groups. Two or three middle-aged couples who obviously knew what they were doing danced properly in the middle, incongruously able in the midst of the melee.

Rob dragged Susannah, protesting and laughing, into the throng, and then pulled her to him, one arm tight around her waist.

'I can't.'

'We can.'

She put her arms around his neck, and kissed him. His response was an unexpected dip, which elicited another squeal from her. But then they were dancing, holding tight to each other, suddenly oblivious to their surroundings.

'I remember the first time we danced,' he whispered into her ear. 'Do you?'

'Of course. I remember the song, and what you were wearing, and how it felt.'

'And I remember the last time, too.'

Cranwell. At the ball. She didn't remember the song. Just the feeling. The sad, horrible feeling that it was all ending . . .

'It wasn't the last time, though, was it? We're dancing now, aren't we?'

And we were each other's first, Susannah thought, as she nuzzled his neck. Before we belonged to anyone else, we were each other's.

It couldn't last, of course. They both knew it. Not the evening, not the holiday. They danced until Susannah's feet started to hurt, then Rob drove them back to the house. They fell asleep wrapped in each other's arms, and slept soundly.

The next morning, when she checked her BlackBerry, there were emails, texts and voicemails from Douglas, each barely containing his irritation.

Where the hell are you?

She couldn't bring herself to reply.

Her return flight was already booked for that evening, and she knew she had to go home.

She had to be at work.

She had to get back to her life.

They hadn't had enough time.

She had to return the hire car, so Rob couldn't even take her to the airport. He came anyway, following her car in his own, and parking in the big car park in front of the terminal. The flight was displayed, and there was no queue at check-in. Rob went all the way to passport control with her, and then held her tightly in his arms before she went through.

Susannah felt strangely tearful. 'This is stupid – I'm going to see you in two days. I don't know what I'm making all this ridiculous fuss for. I feel as if, I feel . . . I'm just afraid of what is coming, I think.'

'Don't be. I'll call you in the morning. And I'll be back by the weekend. We can see each other then.'

'Promise?'

'I promise.'

She had hoped the house would be empty when she got back. She wanted the chance to sort herself out before Doug came home. But the flight was delayed an hour, of course, and the traffic was terrible coming in from Gatwick, and she saw, with a slightly sinking heart, that the lights were on when the minicab pulled up at the front door. Doug came to the door while she paid the cab, and took her case from her hand, kissing her cheek. He only had socks on his feet, and he'd taken his tie off.

'Drink? I'm having one.'

'Thanks.'

He poured them both a tumbler of whisky and went through to the kitchen to get cubes of ice from the freezer, dropping each one in slowly and deliberately. 'So, where did you go?' He sat down and slid one glass across the table to the place opposite.

Susannah pulled out the chair and sat down. 'France. To Mum and Dad's.'

He nodded, as though he wasn't really listening. He wasn't really looking at her either. 'We had a really interesting internal memo come round . . . oh, when was it? A week or so ago. Two, maybe.'

She didn't know what he was talking about. He was acting strangely. She felt trembly and anxious.

'It was for the family law guys really. Not us. But they circulate most of these things to everyone. *Ignorantia juris non excusat* and all that. Probably a salutary warning, too.'

'What are you talking about, Doug?' She'd always found it irritating when he used Latin phrases. It made him sound pompous.

'It was really fascinating, actually. Apparently texts and emails are the new private eyes. You know – you want to catch someone out, catch someone redhanded, doing what they oughtn't to be doing – it's all there now, in black and white, and emoticons and hard discs. So this was a memo outlining the use of this kind of information in cases – you know, divorces, custodies, that sort of thing.'

'Oh.'

'So, I was wondering, Susannah. If I could hack into your email account. If I knew your BlackBerry's passcode. And I mean . . . I know this is all hypothetical. I can barely switch the computer on. Can't programme the video. Utterly useless at all that stuff. But if I could . . . If I could see all that, would I catch you . . . catch you doing something you oughtn't to be doing?'

'Douglas –'

He interrupted her. 'Because, you see, I know there's something. Something not right. Something going on. Something different. And now I'm thinking to myself. You disappear on me – no explanation, no number to call. Maybe there's someone.' He looked right at her now. 'Is there, Susannah?'

Even as her heart pounded and ached, and bile rose in her throat, there was some relief. She nodded, slowly.

Doug took a deep breath and put his elbows on the table, leaning his chin on his hands.

Susannah waited.

Redness spread across his neck, but his voice was calm. 'And do you love this person?'

Again, she nodded. 'I do.' She thought he would ask who it was. How they'd met. Whether she'd slept with him. All the obvious questions. She was ready to answer them all.

But he didn't ask. Anything. He sat for another moment or two, then he downed the contents of his glass, pushed his chair back from the table and stood up.

This she hadn't expected. 'Doug. Can we talk about this?'

He shook his head, as though a fly was bothering him, his movements sharp and rapid. 'I don't think we can. Not tonight.'

She didn't turn round as he left the room. She heard his footsteps on the tread of the stairs, heard him close the door to his study and then the muffled sound of the Dave Brubeck Quartet coming through the walls.

He didn't come out again that night, and he'd gone by the time she woke up the next morning after a fitful, anxious night where it felt as if she had woken up on the hour. All she wanted to do was talk to Rob. But she couldn't do that. What was it Rob had said, in France? It felt 'disloyal'. The kissing, the touching, the desire and the longing – that all felt right, because it obliterated everything else. It was the talking that felt disloyal.

Doug hadn't come into the room they shared that night – he must have taken the clothes he needed for work before he went up, and then showered in the

369

guest bathroom this morning. Or at the gym. She hadn't heard the water running. Although she'd had a dreadful night. She'd got up around three and taken a pill, but she still hadn't fallen into a deep sleep until after five, and the alarm went anyway at seven, dragging her back from a thousand miles away.

Doug didn't want to see her. He couldn't stand to see her.

She couldn't stay, not after that. It was unbearable. And it wasn't fair. In a way, he'd made it easier for her, by guessing. But it didn't feel easier. The unpicking of something she'd been putting together for nine years felt anything but easy. Everything that had felt so wonderful in France under the cobalt-blue sky felt wretched under England's grey clouds. What had seemed pure was now tainted.

She told herself, sitting on the underground, that she hadn't set out to hurt Douglas. That he'd hurt her. She told herself there were wide cracks in their relationship – too wide and too jagged to repair – long before the June day last year when she'd seen Rob, and maybe seen her future, across the common. She should have left years ago.

But she hadn't. She'd stayed because it was easier than the alternative – better than being alone. Because she'd hoped she could make it better, hoped he'd change, hoped she'd love him again, love him more.

She'd stayed in part for the kids. They were the only kids she had, as imperfect and flawed as their relationships were. They were the kids she'd settled for. And only now, only just now, had those relationships started to flourish. It felt cruel to her, and she knew it would to them, too. Daisy and Rosie.

And now leaving was so much harder.

She went to work to answer emails and return phone calls. Megan peered curiously at her and told her she looked like death warmed over. She said there was obviously a reason Susannah never took all her vacation days – time off didn't agree with her. Susannah thought of her glowing, happy reflection in the mirror in her parents' French bathroom, and readily agreed, claiming she'd eaten something funny on the plane home and that she needed to go home to be near the loo and sleep it off.

At home, she'd packed the biggest bag they had by the time Douglas came home, and brought it downstairs. It was by the front door, and he saw it as soon as he came in.

He rubbed his eyes, and when he spoke his voice was tired, and annoyed. 'Here we go again. Where this time? Or aren't you saying?'

'Can you come and sit down, Douglas? Can we talk? I wanted to talk to you yesterday, but you wouldn't let me. Let me now. Please.'

'I don't want to sit down, Susannah. I don't much want to talk, to be honest with you. Not this time. I just want to know what's going on.'

She sighed. 'I'm leaving.'

'I can see that.'

'No. Leaving. Leaving you. For good.'

He did, at least, appear to be shocked. He put his coat and briefcase down at last, and stepped into the living room, sitting down on the nearest chair. 'Because of him?'

Susannah sat down opposite him. It should be obvious. 'Because of you and me.'

'I don't believe you.'

'You should. I'm telling you the truth. I told you about him, and you've no other reason to doubt my honesty. It isn't because of him. That makes it sound like I'm leaving you for him, and that's not what I'm doing. I'm leaving you because this relationship isn't working. It hasn't been working for a long time. And I've known it. You'd know it too, if you were honest with yourself. And I've been a coward. I should have left a long time ago. A long time, Douglas. It's not him.'

'But that's where you're going, isn't it? That's who you're going to be with?'

'I don't know.' That was true, too.

He was staring at her, hard.

'I hope so.' She wouldn't lie to him about it.

'Shit.' Douglas was shaking his lowered head, and his breath was coming in gasps.

'I'm sorry, Doug.'

'Don't do it.' He suddenly slid forward, off his chair,

on to the floor in front of her, almost putting his head in her lap. 'I don't want you to go.'

Of all the reactions she might have predicted, this was the least likely scenario. She'd expected anger, or some sort of resigned agreement. Not this. This wasn't like him.

'I'm sorry, Susannah. I'm sorry I haven't been who you want me to be. That's it, isn't it? I have been letting you down.'

She was tired, but it wasn't going to work this time.

'I can be, though. That's the thing. I can be that guy. I can change. You just have to tell me what you want.'

'That's the point, Doug. I shouldn't have to tell you. I shouldn't need to ask. If it was right, I wouldn't have to. Nor would you. Can't you see that? It's wrong.'

He shook his head. 'I don't accept that.'

Susannah stood up.

He remained, slightly foolish, on the floor at her feet. It was strangely undignified, and she was glad when he stood up slowly and looked her in the eye.

'You have to. This is happening. I don't want . . . this . . . any more, Doug. None of it. I don't want you. I don't love you. Not like that.'

They stood, facing each other, in silence, until Susannah couldn't bear it any more. She half shrugged – in apology? In resignation? And then, as calmly as she could, all her movements slow and deliberate, she took her raincoat from the chair, picked up her bag, and walked to the front door.

All the while, Douglas stood and watched her, his arms by his sides, palms turned towards her and slightly raised, as though he were about to conduct an orchestra. She closed the door at last, quietly, behind her, without a word, and went to her car, walking faster now she had left the house.

Douglas didn't come after her, but she pushed down the lock on the door anyway. Her hands trembled uncontrollably as she turned the key. She pulled out abruptly, without looking in her mirrors. Behind her, she heard the screech of a car's brakes, and the driver pounded hard on his horn in fear and anger. Susannah's heart was throbbing in her chest, and she was breathless. She half raised a hand in apology and, taking the next left turn, indicated and pulled into a space. She turned the ignition off and put her head on the steering wheel, trying to concentrate on making her breaths long and deep.

She couldn't believe she'd said it. She was stunned to have walked away, in an instant, from the past nine years of her life, since she'd first met Doug. There was nothing like relief in it at this moment, although she had to believe that would follow – she'd been thinking about this, knowing she had to do this, for so long. But for now, she felt sick and dizzy. She closed her eyes, and tried not to think.

When she raised her head, the clock told her twenty minutes had passed. The palpitations had slowed. She didn't know what to do next. In all the imagining, she'd never followed herself out of the door. The daydream had stopped when she walked away. She thought about Amelia, or her parents. She didn't want to be alone. It was getting late.

But when she pulled out again, this time taking care to look carefully behind her, she headed with absolute certainty towards the only place she could imagine going: she headed towards him. Even if it was wrong, even if it was betraying Douglas, and even if he didn't want her there, she headed towards him.

She had never been to Rob's home before, although she knew exactly where it was. He'd lived there with Helena, and she hadn't wanted to before. She hadn't wanted to see, or acknowledge a home that the two of them shared. A kitchen they cooked in, a bed they slept in. A life they'd built. Now she didn't care – didn't care if it was theirs, didn't care if it was selfish.

Rob answered the door with his face full of concern. It was after 10 p.m. now, she realized, and she hadn't called ahead. He can't have been back long. He must be exhausted from the driving.

'I ended it.'

That was all she could say. She had no idea until the moment she stood in front of him how exhausted she was. She'd barely slept at all the night before, and she realized she hadn't eaten today, and now, standing here, she thought she might fall down.

Rob didn't say anything. He just opened his arms, and folded her into his embrace. She let her whole weight rest against his bulk. His hand held the back of her head, and she felt his lips in her hair, silently kissing her head. She was trembling.

He half carried, half dragged her into the living room, and then sat her gently on the sofa, leaning her against the cushions, as if she was a child. He took off her shoes, and she curled her legs up under her. He pulled a throw over her. *News at Ten* was on the television, and the *Times* lay open on the arm of a chair, next to a whisky tumbler, still half full. Susannah closed her eyes gratefully, his hand smoothing her fingers.

He passed her the glass and watched her drink it straight down. 'Tea?'

She shook her head. She just wanted to close her eyes. She was profoundly grateful he wasn't asking her questions. She had never felt so tired in her life . . . he sat on the arm of the sofa, stroking her head gently, and they watched the end of the news, and the weather, without any words at all. It was a weirdly domestic situation, both of them quiet, and calm, for the first time in a long while.

She had no idea when she fell asleep.

When she woke up, the digital display on the television said 5.00 a.m., and she was alone in the living room, still under the blanket. For a gentle, blissful moment, she didn't remember where she was. Or anything that had happened. She existed in the wonderful state of nothingness that adults have for the first minute or so of their day. And then she remembered

— Doug's face as she left, Rob's arms around her when she'd arrived on his doorstep.

The memories came in waves.

She sat up and pushed her hair behind her ears, rubbing her eyes.

Rob was in bed, in his room at the top of the stairs. He'd left the door wide open. He'd fallen asleep half sitting up, with the side light on, and there was an open book on the sheets next to him. He was wearing an old khaki T-shirt with a hole at the neck, and it had ridden up to reveal his slim, muscled stomach, and the dark hair there. For a moment she stood by the bed and just watched him, watched the gentle rise and fall of his chest as he breathed, watched his eyelids flicker slightly in his dreams. It felt as if she'd loved him all her life. Susannah silently picked the book up and closed it, put it down carefully on the bedside table. She reached down and switched the bedside light off. It was already just beginning to get light outside, and the early light cast a softer glow on the room. She slipped her dress over her head, and pulled her bra and underwear off, then she slid quickly under the sheets to lie beside him, naked. She laid her head on his chest, and rested her forearm on the side of his stomach. She thought she might go back to sleep in his arms, and stifled a yawn.

But he began to respond to her before he was anywhere close to awake. One arm snaked slowly around her shoulders and the other pulled her up on to his stomach, so that she was almost lying, naked, along the whole length of him. His hands travelled luxuriously, languorous and sleepy, down her back, and cupped her behind. Unconsciously his hips began to push rhythmically, gently, into her, and she felt him begin to harden beneath her.

She wanted him to see her. She wanted him to say her name. She wanted to know that he knew what was happening, knew what she wanted. At last. She was free to come to him, and she'd come to him, and now she wanted to be as close to him as it was possible to be, closer than she'd ever been. She didn't need to put the thought of Helena out of her head – she wasn't in there. This was right.

His hands were in her hair, pulling her mouth on to his. The kisses were slow and deep, as if they had all the time in the world.

Susannah put the heels of her hands into his chest, and pushed herself up, and away from him. 'Rob.'

He opened his eyes sleepily.

'Rob. It's me, Susannah.'

'Of course it's you. It's always been you. My Susannah. My love.'

'I want you, Rob. I want all of you. Now. Please.'

His eyes were glazed with sleep and desire. 'Are you sure?'

How could he ask? It must be written all over her. 'I've never been so sure of anything. Not ever. Please.'

It was as though she'd released something in him at last, and he wasn't gentle any more. He flipped her over, easily, and that strength was so sexy she couldn't believe it. He was on top of her, covering her, his legs forcing hers apart, so that she wrapped them around his back. She felt tiny and weak. His hands roamed all over her. He kissed every piece of her skin that he could reach. Sucked on her and grazed her with his teeth, scratching her with his beard. His touch was at once familiar and new, as though he'd been touching her this way all her life, and at the same time as though he'd never laid a hand on her before.

When they had passed the point of no return, when they couldn't have stopped if they'd tried, he entered her, so slowly, raised up on his elbows, staring into her eyes, and the moment seemed so enormous, so important, that she wanted to stop, be still, and concentrate on it. This very moment, this had been twenty years in the making. She wanted to laugh, and cry, and shout out loud. She wanted to talk to him about it. But at the same time she couldn't have stopped moving if her life depended on it. She came, almost immediately, though she hadn't known she was so close. The orgasm shook her, seeming to travel through her arms and neck and spine and to explode out through her legs. She felt her toes flex and curl. But there was more, much more. Their bodies fit together, and their movements matched each other, stroke for stroke. It felt delicious.

Much, much later that same morning, Saturday, the two of them lay together under the duvet eating bacon sandwiches and drinking hot, sweet tea. They'd made love twice more in the early morning light, unable to get enough of each other, and fell asleep at last sometime around the time she would normally have been waking up. Susannah's legs were aching pleasantly. When she'd arrived last night, her head had been so full of thoughts and feelings, it had all seemed overwhelming. The sex had wiped her mind clear of everything except the sensations she was giving and receiving. And now it felt like the storm had passed – the air was crystal bright and clean and the seas were calm, and the way forward was utterly clear.

'I want us to be together.' She said it first.

'That's what I want, too.' He nodded decisively, as though they'd reached agreement, then fell silent for a few moments.

She knew where his mind had gone.

His fingers stroked her shoulders. 'I can't tell Helena while she's away. I won't do that to her.'

'I know.' She did know.

Neither of them said it, but they both remembered.

'She's back in a couple of months. I'll tell her then.'

'And while we wait?'

He turned so that their faces were close together. 'I should stay away from you. We've waited this long – that's how it feels – and I should be strong enough to wait a while longer.'

'But . . .' She stopped breathing. It seemed impossible to be away from him now.

He kissed her. 'But I don't think I can.'

She nodded.

'I'm not proud of it. She can never know.'

'She won't.'

'What are you going to do?'

'I'm going back to my flat – my own place.'

He looked relieved.

'I know we can't be together here.' She looked around. There weren't many feminine touches in the room – no women's novels on the nightstand, no perfume bottles on the dresser. But it was still Helena's room. There was a single photograph of the two of them in a big silver frame on the chest of drawers. It must have been their wedding. She couldn't look at it. Earlier, in the bathroom, she had stared at herself in the mirror, wondering what might be in the cabinet behind it, on the shelves. Helena's things. Last night she hadn't really been aware of where she was. This morning it wasn't so easy not to be.

'No.'

'I expect it will be good for me to have my own space.' But Susannah didn't believe it, even as she said the words. She didn't want to be anywhere except with him, wherever it was . . .

He nodded.

'I can't stay here.'

He didn't say anything. And it wasn't a question.

Susannah had promised to meet Elizabeth for lunch. Her god-daughter didn't often ask for an audience, but she'd called just before Susannah had gone to France (apparently unaware of the argument at that time) and asked if she could see her. Susannah wished it was any other day but today. She was pretty sure she wasn't thinking entirely straight. There were a million things to sort out. First, she needed somewhere to live. Thank God she hadn't sold her flat when she moved in with Douglas. She'd rented it out on occasions over the years – informally, to friends of friends – but it was currently empty. She shuddered at the thought that she could have made herself homeless by leaving Doug.

She really hadn't thought it through at all. Of course she couldn't stay with Rob – or Amelia either. Not while this horrible fight hung over them. She hadn't called her yesterday, and for all she knew, Amelia might still be furious. Going home to her parents was entirely out of the question, and she wasn't at all sure she was ready to call Alex and Chloe and beg for their sofabed and their silence. Things were pretty loved up and nesty around there, she gathered from Alastair, and she didn't know if she could face that. Her old flat was the only option she had, for now. She was trying to make herself think a day at a time.

It was a long time since Susannah had lived alone. She'd gone from her childhood home via university and law school to the London flats, shared with Amelia, that were always full of people. Then to her married home – the place she and Sean had bought together. He'd left when the marriage ended, and that was the last time she'd lived as a singleton. That didn't entirely count – Alex had camped out for months at a time, and she'd spent countless nights at Amelia's, and, after Alastair and Kathryn had married, at their house. She had a sketchy memory of that house, and scarcely any recollection of being there by herself. It had gone straight on the market when they divorced, but it had taken ages to sell. She'd completed on the purchase of her flat a few weeks before she'd met Douglas, and she'd put all her plans on hold when he'd asked her to move into the house in Islington. They'd never changed things formally. She'd never asked, and he'd certainly never suggested it. He'd continued to pay the mortgage. She'd taken on some of the utilities and paid for most of the food. And that had worked, although it seemed pretty stupid and careless now. She was in her forties, the owner of a starter flat that had suited the life she thought she was embarking on nearly a decade ago. She couldn't even begin to think, properly, about whether the flat might suit the future that now beckoned to her – a future with Rob. This was temporary.

The flat was somewhere to be with Rob where no one else could find them. They'd played house in France. Here they could do it for real. It was small but spotless. She'd seen bigger places, but they'd been grubby and tired, with stained upholstery and scuffed walls. She had wanted something new to go with her new life. It was a one-bedroom on the third floor of a mansion block. It had recently been renovated by the owner, and everything was clean and fresh. There was a living/dining room with a small Juliet balcony between two sets of floor-to-ceiling windows, and a tiny kitchen with simple white units and black stone worktops. The bedroom had another huge window, and the bathroom had black and white marble tiles. Everything was neutral and plain, from the white-washed walls to the sandy sisal carpets throughout. It was simply furnished – Susannah hadn't had the time or inclination to do much with the interior. She'd been excited to move into Douglas's house back then, back when she thought he'd want her to put her stamp on it. There were just a few simple pieces – a big sofa with a cream twill cover, a cast-iron bed. White cotton curtains hung at the windows and, from some, you could see the tops of trees.

It was a warm, sunny day, now, as Susannah contemplated her future. She daydreamed, conjuring up images of herself drinking coffee on the sofa, reading the Sunday papers, curled up with her feet in Rob's lap.

She sent an email to Douglas, letting him know she'd like to call by and pick up the rest of her stuff. He replied tersely, saying he'd be gone all day and suggesting she collect her things that evening. He asked her to leave the key on the table before she left. His hurt and anger were written large in each brief line.

She was glad she wouldn't have to face him.

*

Walking into the restaurant, she barely recognized Elizabeth – Amelia was right, she looked scarily grown-up. She'd chosen the restaurant – Livebait, in Covent Garden, which was where Susannah had taken her when she was little, after a ballet or a show – and had booked the table.

She was relieved when Libby stood up and gave her a warm hug. She didn't know what Amelia might have said to her. 'How are you, sweetheart? How are things?'

'Comme ci, comme ça,' the girl responded.

The waitress came up to offer drinks – Susannah ordered a glass of white wine, and Elizabeth a Diet Coke. They busied themselves with the menus, choosing what to eat.

Once they'd ordered, Susannah sat forward, resting her face on her two clasped hands. 'How's things? What's going on? Talk to me . . .'

'Well . . . in some ways, things are great. Dad's home, and that's *amazing*. He's *so* happy – and Mum, too. They're like a pair of kids.'

This from a kid, thought Susannah.

'Kissing in the kitchen, that kind of stuff. Gross. But good gross.'

Susannah couldn't help laughing.

'But I think I'm mad at you.'

'You are?'

'You're in some huge fight with Mum, aren't you?'

'What has she said to you?'

'Not much. But I know. I heard her talking to Dad about it.'

'And what were they saying?'

'Mum was crying. She said you'd been screaming at each other. In the hospital, was it?'

Susannah didn't answer.

'How could you? I mean, Susannah – come on. In the hospital.' She sounded very adult.

Susannah felt suitably admonished. There was no vestige of the righteous anger she'd felt at the time. How could there be? Amelia had been right.

'What's it all about?'

'I'm not sure you'd understand, Libs. It's all a bit complicated.'

'Well, could you uncomplicate it, please? And go back to being friends. Mum needs you, Suze. I know she's got Dad again, and everything. Gran. Us. But you're her best friend. Nothing is really right with her when things aren't right with you two. You're like Tweedledum and Tweedledee.'

'Thanks for that.' Susannah grimaced.

But Elizabeth was serious. 'She misses you.'

'Has she said so?'

'She doesn't need to. I know.'

'Look, Lib. I love your mum. You know that. She loves me, too. We've never, in all our lives, had a fight so bad that I doubt that – and we've had some fights, believe me. We disagree about . . . about something, right now . . . that's all.'

'She said, to Dad, that you were being naive and foolish.'

'She did, did she?'

Elizabeth nodded solemnly. 'And that it was all going to end in tears. That she was frightened for you, Suze.'

Under the shower, later, after Susannah had gone, Rob laid his head against the cool tile and felt panic rise in him. When she was here, when she was in his arms, she was all he wanted, all he was capable of thinking about. Now, without her here, Helena's trusting, smiling face was all he could see when he closed his eyes. He felt sick. What had he done? What did he still have to do?

He was drying himself off when the phone rang, so lost in his thoughts that its shrill ring jolted him. He picked it up on the third ring, somehow assuming it was Susannah, but it was Helena's voice he heard, distant and fuzzy.

'Rob?'

'Helena?'

'How are you?' He was instantly acutely aware that he was leaning against an unmade bed where only hours ago he'd been lying in sex-tangled sheets with another woman.

'Great, great.' He concentrated on keeping his voice normal. 'You?'

'I'm okay. Fine. Bit knackered. I just missed you,

Rob. I wanted to hear your voice. Talk to me, will you?'

He had nothing to say to her: guilt had tied his tongue. He had never felt so little like himself. He took a deep breath and forced himself into small talk. He knew which questions to ask, when he dug deep. The weather, the camp, the kit, operations and exercises . . .

They talked easily enough for a few minutes. There'd been a lot of rocket attacks on the compound in the last few days, Helena said – nothing serious, no injuries yet. But they were exhausting, he remembered. They kept you on edge, and made a mess. They made you want to come home.

Eventually she asked, 'Are you sure you're okay? You sound a bit weird.'

'Do I?'

'Yes, you do. Distracted. Are you watching the telly?'

'Course not.'

'What, then? Is everything alright?'

No, no no. Nothing is alright. 'Nothing's wrong. Everything's fine. Honestly. I'm a bit tired, too, that's all.'

'Rocket attacks on the King's Road?' She sounded briefly sarcastic. 'Sorry – that's mean. Have you been out getting pissed with your old mates again?'

He'd forgotten he'd told her that a couple of times to explain evening absences from home. He made a sound like a yes.

'Poor you.' She thought he was hungover. 'Hair of the dog. That's what you need. Or a huge fry-up.'

'Probably.'

'How's your dad?'

'I'm going to go and see him this weekend. I'll send you an email.'

'Give him my love, will you? And your mum.'

'Course. Is your mum okay?'

'You know Mum. Same as always. She asked after you, when I talked to her.'

He'd called his mother-in-law every week, when Helena first went away. But he hadn't spoken to her in almost a month now. How could he call her? He heard the question in Helena's voice, but he ignored it.

'I miss you, Rob.'

'I miss you, too.'

'Not long now, though, is it? I'll be home before you know it. Can't wait. D'you know what I want? A long soak in a hot tub, a Chinese, and a day in bed. Not just sleeping, if you know what I mean . . .'

After Rob put the phone down, he sat on the edge of the bed with his towel still wrapped around him, until he was so cold he had goosebumps.

The phone rang again. This time, he thought it would be Susannah. Helena wouldn't ring back. He couldn't talk to Susannah right now. He let the phone ring out, relieved when it stopped. He was lost in his thoughts when the phone beside him started ringing again. He answered reluctantly.

It was his mum, and she was crying. 'Thank God. Rob. I thought you were never going to answer.'

Rob thought he knew and understood exactly the pattern of his father's deterioration. Thought he was dealing with the shock and horror of his dad's shrinking away from him. Until he saw him in a hospital bed. He might not even have recognized him, if his mother hadn't been sitting beside him. And the shock almost made him stagger backwards.

He hadn't seen the flashing light on his telephone answering machine. He'd been exhausted and preoccupied when he got to the end of his long drive home from France, and he hadn't looked. And then Susannah had turned up . . . and he couldn't think about that any more. Lois hadn't called his mobile phone. She'd never mastered that number, and he knew the technology frightened her. She wouldn't have had the capacity to email or text him – she didn't have a mobile phone of her own, and his parents had always resisted buying a home computer, saying they could never use it enough to justify the cost. So she'd had to rely on the landline. And he hadn't looked at the damn machine. After he hung up, he'd played the messages while he ran around the flat throwing clothes on. She'd left five. Each one more desperate and heartbreaking. The messages told the story of his father's deterioration. In the first, she was worried about his breathing, which sounded different in his sleep, and she was calling the GP to make a home visit – and would Rob call her, please? The fourth message was panic-stricken. She was almost shouting. Where was he? Why wasn't he answering? She needed him. She couldn't decide things without him. Where was he? Please? Her voice was full of sobs. It almost killed him to hear it. By the fifth, it was done. He was intubated in the hospital. A machine was breathing for him, and would be until the moment he died. He'd never speak to either of them again.

Rob got to the hospital as fast as he could, loathing himself with a ferocity that scared him, and more frightened than he'd ever been in his life. He'd failed both of them. He'd failed completely and utterly.

How could this have happened so fast? He'd asked his mother, he'd asked the doctor – the young, slick doctor who'd come to the bedside and told him what had happened, as if he was talking to a child. It was the nature of the disease, the doctor said, not quite meeting his eye. Unpredictable. No prognosis was the same, and no pattern, time-wise, consistently emerged. This had been fast, yes, but he'd seen faster. No, there was nothing he could do – no reversal. Rob knew that, really. He knew enough about the disease to under-stand that much, at least.

Sobs racked his body and he hated himself for crying in front of his mother. But she'd already forgiven him. She'd deflated like a week old party balloon the moment he'd walked on to the ward. She'd so obviously been staying strong with every ounce of willpower she possessed, and it had deserted her when she saw him. For now, she had no comfort to offer him, and so they sat, on either side of Frank's bed, and Rob cried until his ribs hurt for his father, whose voice he would never hear again, and for his mother, who had just, effectively, lost the man she had loved for more than forty years.

Susannah knocked on the front door for the first time in years. She'd promised Libby she'd make amends with her best friend, and she realized she needed to put things right with Amelia before she could move on. She usually just went straight in, and almost always remonstrated with Amelia straight afterwards for not having a chain on the door. It was the middle of the afternoon, and she knew the kids and Jonathan were likely to be on a Saturday outing somewhere. She was banking on Amelia's mum not being there either.

Amelia came to the door. She'd lost more weight since Susannah had seen her, and it wasn't that long. She looked utterly vulnerable. She was wearing a fleece Susannah presumed belonged to Jonathan, and it swamped her. She had nothing on her head today, and the baldness seemed stark and ugly.

The door had clear glass panels, and Susannah watched her friend walk towards her, remorse and sorrow welling up in her. Amelia didn't open it straight away – she stared at Susannah through the glass. Susannah couldn't decide whether she was still angry.

For a moment she wondered whether Amelia was actually going to let her in.

But then she turned the handle and opened the door, stepping aside to let Susannah in.

'No chain?'

The two women stood in the hall.

'I'm sorry, Meels. I should never have left.'

'I sent you away.'

'I shouldn't have listened to you.'

Amelia snorted.

'And I'm sorry because a lot of what you said . . . you were right . . . I didn't want to listen.'

Amelia stepped nearer, and opened her arms, and the two of them held each other for a short while. Susannah could feel all of Amelia's ribs, even under the voluminous fleece.

'I was right. But I'm sorry, too. You didn't need tough love that day. I know that. I was itching for a fight. Took it out on you. Can't help myself, sometimes. I'm so fucking angry some days I could rip someone's head off.'

'So, I actually got lucky?'

'Pretty much.' She sniffed and pulled back. 'Tea? About all I'm keeping down this week, and I'm not making any promises about that.'

'Tea. I'll make it.'

'Oh yes, you will.'

The two of them walked down the corridor towards the kitchen.

'So, what's with the Sinead O'Connor impression?'

'Do fuck off.'

Amelia sat curled up on the deep sofa to direct proceedings, while Susannah filled the kettle and plugged it in to boil, and described how she had walked out on the life she'd built with Douglas – a life she'd outgrown but hadn't had the courage to discard.

Until Rob. But she sensed now wasn't the time to mention his new role in her life. There'd be time for that.

'This is so weird,' Amelia offered, watching Susannah opening cupboards.

'Me waiting on you, or this motley collection of tea bags you've got on offer?' Susannah read off the labels from the boxes in the cupboard. 'Nettle. Fennel. Chamomile. Yuck. What, no PG tips?'

'It's the holistic approach.' Amelia laughed.

'You're off your rocker. All British people know that good old builder's tea is the great cure-all. Weird is right.'

'I didn't mean that . . . I meant all this.' She flung her arms out in an all-embracing gesture.

Susannah looked at her quizzically.

'You're going to be living on your own. Jonathan's moved back in. Total reversal. You're going after what you want. I'm compromising . . .'

'Is that how you see it, you and Jonathan?'

'Oh, I don't know. It all seemed cut and dried, before this wretched illness.'

'Were you ever completely out of love with him? I

mean, I know you had your reasons. What was it —
something about him not liking how you sang in the
car . . . ?'

Amelia threw a cushion in Susannah's direction.

'I'm kidding . . . I know why you did it. But . . . were
you?'

'Out of love?' She paused. 'I suppose not . . . not
completely. I don't know if you ever can be. We were
together for so many years. We had three kids, for
God's sake.'

'So, did you — somewhere in the deepest recesses
of your mind — did you think there was a chance you'd
get back together?'

'I don't know. Would I have gone through with the
divorce if I had? Did I see us as some kind of Burton
and Taylor? I don't know.'

'How did you feel about Jess?'

Amelia laughed. 'Well, if we continue with the
Hollywood comparison . . . I saw her as . . . nothing
more than the Sally . . . I was the one with the Krupp
diamond, dahling . . .'

Letting herself into Douglas's house felt so strange.
This house had been Susannah's home for years — it
was full of her things — but it felt alien to her now, so
quickly. She walked slowly from room to room,
remembering. In the doorway of the bedroom she
and Douglas had shared, she stood for a while, staring
at the bed, thinking of the two of them in it, sleeping,

making love, reading. The decorative pillows were gone, and she smiled at the messy way the duvet had been pulled up, the pillows left askew. There was a bed making a statement if ever there was one – Tracey Emin would be proud.

It hadn't been all bad. They'd been happy, and they'd loved each other. And if, now, drunk on her feelings for Rob, she couldn't claim it was as strong a love, as lasting a love, as good a love, she could – at least – admit it had been love. If it had a memory-foam mattress – and how well she remembered the argument they'd had over one in the bed shop – the bed would remember well the years when the two of them slept entwined in the middle, and then the long time, towards the end, where they crept inexorably towards the edges.

There wasn't all that much really. Clothes, and shoes – stuff like that. She packed the contents of the two wardrobes into the plastic boxes she'd carried in from the car, filling a black bin liner with things to give away, and another with things for the cleaner, smiling at her own burst of efficiency. In the bathroom, he'd already herded all her lotions and potions into one corner of the vanity unit – she swept them with her arm into another plastic container.

From the rest of the house, she took very little. It didn't feel right – taking things from the kitchen and the living room felt petty and vindictive. She didn't want to divide up the books or the DVDs or the good glasses. It felt unutterably sad. She took one photograph – a picture of the two of them with the three children in wetsuits peeled to the waist that had been taken with the tripod a few years ago on the beach at Salcombe. She didn't know what she'd do with it, but she laid it on top of a box of coats, remembering the hot sunny day, and the happy feeling.

When she'd finished, and had carried all the boxes out to her car under the steady gaze of the old woman who lived in the house across the road, she made herself a cup of tea and sat for the last time at the kitchen table, spinning the house key between her fingers, and wondering whether or not to write a note.

She heard a key in the lock. Looking up at the kitchen clock, she saw that it was 6 p.m. She hoped Douglas hadn't changed his mind. She'd been more upset by the process than she'd expected, and she wasn't ready for a scene.

But it was Daisy. 'Hiya.' She pulled off her backpack, and sat down in the opposite chair.

'What are you doing here?'

'Dad said you were coming to clear out your stuff today. I wanted to see you.'

'Oh.' Susannah stood up. 'Do you want some tea?'

Daisy shook her head, then sat forward in her chair, resting her face on her elbows.

'How's Seth?'

'Fine. Good.'

'Rosie?'

She shrugged. 'Okay, I suppose.'

397

'Have you come to see me, Daisy?'

She nodded, twisting her earring in her earlobe, and pulling her sleeves down over her hands. 'I want to ask you not to leave.'

'Daisy . . .'

'Don't leave Dad. Don't leave us.'

'Daisy, please.'

'I mean it, Susannah. Dad loves you. I think he knows he's been crap. He can change, I know he can. If he wants to. And if changing meant he could keep you, I think he'd want to.'

'Did your dad ask you to come and talk to me?'

Daisy snorted. 'No. God. He's got no idea I'm here. All my own idea. Not just for Dad, either. I love you, Susannah. Rosie and Fin do, too. We don't want you to go. And you're choosing to leave us, too.'

Now Susannah's eyes filled with instant tears. Daisy had never said anything remotely like this to her – not even last year, after all that business with Seth.

'I know it sounds weird, but you've been more of a parent to us, sometimes, than our real mum and dad have been. That stuff with Seth – I couldn't have gone to either of them about that. You helped me, Susannah. You. Same with Rosie. What are we supposed to do if you go?'

She had started to cry herself now.

'And I know we haven't been all that great to you. I feel so stupid now. I took it for granted, you know, even though you and Dad weren't married – I just assumed you'd always be here. I feel like I was just, you know, really getting to know you. I like coming here. I like having you to talk to.'

'We can still be friends, Daisy.' It sounded feeble, and even as Susannah said it, she knew it.

'That's not the same. Besides, you'll move on. You're already moving out. You'll find someone else. You'll have your own kids, maybe. We're nothing to you.' Tears rolled unchecked down her cheeks now.

Susannah went round the table to kneel by Daisy's chair, and wiped away a tear with her hand. She was shaken by the vehemence of what Daisy was saying. 'Don't you ever say that. You're *not* nothing to me.'

'I wish Dad had married you. Then you'd be our stepmother.'

Maybe if he had, things would be different.

'But we might still be splitting up, Daisy. You can see that, can't you?'

'You don't really think that, do you?'

Susannah didn't know. If. If. If. 'It doesn't matter, Daisy. Not really.' She struggled to explain it. 'It's complicated.'

'Adults always say that. It isn't. Not at all. You love someone, or you don't.'

Susannah smiled. In a way, Daisy was absolutely right. Just like her dad had been. Young people understood, it seemed, what old people knew. It was just the ones in the middle who didn't get it. She nodded. 'I don't. Not any more. I don't love your dad any more the way you need to love someone if you're planning to stay with them, spend the rest of your life with them. I don't. I'm sorry, Daisy.'

Daisy stared at her with wide eyes.

'And it doesn't matter why not. You're right. Adults do complicate things. It's irrelevant whose fault it is, or what made it this way. It just is.'

Daisy shrugged. 'So, that's it, just like that.'

'There isn't really any other way for it to be. I can't stay for him, and I can't stay for you guys.'

'I know.' Her voice was very small now.

'It wouldn't be right, and it wouldn't work.'

Daisy nodded and sniffed. Her sweater was pulled down over her hands, like it always was, but Susannah could see that she was wringing them, twisting the fingers around each other, trying to stop the emotion that was pouring out.

She held the girl in her arms for a moment, taking in the smell of her hair, and the slightness of her narrow shoulders. She felt close to tears herself. She hadn't been prepared for this.

Daisy pulled away first, embarrassed. 'So. That's it. I'm sorry I came, I suppose. I didn't want to make it worse.'

'You didn't, Daisy. If it doesn't sound too crap, I'm really glad you came. I didn't know, I honestly didn't, how you felt about me. I'm glad you told me. And . . . if you'd like, I really hope we can still see each other. I'm not just saying that. I mean it.'

'Really?'

'Really. You have my number, and my email address. I'll always be happy to hear from you, Daisy. You can tell Rosie the same thing. Fin, too.'

She didn't cry until much later, when she'd carried all the boxes out of the car and upstairs to the new flat. Not until she'd opened the box with the coats, and seen the beach picture, nestled on the top.

And then she sat on the carpet with her back against the wardrobe door and cried and cried.

On the Sunday, Jonathan looked after the kids while Amelia came with her to Ikea, muttering something under his breath about preferring a chemotherapy session to a trip to Ikea . . . They bought a couple of big, vibrant canvas pictures, snow-white bed linen, a modernist rug, and some new dishes and glasses. They stopped at a florist's on the way back, and Amelia bought armfuls of daffodils and tulips, which she arranged into the new vases they'd bought.

The flat looked much more lived in when they'd finished putting the new things in place.

Before she left, Amelia hugged her friend tight. 'You going to be okay? Want me to stay?'

Susannah laughed. 'Permanently?'

'Just for tonight. Though permanently sounds tempting. Be just like the good old days, wouldn't it?'

'Except for – I don't know – the one bed, the kids you've got at home . . . the mess I've made of my life . . .'

'Your life isn't a mess, Susannah. Your life is clean and clear and accessorized, if I may say so, beautifully. You've made the big, hard decisions, and, at the risk of sounding all Oprah, I'm so proud of you for doing that. And you've got hair. As of right now, your life makes a lot more sense to me than it has done in years.'

Susannah felt a stab of guilt. Amelia might not say that if she really knew. But she wasn't asking. Things were delicate between them, still, and Susannah knew it was easier this way.

Rob would be here in an hour or so. She kissed Amelia, and ushered her out, promising to pick her up on Monday. Rob was coming. She ached to see him. She knew he'd gone home – he'd texted her briefly to say his dad wasn't well, that his mum needed him. She hadn't liked to chase him. It was weird, but she still didn't feel she had rights – despite what had happened between them. So, she knew he was at his mum's and she knew the number, but she daren't ring. In the middle of the night, she had woken up in a panic. He was backing out. He was backing away. But in the morning she felt better. She willed herself to believe that this particular dream was inexorably coming true. That she'd waited this long for him and she could wait a bit longer.

He was coming in an hour. He was.

And he did.

He came. But she knew straight away that something

was very, very wrong. Rob hadn't shaved, and she hadn't seen him with a few days' growth before. He looked older. For a second or two, he held himself aloof from her embrace, his shoulders straight and stiff. But then he crumpled, and let himself be held. She pulled him into the living room, and on to the sofa. She waited for him to tell her, sensing that it was difficult for him to speak and willing herself to stay calm.

'He loves me, he loves me. It is going to be alright.' She almost chanted the mantra out loud.

'My dad died.'

'Oh God, Rob.' She hadn't even thought it might be that. Relief flooded her. And was followed immediately by sorrow. For Rob, for Lois, for lovely Frank – who she had adored. 'I'm so sorry. When?'

'Yesterday. Yesterday afternoon. I've been with Mum.'

Susannah's eyes had filled with sudden tears.

Rob brushed one from her cheek.

'Of course.' She nodded. 'How is she?'

Rob shrugged. 'Lousy. She can't stop crying. It's all she does. It's scary, you know. I can't help her.'

Susannah's tears of pity for Lois came faster now. She struggled to find what to say.

'I'm sure you helped her just by being there.'

Rob laughed, but there was no humour in the sound. 'I wasn't even there.'

'When he died?'

'When she needed me most. I was with you.'

'I don't understand.'

'We were in bed together. After I got back from France. After you left Douglas. She'd been leaving messages. She'd left all these messages. She needed me. Dad's breathing got bad. She had to get him to hospital. She had to let them put a tube down his throat to breathe for him. She wanted me to be there. To help her. But I never got the damn message.'

'Oh my God.'

Rob stood up and walked over to the window.

'Would it have made any difference, if you'd been there?'

He shook his head, but he didn't look at her. 'Not to my dad. If they hadn't tubed him, he'd have died. But it would have made all the difference in the world to Mum. She shouldn't have had to go through that alone.'

Susannah nodded. He was right, she knew.

Now Rob sat down heavily on the chair at the table. 'I can't believe what I did.'

'You didn't do anything, Rob. You couldn't have known.'

'I wasn't thinking about him, Susie. I wasn't think-ing about either of them.'

He was thinking about us, she thought. That's all either of us could think about. We've been in a beau-tiful bubble. She felt it bursting all around them in the room, pricked by their new reality. 'What happened? I mean, if you want to talk about it.'

Rob shrugged. 'Once the tube was in, it was the beginning of the end. Everything shuts down.'

'Did he know what was going on?'

'I don't think so. I looked at him, you know. Stared at him. But he never opened his eyes. Not after I got there.'

Susannah wanted to ask questions – had they taken the decision to switch the machines off, or had Frank died naturally? But she knew it wasn't the time.

'Mum couldn't let go. She sat there and held his hand, and her eyes never looked anywhere at all but at his face. They took the tubes out, the drips and stuff – took it all away and switched off the machines, and still she just sat there. In the end, I had to peel her hand off his. She didn't say anything at all. Not to me. She just kept saying, over and over again "mio amore", "mio amore". It was what he used to call her. When she said it, he laughed at her accent. Not unkindly, you know. Just because it made him smile. She said it to him then. So quietly you almost couldn't hear it. I think the nurses thought she was praying over him or something.'

Rob rubbed his bloodshot eyes. 'I can't believe he's gone.'

She went to him, hugged him from behind, and he took her hand, raising it to his mouth to kiss it. It was a gesture that was pure Frank – a memory from years ago. She kissed the top of his head very gently.

'I loved him.'

'I know.'

They stayed that way for a long while, without speaking. Susannah knew Rob was crying, and she let him, smoothing his hair, her arm tightly around him.

When she was uncomfortable standing that way any longer, she moved round in front of him and pushed him back towards the sofa, looking at him. He looked back. Then he put one hand on either side of her face and pulled her down on to the sofa with him in an unexpected, deep kiss. He almost fell on to her from the sofa, and they lay kissing on the floor, pulling at each other's clothes. He felt a sudden deep need for her, to be connected to her, and she responded, desperate to be whatever he needed her to be. Right now, it felt like proof that he was still alive. This wasn't like the time before. This time was urgent and fast, his hips pumping into her wide-open thighs, her hands on his back. He was only inside her for a few minutes before he came, looking deep into her eyes, and when he did, he sobbed again into the side of her neck, his face hot and sweaty against her skin.

Later, they lay together on the sofa, under a blanket, talking about what was happening. Rob was calm now. Frank never went to church. He was Catholic, of course – baptized, but not confirmed – but Lois wasn't. Susannah hadn't realized. The vicar at St Gabriel's had agreed to do the service – Frank wouldn't want a funeral mass, Lois said, and she knew no one at the Catholic church. She didn't know many people at St

Gabriel's either, but the vicar was kind, Rob said, and obviously understood that Lois wanted this done in the simplest way. He'd be cremated, after the service, at the local crematorium.

Frank was at the undertaker's now, Rob said. They'd taken in his best navy-blue suit, and sorted out the coffin and flowers. There was very little to do – Lois had discovered that Frank had spoken to the undertaker already, just after his diagnosis, and paid for what he'd chosen, and that had caused fresh tears. 'He'd thought of everything to make my life easier,' she said, wringing a handkerchief in her hands, 'but he couldn't fix the one thing I cared about, bless him.'

There weren't many people to notify. Rob had called a cousin, and asked him to spread the word among what family remained.

'Will Helena be able to come home?' Susannah asked, terrified of the answer.

'She could. For the death of a parent-in-law – you'd get compassionate leave for that, if you asked for it.'

'And so, has she asked for it? Will she?'

'I haven't spoken to her yet. I'm going to ask her not to come.' Rob wondered whether he meant ask her, or tell her. Either way he knew he didn't want her to make the journey.

He wasn't letting himself think about whether that would hurt her.

Rob felt almost panicked by his distress. Everywhere he turned there was mess, and he felt as if it was all his fault. A line he thought he'd remembered from some action or war film kept running through his head . . . something about the enemy threatening to inflict a world of hurt and pain . . . ?

'I'll come. If you like. I know . . . I mean, I know I can't sit with you. I wouldn't want to do that. I just . . . if you'll let me, I'd just like to be there, for Frank. For you.'

And he couldn't tell her no.

May

St Gabriel's wasn't full for Frank's funeral – people only occupied the first four or five pews. Empty churches were maudlin. He and Lois hadn't had all that many friends, Susannah remembered. They hadn't seemed to need much beyond each other. Most of the people were relatives, she thought. While the organist played, six undertakers carried the oak coffin in on their shoulders, performing the awkward, slow three-point turn at the front of the church that always made a coffin wobble worryingly, and then laid it on the wooden stands set up in front of the altar. It was adorned with a simple wreath of yellow roses. Lois had arrived first, and was sitting in a front pew with her back to everyone. Rob threw her a brief, sad smile as he passed, then walked to the front to sit beside her, and she leant into him a little.

Susannah was sitting alone in a pew very near to the back. She'd driven down this morning, telling no one where she was going, and she'd drive back afterwards. She knew she wouldn't be able to talk to Rob today, nor to touch him, but she needed to be near him.

As the organist began playing the first hymn, her mother slid into the pew beside her, dressed in a neat black shirt dress. Susannah should have realized Rosemary would know what was going on at St Gabriel's, but she was surprised to see her. Rosemary kissed her daughter on the cheek, and held her hand as she sang, with vigour, in her tuneful soprano.

After the service, the two of them sat still and quiet while the mourners filed out behind the coffin. Rob didn't look up, nor did Lois seem to see her. After a minute or so, just the two of them remained in the cool church.

Rosemary bent her head in a last, silent prayer, then stacked her hymn book neatly on the shelf, unable to resist a quick dust check with her index finger as she stood up. 'Shall we?' She was gesturing at the back door – the same escape route Susannah had taken with Alastair after Alex's wedding, all those months and all those decisions ago.

They sat on the same bench outside. It was warm.

'How did you know I'd be here?'

'I'm not daft. Not as daft as you think I am, at any rate. I put it all together. Your dad told me about you going to France. Told me about Rob. It wasn't difficult to figure out.'

'You got me.'

'No one's trying to "get you", Susannah. We just want to help.'

'I don't think you can, Mum.'

'I could try. If you'd talk to me.'

Susannah sighed. She wasn't even sure where to begin. Wasn't sure, any more, where this story originated. Was it with Douglas or with Rob? Falling out of love, or into it?

'Can you try, love? Just try?'

She looked at her mum's concerned face, and felt her own contort with sudden tears. 'Oh, Mum. It's all such a huge bloody mess.'

'What is?'

'My life. My entire life.'

'Sweetheart!'

'It's all going wrong. It's all running away from me. I can't control any of it.'

'That's not true. You've left Douglas, I take it?'

Susannah nodded.

'Well, that needed you to take charge of it, God knows. Your dad and I have known for ages that he wasn't making you happy.'

'You knew?'

Rosemary nodded. 'Of course. We all did. It had been such a long time since the two of you had been properly together. I hated to see it.'

'You never said.'

'You wouldn't have listened. You had to get there on your own.'

'Well, I got there. I moved out. It's all over.'

Hurt flashed briefly across Rosemary's face.

'I'm sorry I hadn't told you, Mum.'

She swiped the apology away. 'It doesn't matter. The important thing is that you did it. You'd have told us, when you were ready.'

Susannah wondered whether Rob would come looking for her – wondering why she hadn't filed out of the church door with the others – but it was quiet.

'And Rob? What about him?'

'Rob's married, Mum.'

If Rosemary's middle-class suburban sensibilities were ruffled, she had the presence of mind not to let her face betray her, and even in the midst of her distress, Susannah was grateful for that.

'But he loves you?'

Susannah nodded. He did, didn't he? Hadn't he said so? 'And I love him. I know what we're doing is wrong, Mum. I know it. I don't want to hurt anyone. Nor does Rob. But I'm doing it anyway. That's what I mean about my life being out of control. That's not me – that's not who I am . . .'

'So, why . . . ?' Mum's tone wasn't judgmental, or even harsh. She was trying, Susannah knew, really trying to understand.

But Susannah struggled to find the words to explain

it. 'Because I have nothing else, Mum. Because I'm forty years old, and I've missed it all. I haven't got anything. I haven't got a husband or a child. I haven't got a proper home any more. Christ Almighty – could I sound *any more pathetic*? But this is where I am. Because it feels like he's the only man who ever loved me properly. Because grabbing at second chances feels like all I have left.'

And so now, because he seemed to need it, and because she didn't know what else to do, Susannah gave Rob space to do what he needed. It was ironic, really. It was one of Douglas's big words. Space. That's what he needed, when he retreated upstairs, away from her and the kids, to the whisky and the jazz. That's what he claimed he was giving her, even though at the time she hadn't wanted it.

She didn't want it now. She wanted to be with Rob. She wanted to hold him while he cried, and feed him and clean his clothes. Dress him, and smooth his hair.

He had practical things to do. Things to sort out. Lois was his priority, and she understood that. At least, with whichever part of her brain wasn't screaming and crying for his attention. It occurred to her, one long lonely evening with too much red wine, that maybe Helena felt exactly that way, sitting in desert fatigues, thousands of miles away, unable to comfort her husband. That they had this feeling in common. They both made him feel guilty, too – too much for either of them to help now. They had that in common as well.

And this new life went on, with its unfamiliar landscape. If my life were a film, she thought, this would be the section with no dialogue, where they play an apposite soundtrack over me going through my everyday routines. Here I am at the drycleaner's. Now I'm finding out where in my new neighbourhood sells the freshest fruit. I'm on the underground, and then I'm sitting in a meeting, gesticulating, maybe even smiling, though be sure that the camera will catch my far-off look when no one else is watching. I'm sticking a ready meal in the microwave and pouring a glass of wine. I'm lying awake in the bed, moonlight on my sleepless face. Here I am with my best friend, who is really just a pale, wan, weak shadow of the bright firefly she used to be before this illness and the treatment for it, and we're so used to this by now, this new Amelia, that we don't even look horrified. I carry the coffees and the magazines and she just tries to keep her head high and we talk about anything and everything – except him, because the peace between us is precious and hard won. *And all of this time he's not with me.* What would the song be? And what might the audience think of me? When I'm crying on the sofa, hugging myself because there is no one else here to hold me, do they feel sorry for me, or do they condemn me to all that I deserve?

She avoided home. She was embarrassed by breaking down with her mother, ashamed to see her father.

Dad took to leaving messages on her answering machine in the flat. One every couple of days. He rang when he knew she wasn't there, in the middle of the day. 'I know you don't feel like talking, love,' he said, the first time. 'But I thought listening might be okay. I just wanted to say that I love you. And so does your mum. And we're here.' And he was right, as he so often was. Listening was okay, and she was grateful.

Alastair wasn't so respectful of her desire to be left alone. It was Millie's birthday, and they were having an animal party next Saturday afternoon, and she was coming, he said, whether she wanted to or not. In costume, ideally. Susannah knew from the tone of his voice on the machine that Mum had told him (everything, she guessed, knowing Mum), but she couldn't even be angry. It was almost a relief that he knew, and that she didn't have to explain it all.

She wore a brown stripy sweater and brown cords and said to Millie, who answered the door, a resplendent ladybird, that she'd come as an earwig. Millie wrinkled her nose in distaste, but hugged her anyway, before shrieking and squealing and running off back to the conservatory, where her friends were. Kathryn wasn't far behind her daughter, in a black mini dress, with yellow and black stripy tights and an antenna headband.

'Mole?' She looked her sister-in-law up and down appraisingly, her hands on her hips.

Susannah shrugged. 'Earwig.'

'Pathetic.'

'Hey! I'm here, aren't I?'

Kathryn laughed and kissed her. 'And thank God. It's like a zoo in here. Literally. Come on in . . . Al's expecting you . . .'

Al was in the conservatory, small children running amok around him, chatting to a guy in a safari suit and a pith helmet. When he saw his sister, he excused himself and came over, holding her in a long, wonderful hug.

'I needed that.'

'Thought you might.'

'You thought right.'

He held her shoulders and smiled at her. 'Nice costume.'

Susannah ignored him and gestured towards the guy he'd been talking to. 'Dr Livingstone, I presume?'

Alastair sniggered. 'He's the entertainment.'

'What's he going to do?'

'See that box?'

Susannah nodded.

'A tarantula, a python, a scorpion . . .'

'For real?'

'I hope so. He costs a fortune, and comes highly recommended, Kath says.'

'Bloody hell! Won't he scare them to death?'

'I just hope he holds their attention for twenty minutes and keeps the racket down to a dull thunder . . .'

Susannah realized they were having to shout at each other to make themselves heard. How could small people make so much noise? 'Whatever happened to balloon animals and rabbits in hats?'

'We never even had that, did we?'

Susannah laughed. 'No. You're right. We played that game where you had to cut cold chocolate with a knife and fork . . .'

'And bob for apples . . .'

'And eat marshmallows hanging on string . . .'

'You'd be laughed out of the PTA for that nowa-days.'

'Bollocks. I bet the kids would love it.'

'Well, I suggest you suggest it to Kath . . .'

They both looked at Kathryn, across the room, arranging trays of fairy cakes and pineapple hedge-hogs on a table.

'Perhaps not today . . .'

Susannah wasn't sure whether the children were paralysed with terror or genuinely fascinated by the animals, once the show started, but they were certainly quiet. Kathryn shot a video of Millie with a tarantula on the top of her head, Sadie watching with her wide mouth open in wonder. Oscar, still steadfastly refus-ing to walk at eighteenth months old, shuffled around at warp speed on his bum, drooling on everything in his reach, and chatting happily to himself.

I want this, Susannah thought to herself. I want this.

Much later, when the circus had left town, Kathryn put the three exhausted and sugar-crashing kids in front of a video, and joined the two of them and a bottle of wine in the kitchen, pulling off her headband and plopping into a chair gratefully, beaming with tired satisfaction.

'Thank Christ that's over.'

Susannah knew she didn't entirely mean it. Kathryn was in her element doing stuff like this. She was an amazing mother – calm and fun, imaginative and energetic, warm and funny. And lucky. So lucky.

'So, how are you doing, Sis?' she asked, turning now to focus on Susannah.

Al poured her a large glass, and Susannah watched him kiss the top of her head as he handed it to her.

'I guess Mum's told you guys what's going on?'

Kathryn nodded. 'Pretty much. Sorry. You know its eighty-five per cent concern, fifteen per cent gossip, right?'

Susannah laughed. Kathryn knew her mother-in-law very well.

'And your dad – he's one hundred per cent concern.'

'Not even five per cent disapproving?'

Alastair shook his head vigorously. 'None of us is judging you, Suze. I promise.'

'I don't know why not. I'm judging myself.' She smiled a tight smile.

'Okay.' This was Kathryn, who'd sat forward and taken a deep breath. 'I'm judging you, just a bit. I love you. I love you a lot. But . . .'

'I know. He's married.' She was relieved Kathryn was being honest.

'And it's not a level playing field, is it? She doesn't know about you. It's not a fair fight.'

'Is it a fight, then, do you think?' Alastair asked.

Susannah shrugged. 'I don't know what it is. I'm trying to give him some space. You're right, Kathryn. Thank you for being honest.'

Kathryn reached over and squeezed her sister-in-law's hand.

'He *is* married. This isn't who I am. What I do. And I'm not going to cry.' She made a fist with her hand, willed herself to stay in control.

'What are you going to do?'

'I can't do anything now, can I? I have to wait. I'm not holding any of the cards. If I deserve to be punished, then I promise you I am being.'

'He needs time.' This was Alastair. 'Look, I know I don't know this guy as he is now, but there was a time when I knew him pretty well. There's something about all of this that is somehow completely unsurprising to me. I was saying, to Kathryn. You two were never properly resolved. I don't know, don't remember, don't even want to know what went on, all those years ago. But you were never really finished with each other. And I don't know what's going on with him now. But I do know that you've been miserable, stuck in a sterile, crappy relationship for years. You were vulnerable, Sis. It makes sense – perfect sense to me – that he comes back now, that your life isn't where you want it to be, that you fall for him again.

You never fell out. Not really. Not through Sean, not through Douglas. I should have seen it coming last summer.'

'That's quite a speech, Al.'

'I've been thinking about it . . .' Kathryn nodded.

'But you don't have answers . . . ?'

'Course not. But I know what you should do.'

'And that is?'

'Give him time. He's a thinker. He always was. And he's a good guy. He's not a cheater either. He always had more moral fibre than the rest of us put together.'

Susannah remembered the caravan, and Alastair and Amelia, a thousand years ago.

'So, you know he's got to be in just as big a mess as you. Throw the Greek tragedy of his dad dying while he's with you into the mix, and that's one hell of a lot of crap to deal with. Give him time.'

'And if it is right, he'll come back? Is that what you're saying? Set it free if you love it? Because you're sounding dangerously like a Sting song . . .'

Alastair shrugged. 'I didn't say it was an original thought. But I think I'm right. And Sting's right.'

'Not about the tantric sex, he's not.' Kathryn, draining her glass, broke the tension beautifully. 'We tried it once. Both fell asleep before anything whatsoever happened in the loins department.'

When Rob's mobile phone number flashed up on the caller ID, Susannah's heart leapt like a schoolgirl's. She wondered whether she'd always feel that way, almost running across the room to answer, wrapped in a towel after the shower, and throwing herself into the sofa, eager to hear the sound of his voice. Maybe he was running late . . . or early. She'd longed for him all day. She hadn't seen him since Frank's funeral, and her meltdown with Mum. She was desperate. It was an ache – a delicious, throbbing ache.

'Susie? It's me.'

'Are you okay?'

He sounded frightened and tense. Susannah sat up immediately, clutching the towel to her.

'It's Helena.'

She'd found out. She must have done. How? 'What's happened?'

'She's been injured.'

'Oh my God!' Thoughts raced through her brain. 'How badly?'

'I don't know . . .' Rob sounded desperate.

'Well, what did they tell you?' He knew people – he had to have more information than that.

'Just that. She's being flown to Germany now, to the military hospital. I only know that because a mate called me. If I was a civilian I'd still have no clue anything was up.'

'I didn't think she was in a dangerous place.' He'd said she would be safe.

'For fuck's sake, Susannah – the whole place is dangerous. It's Afghanistan. It's a combat zone.'

'I'm sorry. Of course.' Her tongue felt thick, and she couldn't find words.

'No – I'm sorry. I don't mean to snap.'

'You're worried.'

'Worried, and frustrated as hell. I can't get through to anyone who can tell me what's happening.'

'Do you think . . . I mean . . . is there a possibility she could be . . .'

She couldn't bring herself to say it, but Rob did, and the word sounded flat and harsh.

'Dead? No – they don't airlift them out straight away if they're dead.' It sounded so matter-of-fact.

She told herself she couldn't help the thought that snaked into her brain. She couldn't even quite translate it. Did she wish Helena was dead, because it would make things easier – clear the way for her and Rob? Just for a moment? Could she be that cruel about a woman she'd never met? She couldn't tell what Rob was thinking, and he wasn't speaking. She wished she could see his face.

'Listen – I'd better go. I need to make some more calls.' He wanted to get off the phone.

She couldn't help him. Or reach him. 'Of course. You're not coming tonight?' It was only half a question. She sounded like a whiny child, even to herself.

'I'll call you, okay?'

He hung up before she could say anything else, leaving her sitting on the sofa, wrapped in a towel, staring at the wall.

For the first time in a very long time, she thought of Ichabod, their old English teacher, and a quote – was it Shakespeare? – dredged itself up from somewhere long forgotten. Something about sorrows coming not single spies but in battalions . . . She was reeling . . .

It was two long days before he called again. Two long days in which she barely slept. Her life with Rob played like an old cine film in her head whenever she lay down to rest.

She couldn't believe it. That these two things would, could happen so close together. Their old life, this new life they'd begun to build . . . the life she hadn't been able to stop herself imagining for the pair of them . . . going forward into the future . . . She didn't want to think about it, but she couldn't help it.

His voice sounded different. He was calling because he had to. Not because he wanted to. She could tell from his tone.

'Susie?'

'Rob. God. I'm so glad to hear you.' She tried not to respond that way. But she couldn't help that either. She'd never been so helpless, it seemed.

He didn't answer.

'How is . . . how's Helena? Are you with her?'

'Yes. She got back yesterday.'

'How is she?'

His voice almost broke then, and so did Susannah's heart.

'She's going to be okay.'

Susannah remembered Rob not wanting to talk about Helena, when they were in France. Saying it felt disloyal. She wasn't sure what to say. 'Was she . . . badly hurt?'

'Yes.' He sounded like he was fighting back tears.

She wondered who they were for. 'But she's not . . . in danger?'

He sniffed, hard. 'No. She's out of the woods.'

Again, silence.

'Thank you for letting me know.' She sounded bizarrely formal.

'I said I'd call. I don't know when I'll be able to call again.'

'I understand.' What choice did she have? 'Rob?'

'Yes?'

'I'm thinking of you. Both of you.'

'Thanks, Susie. Bye.'

The letter came later that week. It was waiting for her when she came home from work, lying among a pile of utility bills and catalogues. He hadn't called. She hadn't slept well – lying for hours, hot and wide awake, under twisted sheets, checking her phone every few minutes for a text. A letter felt ominous and important, and she couldn't bring herself to open it straight away. She laid it against the fruit bowl on the round table, and poured a glass of wine, staring at it.

Dear Susie

Helena is recovering. We know more now, more about how it happened. It was a classic situation. She was in a helicopter, being transferred between bases, when it was hit by a rocket. Helicopters are noisy targets. It's easier for rockets to hit them and cause damage than to hit the camps — where they don't do much, most of the time. I remember that now. The explosion killed three of the people with her, but most of the others were uninjured, including the pilot, thank God. She was pretty badly hit — she and the dead guys caught the worst of it, apparently, but she's going to be okay. At first they were worried about how much blood she had lost, but she pulled through. She's got a lot of cuts and bruises. She's lost her right leg. It was blown away at mid-calf by the explosion, but they have amputated to just below her knee. It could have been a lot worse — and I know that sounds callous, but loss of limb is one of the most common injuries in this whole war, and they're really well set up for convalescence and rehabilitation. And it's much easier to relearn if you still have a knee. She'll wear a prosthetic, eventually. Walk without crutches, just a limp.

But they always say — and I know something about this — that the injuries you can't see are the ones to really worry about. She went through a lot out there, and it will be a while before she's okay again. She still

424

can't speak much about it, not yet. They've got her pretty doped up, and she's still quite out of it.

She's in Selly Oak, the forces hospital in Birmingham – for the next while, at least. I'm here with her. I've taken leave from work, and I'll be here while she is. Her mum is here, too.

I can't tell her about us now, Susie. I don't know when I'll be able to tell her. Or if. This changes things for all of us. She's my wife, Susie, and I have to take care of her now. What I feel, or what I want – that doesn't seem to matter as much right now.

I hope you understand. I hope you can forgive me. I'll be in touch when I can. Trust me.

I do love you. I always have. I always will.

Rob

Helen had brushed Helena's hair, grown longer since she'd seen her. It curled becomingly across her forehead now, and below her ears, at her neck. The gash on her forehead had been restitched at Selly Oak – invisible inside stitches held the sides together. Helen had gently wiped away the crusted blood, too, so that there was only a purple line really, about three inches long, with a shadow of yellow bruising running along it. It came perilously close to her left eye. Small red scabs, each about a centimetre across, dotted her cheeks and neck. The doctor said they'd leave only very faint scars – they were superficial.

The real wound was beneath the blankets. Rob had made himself look, the first time they'd been alone. There was nothing to see, of course. The stump of his wife's right leg was bound tightly with pristine bandages, rounded and smooth – a careful job.

He and Helen were taking turns sitting with her. They had a relatives' room two floors down – a single bed they shared, one sleeping while the other stayed with Helena. Helen had arrived before him – he'd called her as soon as he knew they were bringing Helena here, and Helen was closer. She was tough, Helen. He'd forgotten – or maybe he'd never known how tough. She hadn't cried – at least, not in front of him. She fixed each doctor they saw with a steely gaze, asking pertinent questions. She'd asked the nurses to let her wash Helena herself, and she'd done it as gently as if she were washing a newborn.

Rob had stood and watched her, touched deeply by her tenderness. 'They said they'd given her a wash in the hospital, after she was born,' she said to him while she worked. 'But she wasn't clean. She still had that stuff – that white stuff, you know? – all over her. In her ears, all through her hair. They said I didn't need to do anything else. So I waited, until they'd gone. Until they thought we were all asleep. And I took her into the bathroom then, and ran a sink and washed her myself. Washed her properly. Dried her in my dressing gown. Then she was gorgeous. You were gorgeous, weren't you, darling? You were then. You are now.'

426

Helen did the days. She wanted to be there, she said, when the doctors did their rounds. He was glad she wanted to do that. It left him with the nights. He slept fitfully, restlessly, in the narrow single bed during the day, and sat in the garden nursing endless cups of bad hospital coffee. Sometimes he sat with Helen, and listened to stories about his wife when she was a girl. But the nights were his.

In the beginning they kept her unconscious, and she lay very, very still in the bed. Then, when she was first conscious, she still hardly moved. She groaned a little, and from time to time her eyelids flickered open, but she retreated quickly back into sleep. He watched her face while she slept, watched her eyeballs move from side to side under her closed lids in dreams. He wanted to know what she was dreaming.

She used to have nightmares, sometimes, before this happened. She'd had one on their honeymoon. He'd woken up to the sound of her grinding her teeth, her fists balled by her side, gripping the sheets tightly. He'd worried about waking her, knowing it could be dangerous, but then she'd sat bolt upright, her eyes open in fright. He'd sat up, too, and folded her into his arms while her breathing subsided and her chest stopped heaving – and while she recounted the illogical, evil terror of her dream to him – and he promised, as though she was a child, that he would protect her and take care of her. It had moved him to see his confident young wife look up at him with gratitude and trust and love in her eyes.

He knew now that what he was feeling wasn't pity. As he drove up the M1 to find her, he had examined his feelings, worried it might be pity after all. But it wasn't. It wasn't guilt either, though he felt that in spades through the long quiet nights. It had nothing to do with her accident, or her pathetic stump, or her long road to recovery. He loved her. Not the way he loved Susannah, he knew. But he loved her.

He was waiting for her to wake up from this nightmare. He was going to be there, just as he'd promised her he would be.

June

When the doorbell rang, and Susannah went to answer the door, it didn't occur to her to be surprised to see Lois on her threshold. She wondered if she'd got her address from Rob – or had she spoken to Mum and Dad? It didn't matter . . . somehow, it felt as if she'd been expecting her. This time, though, there was no encompassing, warm embrace. Lois had lost weight, even since the funeral. She looked slight and old standing there, with no make-up on. Susannah guessed that she knew everything. Or knew enough.

She stood back, and ushered her in. 'How is he? How's Helena?'

'She's going to be okay. She has a fair amount of pain, and she's still a bit confused.'

'Where is she?'

'She's still in Birmingham, at Selly Oak. It'll be a goodish while, I expect. Rob's there, too.'

'Of course. Is he okay?'

Lois shook her head. 'No. No, Susannah. He isn't okay. He's a mess.'

'I'm sorry, Lois. I'm really sorry.'

Lois put her hand on Susannah's arm. 'I didn't come here for that.'

'But I am.'

'It doesn't matter, love. It doesn't help.' She wasn't angry.

'But I can't help, can I? I know that.'

'Oh, but you can. You can. You can stay away from him. Leave him alone. When he got back from France, when he found out he'd been with you, you know, when his dad was taken into the hospital . . . when he saw the tube, and he realized he'd never talk to him again . . . Well, he was devastated. I'd never seen him so upset.

'And now, he's got all this with Helena to deal with. And that's what he wants to do, and that's what he needs to do.'

'Did he send you to talk to me?'

'No. I daresay he'd be furious if he knew I was here. I'm here because I need you to help him.'

'You just asked me to leave him alone.'

'Same thing, Susannah. I don't know if he can stay away from you on his own. I don't know exactly what's going on between you two – but I know it's got him all twisted up.'

'Both of us.'

'But I can't worry about you, lovely. I can only worry about him. He's all I have now. And I may just be an old lady, but I know one thing about him for sure. If he leaves Helena now, if he leaves her for you – he'll never forgive himself. And you'll never be able to be happy without that. It can't work. Don't you see?

'Your time – the time for the two of you – has passed, Susannah. It's gone.'

It was amazing how life went on as normal. Every morning the alarm clock went off, and Susannah got out of bed. She showered. She ate breakfast, watched the news. She got dressed, and dried her hair and put on her make-up. She just never looked herself in the eye in the bathroom mirror. Because it hurt too much. She went to work. Out to lunch with colleagues. To business meetings where she spoke to long tables of listening faces. She shopped for food, but she didn't cook it. At home, at night, she sat in front of the television for hours, though she couldn't have told you afterwards which programmes she watched. The phone rang, and she always leapt for it, but if she saw Mum and Dad, or Amelia on the caller ID, she didn't answer. It took six rings before the phone went to the machine, and she counted them. The last four rings reproached her. She knew they were concerned for her. But she had no energy for conversation. She had never been so exhausted. She felt like the bloke who walked the London Marathon course in a diving suit. A thousand pounds heavier, ten times slower than her normal self. The rest of the world was muffled and distant. She could hear her own heartbeat in her head. All the time. Hear each breath.

Pushing an almost empty shopping trolley aimlessly down the aisle of Tesco's late one evening, she vaguely remembered needing shampoo. In the toiletries aisle she stopped suddenly in front of the tampons and towels. The realization that she'd missed a period cut a streak of vivid lucidity through the fog in which she had been existing. She tried counting backwards in her head, but she got muddled, so she pulled her diary out of her handbag and stood in the aisle, counting days.

It was possible.

She picked up a pregnancy test. It was the second one she had ever bought. Sean's baby – that had been the first, and that had been a long, long time ago. She read the back of the box. Remembered.

And her thoughts raced. Faster than she could keep track of them. A baby would be born in the winter. In time for Valentine's Day, maybe. She'd be heavily pregnant for Christmas. A boy or a girl? Twins? Her heart pounded.

She should call him. He had a right to know. She had a right to tell him. Should she tell him she suspected, or should she take the test and tell him once she knew for sure? She smiled to herself. An older lady walking past saw the smile, saw the box, smiled back conspiratorially.

But the daydream died as quickly as it had been born, and she turned her back on the woman. She had no rights. She knew that, even before Lois's visit. Before Mum, and Amelia, and everyone else told her, she already knew. And she couldn't tell him. She couldn't do that to him.

At home, she put the pregnancy test on a shelf in the bathroom cabinet. She wouldn't take it yet. She couldn't bear to.

July

Susannah awoke sometime after midnight. She'd fallen asleep on the sofa hours earlier, with the television still on. This was a new, and bad, habit she'd slipped into. She didn't like going to bed – the dark and the quiet were perversely stimulating, and she lay there feeling her eyes wide open, unseeing, and her mind racing. She rifled through her memories of Rob, sometimes in date order, more often randomly – some vague, some so vivid. So she stayed in the living room, with a side light, and *Newsnight*.

But on this night it wasn't the television that woke her. It was the familiar, wretched nagging ache low down in her belly. She half ran, half stumbled to the

432

toilet, and switched on the light, her eyes closing involuntarily against the unfamiliar brightness. Sitting down heavily on the loo, she stared disbelievingly at the dark red smear of blood in her underwear.

No baby. There never had been. Just an idea, a dream of a baby.

She sank down to the floor and hugged her knees and sat there in the bright bathroom. She couldn't even cry. She certainly wouldn't have been able to put into words – words that made sense, at least – how intense her sense of loss was. This was so, so much harder than the miscarriage she'd had when she was married to Sean. She was years and years older. This might have been her last chance. And this baby . . . this baby would have been hers and Rob's.

It was slipping away. It was all slipping away from her. She was terrified, and she was sad, and she was powerless to stop it.

Rob

He didn't have to tell her. She need never know. He remembered how much Susannah's confession about Matt had hurt him, all those years ago, and he winced physically at the thought of doing the same thing to Helena.

But if he didn't tell her, the rest of their life together would be based on a lie. And he knew he couldn't live with that. Telling her was part of his penance. Part of his route towards forgiving himself for what he'd done – because he knew with certainty that if he didn't forgive himself, he'd be forever changed by it, and no one would be able to love him.

And so he told her. He told her on a Wednesday afternoon. She was well enough to be wheeled out in a hospital chair now, and to sit in the fresh air for a while with a blanket over her knees. Helen had bought her a bright plaid cotton dressing gown from Marks & Spencer and she wore that. She had colour in her cheeks again, and the beginnings of a tan.

He sat on a bench beside her and spoke softly and calmly. He didn't tell her about thinking of Susannah as he pushed the wedding ring on to her finger, and he didn't tell her Susannah was in the church while his father's funeral went on. Those two things seemed the most unforgivable, and the most hurtful. He wouldn't lie – not about the funeral, at least – but he hoped she wouldn't ask.

She didn't ask anything, at first.

Helena had been very calm during her time in Selly Oak. She hadn't once wailed or railed against what had happened to her. And the nightmares he had been waiting for still hadn't materialized. She'd been stoical about her pain, and even joked about the phantom limb syndrome the doctors warned of. She'd started some gentle rehabilitation a few days earlier, and he'd watched her go through her paces with determination and grit. She hadn't said much about the accident – she didn't remember much, she said. She woke up in the field hospital, having passed out almost immediately after the rocket attack, and she had no recollection of her friends' bodies lying dead and dying around her. She'd cried a little, telling Rob that one, Justin, was due to marry his girlfriend at the end of his tour, and that another, Steve, had carried pictures of his three young daughters in his pocket and showed them to anyone who'd stand still long enough. But generally she seemed, in the words of the ward doctor, 'fantastically well adjusted'.

He wasn't sure that was how she was when confronted with what he told her. But she was calm. For the longest time – an almost unbearable time, for him – she sat staring at the trees across the green, saying nothing at all.

Then she asked him. 'Are you leaving me, then, for her?'

He shook his head slowly. 'No.'

'Why not? You love her, don't you?'

'I love her, but I love you, too.'

'And I win on the pity tiebreaker, do I? Lose a leg, keep a husband.'

'It's not like that.'

'What's it like, then?'

'I want to stay with you. I made promises.'

'You broke them.'

'I won't break them again.'

'How do I know that, Rob?'

'Because I know it. And you have to believe me.'

'Why should I believe a word you say?'

'Because I didn't have to tell you, Helena. I'm telling you because I want to make a clean break. I want us to have a fresh start. No lies.'

'You want me to know that you chose me, is that what you're saying? I'm supposed to be grateful, am I?'

'Not grateful. No. I can't tell you what to be. I can only tell you what I want. And how sorry I am. How very, very sorry.'

'But I don't understand, Rob. You can't love two women. Not be in love with them both. You can't.'

Oh, he begged to differ. He cried out to differ.

'I want to understand, Rob. I really do.'

'And I want to make you understand.'

'But you can't.'

'It's as if . . . it's as if she's my past. You're my future.'

'And we've both been your present for a while. Boom, boom.' A bitter, tight smile broke out briefly on Helena's face. Then she looked at him for the first time. 'Will you go away now, please, Rob?'

'I can't leave you here.'

'Tell my mum where I am. I want to be by myself for a while.'

'I don't want to leave you.'

She sighed. 'Don't be so bloody melodramatic. I'm

talking about leaving me on a bit of sodding grass. Just get lost. Please.'

He turned back to look at her, from the edge of the car park – about a hundred yards from where she sat. But she was still staring impassively out at the trees, and he couldn't see her face clearly.

Strangely, he slept that afternoon, and awoke feeling more refreshed than he had done for a while, although reality slapped him across the cheek before he'd even sat up in the bed. He may have experienced some relief from his confession – he couldn't imagine why else he'd slept – but he hadn't fixed anything. He'd still done it. He'd still done all of it.

When she came into the bedroom they'd been bizarrely sharing, Helen slapped him hard across the other cheek. 'She's told me everything.'

'I thought she would.'

'Well, she has. You bastard.'

He felt more comfortable with anger. 'I'm sorry, Helen. I'm really sorry.'

'Doesn't fix much, does it, that?'

'I know. But I do want to fix it. I want to stay. I want to make it up to her.'

'She thinks it's because she's lost her leg that you want to stay. You know that, don't you?'

'But it isn't.'

Helen squared up to him, and looked long and sharp into his eyes. 'Good. It better bloody not be. I'll skin you.'

'What did you tell her?'

'You don't know my daughter very well if you think she listens to me.'

'You know she listens to you. What did you tell her?'

'I told her you've been a total shit. I told her I wouldn't blame her if she told you to piss off permanently and meant it.' She narrowed her eyes at him. 'Then I told her that, for what it's worth, I've watched you with her, these last days. Watched you sitting with her, watched you touch her, watched you look at her. And that I don't think your wanting to stay with her has anything at all to do with the damn leg.'

Susannah

Susannah knew her happy ending wasn't going to happen. She knew before he called. She'd been so afraid he'd just send a letter, or do it over the phone. But, of course, he wouldn't do that. He was Rob. He did call – to ask her to meet him. They met on the Embankment, about half a mile away from where he'd fastened the locket around her neck on her eighteenth birthday. As she walked, she realized that, for the rest of her life, this stretch of river would remind her of him. It was an inappropriately glorious day – hot and sunny, the blue sky dusted with white clouds.

Even though she knew, when she saw him, hope betrayed her, leaping in her stomach. He hugged her

438

to him, so hard she couldn't breathe for a moment, and so hard he killed the hope. When he pulled back, she knew again what he'd come to say.

He'd lost some weight. His cheeks looked hollow, and he was pale, for Rob. He looked tired, too. He hadn't shaved for a while, and his stubble was flecked with grey. It made her sad. She wanted to save him from having to say it, knowing that it cost him almost as dearly to articulate it as it did her to hear it.

'This isn't going to happen, is it – you and me?'

He shook his head, and she bowed hers.

When he spoke, his voice was small. 'I can't leave her.' He shook his head, as though that wasn't quite right. 'I don't want to leave her. I won't do it.'

Which was it?

'I know.'

It was all of them. She understood. She was just fighting herself. *Can't* was too passive. He was being honest. *Wouldn't. Didn't want to.*

He couldn't. They couldn't. She'd known.

She forced herself to meet his eyes. They were full of tears, and even in that horrible, wretched moment she drew a minuscule crumb of comfort from knowing that it hurt him this much.

And at the same time, she wanted to help. 'I know. I know. It's okay, Rob. It's okay. I know because I know you, and I know that it couldn't ever be right. If you were the kind of man who could do this, I wouldn't love you the way I do. The way I think I always will.'

'All of that, all of what you just said – that's true of you, too, you know.'

Was it? It didn't used to be. But she *was* different now. She knew he was right. She could beg, she could cry. She might be able to persuade him – now, in this moment, when his love for her was this strong, when the feelings they had were this intense.

Once, she'd have done just that. Used every weapon in her arsenal. Sung her siren song at the top of her lungs. Not now. She saw now, so clearly, that it would be another kind of settling. He wasn't free to be hers. It could never be right.

'We've got to let each other go.'

This had to be a clean break, she knew. For ever, for good. It was hard to conceive of not seeing him again. Beyond the limits of physical pain to even imagine it.

He put his arms around her again. 'I'll never be sorry, Susie, that it happened. I hope you won't be.'

How could they be?

'I'll love you for ever.'

'And I'll love you.'

There was much more, they both knew. He'd love Helena, and she'd love . . . she'd love someone . . . someone who was free. Someone who'd love her back with everything he had.

But it was too soon for all that. It was a lurking shadow at this moment. This feeling – the one they had now, this minute – would never go away.

And so, there was nothing more to say. Nothing

more to do. Anything else would prolong the inevitable, draw out the pain too much. Rob kissed her once more – his dry, soft lips quickly on hers – and then he stood back from her, his arms by his sides.

It took strength she didn't know she had to turn, walk away, and not look back.

Epilogue

When Susannah didn't answer a ringing phone or a text marked urgent for two straight days, Amelia drove round to the flat and knocked on the door until she got a response. She was more shocked than she expected to be when Susannah finally answered – and she'd known it wouldn't be good. Her friend was pale and gaunt, and there were dark hollows beneath her eyes. Her hair was greasy and limp on her shoulders, and she was wearing jogging bottoms and a T-shirt, with a blanket from the sofa – one they'd bought at Ikea a few months ago – around her shoulders.

Susannah let herself be held in the doorway for a moment, and then guided inside on to the sofa. The flat was weirdly spotless and tidy – as though it, too, was waiting, ready for something.

'Why didn't you tell me?'

Susannah shrugged. 'I was ashamed, I think.'

'That's ridiculous.'

'You were so cross with me, Meels.'

'Yes, I was cross. But I'm still your best friend, you daft bugger. Do you think I wouldn't have come straight round, cross or not?'

'You couldn't have done anything.'

'I could have been here.'

Susannah smiled. 'You're here now.'

They sat down on the sofa, each curled into a different corner, just looking at each other. After a moment, Susannah started to cry. For the longest time, she cried, and Amelia said nothing, just watched her. She took her friend's hand, and held it as they sat there. She fumbled in a pocket for a tissue and passed it to her. She didn't try and stop her sobs, she didn't offer platitudes, and they didn't speak. She just went through it with her, as Susannah had been through things – different things – with her.

Susannah cried like she had never cried before. Cried for herself, for Douglas, and for the kids that weren't hers. Cried for Rob and for Helena. Cried for the mess they'd made of it all. For the babies that had never been – hers and Sean's, hers and Rob's. And for the babies that might never be. Cried until she couldn't cry any more.

And then, at last, a calm descended – a calm Susannah hadn't felt in so many days.

'Are we going to talk about it?' Amelia asked at last.

She shook her head. 'Nothing to say. It's done. We're done.'

'For good?'

She nodded. 'For good.' And knew that it was true.

All those dreams were over. She was awake again, for the first time in years. There would need to be new dreams. Not just yet, but soon.

'Did I tell you this thing I read recently? That the

cracks in your heart are there so that the light can shine through?'

'Bugger off.' Susannah laughed, in spite of herself.

Amelia pulled open the capacious handbag motherhood seemed to require and pulled out a half-bottle of Moët et Chandon champagne.

'What's that for?' It was staggeringly inappropriate and utterly Amelia.

'It's for us, though I think you should probably have a piece of toast before you drink any . . . looks like you haven't eaten anything in a while, and I don't want you falling down on me.'

'What are we drinking to?' Susannah knew it was pointless to argue. She padded to the kitchen cabinet and took down two glasses. 'Haven't got any champagne flutes, I'm afraid. Will these do?' She handed Amelia two stemless wine glasses.

Amelia was pulling off the foil, and untwisting the cork. 'They'll have to. We've drunk it out of worse . . . Remember those tooth mugs in Paris that time?'

'Yeah. So . . . what are we drinking to?'

Amelia was pouring. The bubbles fizzed up and over the top of the first glass, pooling on the coffee table. She picked it up and dried it on her leg before she handed it to Susannah and filled the second glass.

Then she clinked hers against Susannah's. 'To life, Susannah. Your life. Mine. The future.'

Amelia took a big gulp, but Susannah didn't drink.

'I'm cancer free.' She made inverted commas in the air. 'Just found out.'

Susannah's face crumpled again, although there were no tears left. The relief hit her like a heavy blow. 'Oh, thank God. Oh, Amelia.' She threw her arms around her friend, sending champagne flying over both of them, and the sofa. 'I'm sorry – I've been so up my own bum, I'd forgotten. When did you find out?'

'You've absolutely been up your own bum, but we all get that way. I can live with that, so long as you come out eventually. Besides, did you hear me? Cancer free, baby!' She punched the air triumphantly. 'Who the hell cares about anything else today?'

Susannah kissed her on the cheek. 'Congratulations. I'm so, so happy for you. I'm so happy for me.' She was. Life without Amelia was something she was not strong enough to contemplate. 'I'm gonna miss those sessions on the oncology ward, but I'll cope.'

'Phooey. We can still have the sessions. Just maybe we'll have them in the Porchester Spa, or the fifth floor of Harvey Nicks, or . . . anywhere bloody else but that hospital.'

The two women hugged again.

'I mean, there's that five-year rule, before you can really exhale, but right now, I'm clear, and he doesn't think there's any reason to suppose I won't stay this way. And I'm going to get my hair back . . .'

Susannah saw that Amelia's eyes were full of tears. 'You've been so brave. Have I told you that?'

446

'Yes, I have. Yes, you have. Over and over. And I'm so grateful for that. I did it for you, you know?' She winked at Susannah. 'Knew you couldn't cope if I wasn't . . .'

Susannah laughed. She was right, of course.

'And you're going to be brave now, too, aren't you?'

Susannah stared into the contents of her glass.

Amelia nudged her knee with her own. 'And it isn't going to be easy. I know that. I'm not making light of it, Susannah, honestly I'm not. I know what Rob meant to you. At least, I think I do. But look at you. It's all there.'

'What do you mean?'

'I mean you're young, and you're healthy. That's something people say, isn't it? But you have *no* idea how important that is – nothing else is as important. You've got this great flat. You're solvent, and employed and still, frankly, kind of foxy. Not today, obviously. Today you look rough as hell, and I suspect that you may smell.' She looked her up and down appraisingly. 'But it's nothing some kip, a hot shower and a bit of lippy can't fix.'

'You make it sound easy.'

'Don't mean to. I know it's bloody hard. I know what it's all meant. But you've done the hardest stuff. You left Doug. You've realized what you want from life. And you've lost Rob again. You survived that once, and you can survive it again. But this time . . .'

'This time?'

447

'This time, no settling. You deserve it all. Have it all, Susannah. You've got to promise me that.'

Susannah didn't say anything.

Amelia leant her whole body into her. 'Promise?'

And this time, when she looked at her friend's face, and raised her glass, she promised.

Acknowledgements

I gratefully acknowledge the invaluable help of so many people throughout this process, most particularly Jonathan Lloyd, Mari Evans, Shân Morley Jones and Annabel Robinson.

Others who have contributed know who they are, and how thankful I am. I hope.

David, Lulu, Tillie, and Mum and Dad – I love you all.

Come and enjoy
www.ElizabethNoble.co.uk

Welcome to a place where you can find out more about Elizabeth, read extracts from her novels and watch video messages to her readers.

The site also offers the opportunity to share your own stories about your mother, daughters or sisters. Hundreds of women have already done so after reading the heartbreaking *Things I Want My Daughters to Know* and there are many inspiring messages of love and wisdom for you to see.

And as an added treat, not only can you pick up some skin savvy tips from our friends at Dermalogica, but if you sign up for Elizabeth's regular newsletter you can win goodies from them in our exclusive competitions.

Elizabeth Noble – so good you have to share her